The Year
I Turned
Sixteen

The Year I Turned Sixteen

*Rose, Daisy,
Laurel, Lily*

Diane Schwemm

Simon Pulse
New York London Toronto Sydney

SIMON PULSE

An imprint of Simon & Schuster Children's Publishing Division
1230 Avenue of the Americas, New York, NY 10020
This Simon Pulse paperback edition January 2010
Rose copyright © 1998 by Daniel Weiss Associates, Inc., and Diane Schwemm
Daisy copyright © 1998 by Daniel Weiss Associates, Inc., and Diane Schwemm
Laurel copyright © 1998 by Daniel Weiss Associates, Inc., and Diane Schwemm
Lily copyright © 1998 by Daniel Weiss Associates, Inc., and Diane Schwemm

alloy**entertainment**

Produced by Alloy Entertainment
151 West 26th Street, New York, NY 10001

For information about special discounts for bulk purchases, please contact Simon & Schuster
Special Sales at 1-866-506-1949 or business@simonandschuster.com.
The Simon & Schuster Speakers Bureau can bring authors to your live event. For more
information or to book an event contact the Simon & Schuster Speakers Bureau
at 1-866-248-3049 or visit our website at www.simonspeakers.com.
Designed by Mike Rosamilia
The text of this book was set in Mrs Eaves.
Manufactured in the United States of America
11 13 15 17 19 20 18 16 14 12
Library of Congress Control Number 2009927164
ISBN 978-1-4169-8597-6
ISBN 978-1-4169-9873-0 (eBook)
These titles were previously published individually.

Contents

Rose

For Heather and Laura,

my sisters

and best friends

One

SOMETIMES I WISH I didn't live in a small town.

Hawk Harbor is the kind of place where everybody knows everybody else. There's one grocery store and one gas station and one bank. We have to share a high school with a bunch of other towns. We don't even have our own exit off the Maine Turnpike.

And needless to say, the nightlife is rather limited.

Now and then I find myself wondering what it would be like to live someplace crowded and exciting. Those are the days I can't wait to graduate and move to New York or L.A.

Then there are days like today, May 21, my sixteenth birthday, when I can't imagine living anywhere else. This afternoon on my way in from school I stopped on the porch of my family's Victorian house. Standing on tiptoe, I could see a distant sliver of the Atlantic, past the pines and the rocky shore. The water was speckled with sailboats and fishing trawl-ers that reminded me of my dad's old boat, the *Pelican*.

Summer is just around the corner, and that means pretty soon I'll be heading off to be a counselor at Wildwood, a camp in Vermont. I can't wait. I want to be a singer, and Wildwood is a performance camp—I won a scholarship there a few years ago, and I've been going every summer. There aren't many opportunities to get musical training in rural Maine, so Wild-wood was a total stroke of luck. Plus it's my only opportunity all year to get a taste of independence.

Inside the house I could tell right away that my mother, Maggie Walker, had been chopping and roasting and sifting and baking all afternoon. She's an awesome cook and always goes all out for special occasions, but this morning I'd told her it was fine if we skipped the festivities. After all, no one's been in the mood for a party for three months. Why would anything be different today? But she just hugged me and said, "My oldest girl is turning sixteen. That only happens once in a lifetime."

Seeing the tears in her blue eyes, I felt I couldn't argue with that.

I dumped my backpack on the living room couch and fol-lowed my nose to the kitchen. "Happy birthday, Rose," my thirteen-year-old sister, Daisy, called out from the dining room.

"Happy birthday!" echoed ten-year-old Laurel and eight-year-old Lily.

"Hi, everybody," I responded. "Smells great, Mom!" I walked

into the dining room and watched Daisy set the table with the good china, carefully placing every napkin and utensil just so. Her long blond ponytail was pulled through the back of her Boston Red Sox cap, which I suspect she sleeps in. (I know for a fact that until she was eleven she slept with her autographed Nomar Garciaparra baseball mitt under her pillow.) I couldn't help noticing that in spite of her usual uniform of gym shorts and T-shirt, she's starting to get really pretty. Of course, she'd probably punch me if I said so. When the guys on her baseball team started telling her that last year, she switched to all-girls' softball.

I opened my mouth to tell Daisy how nice the table looked but was interrupted. "It's my turn to lick the beaters," Lily whined from the kitchen.

"Uh-oh," I said, and Daisy rolled her eyes in a here-we-go-again look.

We both peeked through the doorway into the kitchen, anticipating a good show. Sure enough, Mom had just made the chocolate frosting for my birthday cake and Laurel had, naturally, seized the beaters. She's going through a growth spurt or something and consumes about half her weight in food a day. She's currently about a foot taller than Lily. So there was Laurel, holding one beater high above Lily's head and licking the other while Lily danced up and down, fuming.

I couldn't help laughing. Lily likes to dress up, and the costume du jour consisted of the calico skirt I had worn in our high school production of *Oklahoma!* last year, a hot pink tube top that wasn't staying up very well, and clip-on pearl earrings. For some reason her blond pigtails were sticking straight out from the sides of her head. Laurel was a sight, too: cutoff jeans, scraped knees, and a grass-stained shirt. "Personally, I wouldn't want to eat anything she just touched, but that's me," I said to Daisy under my breath.

Laurel turned bright red. She doesn't like to fight, but she has a real stubborn streak—especially when she knows she's right. "It's not your turn," she informed Lily. "You got the beaters when Mom made carrot cake for the church potluck two weeks ago."

"No, I didn't!" screeched Lily—who does like to fight—as she stamped her small feet.

"Time-out," called Daisy. "Hand one over, Laurel."

"Why should I?" asked Laurel. "Possession is nine-tenths of the law, and Lily doesn't have the right to—ow!"

Laurel's speech was interrupted by the kick in the shin Lily gave her. With a yelp Laurel dropped both beaters on the kitchen floor and started hopping around in pain.

"Okay, that's enough," Mom declared, scooping up the beaters and dumping them into the soapy water in the sink. "If you can't agree, then nobody gets any beaters. Now, take it outside, you two. And don't come back in until you've made up."

Lily and Laurel disappeared, but I could still hear them bickering as I headed upstairs to my room. Oh, well, what can you do? *Sisters.*

Since I was going out later, I put on the blue sleeveless dress

I'd just bought on sale at Harrington's Department Store. It had taken all the birthday money my grandparents in Florida had sent me, but it was worth it.

As my family gathered for dinner I noticed that my sisters looked relatively presentable, too. Of course Mom looked beautiful—she always does. She'd tossed aside her apron and brushed out her shoulder-length blond hair. With her, that's all it takes. Lily had added a rhinestone necklace to her ensemble, and Daisy had taken off her baseball cap. Laurel was wearing a baggy but clean chambray shirt . . . with a suspicious bulge in the pocket.

"Oh no, you don't," I told her. "Henry is not invited to my birthday dinner."

Laurel stood there acting wide-eyed and innocent, but Mom stared her down. Sheepishly Laurel stuck a hand in her shirt pocket, removing a small brown field mouse. Henry scampered up Laurel's arm to her shoulder as if he were about to make a nest in her hair.

"Out," I commanded, and Laurel disappeared.

"Why does she always carry that rodent around with her?" I asked.

Mom gave a gentle smile and said, "You know your sister doesn't make friends easily. Her animals are her friends."

"I wish she weren't so shy," I replied. "Why can't she be more normal?"

"I'm not shy," Lily put in.

"If she weren't shy, she wouldn't be Laurel," Daisy said, and my mother nodded.

Just then we heard Laurel washing her hands in the kitchen—thank goodness for antibacterial soap. When she returned, we all stood for a moment, admiring the table. There were candles and a vase of pink roses in the middle and a single white rose along with a small, gift-wrapped box next to my plate.

"Happy birthday, Rose," Mom said, smiling at me.

I smiled back, but as I pulled out my chair and sat down I knew the same sad feeling was settling over each of us. I miss Dad all the time, but there are moments when it hits me more that he's really gone. Dinner is the worst. Mom always sits at the foot of the table so she can zip into the kitchen; Daisy and Lily sit on one side, Laurel and I on the other. Which leaves the captain's chair at the head of the table empty.

I tried not to look at it.

Mom served the roast beef while Daisy passed the platter of potatoes and vegetables. Laurel buttered a roll, and Lily swished a straw around in her glass of chocolate milk. Everyone looked solemn. No one spoke.

"Hey, this is a party," I reminded them, trying to sound cheerful. I tasted the roast beef. "It's delicious," I said. "Thanks for going to so much trouble, Mom. I really didn't expect it."

"This is a special day. Nothing can change that," she replied, but this time when she smiled, I could tell it took an effort.

I did my best to keep the conversation hopping. It wasn't all that hard because Daisy and Lily both like to gab, and if you bring up the right topic, Laurel can, too.

"How was school, Toad?" I asked, using the nickname I gave her when she was six and spent the whole summer collecting slimy things in mason jars. "Did you finish your biology project?"

"We finished it today. Last week we fed the caterpillars all these leaves," Laurel reported, "and then they made chrysalides. Well, today the butterflies started to come out! It was so amazing. Next week we're doing tadpoles."

"How appropriate," I said. "Sounds perfect for you." She smiled and stared down at her plate.

"Ask me about my day!" Lily urged me.

"Okay, how was your day, Lily?"

"I did my book report on *Pippi Longstocking* and got an Excellent!"

"That's wonderful!" Mom told her. "Congratulations." Lily beamed.

I laughed. "Now I get it. That's what the pigtails are for, right?"

Lily nodded, pleased with herself. "I acted my report out for the class. All the girls in my class said they wished they'd thought of it. The only person whose report was half as good as mine was Amanda Waterston's, and you could tell that her mother helped her make her shadow box."

"It's better to do all the work yourself," I told her. "Good job."

"Maybe I can go to Wildwood next year," Lily said. "For acting! I'll be old enough."

"That would be great," I replied warmly. "I'd love to take

you with me, Lily. It's so much fun, but I missed you guys last year." We grinned at each other a moment, then I looked at Daisy. "Okay, Daisy, your turn."

Daisy had already eaten a humongous slice of roast beef and was now halfway through her second serving of mashed potatoes. She paused just long enough to say, "Softball practice was canceled—Coach was sick. I wish that I had someone to play catch with when I can't practice with the team." Daisy's been a star athlete since toddlerhood, but the rest of us just aren't interested in sports.

"Have any of you girls met the new boy who's moved into Windy Ridge?" Mom wanted to know. Windy Ridge is the big old house at the end of Lighthouse Road—it's been vacant for almost a year. We all shook our heads. "Maybe he's interested in sports, Daisy."

"I don't know. I've seen him around—he seems too young to me," Daisy said. "He looks around Laurel's age."

"Maybe *you* could go introduce yourself, Laurel," Mom said.

Laurel flushed slightly.

"But you don't have to," Mom added hastily. Laurel looked relieved.

When we finished eating, Daisy cleared the table, then brought in clean plates for dessert.

"Before we cut the cake, why don't you open your gift, Rose?" Mom suggested.

That was the only invitation I needed. I'd been dying to tear into the wrapping paper but didn't want to seem too eager.

Reminding myself that I was sixteen, not six, I opened the box with painstaking slowness. "Hurry up, Rose!" Lily said, but I just glared at her. I wondered what the gift would be. We've never been rich, but I had always dreamed that there would be a brand-new car in the driveway with a bow on top of it for my sixteenth birthday. Even though I knew it wasn't very likely, I couldn't help hoping briefly that the small box held a set of car keys.

But when I saw what was lying on a puff of cotton inside, I gasped. "Mom, it's beautiful!"

Everyone leaned in for a look. I held up the necklace so my sisters could admire it: a tiny gold rosebud suspended from a gold chain so delicate it was nearly invisible. "The rose was on your great-grandmother Walker's charm bracelet," my mother explained.

I fastened the clasp around my neck, then jumped up and ran to look at myself in the mirror over the sideboard. I loved what I saw. The necklace was pretty against my skin—just what the new dress needed. It might not be keys to my dream car, but I loved it.

Returning to the table, I wrapped my arms around my mother. "This is really a treasure. Thanks, Mom," I whispered.

We both had tears in our eyes. Mom hid hers by rising to her feet and disappearing into the kitchen. "Cake time," she called. "Dim the lights, Daisy, would you?"

As my mom carried the chocolate cake into the dining room Laurel ran into the living room to thump out an extremely off-key rendition of "Happy Birthday to You" on the piano. (I got all the musical talent in this family.) As everybody sang along Mom set the cake in front of me. Lily clapped, urging, "Make a wish!"

I drew in a breath, preparing to blow out the candles. I wish . . . I wish Dad were still alive.

Oh, God, what kind of birthday wish is that? I thought, shocked at myself. No matter how much I wanted it, there was no point wishing for something that couldn't possibly come true. I couldn't wish away the unexpected nor'easter that had swamped my father's fishing boat. I couldn't wish Dad back again. If only I could.

Shaking my head, I tried to come up with something else. Luckily for impatient Lily, another wish, one relating to my new boyfriend, Parker Kemp, and the possibility that someday my initials might be R. W. K., came quickly to mind.

I smiled and blew out the candles on my birthday cake—all sixteen of them at once.

HALF AN HOUR later I'd put on some makeup and perfume and brushed out my long blond hair, ready to head out the door as soon as Parker rang the bell. I stopped on my way past the kitchen.

The dishwasher was humming, the counters were spotless; even the blue-and-white-checked dish towels were hanging neatly from their pegs by the window. That's my mom—neat to a fault. But the drop-leaf table in the breakfast nook . . .

"Mom, what are you doing?" I asked.

She was sitting with her shoulders hunched forward, gnawing on a pencil. The table was piled high with file folders, checkbooks, and shoe boxes full of paper scraps.

Mom poked at the buttons on a calculator with the eraser end of a pencil, then glanced up at me distractedly. "Our income tax return," she answered. "I filed an extension last month, but I can't put it off indefinitely."

I wrinkled my nose. "Is it complicated?"

She sighed. "I loved your dad, but he was not a businessman. He left the finances in a mess. I can't make heads or tails of any of it."

"Well, don't stay up too late," I advised.

"Don't forget you have a curfew," she replied.

"I won't. Night, Mom."

Outside, I sat on the top porch step, hugging my knees and humming a Taylor Swift song. When a pair of headlights bumped down the gravel driveway, I stood up, my heart pounding with anticipation.

Whenever I go out with Parker, I feel like I'm entering a fairy tale. He whisks me into a different world.

He stepped out of his black Jeep Wrangler, leaving the engine running. Before helping me up into the passenger seat, he bent me back slightly against the side of the Jeep for a kiss. "Hey, birthday girl," he murmured, his mouth smiling against mine. "Nice dress."

It's hard to explain the effect Parker has on me, I mean without resorting to clichés like he makes my knees weak and all that. He looks like a Ralph Lauren model—blond hair and blue eyes and the kind of smile that stops you in your tracks. He's tall, too—six-foot-one—with a lean, muscular tennis player's build. At the risk of sounding totally conceited, I have to say we look great together. Not that I'm obsessed with appearances or anything, but he's the first Seagate Academy guy I've gone out with, and that's kind of a status thing in Hawk Harbor.

"Do you know what day this is, besides my birthday?" I asked.

He scratched his head, pretending he didn't. "No, what?"

"It's our one-month anniversary," I reminded him, pinching his ribs playfully.

His face broke into a grin. "Of course I remember. I'll never forget the first time I saw you," Parker said.

I smiled up at him a little wistfully. I'd been feeling really sad about Dad that day, so I'd gone for a walk along the shore. That's where I feel closest to Dad because he spent so much time out on the ocean. I started walking at the public beach, too busy crying to pay attention to where I was going. I just kept climbing across rocks and jumping over tide pools and slogging through piles of seaweed as if I could somehow walk off my grief. Suddenly Parker had appeared before me.

"You looked so beautiful, but so sad," Parker went on.

I'd been kind of blown away when Parker told me we were standing on his family's private beach—that he lived in the mansion on the cliff above us. Maybe that was why, when I told him my father had died in a boating accident, I'd left out the fact that Dad had been a commercial fisherman. Of course,

I'm sure that Parker could tell we weren't the kind of family that would have a yacht, but he never asked what kind of boat it was. And I never enlightened him.

Now I sniffled, feeling sentimental. A month ago on the rainy beach Parker had put an arm around me and pulled me under his umbrella. We'd been inseparable ever since. "I'm the luckiest girl in the world," I whispered softly.

"You're the prettiest girl in the world," said Parker, kissing me.

"So, where are we going?" I asked a minute later as Parker backed out of the driveway.

He gave me a sideways glance, smiling. "You'll see."

I settled back in my seat with a happy sigh. Parker has his own charge card, and he always takes me to pretty nice places. So I wasn't surprised when he pulled up in front of the Harborside. But I was surprised when he led me through the restaurant to a private room in the back. A room packed with kids wearing party hats who threw confetti into the air and shouted, "Surprise!"

I blinked. "What on . . . is this for . . . ?"

"Yep, it's for you," Parker said. "Happy birthday!"

Sliding an arm around my waist, he steered me into the crowd. I couldn't get over it. It wasn't just that Parker had thrown me a surprise party. It was a surprise party with armfuls of red roses in crystal vases all over the place, and a waiter passing a tray of hors d'oeuvres, and a two-tiered cake garnished with real rosebuds on a silver pedestal. It was a far cry from my fifteenth birthday party, which had consisted of pizzas and pitchers of Pepsi with my now ex-boyfriend Sully and other friends at the Rusty Nail, a very casual hangout in town.

"You really shouldn't have done this," I said to Parker, feeling a little embarrassed.

He shrugged as if it were nothing. "Come on, I want you to meet everybody."

We made a quick tour of the room. I mostly just smiled, trying to remember names—Chip van Alder, Cynthia Ferris, David Shuman, Valerie Mathias—and trying not to panic over the fact that I was the only girl in the room wearing a cotton dress. I took mental notes for future reference, not that I could afford to copy these girls' outfits. Seagate Academy girls obviously didn't shop the sale rack at Harrington's.

"Here." Parker pressed a glass of punch into my hand. "Be right back."

For a minute I stood alone by the buffet table, sipping my punch. It seemed a little strange—here I was at my own birthday party with no one to talk to. I edged up to a conversation. "So if I can score some tickets, maybe we could road trip to Boston for the concert," David was saying.

"What concert?" I asked brightly.

"We could crash at my cousin's dorm," Cynthia went on, as if she hadn't heard me. She was looking from David to Chip. "If we stay over Saturday, we could go to some Harvard parties."

"I don't want to miss the crew regatta, though," Chip told Cynthia. "What if we—"

They didn't seem to need me, so I backed up a step or

two. "I think I'll have some cake," I said to no one in particular. I looked around for Parker, but he was on the far side of
the room, talking to Valerie. "Yes, it's cake time," I decided,
turning to the buffet.

As I contemplated the cake someone behind me said, "It's
almost too beautiful to cut."

I glanced over my shoulder at a tall guy with deep brown
eyes. He had thick, dark hair and small wire-rimmed glasses.
He looked like a future professor in spite of the fact that he
was incredibly handsome.

"Yes," I agreed, feeling a little ridiculous about the fact
that this person was at my party and I had no idea who he was.
I turned back to the cake. Oh, well, I thought. Let them eat—

"Cake," the guy said.

"What?" I asked.

"Let them eat cake," he repeated. "I'm sure the chef would
hate to think that he went to all the trouble of making it taste
good for nothing."

"You have a point," I said. Smiling, I grabbed the silver
knife on the table and sliced into the cake. I offered him the
first piece. "By the way, I'm Rose," I said.

"Sorry. I should have introduced myself sooner." He actually blushed. "Stephen Mathias," he said as we shook hands.

"Mathias. Then you must be Valerie's"—I inspected him
more closely. Valerie is the same age as Parker and me, sixteen, and a sophomore. This guy looked a little older—"big
brother?"

"Right," he said. "I'm a junior."

I don't usually have trouble talking to people, but this guy was a little intimidating. He was staring at me kind of intensely, as if he was trying to figure something out, which was making me worry that maybe I had a blob of frosting on my face or something. I glanced around for Parker, hoping he'd rescue me. Suddenly Stephen remarked, "You don't go to Seagate, do you?" Now it was my turn to flush slightly. "I mean," he added quickly, "I'd remember seeing you around."

"No, I go to South Regional," I admitted, naming my public high school. It was pretty obvious that I didn't fit in with this crowd, and I hated the fact that it bothered me so much.

"Well." He rocked back on his heels. "This is quite a party."

I nodded. "Unbelievable."

"It was a surprise, huh?" he asked. I couldn't read the look on his face.

I nodded again.

"So, where are your friends?"

"I wouldn't have expected Parker to invite people he's never met," I said a little defensively.

"You two haven't been dating that long, then?"

"Well, a month, but—" I stopped, frowning. A whole month and Parker still hadn't met my best friends. Why not?

At that moment someone who smelled like expensive men's cologne came up behind me and wrapped his arms around my waist. "Don't eat too much cake," Parker murmured, his lips on my earlobe.

I put my plate down fast and turned to face him. "Ready for your present?" he asked.

"You mean this party isn't my present?"

"Of course not."

He pressed a robin's egg blue box into my hand. "For me?"

Parker laughed. "Who else? Open it."

Stephen had drifted away, but Cynthia and a few other girls crowded around to watch. I heard Valerie say, "That's a Tiffany box." Self-conscious, I opened it. When I saw what was inside, I almost fainted. I lifted out the heavy silver necklace.

"Parker," I whispered, "it's lovely."

Removing the necklace my mother had given me earlier in the evening, Parker fastened the clasp of the Tiffany one around my neck. "Now, that does you justice," he said, bending forward to kiss me. "You're so beautiful. I love you, Rose."

It was the first time he'd said that. My eyes widened in surprise, but I closed them as our lips touched. Parker Kemp loved me!

Our kiss went on and on. Parker's friends clapped and whistled, but we still didn't draw apart.

Fifteen had been a terrible year—I'd lost my father. The year I turned sixteen was bound to be better. One thing's for sure, I thought, dizzy with happiness. It's off to a great start.

IN THE MIDDLE of the night something woke me up. For a few seconds I lay with my eyes closed, trying to get back into the dream I'd been having. It was about Parker, of course. Then I heard the sound again. "Daddy!" someone cried. "Daddy, come here!"

Lily, I thought groggily. My youngest sister has a seriously overactive imagination—she has nightmares all the time, and Dad's the only one who can calm her down. I lay in the dark, waiting for the sound of his footsteps plodding down the hall. Lily kept crying, "Daddy, I'm scared!"

A minute passed, then two, and I was starting to wonder what was taking Dad so long.

And then I remembered.

Hopping out of bed, I hurried to Lily's room. She was sitting up in bed, a pillow clutched to her chest and tears sliding down her face. I sat down on the mattress and put an arm around her, wondering what to say. "It's okay," I murmured.

"Where's Daddy? I want Daddy," Lily sobbed.

I wished I didn't have to tell her the truth. "Dad's not here," I reminded her at last, "and Mom's still asleep. She was really tired tonight."

Lily sagged against me, her head on my shoulder. Her tears wouldn't stop. "I had this awful dream, Rose," she whispered, sniffling. "I was wading in Kettle Cove looking for clams and this big shark swam up and I . . ."

As Lily went on, I could feel her still shaking with fear. What had Dad done in this situation? I wondered, feeling helpless. I wasn't used to playing this role.

"There, there," I murmured.

Lily kept crying. I was totally at a loss. Help me, Dad, I thought.

Dad always believed in being as rational as possible. I took a deep breath. "It'll be okay. There aren't any sharks in Kettle Cove."

Lily looked up at me. "There aren't?" she asked with another sniff.

"Definitely not," I declared. "They like the beaches down on Cape Cod. In fact, they prefer . . ." and I went off on some long, rambling explanation that was half remembered from an old science textbook and half invention.

Believe it or not, it worked. I held Lily until her eyelids drooped sleepily. Then I tucked her back in.

As I was closing the door Lily woke up again. "Where are you going?" she asked.

"Back to my room," I said.

She thought about this for a minute.

"I'll be right down the hall," I added.

"Okay," she said. "Thanks, Rose."

Oh, Dad, I thought, what was it you used to say? "Anytime," I whispered.

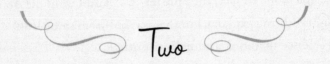

Two

S TOP MAKING ME laugh," Catherine Appleby begged Sumita Ghosh as we headed out of school the next day after concert choir. "Or I'll wet my pants."

Mita had been mimicking the way Mr. Arnold, the music director at South Regional High, instructs the sopranos by singing their parts in this quavery falsetto. It was hilarious. Mita's from India. She has this totally cool British accent, but she can imitate anyone.

Cath was doubled over. She did look close to losing it, so Mita took pity on her. "Okay," Mita said, putting one arm around me and the other around Roxanne Beale. She started belting out the raunchy lyrics to a rock song. We all joined in at the top of our lungs—it felt great after an hour and a half of practicing prim songs for the spring concert. People call us the "Fab Four" because there are four of us and we're always singing.

"Who needs a ride?" Cath asked when we got to the student parking lot. She jingled the keys to her father's blue Dodge pickup.

I dropped my backpack on the sidewalk, then took a seat on the curb. "Not me," I replied. "Parker's picking me up."

"Ooh." Rox wriggled her light eyebrows. She has strawberry blond hair and is very fair. "Parker."

"The man," teased Cath, her green eyes sparkling.

"Did Prince Charming make your birthday extra special?" Mita asked suggestively.

I rolled my eyes. "As a matter of fact, he did. He threw this amazing party at the . . ." I remembered Parker's oversight and stopped, embarrassed. "I wish you guys could have been there, but it was a pretty small party, actually," I finished lamely. "Low-key. We didn't even dance."

"Hey, no big deal," Rox assured me.

"He doesn't even know us," Cath pointed out.

"We want to do something for you, though," Mita said, "to celebrate."

"How about Pizza Bowl?" Cath suggested. "We'll round up everybody this Friday night."

"We could invite Parker," Rox added charitably.

I tried to picture Parker at the bowling alley, munching a slice of pepperoni with extra cheese, but my imagination couldn't stretch that far. "Um, I'll ask him, but I think he's going away this weekend," I improvised. Parker's family has a house in Boston, too, so it wasn't hard to come up with a story. "Yeah, I'm pretty sure he'll be in Boston."

To my relief, they dropped the topic and we moved on to our favorite joke fantasy: forming an all-girl singing group after we graduate in two years. Mita put forth her argument for opening our first set with a Rolling Stones cover.

We decided to try it out and started singing "Start Me Up"—Mita even threw in some Mick Jagger moves. Just then a black Jeep pulled into the parking lot. Abruptly the husky musical notes died in my throat. I jumped to my feet, one hand flying up to smooth my hair, the other quickly flicking the dirt off the seat of my jeans. The grunge look is cool in some circles, but not at Seagate Academy. Parker always looks totally crisp, as if his clothes get dry-cleaned—with him in them.

I grabbed my bag, swinging it over my shoulder, and started toward the Jeep. Then I turned back. "Come over and meet Parker," I said to my friends, who didn't need to be asked twice—they'd been dying to meet Parker. It was about time, wasn't it?

I strode over to the driver's side of the Jeep with Cath, Mita, and Rox at my heels. "Parker, hey." I gave him a quick kiss. "These are my friends. Cath Appleby—you know Appleby's Hardware in town? And Roxanne—her dad used to . . ." I caught myself before saying "her dad used to fish with my dad." For some reason I didn't want Parker to know that. "Her dad's a fisherman," I went on, "and Mita's parents run that really excellent Indian restaurant in Eastport."

Rox, Mita, and Cath took turns shaking Parker's hand, as if he were fifty years old or something. Parker gave them a smile, but it wasn't his usual turn-your-bones-to-butter smile. Why is this weird? I wondered. Did I say something wrong?

"Nice to meet you," Parker said.

"Nice to meet you, too," Mita, Rox, and Cath replied.

An awkward silence fell over us. "Yeah, the Bombay Palace," I went on in an attempt to jump-start the conversation. "Have you ever eaten there, Parker?"

"Haven't had the pleasure," Parker said.

I faltered. "Well. Um . . ."

"Hop in," Parker suggested. "Nice to meet you," he said to my friends.

I got into the passenger seat, confused and disappointed. So there hadn't been instant chemistry between Parker and my girlfriends. So what? When they get to know one another better, it'll be cool, I told myself.

"See ya," I called out the window to Cath, Rox, and Mita.

"See ya," they replied, waving as Parker and I drove off.

P ARKER AND I went to the Seagate library and then out for a snack. It was six o'clock when he dropped me off at the house. Mom was just putting dinner on the table. "Will you join us, Parker?" she invited, smiling at him from the dining room.

We were still standing in the front hall. "It's just stew, but my mom's is the best," I whispered.

Parker checked his watch in a kind of exaggerated way—stretching out his arm, then bringing his hand back in with the wrist cocked. "I really need to get home," he told me. "Can't, but thanks, anyway, Mrs. Walker," he called.

After Parker left, I took my place at the table. Lily, Laurel, and Daisy were already in their chairs, rattling silverware and reaching for the serving bowls and platters. I piled my plate high; I was starving. Parker and I had stopped at a coffee shop in town, but I hadn't wanted to seem like a pig—I'd just ordered a diet soda.

"Parker never hangs out here," Daisy remarked, buttering a corn muffin.

"Yeah, well . . ." I considered this statement. It was true. "He has . . . lots of things to do."

"Is his house more fun or something?" asked Lily.

I thought about Parker's house: the awesome CD and DVD collection, the big-screen TV, the pool, the sauna. It was more fun. Before I could answer Lily's question, though, Laurel said, "I guess he doesn't have to talk to us if he doesn't want to."

I looked at Mom, wondering what she thought about all this. That's when I noticed that five minutes into the meal, she hadn't touched her food. "Are you feeling okay, Mom?" I asked.

Mom propped her elbows on the table, chin on clasped hands. Her blue eyes were somber. "I need to talk to you girls about something," she said, "but I don't know where to start."

"What is it?" Daisy asked.

Mom paused before speaking. "It's about our . . . finances."

"Finances?" Lily repeated, puzzled.

"That means money," Daisy told Lily.

"What about our finances?" I asked.

"Your father had a life insurance policy, but it was small," Mom began. "It covered his funeral expenses, some old debts from the fishing business, and a couple of household bills. That's all."

"But you have a job now, Mom," said Daisy. "And we've been economizing. Right?"

I scowled at the word *economizing*. That's what we'd been doing since Dad died, and it wasn't fun. Economizing meant spaghetti for dinner every other night. It meant no renting movies and no more going out for pizza and ice cream on Friday nights like we did when Dad was alive. No new clothes, no new anything.

"I have a job," Mom agreed. She worked at a local real estate agency, answering phones and filing. I knew she felt lucky to have landed the position—she and my father married young, and she never went to college. Being a mom had always taken all her time. "But I'm still only part-time, and my salary doesn't come close to meeting our expenses. The upkeep on the house—food—utilities—taxes . . ."

Mom stopped. The four of us girls sat quietly, waiting. Where was all this leading?

"We'll be all right," she said at last. "We'll pull through. I'm trying to get more hours at work. But in the short-term I'm going to have to apply for . . . assistance."

Daisy tipped her head to one side. Laurel and Lily exchanged a confused glance. A sick feeling bubbled in my stomach. Maybe my sisters didn't know what Mom meant by *assistance,* but I did. Welfare, I thought numbly.

"Couldn't we ask Gram and Gramps for money?" Daisy said.

Mom's parents retired to Florida—my other grandparents are both dead. "No," Mom answered Daisy. "Grampa's pension from the telephone company is barely enough for the two of them."

I opened my mouth to ask if the bank could lend us some money. Mom turned to me at the same instant and spoke first. "Rose, I've been meaning to talk to you about Wildwood."

A chill ran over my entire body.

"I know how much you love it," she went on. I nodded, unable to speak.

Mom chewed her lower lip. "The thing is, honey," she said apologetically, "camp counselors don't get paid much. Hardly anything, really. And now that you're sixteen . . ."

I stared at her for a minute before putting into words what she obviously couldn't bring herself to say. "You want me to give up Wildwood and find some other job that pays more?" I asked, although it wasn't really a question.

"It's your choice," Mom hurried to assure me. "But whatever you do, you'll need to start putting money aside for college. I won't be able to cover your clothing allowance anymore, either, or your spending money. I know this is hard for you, Rose."

My sisters were gaping at me. I looked down at my plate, my jaw clenched. I was fighting back tears. Wildwood was the best part of the entire year. It was my only chance to study with people who knew about music and performance. I remembered how excited I'd been when I got the letter from the camp director offering me the job. Right away I'd called Julianne Greenberg, my camp friend from Connecticut. She'd gotten a letter, too, and we'd talked for an hour about how much fun this summer was going to be.

I knew that I shouldn't take it so hard, but I couldn't help it.

"I'll look for a job in town," I managed to say after a minute that felt like a month.

"I'm sorry, honey," Mom said. "I really am."

"Excuse me, I'm not hungry anymore," I mumbled, pushing back my chair. Turning my head so no one would see the tears that were flowing down my face, I hurried from the table.

N O, THAT'S NOT right." I shifted the key from major to minor, humming as I played.

It was a rainy afternoon a week after Mom broke the bad news about going on welfare, and I was sitting at the piano trying to write a song for Parker. I wanted it to be upbeat, obviously, a song about being madly in love, but the words and notes kept coming out gloomy. I'd been feeling down all week and—with the exception of the night my friends and I went to Pizza Bowl—it was a feeling I couldn't seem to shake. "It's a gray day and I'm missing you, wishing you were here," I sang. I scribbled a few notes on the composition pad on top of the piano, then scratched them out, making a sour face. "Blech!"

For a minute I sat with my hands flat on the bench beside me, staring out the rain-streaked window. Then my fingers moved back to the keys and began picking out a melody Jenny Lewis recorded with Rilo Kiley.

With a sigh I gave up trying to be creative. Just as I was stowing my composition pad in the piano bench Laurel burst through the front door into the hall, her hair flying out behind her, Henry clutched in one hand. "Rose, someone's stealing our car!"

Her cry brought Daisy and Lily running from the kitchen. All four of us crowded over to the living room window. Sure enough, there was a tow truck parked in our driveway and a man in an orange mechanic's jumpsuit was attaching a cable to the bumper of our silver Buick, working fast because of the drizzle. Another man walked briskly up to the house. I met him at the door. "Here's the notice from your bank," he said, handing me a rain-spattered envelope. "Sorry, miss."

I closed and locked the door, then rejoined my sisters. "They're not stealing it—they're repossessing it," I informed them.

"That's Dad's car," Daisy said angrily. "I'm going to tell them they can't take it!"

She started for the door. Leaping after her, I grabbed her arm. "Mom must not have been making the loan payments. Just chill, Daze."

"It's not fair," she said, her eyes still blazing.

"I know," I agreed.

We squeezed onto the couch, all four of us, and looked out the window in silence. Dad's car. Funny how we all still thought of it that way, even though Mom drove it and I did, too, now that I had my license. Dad's car.

I remembered the day we bought it, about a year before Dad died. He took us with him to the used car lot, and he acted as if he really cared about our opinions. "What do you think, Rose?" he'd asked me. "Does it look like a fisherman's car?"

"Nope," I'd replied.

He'd grinned, his blue eyes twinkling. "Good."

We went for a test drive. Dad put all the windows down and we cranked the oldies station, screaming along to the Beatles and Beach Boys. When we got back to the dealership, Dad told the used car guy, "You've made a sale." And we drove the car home.

Now I remembered asking Dad why he'd picked the Buick instead of a van or something more practical. "Don't get me wrong," he'd answered. "I'm not trying to be someone I'm not. I just want a nice car for my girls to ride in."

Now Daisy, Laurel, Lily, and I watched the tow truck rumble out of the driveway with the sedan rolling behind it. Daisy picked at the fringe on the crocheted afghan that hung over the back of the couch. "We really don't need two cars, anyway," she said.

Typical Daisy—always looking for the silver lining. No point reminding her that the only car we had left was an ancient and hideous wood-sided station wagon.

Laurel remained silent, cradling her pet mouse against her

cheek. For once I felt too sorry for her—and for all of us—to be grossed out. Lily moved closer to me on the sofa. "What does 'repossessed' mean, Rose?" she asked, her eyes large with fear. "Will those men come back and take more things away?"

I put an arm around Lily without answering. I didn't know how to explain it to her. In my head, though, I ran over the meanings of the word. *Repossessed* meant we couldn't afford to make the payments. *Repossessed* meant we couldn't afford anything.

For days Mom, my sisters, and I had had one conversation after another about money, or rather the lack of it. Sacrifices we'd have to make. Lifestyle changes.

But that wasn't the worst of it. Hawk Harbor was a fishbowl—I bet at least a dozen people could see our car being towed and would immediately begin speculating why.

How long would it be before everyone in town found out?

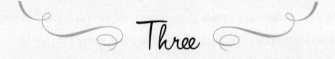

Three

"EVERYONE'S BEING SO nice," Daisy said later that week. "Isn't everyone being nice?"

Saturdays have always been crazy at our house—everybody coming and going, friends in and out, umpteen projects under way. That Saturday was no exception. Daisy was just back from a softball tournament, Mom was washing and ironing curtains, Lily and her friends Mickey and Noelle were staging a play in the living room, and I was recovering. And Laurel was out on a rescue mission with her new friend, Jack Harrison.

Jack was the boy who had moved into Windy Ridge—I had been wondering whether we would ever meet him. When he rang our doorbell that morning, Laurel hid in her room while I answered the door. But Jack had come to tell "the girl who takes care of the animals" that he had found a nest of baby raccoons who needed care. He didn't know what to do. His young face was so serious that I immediately went upstairs and knocked on Laurel's door. Once she understood the situation, Laurel forgot her shyness and rushed downstairs. I expected them back with the raccoons any minute.

As if the house wasn't full enough already! Our neighbor Mr. Comiskey had dropped by to borrow a drill and had stayed to fix some loose shingles on the roof, "since I'm here." Old Mrs. Schenkel from two doors down had just dropped off a wheelbarrow full of canned goods, explaining that she and Mr. Schenkel were about to leave on a cruise and she was "cleaning out her cupboards."

Nineteen-year-old Stan Smith from two doors down in the other direction was at that very moment fixing a leaky tap in the upstairs bathroom. Stan's mother, Sue, who's a good friend of Mom's, had walked over with Stan to return a pie dish she'd borrowed "sometime in the previous century."

"And look!" Daisy whispered to me now. Daisy was putting the pie dish away while Mrs. Smith chatted with Mom on the porch. "There's money in here!"

I peered into the pie dish. Sure enough, along with some recipe cards there was a plain white envelope. It wasn't sealed, and when Daisy lifted the flap, we both could see the green bills. Daisy started to count it. "Stop," I exclaimed, snatching the envelope and the dish away from her. "Have some pride, would you?"

I stomped into the kitchen with the pie dish, setting it on the counter with a loud clunk. Then my curiosity got the better of me. I peeked into the envelope, rifling the bills quickly.

Three fives, two tens, and a twenty. Fifty-five dollars! And the Smiths weren't exactly millionaires. Mr. Smith was the custodian at the grade school, and Mrs. Smith sold little jars of homemade jams and jellies through local gift stores. Stan was the oldest of five kids. So if they were giving money to us . . .

Charity, I thought, overcome by an unpleasant mixture of gratitude and shame. People always think about how hard it is to give, but they never think about how hard it is to receive.

The envelope of money turned out to be nothing compared to what we had to endure the following Monday afternoon. Mom, Daisy, and Lily picked me up after choral practice in the station wagon, which still smelled like fish because Dad used it to haul nets and equipment back and forth from the marina. "Just have to make one stop on the way home," Mom announced, turning onto Old Boston Post Road.

The county social services center is on a busy street, with a huge sign—you'd think they could have been more discreet. "This may take a while," Mom warned as she parked in a space right in front where anyone driving by could see us. "They told me on the phone that I'd have to fill out a bunch of forms."

She left the key in the ignition so we could listen to the radio. I tuned it to a rock station, then slumped down in the passenger seat so only the top of my head would be visible. Meanwhile in the backseat Daisy and Lily continued to sit up as straight as they could, gabbing on and on about some stupid book Lily's teacher was reading out loud to the third graders.

"So there's this tollbooth, but it's magic," Lily reported to Daisy.

"The Phantom Tollbooth," Daisy responded with enthusiasm. "I loved that one."

I wanted to yell at them to shut up. Didn't they know what was going on? Didn't they care? I knew it was a horrible thought, but I wanted to drive off, leaving Mom behind. Who needed food stamps, anyway? I'd rather just go on a diet.

I didn't yell, though, and I didn't drive off, and I didn't cry, which was something else I felt like doing. Instead I turned the radio up louder, folded my arms tightly across my chest, and closed my eyes.

W HY CAN'T YOU wear the dress you wore to the homecoming dance with Sully?" Rox wanted to know on Wednesday.

Rox, Cath, Mita, and I had gone into town after school. I needed a dress for the Seagate Academy prom, but I had only eighteen dollars saved up. My friends were having diet soda and candy bars, but I had to do without since I didn't have a dime to spare. We strolled along the sidewalk, discussing my options.

Now that Memorial Day weekend had come and gone, Main Street was starting to wake up from its winter sleep. I paused in front of a new boutique called Cecilia's. "I went in there the other day—they have nice stuff," Cath commented.

"Expensive, though," Mita said.

I turned away from the window. What was the point of even looking? Cecilia's catered to the summer crowd and families like the Kemps—I couldn't afford to shop there.

"I can't wear my homecoming dress," I explained somewhat impatiently, "because it's last year's dress. Besides, it's not even the right season."

"Who'd know?" wondered Rox. "Nobody from Seagate's seen you in it, and it's sleeveless. It could be a spring dress."

"I can't wear it," I repeated firmly. "Besides, Sully spilled a Coke all over me. There's this huge stain on the skirt."

"You could borrow my yellow dress," offered Cath.

I had to smile at that. Cath's yellow dress is gorgeous. Cath, however, is the world's smallest person—I'm six inches taller than she is. "I like short dresses, but not that short," I said.

"Well, they're having another sale at Harrington's," Rox said.

I shook my head, sighing. Even at Harrington's, on sale, I couldn't afford a brand-new dress. That was all there was to it.

I was ready to give up. Then Mita said suddenly, "I've got an idea. Let's check out Second Time Around."

I glanced at her, one eyebrow lifted. "That's a consignment shop," I pointed out, picturing racks of tacky chiffon mother-of-the-bride dresses.

"They sell vintage clothing," Mita corrected me in her precise and refined British manner. I continued to look skeptical. "I've found some funky things there," she pressed. "Trust me!"

I thought about it a minute. Oh, well. What could it hurt? I didn't have many options. "Okay, let's try it," I said.

At the next corner we turned down a side street, pausing to breathe in the delicious smell of Wissinger's Bakery. Second Time Around was halfway down the block.

It was a mild day, and the door to the store was propped open. Jeff Buckley's version of "Hallelujah" wafted out to the sidewalk, along with the smell of incense. Maybe this won't be so horrible after all, I thought hopefully.

Mita yanked me straight to a rack in the back. "How about this?" She pulled out a dress. "Or this?"

Cath and Rox pounced on the dresses. "Oh, I like this one," Cath said. "Check out the lace."

"How about this?" Rox grabbed a hanger with something psychedelic on it. "It's kind of seventies. *Mod Squad,* you know? Groovy, baby."

I started to get excited in spite of myself. I studied the first dress Mita had picked out. "I love the color," I said. "What would you call it, olive?"

"Sage," Mita said. She held the dress against me. "It's perfect for you. And it's only . . ." She flicked the price tag in my direction. It had been marked down a couple of times. I could afford the dress and still have enough cash left over to buy a boutonniere for Parker.

I looked at my reflection in the mirror. "I'm trying it on," I declared.

I marched to the dressing room with Mita, Cath, and Rox trailing in my wake. The four of us crowded behind the curtain together. Their faces were intent as I stripped out of my short denim skirt and T-shirt and pulled the dress over my head.

Choosing a prom dress is serious business.

When the dress was on, though, they all melted. "Oh, Rose, you look beautiful," Cath gushed.

Rox sighed. "It's romantic."

"Parker's eyes will pop out of his head," Mita predicted.

A blush of pleasure stole across my cheeks as I looked at myself in the mirror. The dress was simple and a little bit old-fashioned, but that was what made it flattering. The soft fabric fell straight, tucking in just slightly at the waist, the hem hitting me midcalf. The wide, scooped neckline was edged in lace, as were the sheer elbow-length sleeves. "The woman who first wore this dress is probably a grandma by now," I said with a laugh.

"A sexy grandma," Mita said. "I think you look hot." Her dark eyes sparkled. "Didn't I tell you we'd hit the jackpot here?"

I don't have a problem admitting when I'm wrong. "You were right, O Wise One," I said, grinning.

Mita, Cath, and Rox left so I could change back into my own clothes. First I twirled in front of the mirror, enjoying the way the delicate fabric draped against my body. Then I stopped, a frown creasing my forehead. We'd all agreed the dress was perfect—or was it? Something's not right, I thought. Was it the length? The neckline?

Then I focused on the necklace I was wearing—my birthday gift from Parker. That was the problem, definitely. I wanted to wear the necklace on prom night, but it looked odd with the dress—too ornate. Too Tiffany. Is that possible? I wondered, gnawing my lip.

For a millisecond I considered returning the dress to the rack. Then I shook my head. No, I loved the necklace, but I loved the dress, too. Besides, I could wear the necklace any-time.

After changing fast, I hurried to the cash register with the dress slung over my arm.

PARKER PICKED ME up at my house after dinner that night. We'd made plans to study together at the town library—finals were coming up—but somehow we found ourselves parked at the beach. "And what do you know," said Parker, grinning at me in the twilight. "There's a blanket in the back of the Jeep."

"How do you suppose that got there?" I asked, pretending to be shocked.

Leaving our shoes behind, we walked across the cool sand, aiming for a sheltered spot in the dunes. The sun had just set behind us; ahead the purple sky over the ocean was beginning to sparkle with stars.

Parker spread the blanket and flopped down on it. I stretched out beside him, anticipating a long, warm, wonder-ful kiss. Instead he stayed away from me, propping himself up on one elbow. "So, are things okay at home?" he asked out of the blue.

"Sure," I said, surprised. "Why do you ask?"

"I just heard something about how, like, maybe money's a little bit tight since your dad passed away." His hand traced circles in the sand.

What had he heard? I wondered. A vague rumor or gory details? I acted casual, hoping it was the former. "Yeah, money's

tight, but we're managing. My mom's got a pretty good job."
I should have stopped there, but I didn't. The lies began slipping out before I could stop myself. "I mean, it's not the same without Dad. Like, the Buick broke down and Mom had no idea what to do so she had it towed someplace and who knows when we'll get it back. But you don't have to worry about us," I declared. "It turns out my dad had this big insurance policy. So everything's"—*awful. Terrifying*—"fine."

"Glad to hear it," Parker said, visibly relieved.

I redirected the conversation fast. "I'm so excited about the prom, Parker. I've never been to one! Is it just sophomores? Where is it going to be?"

"Rocky Point Country Club," he replied. "All four classes together—it's a small school. Hey, by the way, have you bought a dress yet? I need to know the color so I can order a corsage to match."

"I did buy a dress," I told him. "It's really pretty, but the color's kind of hard to describe. I'll show it to you when you drop me off."

We kissed for a while, but for some reason I couldn't relax. I kept thinking about the lies I'd told Parker. He'd asked me a straightforward question—why hadn't I been honest?

When it started to get cold at the beach, we went to the library. It was about ten when Parker took me home. I brought him inside, and we stuck our heads into the family room to say hi to Mom, who was watching the news. "I'm just going to show Parker my new dress," I told her.

"Okay. How was the library?" Mom asked.

"Full of books," Parker replied, giving my waist a secret little pinch. Then he pointed to the news program on the TV. "Anything interesting happening in the real world, Mrs. Walker?"

"The usual madness and mayhem," she replied.

"You got to love it, though, just for the contrast," Parker said. "Hawk Harbor can be pretty slow. If my family didn't have a place in Boston, we'd go nuts."

A funny expression flickered across Mom's face. Parker's right—Hawk Harbor can be boring—but it's also home. Mom's lived here all her life. "Show Parker that dress, Rose," Mom suggested. "I think he'll like it."

We stepped back into the hall.

"The dress is in my closet," I told Parker.

"Are you inviting me to your bedroom?" he kidded.

"Sure, with the lights on and the door open and my sisters right next door."

Upstairs, I pulled the dress from my closet, holding it against my body so Parker could admire it properly. "It's kind of green," I said. "Sage. Probably just about any color corsage would—" I noticed his expression and stopped. "The dress looks really pretty on," I assured him.

"Maybe," he said without conviction. "Rose, though, the thing is, the Seagate prom is really . . . formal."

For a moment I didn't know what to say. "You think this dress isn't nice enough?" I asked, crestfallen.

"I want you to have fun at the dance, that's all," he said. He took the dress and tossed it onto the bed, then gave me a hug. "I want you to feel like you fit in. And you're such a knockout. You should be wearing something more . . ." He stepped back, snapping his fingers. "I bet Val has a dress you could borrow."

"Val?" I repeated.

"Valerie Mathias—you met her at your birthday party. She has a closet full of formal stuff."

"How do you know?" I asked crabbily, folding my arms across my chest.

Parker smiled. "I confess—I've been in her room. We used to go out, kind of on-again, off-again."

"Oh, I see," I said, though I wasn't sure that I did.

"Anyhow, I'll take care of it. You'll be perfect—the prettiest girl at the prom," Parker promised, pulling me to him for a kiss.

The prettiest girl at the prom, I mused a little while later as I walked back upstairs. I'd seen Parker out to his car and we'd kissed again and I'd decided to be grateful for his offer to get a dress for me instead of insulted, which had been my first response. Hadn't he said he was just thinking about my feelings? I frowned. If that was the case, then how come my feelings were hurt?

For about the thousandth time since he died, I wished I could talk to my father. It had never seemed quite right, dating a boy Dad hadn't checked out first. I remembered his assessment of Sully a couple of years ago. "Nice boy, but he's not as bright as you." Dad had grinned. "Which is okay in the romantic department. Your mother's twice as smart as I am."

Would Dad have liked Parker? I wondered, trying unsuccessfully to imagine the two of them having a guy-to-guy chat about football or cars. Okay, so maybe it wouldn't have been love at first sight. But Dad was a generous, tolerant person, I thought. He would see Parker's good qualities—how smart he was, and how much he liked me.

How about Parker? It was hard to guess what he'd have thought about Dad since I never discussed Dad with him. Why is that? I asked myself. Am I afraid he'll look down on me or something since my dad was a fisherman and his dad's a stockbroker?

Still thinking about Dad, I headed down the hall to the bathroom to brush my teeth. I passed Daisy's room—it was dark, and so were Lily's and Laurel's rooms. When I heard a muffled noise, though, I stopped.

Was Lily having another bad dream?

Then I realized the sound had come from Laurel's room. "Toad?" I called quietly. "Are you all right?"

She didn't answer, but I heard the telltale sound again and I pushed open the door. Laurel was sitting up in bed, her hair even more tangled than usual. I sat next to her. "What's the matter, Toad? Why are you crying?"

She pressed her face against my shoulder, her body shaking with quiet sobs. "I miss Daddy." She looked up at me, her eyes bright with tears. "I miss him so much. Don't you, Rose?"

I nodded, my own throat suddenly tight with tears. "Yes," I told her. "I do."

Four

VALERIE DROPPED THE dress off on Saturday. It was possibly the most embarrassing moment of my life. "Parker said you needed a dress for the prom," she said, pulling a dry cleaner's bag out of the backseat of her black Saab. "I hope this fits. You're a little bigger than me."

We were standing in my driveway. I took the bag, feeling ridiculous. "Uh, do you want to come in? Have a soda or something?"

"Can't." She glanced over her shoulder at my house. I saw it through her eyes—old and somewhat dilapidated. "Thanks, anyway."

"Thank you. For the dress."

Valerie climbed back behind the wheel of the car. "Just clean it before you give it back, okay?"

"Sure."

She flashed a smile before she drove away. "See you at the prom, Rose."

I went inside, holding the hanger high so the dress wouldn't trail on the ground. The house rumbled around me, buzzing with Saturday sounds: Daisy vacuuming, Lily and Laurel squabbling, a distant radio tuned to the classical music station Mom likes.

In my room I pulled the dry cleaner's bag off Valerie's dress. Now that I could really see it, I caught my breath. It was gorgeous. The strapless bodice was made of light blue satin, and the poofy skirt was soft ivory. I'll wear high heels, pale stockings, and the silver necklace from Parker, I thought excitedly.

I fingered the expensive fabric, imagining myself wearing the dress as I danced with Parker at the Seagate Academy prom. With this dress I would be the prettiest girl there. Parker was right.

Then my happy smile faded. Something was bothering me . . . but what? Was it the idea that the dress somehow mattered more than I did? That in a plainer dress, a secondhand dress, I'd be less attractive, less important, less special?

My gaze shifted to the closet, where the sage green vintage dress from Second Time Around was hanging. Then I looked back at the blue-and-ivory dress. "Don't you want to be beautiful?" I asked myself.

I WAS YAWNING over my cereal bowl on Monday morning when my mother flew through the kitchen, her heels clattering. A car horn honked outside in the driveway. "That's my ride," she said, sticking her arms in the sleeves of a blazer as she hurried to the door. "You can take the wagon today. Would you pick Daisy up after softball? And stop at the grocery store on the way home—there's a list on the counter. Thanks a million, honey."

I rinsed out my bowl, then stuck it in the dishwasher. I still had to brush my teeth and get my books together, and by the time I was ready to head out to the car, I'd almost forgotten about the grocery list. I doubled back to get it.

The list was on the counter as Mom had said, but it wasn't alone. Right next to it was a book of food stamp coupons.

Having my driver's license is a mixed blessing, I decided, eyeing the food stamps with distaste. When I got my license, I was so psyched to cruise around town that I'd volunteered to do errands. I wished I could take back the offer, but it was too late. I hesitated for a second, then picked up the coupons gingerly, shoving them as far down in my bag as possible.

At school I kept the food stamps hidden in my bag, figuring out of sight, out of mind. Instead I couldn't stop thinking about them. By lunch period I'd decided to talk to my friends about my dilemma. Maybe Rox knows about this kind of stuff, I speculated. After all, Mr. Beale had been unemployed for a while a few years back. And what about Sumita's family, when they first got to the United States from India, before the restaurant took off?

The four of us staked out our usual table, near the vending machines by the back wall of the cafeteria. We opened our lunches—we'd all brought from home—and everyone else began eating. I took my time unwrapping my sandwich, considering how to bring up the food stamps. Before I could, though, Mita gestured with a carrot stick. "So, we're all waiting to hear about The Dress!" she declared, giving the words capital letters.

"The dress," I repeated.

"The one you're borrowing from Parker's friend," said Rox.

"I saw it last night," Cath cut in, tearing the paper wrapper off a straw. Cath came over because we were working on an American history report together. "It's strapless."

"Sounds sexy," Mita commented.

"And the fabric," Cath elaborated, sticking the straw into a bottle of grapefruit juice. "It's satin, but not the shiny kind. It just sort of . . . glows."

Cath went on describing the dress, and since she was doing such a good job, I only needed to add a word here and there. As we talked, though, I felt less and less like bringing up the food stamps. It was just such a contrast to the fairy-tale ball gown. I shouldn't be embarrassed around my friends, though, I told myself.

I looked around to make sure no one at the nearby tables could hear me. Then I pulled the food stamps out of my bag and slid them onto the table, keeping them mostly covered with my hand. "Check this out," I said grimly.

Rox, Mita, and Cath peered at the coupon book. "Oh, I remember those," said Rox with a knowing sigh.

Cath looked up at my face, reading me with the ease of someone who's known me all my life. "You're bummed, huh?"

"Wouldn't you be?" I countered.

"It's not the end of the world," Rox said. "Your mom needs some help right now—anyone would. She'll be back on her feet in no time." Rox put a hand on mine and gave my fingers a squeeze. "Don't worry."

I wanted to cry. "It's kind of embarrassing," I said with a sniffle. "I almost didn't tell you."

"That's crazy," said Mita. "I mean, what are friends for? Richer or poorer, in sickness and in health—"

"That's marriage," I pointed out, tucking the food stamps back into their hiding place.

"Whatever. Tell you what. I'll go shopping with you this afternoon," Mita offered. "I don't have to be at the restaurant until five."

"You're the best," I told her, my eyes shining. "All of you. But don't worry about it, Mita. Daisy will be with me, so I'll manage."

We went back to eating our lunches. I was still dreading the grocery store, but it seemed a little less horrible now that my friends knew about it. They'd put it into perspective for me. Food stamps were just one of those things. Maybe my family didn't have a lot of money, but we were managing.

"Back to the prom," Rox said to me. "Tell Parker if any of his Seagate friends needs a date, I'm free that night."

I cracked a smile. "Will do."

* * *

LATE THAT AFTERNOON I picked up Daisy at the junior high after softball practice, then drove slowly back into town. "The speed limit's thirty-five," Daisy pointed out.

I was going about twenty. "Give me a break, okay?" I said. "I just got my license. I don't want to get pulled over."

I couldn't drive much slower than that, though, so eventually we arrived at the Village Market. I parked the station wagon, climbed out slowly, slammed the creaky driver's side door, then took my time locking it even though no one bothers locking a car in the Village Market parking lot. Daisy, meanwhile, had grabbed a shopping cart and was heading into the store.

I trotted after her, shopping list in hand. "Should we split up?" she asked.

"Sure." I scanned the list. "Why don't you grab a couple of loaves of bread and some cereal?" I lowered my voice. "Mom wrote down that the generic cornflakes are on sale."

Daisy strode off, her ponytail swinging purposefully. I wheeled the cart down the produce aisle, grabbing bunches of carrots and bananas and heads of lettuce almost at random. I'd dragged my feet on my way to the store, but now that I was there, I wanted to get this over with as quickly as possible.

In the meat and poultry section I chose value packs of ground beef and chicken. Then I cruised down the dairy aisle, snagging a couple of jugs of milk. Daisy met me near the snack aisle. "How about some cookies?" she suggested.

"They're not on the list," I said, wondering if there was a rule against buying junk food with food stamps. I pictured the checkout clerk frowning at the cookies, then calling the store manager over the loudspeaker. "We should stick to the list," I decided.

"Well, what else do we need?"

I glanced at the list—only one more item. That meant it was about time to head to the checkout counter. I froze, suddenly unable to move my feet. "Rose?" Daisy prompted.

"Um, laundry soap," I told her. "A jumbo box. Whatever's cheapest."

"I'll run and get it. Meet you in line."

"Yeah."

She left me standing near the snack aisle, my heart pounding with dread. *Pull yourself together, Rose Walker*, I thought, wishing I had let Mita come along for moral support. *Have some guts.*

Taking a deep breath, I focused on a boy halfway down the snack aisle. He was of medium height and stocky build and sandy haired, wearing baggy gym shorts, a ripped T-shirt, and a backward Hawk Harbor South Regional H.S. varsity baseball cap. *It's Sully*, I realized, horrified.

My old boyfriend, Brian "Sully" Sullivan, was staring at the shelf in front of him as if choosing between tortilla chips and cheese puffs were the most important decision he'd ever make in his life. Had he spotted me yet? If he turned his head half an inch, it was all over. He'd grab his bag of chips, then saunter over to say hi. Walk me to the checkout counter . . . and see the food coupons. Sully didn't have a mean bone in his body, and that was the problem—he wouldn't think twice about telling people about the food stamps. It would never occur to him that I would care if people knew. The whole baseball team will know by tomorrow, and their girlfriends. And isn't Sam Conover's sister Kate dating a guy whose cousin goes to Seagate? I thought frantically. What if the word gets back to Parker?

Panic struck like a riptide. Abandoning the shopping cart full of food, I sprinted toward the exit.

Daisy intercepted me. "Rose, where are you going?"

Without answering, I yanked the box of laundry detergent from her hand and stuck it on the nearest shelf. I grabbed her arm, but she resisted me. "We can't leave without the groceries," Daisy said. "Mom'll be mad. If it's about the—*you know*—I'll pay for the stuff. I don't care."

Her selflessness made me feel a thousand times worse, if that were possible. "Just come on," I said, choking back tears.

WE DROVE HOME in silence—the only sound the humming of the pavement under the wheels. "What are you going to tell Mom?" Daisy asked quietly as I brought the car to a stop on our gravel driveway.

I shrugged. "I'll think of something. Just keep your mouth shut, okay?"

We went into the house. Mom was in the kitchen, sipping a glass of iced tea while she sorted through the day's mail. I wanted to run straight up to my room, but that would only make me look guilty. And I didn't do anything wrong, I told myself.

"Hi, girls," Mom greeted us, looking up with a smile. "Need help carrying in the groceries?"

Daisy was as silent as a stone. "The groceries," I repeated, pretending I didn't know what she was talking about. "Oh, shoot, the groceries! Mom, I'm so sorry. Choral practice ran over, and I was late picking up Daisy, and then I guess I just . . . I'll run back out," I offered, praying she wouldn't call my bluff. "Do you want me to run back out?"

During this Academy Award—winning speech, my mother watched my face steadily. I managed not to turn red, to blink, or to stammer, and I thought I sounded pretty sincere. Maybe too sincere. Could she see through me?

"That's all right, Rose," she said finally. "I can go tomorrow."

We looked at each other a moment. Her face told me that she understood. If she had called me out on my lie, I couldn't possibly have felt worse than I did at that moment. I turned away, sick with guilt and ashamed of myself. "Well, I'm going to start my homework," I told her. "Let me know if you need help with dinner."

"Will do, Rose."

The way she said my name—so full of sympathy and love— made me want to cry.

But as I headed down the hall toward the staircase another emotion began bubbling to the surface: anger. Why should I feel bad about this? I thought. "It's Mom's fault," I muttered under my breath.

Daisy was right behind me on the stairs. "What's Mom's fault?" she wanted to know.

"That we don't have any money," I practically spat out. "Dad would never have let this happen to us. Maybe if Mom had gone to college like everybody else—"

Daisy's blue eyes widened with shock. "Rose!"

"Well, it's true," I said, kicking open the door to my bedroom. "Why should we have to suffer because she can't get her act together?"

Daisy followed me into my room. "Mom's doing her best," she insisted. "I think she's really brave—and resourceful."

My sister's saintly tone made me even madder. "Whose side are you on?" I snapped.

"I'm not on anyone's side," she answered. "I mean, we're all on the same side, aren't we?"

I shook my head, disgusted. "Thanks for the opinion, Miss I-never-do-anything-wrong!" I stomped across the room to my desk. "If you don't *mind*, I have a ton of studying to do."

Daisy stood in the doorway for a few seconds, biting her lip, her eyebrows furrowed. When I didn't look at her, she finally turned away and disappeared down the hall.

As soon as she was gone the guilt returned. There was no reason to yell at Daisy, I realized. She's just a kid—it's not her fault, either.

Anyway . . . she's right.

With that thought my anger faded, like steam into cold night air. Flopping onto the bed with my Spanish book, I sighed deeply. Who was I really mad at, anyway? It wasn't Daisy's fault we were poor, and it wasn't my fault, and Daisy was right—as good as it felt to blame someone, it wasn't Mom's fault.

I decided that in a little while, I'd hunt up Daisy and apologize. I considered confessing to Mom about chickening out at the Village Market, but I just couldn't. What if she asked me to go back to the store? I wasn't ready for that.

I'm not angry at Mom; I'm angry at the situation. It's nobody's fault, I reasoned as I worked through my Spanish assignment. Nobody's fault, nobody's fault.

Shoving my book aside, I dropped my head onto the pillow and let out another deep sigh. Maybe it was nobody's fault, but it was still horrible.

Five

THE SOUTH REGIONAL junior prom was taking place the same night as the Seagate Academy prom, though it would be held in the school gym, not at a fancy country club. Cath was going with Tony, a guy she'd just started dating, and Mita and Rox were both planning to go to a big sophomore class bash at the beach. We decided to get together at Cath's on Saturday morning for a pre-prom-and-party manicure session.

We set up in Cath's bedroom. She is seriously into being a Beautiful Person and could practically open her own salon—she has a vanity table cluttered with dozens of kinds and colors of makeup, all sorts of hairbrushes and curlers, and enough cotton balls to decorate a parade float. She took turns giving me, Rox, and Mita manicures. Then Rox did Cath's nails while Mita helped me experiment with hairstyles.

"I wish we were all going to the same party tonight," Rox

said as she dipped the nail brush into a bottle of polish and went to work on Cath's left thumb.

"Tony and I will come by the beach later if the dance gets boring," Cath promised.

"Where's he taking you for dinner beforehand?" Mita asked.

"Leonardo's." Cath rolled her eyes. "Italian, of course."

"You'll get spaghetti sauce on your prom dress," I predicted with a grin.

"Give me a little credit!" she said, laughing. "I won't order marinara."

"How about you?" Mita asked as she twisted my hair into a French knot. "Think you'll be able to drag *Parker*"—at his name, she batted her dark eyes playfully—"to the beach when the Seagate prom winds down?"

Parker's not really the type to party on the beach in a tuxedo. "We'll see," I said. "I think one of his friends is having an after-party. He'll probably want to stick with the Seagate crowd."

"So, guess who called me last night," Rox said, her blue eyes sparkling. She placed the nail polish bottle on the vanity to free up her hands for a dramatic gesture. "Kurt Blessing."

"Oooh!" We gave an appropriately enthusiastic group squeal—Kurt Blessing is one of the cutest boys in our class.

"Why on *earth* did he call you?" Mita teased. Guys are always calling Rox—she has big blue eyes, tons of wavy strawberry blond hair, and a killer figure, not to mention a great personality.

"He wanted to be sure I was going to the party tonight," Rox replied.

"Oooh!" we chorused again.

"So what you're saying," Cath said, "is that by the time Tony and I show up, you and Kurt will have disappeared into the dunes for your own private—"

Rox slapped the back of Cath's still drying hand. "Dirty mind."

"What do you think about your hair?" Mita asked me. "Do you like it? Or is it too formal?" She answered her own question before I had a chance. "Maybe you should wear it down. What if you brushed it back like this and then tucked this part and clipped this part and . . ."

I sat quietly while Mita fussed. Rox and Cath were still joking about Kurt. Suddenly I felt a pang. They're going to have so much fun tonight, I thought, feeling left out. I wish I were going to the beach party, too.

Then I caught myself. I was going to the prom with Parker Kemp. Nothing could be more fun than that. Right?

YOUR HAIR LOOKS so pretty," Lily chirped that evening. I was standing in front of my dresser and mirror in my underwear and stockings, getting ready for the dance. Lily had been driving me nuts peeking into my room, so I'd finally invited her in to watch me put on my makeup and get dressed.

I'd decided on a French twist. It was a more formal style than I usually liked, but I wanted to look sophisticated.

I stuck a bobby pin into my hair, capturing a stray wisp. "Do you really think so?" I asked anxiously. Ordinarily my eight-year-old sister wouldn't be my first choice as a fashion consultant, but her opinion was better than nothing. And suddenly, for some reason, I was nervous. About my appearance . . . about everything. Will I look right? Will I act right? What if Parker ends up wishing he'd taken someone else to the dance?

"I really think so," Lily declared.

"Well, then, how about my makeup? Did I put on too much eye shadow?" I blinked, then patted my cheeks. "I'm not tan yet. Should I wear blush?"

"You look fine the way you are," Lily said.

"Fine?"

"I mean, *great*," she corrected herself.

With a wry laugh I reached for my jewelry box. I fastened the silver necklace Parker had given me around my neck and then went to the closet, where Valerie's dress waited for me.

I took the dress from the dry cleaner's bag. I laid it out on the bed and for a moment just looked at it admiringly. Then I unzipped the zipper down the back, careful not to snag the delicate fabric, and prepared to step into the dress.

Ten seconds passed, then thirty. I stood holding the dress for a full minute. "What's wrong?" Lily wanted to know.

I stared at the dress in my hands. What *was* wrong? I wasn't a hundred percent sure, but I knew one thing for certain. "I can't wear this dress," I said quietly.

"Why not?" Lily asked. "It's really pretty."

I bit my lip. Was it because it belonged to someone else, a girl I didn't know very well? I recalled my joking remark to Cath about getting spaghetti sauce on her dress. "I won't be able to relax—I'll be too worried that I'll spill something on it," I said to Lily. "Or rip it or something."

Lily seemed satisfied with that explanation, and I was, too. But was it the real reason? I found myself thinking about my conversation with Parker the day I'd shown him the dress from Second Time Around. I'd been so excited about it, but he'd dismissed it with a glance.

Why did it even matter to him what dress I wore?

"I'm going to wear the other dress," I decided suddenly, sticking Valerie's dress back in the dry cleaner's bag before I could change my mind.

I slipped into the sage green dress and immediately knew I was doing the right thing. It felt soft, silky, comfortable. I didn't look like a supermodel, but I looked pretty. I looked like me.

Lily squinted at me. "Now the necklace looks wrong," she pointed out.

Of course Lily, the costume jewelry queen, was right. I returned Parker's necklace to my jewelry box, putting on the one my mother had given me. The tiny gold rosebud on the delicate chain was perfect with the old-fashioned dress. "There," I said. "I'm ready."

Lily clapped, her eyes shining. "Parker will think you're so beautiful!"

The tiniest of doubts flickered in my heart. I ignored it. He's taking *me* to the dance, not the dress, I reminded myself. "I hope so," I replied.

D AISY, DON'T TALK to Parker about sports, okay? He's not into baseball or any of that stuff. Lily, couldn't you wear something normal for once in your life? And Toad, if Henry or any other rodent comes within fifty feet of this house tonight, you're doomed. Got that?"

It was seven o'clock—Parker would be ringing the doorbell any minute now. Meanwhile, seeing me off on my first prom date had turned into a Walker Family Event. My three sisters were lurking in the front hall. Daisy had an old Polaroid camera, and Lily was clutching the box with Parker's boutonniere. Laurel was without pets—that I could see, anyway—but as usual she carried the faintest whiff of eau de barnyard.

"If I can't talk to him about sports, what should I talk about?" Daisy asked.

"You don't have to talk about *anything*," I said, grabbing a bottle of room spray from the powder room and giving Laurel a quick spritz. "Just, you know, smile." I took Daisy's baseball cap off her head and tossed it in the coat closet. "Say hello and then vamoose."

The doorbell rang. We all jumped. "It's him!" Lily squealed excitedly.

"I'll open it," Laurel offered.

"No, I will," said Lily. A shoving match ensued. I elbowed past them to open it myself.

Parker stepped into the hall, a white florist's box in his hand. He looked incredibly handsome in his black tuxedo and cummerbund. "Hi," I said breathlessly. "You look great!"

I waited for my kiss. Instead Parker gave me an up-and-down look. "What happened to Val's dress?" he asked.

That threw me off balance for a minute. What happened to "Hi, Rose, you look wonderful"? I thought. "I, uh . . . the zipper was broken," I fibbed, blushing. I darted a don't-you-dare-speak glance at Lily. "I just noticed when I went to put it on tonight. Don't worry," I babbled on, "I'll get it fixed before I give it back to Valerie. I'll—"

"It's too bad because . . ." Parker shook his head, then gave me a quick peck on the cheek. "Never mind. You look fine. And hey. What have we here?" he asked in a patronizing tone. "Dorothy from *The Wizard of Oz?*"

This is the moment to point out that Lily had curled her long hair into ringlets and was wearing an old-fashioned blue pinafore with a white blouse and button-up shoes. "*Alice in Wonderland,*" she told him, frowning a little at his mistake.

"Right. You're the one who likes to dress up." Parker turned to Laurel. "And you're in, what, third grade?"

Laurel's eyebrows drew together. "Fifth," she said from her hiding place behind Daisy.

"And you'll be starting high school next year, right?" Parker said to Daisy. "Breaking a lot of hearts, too."

"I *hope* not," Daisy replied, making a disgusted face.

I'd been holding my breath, waiting for one of my siblings to do something humiliating. Henry the mouse hadn't made an appearance, though, so maybe this was my lucky night.

Done with small talk, Parker turned his back on my sisters. I saw them exchange meaningful glances. "Let's get this show on the road," he said to me.

"No, wait." Daisy whipped out the camera. "We need a picture!"

Just then Mom showed up. She'd been at the dining room table, paying some bills. "Let's take a whole bunch," she suggested. "Rose, why don't you give Parker his boutonniere?"

Daisy snapped photos of Parker pinning the corsage to my dress and me pinning the boutonniere to his jacket. Then we posed for about twenty pictures standing with our arms around each other. I felt like an idiot.

Finally Parker said, "We really need to get going, Rose." He put a hand on the small of my back and practically shoved me out the door.

"Bye!" I called back to my family.

"Have fun!" Mom said.

W OW," I COULDN'T help saying when we entered the lobby of Rocky Point Country Club.

It was like a movie set: chandeliers and gilded mirrors, oriental rugs and ornate furniture, glass cabinets filled with silver trophies, and photographs of yachts on all the walls. "Haven't you ever been here?" Parker asked, one eyebrow lifted slightly.

Until I'd met Parker, I hadn't even known anyone who

was a member. "Um, it's been a couple of years," I lied. "I'd forgotten how pretty it is."

The prom was being held in a ballroom that opened onto a stone terrace. There was a view of the moonlit golf course in one direction and of the marina in the other. We had eaten dinner at the Harborside before heading over to the country club, so the dance was already in full swing. As soon as Parker and I appeared we were surrounded by his friends. I spotted Valerie's brother, Stephen, standing at a distance. "Who did he come with?" I asked Parker.

Parker shrugged. "Mathias? He's probably stag. No one's good enough for that guy."

Parker, David, Chip, and the other guys went through the usual routine of high fives and pounding one another on the back. Meanwhile the Seagate girls descended on me.

"Rose, what a sweet dress," exclaimed Tiffany Greer, who goes out with Parker's friend David. "Did you make it yourself?"

"Um," I began.

"I love it," gushed Caitlin O'Connor. "It's like *The Age of Innocence* or something. The Victorian look really looks good on her, don't you think, Amanda?"

"She's braver than me," Amanda Morrow agreed. "I have to go with the trends, you know?"

I'd never heard such backhanded compliments in my life. I should have laughed out loud. Instead I cringed, hoping Parker wasn't listening.

Valerie Mathias strolled by with her date. She was wearing

a very short, sexy, black off-the-shoulder dress. She paused just long enough to note, "The blue-and-white dress didn't work out, huh?"

"Uh—no," I replied lamely.

"Too bad." As she drifted off she lowered her voice, speaking to her date, but I heard her clearly. "I can see why she wanted to borrow something from me."

I decided not to let it bother me. What do I care if the Seagate girls are snobs? I thought. That's not exactly news.

The band was great and I was dying to dance, but Parker wanted to stand around and gab with his friends. I tried to take part in the conversation, but it was hard—there were too many inside jokes. Every now and then someone would clue me in, but instead of making me feel included, it only made it more apparent that I was an outsider. Then they all started comparing their plans for the summer. Aspen, Europe, sailing, tennis. Nobody mentioned a job.

"Let's dance, Parker," I said impulsively.

We danced to a few songs, and I started to relax. It felt good to be in Parker's arms. Then in between songs Valerie appeared. "You don't mind if I borrow your date, do you?" she asked with a sly smile, hooking her arm through Parker's.

What could I say? I'd borrowed her dress, even if I didn't end up wearing it. And Parker didn't look as if he thought having to dance with Valerie was too much of a burden. "Sure," I replied. "Go ahead."

I wandered over to the food. As I poured myself a cup of punch and turned to watch the dancers, I wondered why I was experiencing a feeling of déjà vu. When Stephen Mathias walked up to me, I figured it out. It was just like at my surprise party.

"Would you like to dance?" he asked politely.

I blushed, feeling somewhat idiotic. "We don't have to," I told him. "I mean—"

"I'd like to." Stephen stuck out an elbow so I had to take his arm. "Just a couple of songs."

Just my luck, right then the band started playing a slow song. Stephen took my right hand in his left and placed his right hand on my waist. I just kind of shuffled, but he was doing something fancy with his feet. "You really know how to dance," I observed.

"Ballroom lessons when I was in sixth grade," he told me.

"You're kidding!"

"My mother made me take them. But it comes in handy now and then," he said. "At debutante parties and stuff."

"Oh," I said.

For some reason I found myself blushing again. Stephen's hand was very warm on my waist. "This is a pretty dress," he remarked.

I glanced up at him. "You're joking, right?"

"Of course not. I like it."

"Then you're the only one."

He was still looking into my eyes. "They're just jealous," he said.

"Who?" I asked, wondering if he'd overheard my conversation with Amanda, Tiffany, and Caitlin.

"Because you don't feel like you have to look like every other girl here," he went on. "You have your own style."

I realized that Stephen was right. The Seagate girls had made me feel like the poor relation—I'd almost forgotten that I'd *chosen* to wear this dress. "Thanks," I said softly.

When the song ended, I stepped away from Stephen. "I should go find Parker," I told him, hunting for my boyfriend in the crowded room. "He's probably looking for me."

A funny expression crossed Stephen's face. "I don't see him," he said. He took my hand again. "One more song, okay?"

"Well, okay," I agreed.

We danced one more song, and then I went to the ladies' room. When I came out, I still didn't see Parker, but I did see Amanda. "Three girls have the exact same dress as me," she moaned, sucking in her thin cheeks in irritation. "Can you believe it? And I went all the way to Boston for it just so this wouldn't happen!"

You should have shopped at Second Time Around, I thought smugly. "Bad luck," I said.

"So, I saw you dancing with Stephen Mathias," Amanda said. "That's kind of an honor, you know."

I didn't know. "What do you mean?"

"He used to go out with this Seagate girl two classes ahead of him," Amanda explained as she fiddled with her corsage, which had come unpinned. "Camilla Larson. They broke up right after she left for college last fall, though, so he's available, but I guess none of us meets his high standards or something. He hasn't asked anyone else out this whole year. There." She patted her corsage, then gave me a distracted smile. "See you, Rose."

Amanda melted into the crowd. A minute later I saw her dancing with her date. I glimpsed Stephen, too, standing with a group of guys whom I guessed were juniors and seniors. I studied him thoughtfully. So, he didn't have a date, and he didn't seem to be dancing much, but he had danced with me. How come? Did he feel sorry for me? I hoped not.

I made a tour of the ballroom and finally spotted Parker and Valerie. A song had just ended, but they were still standing close together. Before drawing apart, Valerie whispered something in Parker's ear that made him grin. Parker whispered something back, gave her a little hug around the waist, and then headed in my direction.

He gave me the same kind of hug he'd given Valerie. I tried hard not to notice or care. "Having fun?" he asked.

Was I having fun standing by myself, dodging insults about my dress, and watching Parker dance with someone else? I smiled at him brightly and gave Parker the only answer I knew he would accept. "Sure!"

KNOWING IT WAS a special night for me, Mom had relaxed my usual curfew, so Parker and I went to a couple of after-parties and I didn't get home until nearly four in the morning. After we kissed good night, Parker drove off as quietly as he could, the Jeep's tires crunching on the gravel driveway, and I tiptoed into the dark and silent house.

In my room I left the light off, but the moon was shining

into my window, so I could still see myself as I stood in front of the mirror over my dresser. For a long moment I stared at my shadowy reflection. I didn't look like a girl who'd just been to her first prom with the boy of her dreams. I looked like I was about to cry—which I was.

Disappointment washed over me. Thinking back on the evening, I couldn't find fault with Parker. He'd been the perfect date as always. Sure, he'd danced a few times with other girls, but that seemed to be the Seagate style. His good night kisses had been passionate. He'd told me, not for the first time, that he was crazy about my long blond hair, my big blue eyes, my smooth skin. Shouldn't that make me happy?

Tears welled up in my eyes and spilled down my cheeks. I ripped the drooping corsage from my dress and threw it on the floor. The gold rosebud and chain around my neck glimmered softly in the moonlight—I yanked it off, too, then shoved the necklace to the back of my dresser drawer, thinking unreasonably, I hate this tacky rosebud charm! I hate it! I'll never wear it again.

Quickly unzipping my dress, I wriggled free of it as fast as I could. I crumpled the soft fabric in my hands and tossed it into the corner, giving it a kick for good measure.

I'd been trying to blink back my tears, but now they were flowing. I grabbed a nightgown from my dresser drawer and pulled it over my head, noticing that it was on backward and inside out but not caring. I crawled into bed and buried my face in my pillow to stifle my sobs. Outside my window the sky was gray with light as I finally cried myself to sleep.

Six

Don't you just love summer?" Rox asked me a week and a half later.

It was midmorning on a Tuesday, and we were strolling along the sidewalk in downtown Hawk Harbor, enjoying the still fresh freedom of summer vacation. The sun was shining, and there was a warm sea breeze. Main Street still wasn't too busy—things wouldn't really pick up until Fourth of July weekend—but most of the shops and restaurants were open, and the town had a clean, just-washed look. I pushed my sunglasses up on the bridge of my nose and tipped my head back a bit, shaking out my loose hair. "I love summer, generally speaking," I admitted. "But *this* summer . . ."

"Are you still moping because you can't go to Wildwood?" Rox wanted to know.

I shrugged. Just the day before I'd gotten a letter from

Julianne Greenberg. Camp had only just started, but she already had ten hilarious wish-you-were-here stories. The worst of it was she didn't know the real reason I'd turned down the counselor job, so she assumed I was having a great time, too. When I'd told her the news, I'd whitewashed the situation, throwing in a lie about a family trip. "Have I really been moping?" I asked Rox.

"Maybe not *moping*," she said, "but I could tell you've been bummed."

"I was at first," I agreed, "but I'm trying not to act like a baby about it. I mean, a lot of things had to change with Dad . . . gone." It was still hard for me to say *dead.* It sounded so final.

We were silent for a moment. "But there's a silver lining," Rox pointed out. "Since you're staying in Hawk Harbor, you'll get to see more of Parker."

"Right," I said. I couldn't admit, though, that ever since prom night, thinking about Parker made me so insecure that I felt nauseated. I hated feeling that way. Everyone assumed I'd had a great time at the Seagate prom, and I hadn't disillusioned them. Lying was getting easier for me. "He and his dad have this big just-us-guys sailing trip planned for most of August, but yeah. 'A silver lining.'" I had to laugh. "I sound like Daisy. That's the kind of sappy thing she'd say."

"Hey, it beats the alternative," Rox said. She stopped, gesturing at a storefront. "What do you say we try here first?"

Rox's words reminded me of why we'd come into town in the first place—we were job hunting. Our other friends already had jobs for the summer: Cath would be pitching in at her family's hardware store while Mita would help at her parents' restaurant.

Suppressing a sigh, I peered into the window of Cecilia's. "It doesn't look half bad," I said. And there was a Help Wanted sign in the window. "Okay." I straightened my shoulders. "Let's get this over with."

An hour later we concluded our parade of Main Street with a stop at Patsy's Diner. Rox didn't even have to fill out an application—Patsy hired her on the spot. "I can't believe it was that easy!" Rox exclaimed as we emerged into the sunshine. "Patsy said if I do a good job busing tables, she'll promote me to waitress after just a couple of weeks. Then I'll really be making decent money with tips and all."

I high-fived Rox, meanwhile biting my tongue. Maybe waitresses make good money, but you wouldn't catch me dishing out french fries and tuna melts in a tacky beige uniform. I gave a silent shudder at the thought of what Parker would say.

I'd applied for three jobs. "I hope I get the position at Cecilia's," I confided. "Mrs. King said she'd let me know tomorrow after she interviews a few more people."

Rox hooked her arm through mine. "We'll be working girls," she said cheerfully. "It'll be fun."

Working girls. I tried to look at it the way Rox did, with a positive attitude—the ol' silver lining approach. I'm not going to Wildwood because I'm not a kid anymore. No camp and no hanging out at the beach, either. I'll be working nine to five, five days a week. But I'll be making money, my own money. My expression brightened somewhat. "Maybe I'll even get an employee's discount!"

T HE HOURS ARE pretty flexible," I told Parker two days later. "I won't have to work every weekend. And Mrs. King seems really nice. I mean, like she'll be a cool boss even though she's pretty old, forty-five or so."

Parker had invited me over, and we were hanging out by the pool in his backyard. I was wearing a navy-and-white flowered bikini—last year's, but it still looked good on me.

Parker's house is one of the most beautiful in Hawk Harbor. It's right on the water, three stories high, with a widow's walk and painted white with black shutters. It was what our house might look like if we poured a million dollars into fixing it up. Not that I was envious—well, maybe a little. The Kemps have servants, too, an older couple named Mr. and Mrs. Birtwhistle, who live in an apartment over the four-car garage.

Mr. and Mrs. Birtwhistle do everything—shop, cook, clean, garden, you name it. Which means Mrs. Kemp doesn't have to lift a finger around the house, and she doesn't have a job, so she has plenty of time to sit by the pool, and that's what she was doing right then, just like Parker and me. She was on the opposite side of the pool, though, in a black strapless bathing suit, her eyes hidden behind big Jackie O. sunglasses. She is very blond and very thin and very tan. She kept her nose in a glossy travel magazine, putting it down now and then to make a call on her cell phone. She didn't speak to me or Parker.

I was still waiting for him to say something about my summer job. "Congratulations" or "Nice going" or something. Finally he grunted, "It's too bad you'll be working. We could have a lot of fun out on the boat."

"I won't be working all the time," I reminded him.

"So you'll be what, a salesgirl?"

On the surface it was an innocent question, but Parker managed to make *salesgirl* sound like *prostitute* or something. My cheeks burned. "Yeah, I'll be a salesgirl," I said in a defensive tone. "It's a nice store."

Parker laughed. "For Hawk Harbor. Hey, I'm roasting. Let's get wet."

Parker grabbed my hand and pulled me toward the pool. We dove into the cool water and started splashing around. I dunked Parker. He grabbed me around the waist and kissed me on the lips.

We were soaking wet and nearly naked, and the kiss made me kind of uncomfortable. I shot a glance at Mrs. Kemp, but she clearly couldn't care less what we did.

Parker gave me another kiss, and I tried to enjoy it. I tried not to think about him hating my dress and dancing with Valerie at the prom, about my summer job, about my family, about food stamps.

For just half an hour I wanted my life to be simple and perfect—for it to be nothing more than me and Parker in a turquoise blue swimming pool on a sunny summer day.

* * *

D ARN," MY MOTHER exclaimed.

I was setting the dining room table when I heard a saucepan clatter on the stove, its contents sizzling angrily. I looked into the kitchen at Mom—she'd dropped the wooden spoon and was shaking her right hand in the air. "Are you all right, Mom?" I asked.

She nodded, brushing the hair back from her face with an impatient gesture. "Just clumsy, that's all," she said. "Dinner's ready, Rose. Would you call your sisters?"

I shouted up the stairs and out the back door, and in a few minutes Daisy and Lily showed up. The four of us sat down to supper. "Where's Laurel?" I asked as Mom served the food.

"You remember Jack, who found the raccoons?" she replied, scooping mashed potatoes onto Lily's plate. "Cute kid, very well behaved. He invited her over for dinner."

I was kind of surprised Laurel went. I didn't really expect her to make friends with a boy. "That's great," I said.

"It's too bad she's not here, though," said Mom, "because I wanted to have a family meeting."

Oh no, not again, I thought. "What's up?" I asked warily.

"We just need to talk about chores," she said. "There's a lot of work that has to be done around the house and yard, and we need to do it ourselves. And I could use some help with the housework now that I'm working."

Against my will, I pictured the Kemps' spotless house, with Mrs. Birtwhistle busy in the kitchen and Mr. Birtwhistle busy in the yard. "Sure, Mom," Daisy said. "When Laurel comes home, you can just tell us what we should do."

We all started eating. "Great chicken, Mom," Daisy declared.

We'd been having chicken practically every night. It was always chicken or spaghetti, or at least that's how it seemed. Chicken with rice, chicken with pasta, chicken pot pie, chicken soup. "Thanks, sweetheart," she said. She looked very tired.

Susie Sunshine tried again. "How was work today, Mom?"

"Okay. They're giving me more hours starting next week—thirty-five up from twenty-five. Almost but not quite full-time."

"That's great!" I exclaimed, envisioning an end to our money problems.

Mom sighed, and my spirits sank again. "It's still not enough. Even if I were working forty hours a week with full benefits, I don't think I could make ends meet. Not at this job."

"Well, here," said Daisy brightly. She pulled something from the pocket of her shorts and placed it on the table. It was a wad of dollar bills. "Chores are one thing, but I want to do more. I've been saving my baby-sitting money. It's not tons, but now that it's summer, I'll really start raking it in. I've lined up two steady baby-sitting jobs, plus I put up flyers all over town about doing yard work."

Lily glanced from Daisy to Mom, her face solemn. "Mommy, should I try to make some money, too?" she asked.

"Of course not, honey," Mom said. She turned to Daisy,

her eyes watery. "I can't take your babysitting money, Daisy. There are lots of things you need for yourself."

"I'm going to make more," Daisy insisted. She shoved the bills toward Mom. "Really, Mom. You have to let me help." Daisy's eyes looked misty now, too. "I want to help."

I ate my chicken in silence, my own eyes prickling with unexpected tears.

I thought again about Parker's "perfect" life. I'd rather be rich than poor—who wouldn't? To live in a house like Parker's, with my own pool, my own car, servants. But then I thought about Parker's mother, the elegant, stylish, ice-cold, disinterested Mrs. Kemp, and my heart ached with love for my own mother and sisters. Maybe we had to work hard, but didn't that bring us closer in the end?

Honestly, Rose, I asked myself. Would you trade your life if you could?

Seven

THE SUMMER DAYS sped by, and I fell into a routine that wasn't half bad. I had thought I would hate getting up early every single morning—I thought I'd hate work, period. To my surprise, though, I liked working at the boutique. After a week I stopped moping about Wildwood. Rox made more money than I did, but at the end of the day she had to shampoo her hair for half an hour to get out the french fry smell. No, thanks!

So, my job was fine. Days off were still the best, though. Today Parker was taking me sailing for the first time.

We met at the marina. Parker's family's yacht, *Kiss and Tell*, was moored at slip nine, and Parker was already there, kneeling on the wooden deck with a rag in his hand.

"What are you doing?" I asked, swinging myself onto the boat.

He sat back. "Is what a threat?"

"When I'm not around, you—"

"Hey, you know I don't like to sail by myself. There's always someone else along or usually a bunch of people. If you didn't work so much, you wouldn't miss out. Which isn't to say you're not the one I want to be with. Let's mellow out, okay?"

Parker faced forward again, steering past a buoy. The breeze was picking up, so I took over the helm while he put up the sails. For a few minutes we were too busy to talk, which gave me time to think. Why is it always "I love the way you look"? I wondered. And that crack about the fishing boats. He wouldn't have said it if he knew about my dad, but still . . . There's a lot he doesn't know about me, I realized a little sadly. We'd been going out for three months. Why were we still practically strangers?

THE NEXT MORNING I made a couple of sales as soon as Cecilia's opened. Then during a quiet spell I dusted shelves and unpacked some new inventory—leather belts and other accessories. Mrs. King was letting me experiment with different ways of arranging things, so I decided to loop the belts over a piece of driftwood in the front window, alternating them with knotted silk scarves.

I was working on my display when the little bell over the door jingled. Straightening up, I pushed back my hair and prepared to smile winningly at my customer. Then I saw who it was, and my mouth just dropped open.

Stephen was wearing the standard Rocky Point uniform: khaki shorts, a weathered designer polo, boat shoes without socks, sunglasses. His glossy dark hair flopped down on his forehead. "Hi, Rose," he said.

"Hi," I replied.

I returned to the scarves and belts, ducking my head to hide my face behind my hair. He must've walked into the wrong store, I thought, hoping he'd be gone when I looked up again.

He wasn't. I remembered my position as a helpful sales-clerk. "Um, is there something I can help you with?" I asked.

Stephen leaned against the counter. "I like your display," he remarked. "You're artistic."

I turned red. Did I detect a note of sarcasm? I couldn't tell. "Um, thanks," I mumbled.

"So, yeah, there is," he went on.

"There is what?" I asked, mad at myself for letting him throw me off balance but unable to keep from blushing more.

"There is something you can help me with. If you would," he added politely. He spread his hands and raised his eyebrows in an expression of cluelessness. "My grandmother's seventy-fifth birthday. What should I give her?"

"Hmmm. It depends," I replied. "Is she an old old lady or a kind of hip old lady? We have these paperweights with shells inside the glass. They're pretty. Then we have these scarves—flashier. Or how about a pair of sunglasses?"

"I gave her a Dave Matthews Band CD for her last birth-day," Stephen told me.

I grinned. "Let's pick out some shades."

I expected him to take his gift-wrapped package and jet. Instead he hung out a while longer. "Don't you have to get back to work?" I asked, even though judging by his killer tan, he didn't have a summer job.

"I've got half an hour until my next lesson," he answered, explaining, "I teach soccer."

"You do?" I asked.

"Yeah," he said. "To a bunch of eighth graders." He smiled and added, "They're a handful."

"I bet," I said.

He fiddled with one of the scarves on the rack by the register. "So—what's Parker up to today?"

"Sailing, of course," I replied.

"Who with?"

I shrugged. "Some of his Rocky Point friends, probably. Or maybe your sister and that gang." I tipped my head to one side, wondering why Stephen was interested. "He doesn't always give me a detailed report."

He looked uncomfortable, as if he wanted to say more, but he just shrugged. "Well, hey," he said. "I'll see you around."

I nodded. "Right."

"Thanks again for helping me pick out a gift."

"That's what they pay me for."

He was still standing there, his eyes on my face. Once again I felt a flush creep up my neck to my cheeks. "So long," he said, finally turning toward the door.

"Bye," I said.

S O, WHAT DOES everyone feel like doing?" Parker asked.

It was Saturday evening, and a bunch of people were

flopped on chairs around the swimming pool in Parker's backyard, munching chips and salsa and watching the sun set. We'd spent the afternoon playing round-robin tennis at the country club, and everyone was beat. Beat and bored—at least I was. I'm not much of a tennis player and couldn't see the point, frankly, of playing game after game after game, but I'd gone along with it. If I'd sat out, Parker would've chosen another partner—maybe Valerie, who unfortunately was part of the group, as was her brother, Stephen. My impression was that Stephen didn't hang out with Parker and Valerie a whole lot, but he'd brought along some of his own friends for tennis, who were cool. Stephen had won more games than anyone, even Parker.

"There's a new Italian restaurant in Kent," Valerie said, snapping a tortilla chip in two and carefully eating half of it. "How about going out for dinner and then seeing a movie?"

"We could just stay here," Chip suggested, stretching his arms over his head and yawning widely. "Get takeout and delve into Kemp's video collection."

"Fine with me," David said.

"Oh, come on," wheedled Valerie. She crossed her slim, tanned legs. She was wearing a very short white tennis dress that managed to be prim and sexy at the same time. "Don't be such a slug. Who's up for trying La Trattoria?"

I stifled a yawn of my own. Another night sitting around a table in a stuffy, overpriced restaurant, I thought. I looked at Parker, who was looking at Valerie. I could tell he was about to vote for La Trattoria. "I've got an idea," I burst out.

"You do?" said Parker, sounding surprised. Usually when we're with his friends, I just go along with whatever he wants to do.

"Have any of you guys ever been to the Rusty Nail?" I asked. "I think some friends of mine might show up there tonight. Why don't we all go?"

"Isn't that the dive on Old Boston Post Road?" Chip asked. "I mean, it's just townies, isn't it? I mean—" He broke off, apparently realizing for the first time who he was talking to, his face red under his tan.

"Don't knock it if you haven't tried it," I said lightly, although my blood was boiling. "It may not look like much from the street, but they have pool tables and video games, and on Saturday night there's a deejay who plays great dance music. It's a lot of fun," I promised, turning to Parker.

I waited for him to render a verdict—we were all waiting. But Stephen was the one who spoke up first. "I read something in the paper about the Rusty Nail," he said. "It sounds like it rocks. Let's do something new."

Parker shrugged carelessly. "Sure. I'm up for it."

"Cool," I said, flashing Stephen a grateful look.

Out of the corner of my eye I saw Valerie purse her lips—she looked as if she'd just bitten into a lemon. I smothered a triumphant grin.

CHIP WAS PARTLY right—the Rusty Nail *is* kind of a dive. There's no interior decoration to speak of: bare wood walls and floors, exposed beams in the ceiling, no-nonsense tables and chairs. But it's the only place anywhere near Hawk Harbor with live music that lets in kids under eighteen, and because it looks like somebody's unfinished basement, you really feel like you can let loose and have a good time. And that's just what my friends and I like to do.

I spotted Rox, Cath, and Mita along with a mob of other people I knew, and we spent a few minutes greeting one another noisily. Parker stayed with me, but he didn't say much, just smiled politely at everyone. Right away it was obvious that he and the prep school/summer house crowd were fish out of water. A couple of them at least made a good-faith effort to unbend a little and have fun—Stephen grabbed a cue and challenged Cath's boyfriend, Tony, to a friendly game of pool, and Amanda accepted Sully's invitation to dance. But the rest of Parker's cronies stayed on the fringes, not even bothering to hide their disdain.

Parker's reaction was hard to read. For some reason I really wanted us to have a good time, and I wanted us to have it at the Rusty Nail—on my turf, among my friends. I realized in a flash that I wanted Parker to prove something to me: to prove that he really did love me. Me, Rose Annabelle Walker, a local girl.

He hadn't spoken since we entered the Rusty Nail except to say a polite hello to my friends. Now I turned to him and took his hand, leaning close so I wouldn't have to shout. "Want to dance?"

"Actually I was just wondering how long we needed to stick around here," he said.

I wrinkled my forehead. "I thought you were up for trying something new."

"No offense," Parker said. "But is this really your kind of place?"

"My friends and I come here all the time," I told him.

"Okay. Forget I said that." He slipped an arm around my waist. "You want to dance? We'll dance."

I gave Parker a thank-you kiss. For a minute or two after we started dancing, I thought everything was going to be okay. Parker seemed to be loosening up, and when the song ended, he actually gave me a smile.

Just then the deejay made an announcement. "Saturday is open mike night," he bellowed into the microphone. There was a lot of clapping and whistling. "Who's got a guitar? A harmonica? A few good jokes?"

"Oh, man," Parker said. "I can't wait to hear what this crowd does for open mike night."

I flinched a little at that but made no comment. Maybe he didn't mean anything by it. After all, the crowd *was* a little rowdy.

"I'm heading to the bar for some soda," Parker said. "Want anything?"

I asked for a Coke and made my way over to Mita, Cath, and Rox.

"Hey, Sully, get up there and flex your muscles," Tony yelled. Everybody but Parker's posse burst out laughing.

Sully yelled something back, his language slightly off-color, to put it politely, and we laughed harder. Then this guy who'd just graduated, Jeremy Pratt, swaggered up with his electric guitar. He plugged into an amp and deafened us with a screeching guitar solo that we all bopped to wildly even though he couldn't carry a tune for his life. Then another guy told a bunch of really stupid jokes, which we laughed at because sometimes when you're in the right mood, anything's funny.

A guy moved up next to me. Assuming it was Parker, I put a hand on his arm. Stephen looked down at me and I pulled my hand back quickly, blushing at my mistake. "I wish I had the guts to get up there," he said.

"Go on, do it!" Cath urged.

He shook his head, smiling kind of shyly. "I'm not that good."

"All it takes is enthusiasm," Rox said.

"What have you got to lose?" Mita agreed. "You couldn't be worse than what we've already seen."

Stephen didn't budge, though, so they started working on me.

"Come on, Rose," Cath coaxed. "Get up there and sing."

"No way," I said, although I was secretly tempted.

Parker reappeared and put an arm firmly around my waist just as Mita shouted, "She's got a great voice!"

"Yeah, Rose, sing something!" Sully bellowed helpfully.

The crowd started to chant my name. I looked up at Parker for encouragement. He rolled his eyes.

"Rose doesn't want to sing," Parker announced loudly.

"Whoa, hold on." My eyes widened in surprise. "How do you know what I—"

"Just a little touch-up," he answered. He screwed the top back on a jar of wax. "There's always some little project, you know?"

"Yeah," I said, intrigued by the fact that Parker didn't mind working—when it came to the boat.

I popped a CD—John Mayer—into the boom box while we motored into the harbor. "When will you put up the sails?" I asked Parker.

"As soon as we get beyond that buoy." He pointed to the channel marker. "Man, those fishing boats stink. There should be a law."

Two lobster boats passed us, heading in the opposite direction. I knew both the fishermen—one was Nathan Beale, Rox's dad. A year ago one of those stinking boats might have been my father's. Which of course Parker didn't know because I'd never told him.

I looked at Parker, about to tell him off. Those are real boats and real people, trying to make an honest living. How dare you? But the words died on my lips.

Parker was smiling fondly at me. "Did I ever tell you I love the way you look on this boat?"

For once I wasn't pleased by the compliment. "I'm just here for decoration?" I asked somewhat testily.

His left hand on the wheel, Parker reached for me with the other, laughing. "Yeah, and if you're not available, I'll call up some other gorgeous, bikini-clad blond," he teased.

Parker nuzzled my neck. I stiffened. "Is that a threat?" I asked him.

"Let's go, okay, Rose?" Parker cut in.

His arm was still around me, but I pulled away from him before he could propel me toward the exit. "I don't *want* to leave, Parker," I said.

"You're not going to sing, though, are you?" He was pleading with me.

We stared at each other, and for a second I hesitated.

I wanted Parker to love me and be proud of me. But I had to wonder why it mattered so much what I wore and what I did. Besides, I love to sing. That was one of the many things Parker didn't know about me. It's time for him to see the real me, I thought. At least *part* of the real me.

I took a deep breath. "I am going to sing," I told Parker quietly. Tossing back my hair, I strode forward. "Hand over that mike!" I told the deejay.

My friends went nuts.

Microphone in hand, I avoided Parker's gaze as I called out, "Any requests?"

"Mariah Carey," someone suggested.

"Joss Stone," someone else said.

"The Beatles," Rox said. "'If I Fell.'"

That's one of my very favorite songs, but it's on the slow side. "Too mellow," I replied. I made myself look at Parker. I'll sing to you if you let me, I pleaded with my eyes.

Parker didn't smile. For a split second I was tempted to drop the mike and walk away. Then my gaze shifted to Stephen, whose whole face was shining with encouragement. "I've got it," I told my audience. "This is by the late, great

Janis Joplin. Who's going to play backup? Jeremy, get up here with me!"

The instant I started to sing, I forgot about Parker's disapproval. My voice is a lot like Janis's—gritty, deep, and strong— and I gave the song all I had, filling my lungs and shouting the lyrics. "Take a . . . take another little piece of my heart, now, baby," I sang, tossing back my long hair.

My friends started singing along. I danced as I sang, getting totally into it. "You know you've got it," I sang, and the whole place joined in on, "if it makes you feel good!"

I sang another stanza, then repeated the refrain, this time throwing in a Janis Joplin–type scream. "You know you've got it—yeah! Take a . . ." The crowd went wild.

When I finished the song, I took a deep bow, my hair flopping forward and brushing the floor. I stood up again, grinning. Mita, Cath, Sully, Rox, Kurt, and Tony were clapping as hard as they could. Stephen was, too.

But the rest of the Seagate crowd—including my boyfriend— had bailed.

Parker was gone.

Eight

"DO YOU NEED a ride home?"

It was closing time, and the Rusty Nail was emptying out. I turned to see who had spoken. It was Stephen. "Yeah, I guess so." I stuck my hands in the pockets of my jeans, trying to smile. It was hard—my emotions were all over the place. I'd had a blast singing, but Parker had really hurt my feelings and made me angry, too. "My date left a long time ago, as you may have noticed."

Outside the Rusty Nail, I said good-bye to Cath, Rox, and the others and climbed into the passenger seat of Stephen's car. When Stephen started the engine, a song came on the CD player. "You like the Yeah Yeah Yeahs too?" I asked as we drove out of the parking lot. "This is one of my favorite CDs."

He nodded. "Their vocalist is almost as good as you."

I slumped down in my seat. "I shouldn't have done it," I mumbled.

"Are you kidding? You were great!"

"But look where it got me." I gestured at his car. "Hitchhiking home."

I couldn't help it—I started to cry. Stephen shot me a worried glance. "Hey, maybe it's not as bad as it seems," he said. "I mean . . ."

"Parker *ditched* me," I reminded him, searching in the glove compartment for some Kleenex. "I just don't get it. How could he do that?"

I blew my nose loudly. Stephen was quiet for a minute. "Parker cares a lot about appearances, how things look, whereas you don't," he said finally. "You two are just . . . different. Maybe opposites attract at first, but in the long run, if you don't see things the same way, it could be for the best if . . ."

My body went cold, then a white-hot flash of anger tore through me. Who does this guy think he is? I thought, throwing the tissue on the floor of the car. "I'm not good enough for Parker, is that what you're saying?" I demanded. "We should break up because he's classy and I'm not?"

"I didn't say that," Stephen said. "That's not what I meant at all."

I folded my arms across my chest, and Stephen gripped the steering wheel tight with both hands, and we sat in stony silence for a while, listening to Katy Perry. I was wishing I'd gotten a ride from Mita and Rox or Cath and Tony instead of Stephen when he remarked, "You really do have a fantastic voice, Rose." He tapped the brakes and pulled into my drive-way. "I think it's great that you weren't embarrassed to get up and sing in front of all those people. Seriously."

Is that supposed to make me feel better? I wondered, even more upset than before. "I guess that's one of the many *differences* between you and me," I pointed out, giving the word he'd used a heavy, sarcastic emphasis. "Just like between me and Parker."

The car hadn't totally stopped yet, but I grabbed the door handle, anyway. "Rose, I didn't mean—," Stephen began.

I got out of the car and slammed the door without waiting for him to finish his sentence and without saying good-bye.

SUMMER IN COASTAL Maine can feel like winter anyplace else. The next day started out sunny, but over the course of the morning the little white clouds that had speckled the sky multiplied and darkened until they blotted out the blue altogether. Meanwhile the temperature dropped steadily—by lunchtime it was only in the fifties, so I put on a jacket to go to the marina to look for Parker.

I'd waited an hour or two that morning before calling, hoping he'd call me first. When he didn't, I dialed his number with trembling fingers. Mrs. Birtwhistle told me he wasn't home—she thought he'd gone to work on the boat.

I walked fast, trying to beat the rain. I didn't. As I hurried along the dock toward slip nine fat drops began to fall. I folded my arms over my head, trying to keep my hair dry so I wouldn't look like a total wreck when I confronted Parker about why he'd left the Rusty Nail.

But I shouldn't have bothered worrying about how I looked. When I got to the boat, I saw Parker with his arms around another girl. A girl with black, chin-length hair. Valerie.

I felt sick. My experiment showing Parker "the real me" had backfired. He'd found someone who wouldn't embarrass him in public. Someone who wouldn't have to borrow a dress for the prom. I ran back up the dock before they spotted me, dodging the raindrops and trying not to cry. I knew now why Parker had abandoned me—and for whom.

THE DOOR TO the boutique opened just as I was getting ready to leave at the end of the day. "We're closed," I started to say. Then I saw who it was. "Parker!" I said, surprised.

"Want to grab a bite to eat?" he asked, smiling as if nothing had happened.

I nodded dumbly.

We climbed into the Jeep. "Lousy weather, huh?" he said as he shifted into reverse, ready to back away from the curb.

"Too wet to go sailing?" I asked.

"I worked on the boat but didn't take her out."

I swallowed hard. It was time for the moment of truth. "I know you did," I told him. "I saw you. You and . . . Valerie."

Parker glanced at me. "Yeah?"

"Yeah."

"And . . ."

"You were kissing her," I burst out. "I saw you!"

Parker slid the Jeep back into the parking space. "Val was

there," he admitted. "Maybe I gave her a hug or something. We're close—I've never pretended otherwise."

"You said 'on-again, off-again,'" I reminded him. "So which is it?"

"Can we talk about this later?" he asked. "I'm starving."

"I want to talk about it now," I insisted.

"We'll discuss it at a restaurant, okay?"

"Fine," I said sharply. "How about Patsy's?" I suggested, naming the diner where Rox is a waitress.

"That greasy dump?"

"Okay, you pick a place," I retorted.

"Do they serve dinner at the Rusty Nail?" he asked in a sarcastic tone.

I raised one eyebrow. "I don't think so."

"So what was that all about last night?" he asked.

"What was what all about?"

"Your lovely little performance."

"I was trying to have fun," I replied, my face growing warm. "Sorry if I embarrassed you. Not that you stuck around long enough for that."

"I saw enough," he said. "Look, let's not fight. You made a mistake, I made a mistake. They cancel each other out."

I stared at Parker. "You're kidding," I exclaimed. "I sing one stupid song and you cheat on me with another girl and those two things are equal?"

"I'm not cheating on you," Parker insisted. "You're over-reacting. Why are we even discussing this?"

I remembered Stephen's comment as he drove me home

the night before, about the differences between Parker and me. Stephen had been right. "Maybe we don't have as much in common as we thought," I said quietly.

"It's this dumb job of yours," Parker decided. He gestured to Cecilia's. "It takes up all your time—I hardly ever see you. Why don't you quit?"

The engine was still idling, and the windshield wipers swished back and forth. Did he really just ask me that? I wondered disbelievingly. "I *can't* just quit," I told Parker. "I need the money. I *have* to work."

Parker turned in his seat so we were face-to-face. I looked him straight in the eye and went on talking. "Yeah, isn't that funny? Having to work? But I do. My family's broke—my mom can't support all of us by herself. We're getting food stamps! Isn't that a riot?"

I tried to laugh, but pain closed my throat, choking me. Now he knows, I thought, dropping my eyes. No more secrets.

I looked down at my hands, which were folded on my lap, and waited for Parker to say something comforting, to apologize, to reach out and hold me. Ten seconds passed, then twenty. Finally I looked up at him again.

"Are you serious, Rose?" he said at last.

"Yes, I am."

He wrinkled his forehead. I wanted love and sympathy, but Parker just looked confused. He didn't touch me or speak. He didn't have to—I knew what he was thinking. Since I was pretty, he could forgive me for being a "local" and for going

to the public high school. He could even forgive me for singing Janis Joplin at the Rusty Nail. But he couldn't forgive me
for being poor.

Tears stung my eyes. "Sorry, Parker. I'm not Val Mathias
and I never will be, no matter what dress you put me in," I said
quietly.

Neither of us spoke after that. We had nothing left to say to
each other. Parker wasn't Prince Charming after all, or maybe
I just wasn't cut out to be Cinderella.

Shoving open the door of the Jeep, I jumped down, right
into a puddle. It was still pouring and I was instantly soaked to
the skin, but I didn't care.

B Y THE TIME I dried off in the women's room at Patsy's and
spilled my sob story to Rox, the downpour had ended and
the sun was out again. Everything steamed in sudden warmth.

As I rode my bike slowly home an eerie sort of calm settled
over me. Strangely, I didn't feel that upset. It's just shock, I
thought. You'll be really upset tomorrow. The words to a very
appropriate Death Cab for Cutie song—"Tiny Vessels"—kept
running through my head.

As I wobbled into the gravel driveway on my bike I couldn't
help singing out loud. Sometimes songs are so much like real
life, it's scary.

Then I saw that my three younger sisters were scattered
around outside the old barn we use as a garage. Daisy, wearing shorts and a halter top with one of Dad's beat-up caps
pulled on over her long blond hair, was trying unsuccessfully

to start our old gas-powered lawn mower. Laurel and her pal Jack were busy by the row of chicken wire hutches that Laurel had built recently along the outside of the garage. Lily, dressed in a sailor dress and a straw hat with a trailing blue ribbon, was curled up under a nearby apple tree, writing in a notebook.

So much for sneaking up to my room for a good cry. I decided to hang out with my sisters—maybe they could cheer me up. I wanted to do something that didn't involve talking about Parker for a while.

I joined Daisy. "Are you all right?" she asked, looking closely at my face.

"Fine," I replied, taking a deep breath. "What are you doing, anyway?"

"Isn't it obvious?" Daisy gave the mower's handle one last yank, but the motor still didn't catch. "Broken," she observed unnecessarily.

"Think you can fix it?" I asked as she lugged a toolbox out of the garage.

She inspected the screwdriver collection, choosing a tool carefully. "I'd better be able to." She brushed back a wayward strand of blond hair. "The grass is practically up to my knees. And that reminds me. Aren't you supposed to fix those loose boards on the porch? Everybody keeps tripping." I grimaced. That was one of the chores Mom had assigned me, unfortunately. "I'm useless with a hammer and nails," I told Daisy. "I'd probably just make it worse. If you do it, I'll take over one of your chores."

"Like fixing the screen door?"

"Well, no. What else have you got?"

She ticked the tasks off on her fingers. "Washing the storm windows, weeding the garden, and reorganizing the pantry."

I seized on the last one as definitely the least grubby and strenuous. "I'll take the pantry," I said. Then I pointed to Lily. "What about Little Miss Muffet over there? I haven't noticed her doing any work."

Daisy shrugged. "She's only eight." While Daisy fiddled around with the lawn mower, I wandered around the side of the barn, my hands stuck in the pockets of my shorts. Laurel had put Henry back in his cage, and now she was handing Jack a bowl of something that looked like prechewed puppy chow. "Here," Laurel ordered. "Feed the raccoons."

Both of Jack's parents are lawyers, and they're a little bit older. Jack's an only child and he's not a brat, but you can tell just by looking at him that Mr. and Mrs. Harrison treat him like something precious. He was dressed in khakis that actually had creases pressed up the front of the trouser legs. His polo shirt was tucked in and his hair combed neatly over from a dead-straight side part. He looked like a kid from the fifties, like Dick from those old See Spot Run early readers that we have a bunch of on the family room bookshelves.

Anyway, Jack's expression was pretty comical as he took the bowl of disgusting mush from Laurel. Those two were a study in contrasts—Laurel was as grubby as Jack was impeccable. When you're a kid, though, sometimes all it takes to become best friends is living next door to each other—and an interest in animals.

As Jack tentatively offered the mush to the nest of baby raccoons whom he and Laurel had saved—their mother had gotten run over by a car—Laurel stuck some carrot tops into a hutch containing a wild brown rabbit with a tiny splint on one of its paws. I glanced down the row of cages—no vacancy in Laurel's animal hotel. "Since when did you turn into Doctor Dolittle?" I wanted to know.

Laurel shrugged. "I just keep finding animals that need taking care of," she said.

I wrinkled my nose. A musky, zooish smell competed with the cleaner scent of rain-washed grass. "Are you sure it's . . . sanitary?" I bent over to peer into a hutch. A squirrel rose up on its hind legs and chattered angrily at me. I jumped back. "I mean, Henry's almost tame, but don't these wild ones bite? What if they have rabies or something?"

"They don't have any of the symptoms, and I'm super-careful," Laurel said, her eyes flashing.

I decided to keep my distance, anyway. Giving Jack a sympathetic look, I returned to Daisy.

She wasn't alone. Kyle Cooper lives a block away—his sister Maeve's in my class, and he's in Daisy's class. Kyle must have been riding past—he'd dropped his bike on the grass and was leaning against the fence, talking to Daisy, whose face was red from working on the lawn mower. At least I thought that was why it was red. "Well, don't break a fingernail, Daisy," Kyle cracked, his tone sly.

Daisy responded with a dirty look. As soon as Kyle had pedaled off she erupted like a volcano. "What a jerk!" she exclaimed. "I do not grow my fingernails. Can you believe he said that?"

I laughed at her indignation. "He didn't mean anything. He was just flirting with you."

"Flirting? With me?"

I laughed again. "Well, that shirt, Daze. I'm sorry to tell you, it's on the sexy side."

Daisy glanced down at herself, mortified. Suddenly self-conscious about her shape, Daisy hunched her shoulders forward and attacked the lawn mower with renewed energy. I smiled to myself.

I wasn't in any hurry to go inside. Lily was still sitting under the tree, so I called to her, "Hey, Lil, what are you writing?"

Lily clutched her notebook protectively to her chest, as if I had Superman vision and could read it from twenty yards away. Then she jumped to her feet. "None of your business!" she shouted, and darted into the house.

"What's with her?" I wondered aloud.

The sun had dropped behind the trees, and the yard was drenched in warm yellow light. I flung myself down on the grass under the apple tree Lily had just deserted, lying on my back with my arms folded behind my head. Thinking again about Parker, I suddenly realized that instead of being depressed, I felt kind of relieved.

I closed my eyes and let the evening breeze cool my skin. Fall was coming soon. My relationship with Parker was over, and that meant my charade was over as well. I didn't have to pretend anymore. I could be myself. I could hang out at the Rusty Nail with my friends, my real friends, kids who had summer jobs at hardware stores and diners. Back to my imperfect life, I thought . . . and smiled.

Nine

OF COURSE, IT didn't take long for my family to find out that I had broken up with Parker.

"Breakfast in bed?" I said. It was a sunny Saturday morning, and I'd been about to jump in the shower when Lily appeared at my door with a tray. "It's not my birthday," I pointed out, yawning. "What's the occasion?"

"I'm just being nice," Lily answered. "Look—it's French toast. I made it myself. And fresh-squeezed orange juice!"

"Wow," I said as she placed the tray on my lap. There was even a wilted daisy in a bud vase. "Lily, that was really sweet of you. Thanks!"

She patted my leg under the blanket in a maternal way. "Now, you just enjoy your breakfast and feel better soon."

The French toast was a little on the soggy side, but I ate every bite. This was so nice of her, I thought, deciding that I'd put off yelling at her about never doing the laundry on time— that was the one chore she'd ended up with after managing to goof up everything else.

Fifteen minutes later I got out of the shower. I was walking down the hall in my robe, towel drying my hair, when I saw Laurel dart out of my room. "What are you doing?" I called.

"Nothing," she called back with a secretive smile.

I went into my room. While I'd been gone, someone— Laurel, obviously—had made my bed and left a tiny basket on the pillow. I looked inside it. Sitting on a nest of cotton was a little china squirrel.

I turned around. Laurel was peeking around the door to see my reaction. "Do you like it?" she asked.

"It's adorable. But Toad, you shouldn't be spending your piggy bank savings on me."

"I didn't actually spend anything," she confessed. "Jack gave it to me. But I want you to have it," she said quickly when I started to hand the squirrel back to her. "To cheer you up!" she said, disappearing into the hall.

When I carried the breakfast tray downstairs, I was still shaking my head over Lily and Laurel. They were the best sisters in the world!

I took the tray into the kitchen. Daisy was there, washing up the breakfast dishes. "Check out the car," she suggested.

I looked out the window to the driveway, where the station wagon was parked. "Yeah?" I said. "What about it?"

"Check it out," she repeated.

I went to the door, sticking my feet into clogs as I went.

Outside, I folded my arms across the front of my sweater—it was sunny but cool. As I walked over to the car I could see that it was dripping. Someone washed it, I guessed. Daisy. And not only that. The inside was clean, too. She'd thrown out all the trash, and cleaned the upholstery, and vacuumed the floor mats, and washed the windows, and somehow she'd even gotten out the old fish smell.

I went back inside. "Daisy, you are too much," I declared. "Were you scrubbing for hours?"

"Looks like new, doesn't it?" she said, pleased.

I laughed. "Well, that would be pushing it," I said. "But it looks better than it has in years."

"Mom said you can have it all weekend," Daisy told me. "If you want to go to the Rusty Nail or someplace with your friends tonight."

"And if you do go," Mom herself said as she entered the kitchen, "here's something to wear."

She held out a dusty-rose-colored sweater. "Mom, your chenille top," I said. I'd always loved it and had even borrowed it once or twice.

"I think it should be your top." She smiled. "It's your color, after all. And look. I altered the skirt for you. Does the length seem okay?"

I examined the matching skirt. Mom had taken it in at the waist and hemmed it so it would fall just halfway down my thighs. "It's perfect," I exclaimed. "Wait until Rox and Cath and Mita see this outfit! We'll definitely have to go out tonight so I can show it off. I can't wait to—" I stopped. "Wait a minute. What's going on here? How come everybody's doing such nice things for me?"

"We just thought it should be Be Nice to Rose Weekend," Daisy explained.

"You've been on a bit of an emotional roller coaster the last few months," Mom added. "We want you to head up again and stay up."

I hugged the skirt and sweater to my chest, gazing at my mom and sister with misty eyes. I'd been feeling sorry for myself lately, but it was time to snap out of it. I had a lot to be grateful for. Maybe we don't have money, but our life is rich, I thought. "Thanks, guys," I said. "You're the best."

S OMEONE'S HERE TO see you, Rose," my mother said the next night.

We were all sitting in the family room, watching *Pride and Prejudice* on the public television station. Mom's announcement made my heart jump into my throat. If it was one of my girlfriends, she'd have said the name. But "someone" . . . It might be Parker, I thought, steeling myself for a confrontation.

There was a tall, good-looking guy in khakis and a polo shirt standing just inside the front door, but it wasn't Parker. "Stephen?" I asked, surprised.

He shifted his weight from one foot to the other. "Uh, hi," he said.

I waited for him to explain why he was there. The last time I saw him, we didn't exactly part on friendly terms. When he didn't speak, I said, "What's up?"

"Can we sit outside?" he asked, looking at something over my shoulder.

I turned around. Lily had followed me and was peering around the bend in the hall.

"Sure," I said, ushering Stephen out to the porch and then shutting both the screen door and the inner door so my sister wouldn't be tempted to eavesdrop.

I sat down on the porch swing. Stephen hitched himself onto the railing. He still looked uncomfortable—almost nervous. "Rose, I just wanted to tell you that I heard about you and Parker. And I'm really sorry . . ."

The second he started talking, something in my brain clicked. I'd almost forgotten exactly who Stephen Mathias was.

"You knew all along, didn't you?" I asked him quietly.

"What?" said Stephen, his eyebrows drawn together.

"Valerie's your sister. You had to have known about her and Parker. Why didn't you tell me?" My mind was reeling as I tried to put the pieces of the puzzle together.

"I didn't think it was my place to—"

"You *did* try to tell me . . . ," I said slowly, and the guilty look on his face confirmed my suspicions. "That day at Cecilia's. When you wanted to know what Parker was up to. And that night—in the car, when you told me that Parker and I were different. You were . . . warning me." I laughed harshly. "You must think I'm an *idiot*," I went on. I pushed off from the wood floor with my bare feet, making the swing rock crazily. "I suppose everyone from Seagate knew Parker was seeing Valerie behind my back. Well, you can go back and tell them that I fell for it. I never suspected a thing! Okay?"

"I'm not going to tell anyone anything."

"Oh, come on, Stephen," I said. "What are you here for? To say I told you so? Well, you were right—Parker found someone who isn't so *different* from him, after all. You were so right—I see that now."

"You don't *see* anything," Stephen blurted. "I'm here because I care about you. *That's* why I'm here."

I stopped swinging, my feet planted on the floor. "W-What?" I stammered.

Stephen looked hurt. "Maybe I should have kept my mouth shut. I think I'd better go."

"What?" I asked again, my own face scarlet. What was happening? Stephen cared for me—and now he was leaving? But didn't he think . . . didn't he think we were different? I'd never been so confused. I sat on the swing, not knowing what to do or say.

"Good night," he said, and walked down the steps to the front path.

"Good night," I echoed as he disappeared into his car and drove away.

WHAT DO YOU mean, you 'accidentally' opened the doors to all seven hutches?" Laurel screeched.

At the same moment Daisy bellowed, "What do you mean, you 'borrowed' my Nomar baseball mitt and now you can't find it?"

It was breakfast time, two weeks after my breakup with Parker. The object of Laurel's and Daisy's wrath was seated at the kitchen table, digging into a huge bowl of Rice Krispies. Not inappropriately, she was dressed in a witch costume complete with tall black hat.

"Those baby raccoons aren't ready to take care of themselves." Laurel was near tears. "How could you?"

"If they really liked you, they wouldn't have run away," Lily replied.

Her hands balled into fists, Laurel stormed out of the kitchen, heading in the direction of her now empty animal B&B. Lily turned to Daisy. "I don't know why you care about that scrungy old thing," Lily said. "It smells."

"You'd better find that mitt," Daisy warned, glaring, "or I'll throttle you, I really will."

Lily's lower lip pushed out in a theatrical pout. "Mom!" she wailed. "Daisy's scaring me!"

Mom was trying to drink a cup of coffee, eat a piece of toast, and read the manual for our malfunctioning dishwasher all at the same time. She paused just long enough to frown at Lily. "Young lady, I don't need trouble from you this early in the day. You know you're not supposed to take your sisters' things without asking first."

"And the mitt's not all," Daisy went on, launching into a list of complaints now that she had Mom on her side. "Last week she broke my favorite—"

"I'm out of here," I sang, pushing back my chair. Lily drove me nuts sometimes, but I didn't feel like sticking around for the rest of her trial. "I'll wash the dishes when I get home from work, Mom. See you."

Compared to the chaos at home, my job at Cecilia's was looking better and better all the time. It's not so bad being sixteen, I thought. If I were only thirteen, like Daisy, I'd have to stay home and take care of Laurel and Lily all day. Ugh!

I had some extra time, so on my way to the boutique I stopped at Wissinger's Bakery for a few doughnuts, then parked my bicycle in front of Appleby's Hardware. The door to the store was propped open with a bag of lawn fertilizer, and Cath was lugging out wheelbarrows, rakes, and other garden tools to make a display on the sidewalk. "Got any hot apple cider to go with these?" I asked her.

"Only if you brought jelly doughnuts," she replied with a smile.

Appleby's always has a pot of hot cider on for the customers—it's one of those old-fashioned kind of stores. Cath filled two plastic foam cups and we sat down on the steps out front, both of us reaching into the greasy bag of still warm doughnuts at the same time.

I had gotten jelly—I knew they were Cath's favorites. She bit into one, chased it with a slurp of hot cider, then tilted her face up to the morning sun. "This is going to be a good day," she said.

It seemed like a safe prediction. Slouching back with my elbows propped on the step behind me, I sampled a choco-late glazed—my own personal favorite. "I can't believe I'm eating this."

"Why?"

"I already had breakfast at home."

"You'll work it off," Cath said.

"You'll work yours off—I just stand around at my job."

Cath eyed me speculatively. "You have gained a couple of pounds in the last few weeks."

"I have?" I asked, worried.

"It looks good," she asserted. "Your face looks better. You were getting too thin, trying to fit in with Parker's crowd. He was never good enough for you, anyway," Cath declared.

I wanted to hug her, but I would've gotten doughnut crumbs all over her. My friends had been so great since Parker and I had broken up, taking me out every couple of nights, calling to check up on me, doing nice things for me, giving me pep talks. "It's not a question of good enough," I concluded. "He wasn't right for me, that's all."

"You'll meet someone a million times nicer."

"That reminds me." I'd told her and Rox and Mita about my very strange conversation with Stephen. "He called me last night. What's going on with that guy?"

"Duh. He likes you," Cath said.

"But why?"

She raised her eyebrows. "Could it be because you're beautiful, smart, funny, and talented?"

I shook my head. "I just don't get it. I'm not ready to date someone new, anyhow. Especially not another rich preppie."

"Then don't," she advised. "Have another doughnut."

We talked for a few more minutes until the doughnuts and

hot cider were gone and my watch told me it was time to hustle over to Cecilia's. I knew Cath was right when she said I looked better—I felt better, too. I was back to my old self, comfortable in my own skin and in my slightly-less-than-the-latest-fashion clothes. And I planned to stay that way.

WHEN I GOT home that evening, the kitchen smelled like roasting chicken and my mom was sitting at the kitchen table, the newspaper classified section open in front of her and a pen in her hand. "What are you doing?" I asked, dropping into the chair next to her.

"Going through the help-wanted ads."

"Why?"

"Because I hate my job." She circled one ad and scrawled a question mark next to another. Then she threw down the pen. "But the problem is, I'm not qualified for anything else. If I call up these places, they'll ask right off the bat if I have a B.A. and when I say no, they'll say forget it."

"You don't know until you try," I reminded her.

Mom shook her head, sighing. "I'm sorry, Rose. I really am."

"Sorry for what?"

"For this." She spread her hands. "For not being able to find a better job and for shifting so much of the burden onto you and your sisters. Your dad and I should have saved for a rainy day, but we just never expected . . ."

Her voice trailed off, and she rubbed her face with her knuckles. When she lowered her hands again, the delicate, shadowy skin under her eyes glistened with tears.

Guilt pierced my heart as I thought about how I'd blamed Mom for our troubles. It wasn't fair—she was trying her hardest. And I hadn't been helping nearly as much as I could. "It's okay, Mom. Don't worry about me, anyway. I don't mind working at Cecilia's."

She gazed at me, her forehead creased. "You don't?"

"No." And just then I realized something. I wasn't just saying that to make her feel better. It was true. "I like earning my own money. I like doing something productive with my time instead of just hanging out."

She smiled wryly. "Get out of here. Kids love just hanging out."

"Well, then I'm not a kid anymore," I informed her. "I can loaf on my days off like a grown-up. And you know what else, Mom? Maybe you don't have a college degree, but you're really smart. You'll find a good job."

For a moment we just looked at each other. It was the most we'd talked in months. The role reversal was a little weird— here I was, supporting my mom the way she'd always supported me—but I didn't mind.

"Thanks for the pep talk," she said.

Leaning forward, I wrapped my arms around my mother. "Anytime, Mom."

Ten

W E WERE HAVING a big end-of-summer sale at Cecilia's
and had been busy all day, so when Stephen came in, I
didn't notice him at first. All of a sudden there he was, standing in front of the cash register.

"Can I help you?" I asked. Then I added, "Don't tell me—
it's your other grandmother's birthday."

"No, I just have a quick question," Stephen said in a busi-
nesslike tone. "When do you get off work?"

"Five-thirty. Why?"

"Just wondering." With that he strode out of the store.

Five-thirty rolled around, and I was slinging my bag over
my shoulder when the bell over the door jingled and there was
Stephen again. Coincidence? I don't think so.

"On your way home?" he asked.

I couldn't help smiling. "You know I am."

Stephen has a serious expression—when he smiles, it's a pleasant surprise. He smiled now. "Okay, so, another question. Would you like to go for a drive?"

"A drive?" I repeated.

"Yeah. Like, in a car."

"Your car?"

"Sure."

"Where would we go?"

"No place special. Up the coast, maybe. Just for fun. A chance to talk."

"Okay, here's a question for you," I countered. "Why do you like me so much?"

I looked Stephen straight in the eye, my hands on my hips. I wanted an honest answer. If he says that he likes me because I'm pretty, like Parker did, I thought, he's history.

"Because you're beautiful," he said, and I felt like I'd been punched in the stomach. Why did everyone only care how I looked? I opened my mouth to tell him off, but then he interrupted, adding, "The way you're kind even to people who hurt your feelings, and the way you always gave Parker the benefit of the doubt, and the way you aren't afraid to sing in front of a group of people," he said, "is beautiful. I really admire you, Rose. I want to get to know you better."

For a moment I was breathless. "Really?" I choked out finally.

"Really. But it'll only be fun if you want to get to know me better, too."

I nodded. "I think I do." Then, in case I sounded too

agreeable, I added, "I mean, you're just going to keep asking until I say yes, right? I'm saving us both a lot of trouble."

"Right," said Stephen, laughing.

We headed north in Stephen's black Saab—the one I'd seen Val drive—taking a country road with views of rocky beaches and lighthouses.

"How long have you lived in Hawk Harbor?" Stephen yelled over the roar of the wind.

"Forever," I yelled back. "How about you?"

"Just a few years. My parents wanted me and Val to go to Seagate—my dad went there—but they didn't want us to board." He flashed me a grin. "Boarding school kids get into too much trouble."

"Your father commutes to Portland?"

"Boston. He just comes home for weekends."

Slowing down, Stephen turned down a side road, which made it easier to talk. "That must be weird, only seeing your father on weekends," I remarked.

Stephen shrugged. "It's better than nothing."

He must have noticed my expression out of the corner of his eye because he stepped on the brakes, almost bringing the Saab to a halt. "I'm sorry, Rose," he said. "That came out wrong—I wasn't thinking. I know about your dad. I was sorry to hear about his fishing accident."

I gave him a sidelong glance. How did he know about my father? I wondered. I guessed he must have asked around. Stephen *wanted* to know about my life, I realized.

"It's just . . ." He accelerated again. "My dad's a workaholic.

Even when we all lived in Boston, Val and I hardly ever saw him."

"That's too bad." I was interested in what he was saying, but I wished he'd stop mentioning his sister. It kept reminding me of how bizarre the connection between us was.

"Maybe we should head back," I said suddenly. "I'm supposed to cook dinner tonight."

"Whatever you want," Stephen said. He looked a little disappointed, though.

As we drove back to Hawk Harbor, Stephen flashed me another one of those surprising grins. "So, Rose, if I turn on the radio, would you sing along?"

"Are you giving me a hard time?" I asked.

"No way. You have a great voice. If you've got it, flaunt it."

"Yeah, well." I had to laugh. "Obviously that's my philosophy, too."

"Do you take singing lessons?"

"Not anymore. I'm in performance choir, though."

"Who's your favorite singer?"

"Do you really want to know?"

He shot a glance at me. "Yeah, I really want to know."

I folded my arms. "Okay, then, guess."

"Um . . ." He was obviously thinking back to the Rusty Nail. "Janis Joplin."

"Nope."

"Uh, Luciano Pavarotti."

I laughed. "Try again."

"Frank Sinatra?"

I groaned. "No, you're right," Stephen decided. "It's probably a woman."

"It's a woman," I confirmed.

"Ani DiFranco? Ella Fitzgerald?"

"Somewhere in between," I said. "Sheryl Crowe."

"How come Sheryl Crowe?"

I thought about it for a moment. "Well, she doesn't have the prettiest voice, but she puts her heart and soul into it. She writes great songs, and she really rocks. That's what I want to do."

"I bet you will someday," he said.

A few minutes later we were parked in my driveway. I kind of wished I hadn't told Stephen to turn around. "So long," I said as I stepped out of the Saab.

"This was a good start," Stephen said.

"A good start to what?"

"Well, I think you're starting to like me a little, aren't you?"

I was. "A little," I told him, and smiled.

Stephen drummed his fingers on the leather steering wheel. "So, Rose. Do you think if I call you again, we could . . . ?"

"Go out for real?" My smile widened. "Try it and see."

HE SAID HE'D call, I thought the next day, which was Saturday. So when is he going to call? Today? Tomorrow? Next week? Next month?

As I made myself a sandwich for lunch I told myself I didn't care. The last thing I wanted was to date another guy who went to Seagate. And Stephen was Valerie's brother . . . we were talking serious bad genes!

Stephen's different, though, I reflected as I spread some of Mrs. Smith's wild blueberry jam on a piece of bread. His family was rich, but he wasn't stuffy and self-centered like Parker. When we talked, he really listened to what I had to say.

I carried my sandwich to the table, where Lily and Laurel were eating clam chowder while Mom thumbed through a pile of cookbooks. "Can't decide what to make for dinner?" I asked her.

"Just getting ideas," she answered, penciling something in the margin of one of the books. "The Schenkels have asked me to cater their fortieth anniversary party, can you believe it? I want to run a menu by Vera this afternoon."

"That's cool," I exclaimed. "And yes, I can believe it. You're the best cook in Hawk Harbor, Mom."

"Well, I don't know about that," she said modestly. "It'll be a challenge cooking for thirty people instead of just my family." She sounded a little worried, but at the same time she smiled—I hadn't seen her eyes sparkle like that in a long, long time. "It'll be fun, though."

Just then there was a muttered curse from Lily. She was scribbling in a notebook while she slurped her soup, and she'd splashed clam chowder all over the page. "Watch your language," Mom warned her.

"What are you writing?" I asked.

Lily wiped the paper with her napkin. "A story," she said.

"What about?"

"Nothing." Lily stuck the notebook under her arm and grabbed her soup bowl. "I'm done."

"Wait a minute," said Laurel. "Isn't it your turn to empty the dishwasher and clean up the kitchen?"

"I'm busy," Lily responded, darting from the kitchen before anyone could stop her.

"Well, I'm busy, too." Laurel pushed back her chair. "I'm going over to Jack's. Mr. and Mrs. Harrison are taking us to—"

Laurel stopped. Daisy had just entered the room. "What?" asked Daisy, putting a hand to her head self-consciously. "Why are you staring?"

"Your hair!" Laurel exclaimed.

The last time I'd seen Daisy, her glossy blond hair fell almost to her waist. Now her hair was so short, you could practically see her scalp.

Daisy looked as if she were about to cry. "It was just getting in the way," she said, trying to sound tough. "How could I mow lawns and weed gardens and stuff with stupid long hair falling in my face all the time?"

I was about to ask her if this had anything to do with Kyle Cooper when the phone rang. I jumped up to answer it, my heart jumping, too.

But it wasn't for me. I held the phone out to Daisy. "For you," I told her. I mouthed a name. "Kyle."

Her face flaming, Daisy grabbed the phone, then retreated as far as the tautly stretched cord would allow. I tried to eavesdrop but couldn't hear her because Laurel was talking to Mom. "This really neat kids' museum in Portland," she was saying. "The Harrisons are members, so they get in free. And we'll probably go out for ice cream—Mr. Harrison loves hot fudge sundaes. And if there's time, Mr. Harrison said we could go for a ride on this cool old-fashioned steam train. Oh, I won't be home for dinner—I'm eating at Windy Ridge tonight."

Before Mom could get a word in edgewise, Laurel whisked out the door. At the same instant Daisy slammed down the telephone. "What did Kyle want?" I asked.

"He asked me *out!*" Daisy fumed.

"And that's a crime?" I said.

"Did you say yes?" Mom wanted to know.

"Of course not!" Daisy yelled.

"But why?" I teased. "Your hair's really not so bad. With a little styling gel . . ."

Daisy burst into angry tears and stomped out of the room. "Rose," my mother chastised me.

"With that haircut she'd better learn to take a joke," I replied. I could see Lily still lurking in the hall. "Are you getting all this down?" I called to her. "Great story material!"

The phone rang again. "It's probably Vera," Mom guessed.

"Or Kyle," I said. "He's the persistent type." I picked up the receiver. "Hello?"

"May I speak to Rose?" asked Stephen.

Mom gave a knowing smile as my face lit up.

"Speaking," I said.

W HY DID I agree to go out with him? I agonized just six hours later.

When Stephen asked me out to dinner, I'd assumed we were talking pizza or fried clams. Instead I found myself seated across from him at an intimate table for two at the Harborside, the very same restaurant where Parker had hosted my sixteenth birthday and taken me before the prom bash back when we were a couple.

Stephen was wearing khakis, a white oxford shirt, and a tie—he was dressed way more formally than Parker ever had been except when we went to the prom. My short denim skirt, T-shirt, and sandals, which had seemed cute at home, now seemed way too casual. I was having a Parker flashback—another one of those when-worlds-collide moments.

I opened the menu, telling myself not to feel stupid just because Stephen was dressed better than I was. "Wow, everything sounds good," I murmured, checking out the catch of the day. And expensive!

"If you don't like seafood, the steak is good, too," Stephen said. "I'm thinking about the swordfish myself."

I was thinking about ordering a plain green salad just in case we ended up splitting the check. Now I arched one eyebrow at Stephen. "Are you trying to impress me?" I asked.

Stephen fumbled with his menu, nearly knocking over his

water glass. "No. Why? I just thought you'd like the food here. I mean, it's . . ."

"The fanciest restaurant in Hawk Harbor," I filled in. "We're the only people under thirty in the whole place!"

Stephen grinned. I was glad—I liked that grin. "Okay, guilty as charged. I am trying to impress you. Does that make me a jerk?"

"I guess not," I said, smiling.

"But you'd rather have a burger and fries."

"Sort of," I admitted.

"Then that's what you'll get."

I looked at the menu, confused. "But I don't think the Harborside serves—"

Stephen was refolding his cloth napkin. "Come on," he hissed. "Let's go!"

A minute later we were in the parking lot, laughing hard. "It's okay," Stephen assured me. "We hadn't even ordered. They can't arrest us."

"But I drank from my water glass," I gasped, giggling. "I touched the silverware!"

"You're right. That's a felony in the state of Maine," Stephen joked. He tossed his car keys in the air. "So, the ball's in your court, Ms. Walker. Where to?"

We ended up at Cap'n Jack's, which has the best burgers in town as well as the cheapest, freshest lobster. "My dad used to sell fish to this restaurant," I told Stephen as we dug into a basket of Cap'n Jack's famous onion rings.

"No kidding," he said. "What kind of fish did he catch?"

"Cod, halibut, flounder."

"Did he like it, fishing? I mean, was it a good way to make a living?"

I thought about Mom and the classified ads, about the humiliation of food stamps, about how she and Dad somehow never managed to save for a "rainy day." Then I pictured my father coming home at the end of the day, his smile gleaming in a face brown from the sun, how he'd grab me for a bear hug and his arms would smell like the ocean. "Yeah, he liked it," I replied, my throat suddenly tight with tears. "He liked working outdoors, and he was proud to be his own boss. He was a happy man."

I'd never talked to Parker like this—I must have known instinctively that he wouldn't understand, or wouldn't care, which would have been worse.

Stephen reached across the table and squeezed my hand. "You must really miss him," he said.

I nodded, not trusting myself to speak.

"Did you ever go out on the boat with him?"

I took a deep breath and had to smile at the memory. "I'll never forget the very first time," I told Stephen. "I was about Lily's age—eight or nine. Anyway, we went out to the banks, and Dad was pretty sure we were over a big school of cod, so he set the nets. And there was a ton of fish, so when he pulled up the nets they were all over the deck of the boat, jumping around and totally scary—I mean, it hadn't occurred to me they'd be *alive*, you know? I started to cry—we're talking major hysterics—so there's Dad, in the middle of the Atlantic with a boat full of cod, sitting on the gunwale with me on his lap, calming me down and telling me not to be afraid of the fish."

We were both laughing. Just then Stephen's lobster came. He held up the plastic bib that came with it. "I've only ordered lobster a couple of times before, and it's always been cut up in a salad or something," he confessed. "You're a fisherman's daughter. Do I really have to wear this?"

"Yep. And lose the tie while you're at it," I advised.

We ate so much at Cap'n Jack's, we decided to go for a walk on the beach afterward. It was a beautiful August night—the full moon made the beach almost as bright as day. "Want to take a swim?" I asked Stephen.

Stephen walked up to the water's edge, jumping back when a wave washed over his bare feet. "Are you nuts?" he yelped. "It's like ice."

I laughed. "You're not a native, are you?"

"Hey, I took off the necktie," he said. "That's all I'm taking off."

We walked down the beach, just below the high-tide line, where the seaweed piles up. I felt incredibly relaxed around him, as if we'd been taking moonlit walks on the beach forever. He's such a sweet guy, I thought, a little bit giddy. How come I never realized that?

"So, how are the eighth graders?" I asked.

He sighed "They're okay. The program I work with is for underprivileged kids, so a lot of them have rough home lives. Sometimes they take their problems out on each other, which makes coaching them hard."

"I can imagine."

"Hard but rewarding," he amended. He looked at me. "I can't wait to graduate next year. I'm going to take a year off before college and work with the kids full-time. I just wish I could do more for them, you know?"

I didn't know what to say. After a minute Stephen took my hand. "Is this okay?" he asked.

"Sure," I said casually, hoping he couldn't tell that his touch made me tingle.

"Because I don't want to rush things," he explained. "In case you're still—"

"It's been a few weeks," I reminded him. "What about you and . . . Camilla, right?"

He laughed. "We broke up almost a year ago." I looked at him expectantly. "You want details?" he asked.

"Sure." I smiled. "I mean, you know all the dirt on me and Parker!"

"Fair enough," Stephen said. "Let's see. Camilla left for Williams last September first, and I think it was, like, a whole day later that she called and broke up with me."

"On the phone?"

"Harsh, right?"

"What was she like?" I asked.

"She was smart," Stephen replied. "She read all the time—books, newspapers. You know, the analytical type. We'd go to a movie and then talk about it for hours."

"That sounds nice," I said, secretly a little jealous. A vague doubt entered my mind. Camilla sounded like the polar opposite of me—I wondered how Stephen could have been interested in both of us. "Do you miss her?"

"I did for a while." He glanced meaningfully at me. "Not anymore."

Too soon, it was eleven o'clock. I didn't want the evening to end, and that surprised me. "You'd better take me home. I have a curfew," I told Stephen apologetically.

"That's cool," he said. "Your mom cares."

"It's because she doesn't know you," I explained. "I mean, you could be a real creep."

"I could be," he agreed. "So, am I?"

I shook my head. I had to admit to myself that I'd really misjudged him. Parker had turned out to be a creep, and so were most of his Seagate friends, but Stephen was different. "No," I said softly, "you're not."

Back at my house he parked the Saab, then came around to open my door. We walked up to the porch and stood for a few seconds, not quite looking at each other. Finally Stephen cleared his throat. "Thanks for going out with me, Rose," he said. "I really enjoyed this evening."

"Me too."

"Would it be okay if I . . . kissed you good night?"

I nodded.

Stephen hesitated, then placed his hands gently on my shoulders. I put one hand on his waist so we'd be balanced. I closed my eyes, and our lips met with one of those little bumps that happen when it's the first time.

We stepped apart again. "Good night, Rose," he whispered.

"Good night," I whispered back.

He jogged down the steps. When he was behind the wheel of the car, I pushed open the door to the house. I was feeling a little bit dizzy. I hadn't expected to stay out this late, to have so much fun, to like Stephen so much. What am I doing? I thought. Am I crazy? Didn't getting burned by Parker teach me anything? Stephen and I are bound to be as different as Parker and I were.

I will not fall for Stephen, I told myself. I will not, I will not.

But I'd wanted that kiss to last a whole lot longer. Ready or not, I *was* falling.

Eleven

H E INVITED HIMSELF over for dinner tonight," I told Rox over the phone. It was the last day of summer vacation. "He says he wants to get to know my family!"

"That's good," Rox said.

"No, it's not. My family's crazy."

"Eccentric," Rox corrected.

"Whatever." I remembered the few times I'd gotten Parker together with my family, even for just a minute or two. Talk about oil and water. "Compared to Stephen's family, they're just not normal."

"Val's normal?"

"Well, no. She's evil. But his little sister, Elizabeth, is a sweetheart, and his mom's really nice. I haven't met his dad yet."

"Just relax," Rox advised me. "You have absolutely no reason to feel insecure."

"You're right," I said.

And she was. Stephen and I had gone out on two more dates and had a great time. I was starting to think of us as a couple. It's just dinner, I reminded myself as I hurried downstairs to see if Mom needed help in the kitchen. What could go wrong?

Everything, I decided thirty seconds later when I spotted Lily in the family room, wearing Mom's silk bathrobe and a feather boa and reciting Hamlet's "To be or not to be" soliloquy to an appreciative audience composed of Laurel and Henry the mouse.

"Okay, Lily, Laurel, and Daisy," I shouted. "Gather round."

Daisy had been in the kitchen. She stuck her head into the family room. "What's up?"

"As you all know, Stephen's coming over for dinner," I began, ready to launch into the same lecture I'd given them before Parker's arrival on prom night. "So I want you to . . ."

My sisters waited, their eyes round and expectant. Even Henry seemed to be listening. Suddenly I felt like a rodent myself. What am I doing? I thought. I thought about my prom night lecture. It hadn't really made a difference—Parker didn't even pay attention to my sisters. I remembered how sweet my sisters had been when I broke up with Parker. That breakup taught me a lot. Just as I'd discovered that I didn't want to change for Parker or anybody, I didn't want my sisters to change, either. I didn't need Lily to dress like everybody else, and Daisy looked great with a mohawk, and so what if Laurel smelled like a barn?

"Be at the table on time," I finished.

"That's all?" Daisy asked.

"No problem," Lily said, tossing the feather boa over one shoulder.

"Sure. I just need a few minutes to put Henry back in his cage and feed the baby fox I found the other day," Laurel said.

So that was where we left it. My sisters were going to do their own thing. And I'm not going to worry, I told myself.

D INNERTIME ROLLED AROUND, and even though it was a cool evening, I started sweating. I felt like I was on an antiperspirant commercial. All my resolve not to worry about what my sisters did evaporated the minute the doorbell rang.

And from the minute he arrived, Stephen did everything right—and my family did everything wrong.

He brought my mom a big bunch of flowers and a bag of fresh herbs. "Thank you, Stephen," Mom said, sniffing a bunch of basil. "This is my favorite."

"My mom likes to garden," he explained.

Just then Daisy entered the kitchen, bouncing a basketball. When she saw Stephen, her eyes glimmered mischievously. "Hey, catch!" she shouted, and fake-pumped the ball at him.

Daisy laughed as Stephen gave a startled jerk.

"Do you have to be so rude, Daze?" I asked testily.

"No, that's cool," Stephen said with a grin. "You won't catch me off guard next time."

"I'm Daisy," she told him. "Nice to meet you."

"Same here," Stephen said.

"What's cooking?" she asked, turning to our mom.

"Lasagna," Mom told her. "Would you set the table, Daisy?"

"And wash your hands first," I said.

Daisy tucked the ball under her arm. "Why don't you set the table yourself, Miss Picky?"

"Because I'm making salad dressing with the fresh herbs Stephen brought."

"Stephen, have a seat," Mom invited him, gesturing to a stool at the counter, "and tell me about your plans for fall term at Seagate."

While Stephen charmed Mom, I sliced tomatoes and agonized silently about which of my sisters would cause a scene at the table. Why hadn't I read them the riot act? When we were all seated, though, and Mom was serving the food, it looked for a moment as if the meal might go smoothly. Daisy had washed up, and Laurel hadn't looked this clean in years— her hair was actually brushed back into a neat ponytail. Lily had traded the robe and feather boa for denim shorts and a scallop-edged pink T-shirt.

"The lasagna is delicious," Stephen said.

"It's a simple recipe," Mom replied, but she looked pleased.

"Mom cooks a lot," Lily piped up. "She catered this big party the other night, and it was so good, a bunch of other people have hired her to cater parties."

Lily's voice was perky and proud. Stephen flashed her a

big smile; I wanted to kick her. She would have to bring up the catering, I thought. Having a mother who's a good cook isn't necessarily a plus. I wondered whether Stephen was drawing a comparison to his own family. They had "help"—Mrs. Mathias only cooked when she felt like it.

Stephen talked to Daisy for a few minutes about the Red Sox—I could tell Daisy was impressed by how many stats he knew. Then he turned to Laurel. "I hear you like animals," he remarked.

As if on cue, a small brown field mouse darted across the table right next to the basket of garlic bread. Stephen jumped, dropping his fork with a clatter. I screamed.

Laurel grabbed Henry, stuffing him back in the pocket of her windbreaker. "Excuse me," she muttered.

"Excuse you?" I yelped. "Toad, I'm going to kill you! I can't believe you brought him to the dinner table!"

"Please take Henry back to the hutch outside, Laurel," Mom said calmly. "You know the rules."

As Laurel pushed back her chair Henry hopped out again. For two exciting minutes Daisy, Laurel, and Lily all scrambled around under the table trying to recapture him. When Lily let out a triumphant shriek—"Got him!"—I dared a glance at Stephen. He looked as if he were trying not to laugh; I was trying not to cry.

Laurel carried the mouse back outside, and the rest of us resumed eating—not that I had much of an appetite after the Henry episode. Lily started swinging her feet, kicking the rungs of her chair. "Do you like horror movies?" she asked Stephen.

"You bet," he said.

"Okay, well, I'm trying to write a really scary story. Do you think the main character should die by being torn to pieces by a zombie, or be decapitated by an ax murderer, or have his blood sucked out and his heart and eyes gouged out by a vampire?"

"Lily, that's gross," I exclaimed.

"Not to me," she declared. "I think it's interesting. And so does Stephen, right, Stephen?"

"I like vampires myself," he said to Lily. "Have you read *Dracula*?"

"No, but I've seen the movie," she replied.

Lily continued to toss out gruesome story ideas, as if Stephen had agreed to be her literary agent or something. Daisy must have sensed that I was about to strangle Lily because as soon as there was a lull in the conversation, she turned to Stephen and said, "So, how about some one-on-one after dinner?"

They really did play basketball, so by the time Stephen and I were alone, sitting on the porch swing, his oxford shirt was damp with sweat.

"I'm really sorry about the hoops workout," I told him, trying to read his expression.

"Are you kidding? It was fun," he said easily.

That's just his prep school manners talking, I thought, still worried. "And *dinner.*" I shuddered. "You know, my sisters never act like that. Really. It must be a full moon tonight or something."

"I like your sisters," Stephen said.

"They're embarrassing."

"They're funny."

I shook my head, unconvinced. "You're just saying that to be nice."

"I don't say things just to be nice," Stephen told me. "Well, okay, maybe sometimes, but not to you. I really do like your family, Rose." He turned toward me. "Almost as much as I like you."

As Stephen wrapped his arms around me my worries faded. Of course he meant what he said, and I liked him, too. A lot. In fact, I was almost starting to think that this time it might be love, real love.

Stephen's warm lips touched mine, spreading heat throughout my body. I had just managed to calm down when Stephen pulled away in order to give me a big smile. "I wanted this to be a surprise—I was going to tell you tomorrow, when I introduce you—but I can't wait."

"Tell me what? Introduce me to whom?" I asked.

"Marilyn Hopper, the soprano. Have you heard of her? She's a friend of my parents. She's performing for a few months with the Portland Symphony. And guess what? She's willing to give you voice lessons for free!"

I wrinkled my forehead. "What?"

"I told her about you and about what a great voice you have," Stephen explained, "and she said she'd take you on as a student, once a week in Portland, for free since you're a special friend of the family. Isn't that awesome?"

I stared at Stephen, speechless.

"I thought you'd be happy about this." Stephen frowned, apparently puzzled by my silence. "I mean, that's the point, to make you happy."

I'd always dreamed about taking private voice lessons, but for some reason this unexpected gift didn't make me happy. "You mean, my voice isn't good enough the way it is," I stated flatly.

"Your voice is fine," Stephen said. "It's like anything, though. You have raw talent, but with the right training you could be a star. I mean, I know your family can't afford voice lessons. It's a great opportunity, Rose."

With the right training . . . your family can't afford . . . Stephen's words screamed in my mind like a rising alarm. Does he think I'm some kind of *charity case*? I wondered. That he can *fix me* by giving me something that my family can't afford? All of a sudden I wasn't hearing Stephen's voice and seeing Stephen's face—it was Parker sitting next to me, Parker telling me that with the right dress I'd be the prettiest girl at the Seagate Academy prom, and of course he could arrange everything. Parker making it clear in countless little ways that I wasn't good enough the way I was, that I was rough around the edges.

I'm such an idiot. Why did I think that everything was okay? I wondered. No matter how nice Stephen was, there was no getting around the fact that we were different—just like he'd said so long ago after the Rusty Nail. He had just confirmed all my worst fears. He feels sorry for me, I thought, horrified. Well, he didn't need to feel sorry for me. I didn't need his help. My *family* didn't need his help.

"I don't want to sing with a symphony," I said aloud. Angry tears stung my eyes. "I'm not an *opera soprano*. Don't you get it?"

"What are you talking about?" he asked. "Look, just come over tomorrow and meet her—"

"Come over? And have dinner with you and *Val*?" I demanded, and the sneer in my voice made me cringe.

"What does Val have to do with anything?"

"You think my sisters and I are hicks, and it's up to you to change us—"

"I don't want to change you," he broke in, looking more confused than ever. "I love you."

"You can't love me if you don't appreciate me for the way I am," I insisted. "You said it yourself that night after the Rusty Nail. We belong to different worlds. You'll never loosen up enough to fit in with my family, and I'll never be polished enough to fit in with yours."

"Whoa, hold on. Five minutes ago I was shooting baskets with your sister. If that's not loose enough for—"

I wasn't listening. I knew that no matter what Stephen said, he would never be able to accept me for who I really was. I would never be like Val, and I would never be like Camilla.

Jumping down from the swing, I shouted, "This is never going to work! You can forget about the voice lessons. You can forget about everything!"

I DIDN'T FEEL like going back inside right then, so I hid out by the garage until the sound of the Saab's engine faded into the night. Then I realized I was shivering. Fall was coming.

The night air was cool, and I was wearing only a sundress.

Still dazed by what had just happened, I went inside through the back door. I thought I'd make it to my room without running into anybody, but no such luck. Mom, Laurel, Lily, and Daisy ambushed me at the foot of the stairs.

"Stephen's great," Daisy declared, as if someone had asked her opinion. "Did you see him sink that three pointer?"

"He was so much nicer than that icky Parker," Lily agreed. "I want to show him some of my stories. Can I, Rose?"

"Let's invite him over for dinner again tomorrow night," Laurel said.

"I liked him a lot," Mom told me. She was beaming. "And your father would have, too."

At that I burst into tears.

"What's wrong, Rose?" Mom asked.

"Where is Stephen, anyway?" Daisy wanted to know. "Why'd he leave so early?"

"Because I just broke up with him!" I wailed.

Twelve

C HEER ME UP," I begged my friends.

What a way to start my junior year—in a major depression. A few days after the breakup I was eating lunch in the high school cafeteria with Rox, Cath, and Mita.

"You want jokes?" Mita asked.

"Anything," I said. It had been really hard to refuse all of Stephen's phone calls after we broke up, but I thought we ought to make a clean break. Still, I was exhausted from all the crying I had been doing.

Mita told a couple of really lame knock-knock jokes. They were so bad, they were almost humorous. Cath and Rox laughed—I smiled, but only a little. "Okay, how about making a list," Rox suggested as she unwrapped her tuna sandwich. "The top ten advantages to not having a boyfriend. Who wants to start?"

"I've got one," Cath volunteered, waving a french fry. "You can dance with anyone you want at parties."

"No more waiting by the telephone for That Certain Someone to call," Rox contributed.

"You don't have to shave your legs as often," said Mita, "and if you forget to put on deodorant, who cares?"

"You have more time for your girlfriends," Cath said.

"You have more time for everything," Mita said.

"More time to be lonely," I said glumly. The fact was, I missed Stephen. Did I make a mistake? I wondered briefly. No, I had to stick to my resolve. Stephen will find a Seagate girl, someone like Camilla, I thought, and I'll end up with a South Regional boy and that will be that.

Cath patted my hand. "It'll get better," she promised.

I nodded. Inside, though, I wasn't so sure. I'd bounced back pretty fast after Parker, but not this time.

I just couldn't stop thinking about Stephen.

L ATER, ON A chilly October afternoon, my family visited my dad's grave. Gray clouds scudded across the sky and a cold northeast wind raked the landscape, twisting the gold and red leaves off their stems and making them fall in showers.

As we stood in front of the simple headstone, a sad silence fell over us. Mom placed a pot of bright yellow mums on the grave, then touched the stone lightly before straightening up again. "It's been a while since we were all here together," she said at last, just the tiniest quaver in her voice. "Does anyone want to say something, to share a memory about Dad?"

"I want to know why Laurel isn't here," Daisy spoke up. She wiped a tear from her eye. "Isn't this important to her?"

There had been a scene when Laurel announced that she was going apple picking with the Harrisons instead of going to the cemetery. Now Mom sighed. "I wish she were here with us, too, but Laurel needs to do what feels right to her."

At that moment Lily started to cry. "I don't like the cemetery," she sobbed, her face hidden in her small hands. "Dad's not here. I want to go home."

Mom knelt down and wrapped her arms around Lily. She looked up at me and Daisy, her eyes questioning. I nodded. "It is kind of cold," Mom decided. "Yes, let's head back."

When we got home, the old Victorian house felt almost as cold as the outdoors. "How about a fire in the fireplace?" Mom suggested, rubbing her hands together. "And maybe some hot cider?"

While Daisy built a fire, I helped Mom in the kitchen. By the time we reappeared with a plate of gingersnaps and four steaming mugs of cider, Lily had disappeared. "She went up to her room," Daisy said, reaching for a cookie. "I guess she wants to be alone."

Mom kicked off her black flats and settled down on the couch, tucking her feet up under her. Daisy curled up next to Mom, draping the afghan over both their knees. I took the rocking chair. For a minute we were quiet, sipping our hot cider.

Daisy broke the silence first. "I remember a day kind of like this, last fall. It was really cold, and I had an away soccer game. Dad drove all the way to Kent with a huge thermos of hot chocolate and a couple dozen doughnuts, enough for the whole team."

"Dad liked doing things like that," I recalled. "Remember how he'd put on magic shows and stuff for our birthday parties?"

"And the time he got the whole neighborhood organized to go Christmas caroling," Daisy said.

I laughed. "I thought I would die of embarrassment over those elf costumes he made us all wear."

Just then a draft of chilly air snaked into the living room. The front door slammed, and Laurel peeked in at us. "Hi," she said.

"Sit down," Mom invited.

Laurel hesitated, then came in and perched on the arm of the sofa. "What are you doing?" she asked.

"We're telling stories about Dad," I answered.

"It's your turn," Daisy said to Laurel.

Laurel was still wearing her jacket, and now she hunched her shoulders, tucking her chin in the collar. "I can't think of anything," she mumbled.

"Come on," I urged. "How about the time Mom was mad at you for sliding down the banister, but you kept doing it, anyway, so Dad rigged that buzzer on the newel post and it went off when you got to the bottom and scared you to death?"

Laurel couldn't help smiling. "That's not funny," she said, although you could tell that she thought it was. "I fell off!"

"Dad was always doing goofy things," Daisy said. "Remember that time he made jelly bean and hot dog pizza?"

"And the pancakes shaped like bunnies and stars and boats," said Laurel.

I laughed. "He was *not* a good cook."

"He was a good storyteller, though," said Daisy. "Remember how he used to tell us fairy tales at bedtime, only he'd make us the characters?"

My sisters and I talked until the cider and cookies were gone and the fire had burned down to glowing embers. "You know, Lily was right," Daisy said at one point. "At the cemetery, when she said Dad wasn't there. He's here." Daisy waved a hand. "In all these rooms. In our memories. In us."

We sat quietly, thinking about this. It was true. The house still felt like Dad in so many ways. He was in the kitchen, flipping pancakes on a Sunday morning; he was out in the barn, repairing his nets; he was upstairs in the hallway at bedtime, checking each of our rooms in turn to make sure we were tucked in and sleeping peacefully. During his life he'd always been there, making us feel safe. Dad took care of us, but he also helped us do things on our own. He talked me out of my stage fright before a concert and played endless games of catch with Daisy when she wanted to try out for the boys' Little League team, and he told Laurel she could still climb trees even if she couldn't slide down banisters, and he never laughed when Lily came to the dinner table dressed like Daniel Boone.

I thought about how I hadn't wanted to tell Parker about my dad, about how I had been ashamed that he was a fisherman. Now I was ashamed that I'd ever felt that way. Dad had been honest and generous and steadfast. He'd believed in me—in all of us. Talking about Dad made my heart ache with longing—I knew I'd never stop missing him. But I knew, too, that if I let it, his spirit would always stay with me.

There'd always be an inner voice saying, I believe in you, Rose.

Thirteen

FALL PASSED QUICKLY, and the days grew darker and shorter.

November is the gloomiest month of the year, I thought one Saturday afternoon as I drove down Old Boston Post Road.

When I saw the sign for the social services center, I tapped the brakes and turned into the parking lot. For a minute I sat with my hands gripping the steering wheel, seriously wishing I hadn't volunteered to pick up the month's food stamps. Then I gave myself a little kick in the pants. "Grow up for once, Rose Walker," I mumbled.

I went inside the building, sort of slouching into my oversize U. Maine sweatshirt. I was surprised to see a bunch of people, some waiting in line at the counter and some sitting on orange plastic chairs. For some reason I thought I'd be the only person there, like my family was the only one in the county with problems. How self-centered can you get?

I stood behind a woman who didn't look much older than me. She was holding a baby girl in a pink fleece snowsuit balanced on her hip. A toddler stood next to her, the little girl's skinny arms wrapped around her mother's blue-jean-clad legs.

It was her turn at the counter. "How are you doing, Jane?" the social worker asked her with a warm smile.

The woman shifted the baby to her other hip. "Rick's still out of work," she said in a broad Maine accent. She sounded beat. "And both kids just got over the flu. Some days I wonder how we'll make it until next summer."

The woman behind the counter reached out and touched the young mother's arm. "You'll make it," she said firmly. "You're not alone."

I turned away, a little embarrassed at witnessing such a personal moment. My gaze roamed around the room. Some of the people waiting for help looked like the people who lived on the farms inland from the coast. There were some farm kids at South Regional with me, and I knew farming for them was a tough way to make a living. I can't believe I ever moaned and groaned about not having enough money for clothes and CDs, I thought. My life could be so much worse.

When I faced forward again, the baby was watching me. Her nose was runny, and she wasn't as chubby as babies should be, but when I smiled at her, she smiled back. The baby's mother turned to leave. Her eyes met mine. I smiled again. "Hi," I said.

Her expression was tired and hopeless, but her lips curved up just a little bit. "Hi," she replied.

I stepped up to the counter—it was my turn. "I'm Rose Walker," I told the social worker. My voice was clear and strong.

ON THE WAY home I stopped in town to do some more errands for Mom. Main Street seemed subdued—about a third of the stores and almost all the restaurants were closed for the winter. Hawk Harbor was hibernating and, as snowflakes stung my cheeks, I wished I could, too.

I pushed through the door of the Down East News and Drugstore just as someone else was leaving.

Someone else who happened to be Stephen Mathias.

"Rose!" he exclaimed.

"Stephen!" I said.

We stood awkwardly in the doorway, half in and half out. "Uh, here," he said, holding the door. I scurried into the store, and he followed.

We took up neutral positions on either side of a rack of postcards. "So," I said. "Doing some shopping?"

Stephen held up a paper bag. "Toothpaste."

"Hey, I'm shopping for toothpaste, too. So," I said again, wishing I could think of a way to make this toothpaste conversation last forever.

"What's new?" he asked.

"Not a lot." I picked out a postcard with a picture of a giant lobster on it and started idly reading the caption on the back. "You know, school. Concert choir."

"The usual for me, too," he said. "Classes. Sports. I'm studying pretty hard this semester. I'm not going out much," he added, his tone significant.

It was a pretty broad hint, and I blushed as the meaning sank in. He's not dating anybody, I guessed.

For some reason that knowledge made me ridiculously happy, but I tried not to make it too obvious. "Yeah, well, you're a senior now. You have to get serious if you want to get into a decent college."

"Right." He looked at me a moment. "Hey, how about grabbing a cup of cider somewhere?"

The invitation sounded casual, but I knew it wasn't. Sitting down across from each other at Patsy's Diner would be completely different from bumping into each other in the drugstore. Why start something that can only end badly? I thought.

Even so, it was an effort not to say *yes, yes, yes.*

"I've got to do these errands for my mom," I said instead. "Maybe some other time."

He couldn't hide his disappointment, or maybe he just didn't try. For a moment the longing in his eyes was unmistakable. "Some other time," he echoed.

"See you around," I said.

He smiled faintly. "Sure."

Without looking back, Stephen walked out of the store and disappeared into the dusk.

Still clutching the lobster postcard, I wandered to the toothpaste aisle. I knew what brand Mom wanted, but for the longest time I just stood there, staring blankly at rows of rectangular boxes. I wasn't seeing the toothpaste—I was remembering the look in Stephen's eyes. Now, belatedly, a similar longing washed over me. I wanted to run after him, to touch his hand, to see him smile when I said I'd changed my mind, let's have a cup of coffee. He's really sad, after all this time, I thought. Maybe I was wrong about him. Maybe he really did care.

But I knew that it was too late. I could never make things right with Stephen again. All I could do was stand there in the toothpaste and mouthwash section of the Down East News and Drugstore, wondering if I'd made a terrible mistake letting him go.

WHERE'S MY BLACK ribbed turtleneck?" I yelled down the hall on Sunday morning. "Lily!"

Lily was supposed to fold the clean laundry and distribute it to everyone's room. I'd cut her some slack for a while, but it was getting ridiculous. "How come I have no clean clothes?" I grumbled to myself. "Lily!"

I stomped down to my sister's room. She had to be hiding the laundry somewhere. Lily wasn't in her room, though, and neither was my black turtleneck. But I did spot a tattered cardboard binder. Her notebook, I thought.

I knew I shouldn't, but I couldn't help myself. Sitting down on her bed, I opened the notebook and started reading a story that Lily had titled "Dark Days."

The story was only six pages long, but the problems were piled high for Linda, the fatherless eight-year-old heroine.

First Linda's family was flung into poverty, then her mother got sick and died, and finally the orphaned child was separated from her three older sisters and sent to live with cruel foster parents.

No wonder Lily has bad dreams, I thought. I had spent so much time getting annoyed with Lily for being rude or neglecting her chores that I had forgotten she was just a little kid. A scared, sad little kid.

Just as I was starting the next story, called "The Zombie's Bloody Revenge," Lily danced into the room wearing a pink ballerina's tutu. She spotted me with the notebook. "What are you doing?" she screeched. "Give me that!" She snatched the notebook from me. "You better not have looked inside it, Rose Annabelle Walker!" she cried, her blue eyes flashing.

"I did look inside," I confessed.

Lily stamped a foot. "Can't you read?" She held the notebook up so I could see the label on the cover: Private Property. Keep Out!

"I'm sorry, Lily," I said. "But I wanted to tell you that your stories are great. They're really entertaining and totally wacky."

She scowled. "What do you mean?"

"Well, like in 'Dark Days.' All those bad things that happened to Linda—it's hardly ever that way in real life."

"How do you know?" she asked.

"I just do," I told her. "Like, take us, for example. Sure, lots of bad things have happened to us. We lost Dad, and we are poor. But Mom isn't going to die for a long, long time, and she's working hard to make more money. Besides, we still have each other, and I would never let you go. I'll always be your big sister."

"My nosy big sister," Lily said, looking a little less mad.

"As if you've never snooped in my stuff," I countered.

She started to protest, but I pounced on her, pinning her to the bed in a big bear hug. "You're bossy," Lily complained.

"You're a pest," I replied, and pressed my cheek against hers.

WHEN LILY REVEALED that she'd been sticking the piles of clean laundry into her closet, I chewed her out for spending all her time in outer space and then helped her fold it all. After putting on a clean pair of jeans and my favorite turtleneck, I headed downstairs and flipped through the newspaper, looking for the movie schedule. I was about to call Mita to suggest going to the two-dollar matinee in Kent when I caught sight of Daisy out the window.

She was in the backyard. Having raked and bagged all the leaves—and there'd been tons—she was now cutting the scraggly brown grass with an old push mower. She was never able to get the gas-powered mower to work again.

Guilt crept into my heart. I really wanted to see the new Tom Cruise movie, but . . .

"Mom, can I borrow the car for a quick errand?" I called out.

"Sure," she answered.

Instead of calling Mita, I made a trip to Appleby's Hardware. Cath's dad helped me pick out the parts I needed. Back home, I put on a jacket and a pair of old gloves and went out to the garage.

When Daisy came up, I was taking the lawn mower apart. "You don't know how to do that," she said.

"Give me a little credit, okay?" I mopped my forehead on the sleeve of my jacket. "Mr. Appleby says if I unscrew this"—I tossed aside a greasy bolt—"and put in a new one of these . . ."

Fifteen minutes later we put some gas in the mower and Daisy gave the cord a pull. It started right up. "You did it!" she exclaimed.

"How about that?" I said with satisfaction. "I'm a regular Ms. Fix-it."

"So we've got the lawn mower working." She gave me an ironic grin. Her hair's growing out—it looked pretty cute, although I knew better than to say so. "Just in time for the first snow."

"Better late than never," I pointed out.

I HELPED DAISY finish up the yard work, then collapsed at the table in the breakfast nook with a bag of potato chips. All that work had given me a gigantic appetite. As I was gobbling them down Laurel stopped in to grab a can of generic cola from the fridge. I noticed she was wearing a jacket and scarf. "Going over to Jack's?" I guessed.

"Yep."

"How come you guys don't play at our house?"

Laurel shrugged. "It's quieter over there. He doesn't have any brothers or sisters."

"I kind of like sisters, myself," I said.

"Well, Mr. and Mrs. Harrison *want* me to come over," Laurel said. "They plan special stuff for us to do. Last weekend Mr. Harrison taught me how to play backgammon. Today we're going horseback riding."

Suddenly I had a feeling I knew what was going on with Laurel—why she was running over to Jack's all the time. And I figured something else out, too. This is turning into the day I pay back all the favors these guys did for me after I broke up with Parker, I thought. My sisters have been needing me, I realized, as much as I needed them.

I offered Laurel the chips, and she took one. "It's weird sometimes, just having one parent, isn't it?" I asked after a moment.

Laurel shrugged again.

"I miss talking to Dad about stuff," I continued. "And Mom's so busy now, with work and all, sometimes she's not around when I need her, either."

"It's just not fair," Laurel burst out. "We used to be a perfect family, and now everything's awful."

"So Jack's family is perfect?"

She nodded. "He has both his parents. He gets all their attention. And they can afford to buy him whatever he wants and take him all these fun places."

"He's an only child, though. Don't you think that gets lonely sometimes?"

"Maybe," she admitted, "but I'd still trade with him in a minute."

I crunched one last chip, then wiped my hands on a napkin. "Sometimes I wish I could go back in time to when Dad was alive," I told Laurel. "Stop the clock right there."

Laurel gazed at me, her eyes suddenly bright with tears. "But we can't, can we?"

I shook my head. "No. We have to be there for each other in new ways." I put my arms around Laurel, praying that Henry wasn't in one of her coat pockets. "And if we do that, we'll be okay. We'll make it."

THANKSGIVING CAME AND went and then, suddenly, it was December. By now I figured that Stephen had probably forgotten about me, but I still found myself thinking about him at odd moments, like this Saturday morning as I sat at the kitchen table eating oatmeal and watching the snow falling outside the window. What's he doing right now? I wondered.

Lily breezed into the kitchen, wearing an *I Dream of Jeannie*–style harem costume. "You're eating breakfast?" she asked. "It's lunchtime!"

Yawning, I glanced at the clock. Lily was right—it was almost noon. "I went to a party at Cath's last night," I told her.

She hopped onto a chair next to me. "Well, hurry up. We're going to cut down a Christmas tree!"

"We are?"

She nodded. "Mom said so. Everyone's going, even Laurel. You need to get dressed!"

I spooned up the last bite of oatmeal. "Is that what you're wearing?"

Lily glanced down at her clothes. "I'll put a snowsuit on over it, of course," she said, rolling her eyes.

Fifteen minutes later, decked out in boots, hats, mittens, and parkas, we marched across the snowy lawn, heading for the woods behind our house. Daisy carried a handsaw, Laurel had some rope looped over her shoulder, and Mom pulled the old Flexible Flyer sled.

"Here's one," Lily said, pointing to the first pine we came across.

"Way too small," Daisy judged. "The best trees are farther in."

As we walked on into the woods I remembered past Decembers. Cutting down the Christmas tree was always Dad's project. "I didn't think we were going to do it this year," I confessed to Mom as we took turns hopping over a half-frozen brook. "I thought maybe we'd just buy a tree."

"But it's such a special ritual," she replied. "It's always meant so much to you girls."

"You're right," I agreed. "It wouldn't really seem like Christmas without a tree from our own woods."

We moved on, our footsteps muffled by the snow. Lily and Laurel skipped ahead, Laurel hunting for deer and fox tracks, Lily's green-and-red stocking cap bouncing. Daisy stopped. "How about that tree?" she called, waving a mittened hand.

We circled the evergreen. It was about six feet tall, and its branches were nice and full except for one flat side. "It's a little bald over here," I pointed out.

"We'll turn that side to the wall," Mom said. "No tree is perfect."

"True." I grinned at Daisy. "Okay. Let's start sawing!"

She and I took turns, and in five minutes the tree fell to the snowy ground with a thump. We hauled it onto the sled, securing its trunk with the rope. Then we all grabbed hold of the rope and pulled the sled toward home.

"Let's sing a Christmas carol," Daisy suggested.

"How about 'Hark, the Herald Angels Sing'?" said Mom.

We shouted out the carol, our breath frosty in the cold air. Back at the house, outside the door, we stood the tree up and shook the snow from its branches. "It's a good tree," Mom declared with satisfaction.

Her cheeks were red from the cold, and her eyes were sparkling, and she had snowflakes in her hair—she looked beautiful. I felt a sudden surge of love for her and for my sisters. It had been a tough year, full of change and loss, but somehow we'd made it through. And I loved my mother and sisters more than I ever had before. I remembered last spring and summer, how I'd tried to be someone different to please Parker, how ashamed and resentful I'd been of my family's poverty. Now I knew what really mattered, and this was it.

"It's a great tree," I said, smiling at my mother.

Fourteen

"Deck the halls with boughs of holly, fa la la la la, la la la la," Lily belted out at the top of her lungs.

It was a wintry Sunday afternoon before Christmas, and we were doing just what the carol said, decking the halls. Laurel was winding pine boughs around the banister. Lily stood on a step stool to arrange holly sprigs on top of the mantel while Daisy wove a wreath for the front door. My project was to make a table centerpiece out of fruit and nuts.

"The house looks festive," Mom said, joining us in the living room. "You girls did a nice job."

"We're going to have an awesome Christmas," Daisy predicted cheerfully.

We'd already agreed that this year, to save money, we'd exchange homemade gifts. The holiday meal would be simple. Of course, with Dad gone, everything about Christmas would feel different. But Daisy's right, I thought. We can still be happy.

Her arms folded tightly across her chest, Mom gazed distractedly at Daisy's half-finished Christmas wreath. "Actually, girls, while you're all together," she said, her tone suddenly more serious, "I suppose this is as good a time as any."

"For what?" Laurel asked.

"I have some news," she began, perching on the arm of a chair.

"Good or bad?" Daisy asked.

"A little of both," Mom replied. "First of all, I'm going to be really busy between now and Christmas. I'm catering three parties."

"Mom, that's terrific!" I exclaimed. "You're almost ready to start your own company."

"Well, I'm not going to quit my job yet, but I am thinking along those lines," she admitted.

Laurel reached up and gave her a hug. I beamed at Mom, so proud of her I was ready to burst. "Yippee!" cheered Lily.

"So, that's the good news," Mom went on. "Thanks to the extra income from the catering, we don't qualify for public aid anymore. But it's still going to be a struggle to make ends meet." I saw Mom's arm tighten around Laurel's shoulders; she gazed at each of us in turn. "I've given it lots of thought, and it looks as if there's only one sure way to take the financial pressure off." She paused to take a deep breath. "We're going to have to sell the house."

A shocked silence fell over us. We all stared at Mom with stunned expressions. Lily's mouth dropped open. Laurel blinked. "Sell the house?" Daisy repeated in disbelief.

"I wish there was an alternative, I really do," Mom said. "But the property taxes are just too high."

"But where will we live?" Lily wailed. "Are we going to be homeless?"

"Oh, honey, of course not." Mom hurried over to Lily and scooped her up in a reassuring hug. "We'll rent a smaller place. I've already found a cute three-bedroom apartment right in town."

"Does it have a yard?" asked Laurel.

"I'm afraid not," Mom said.

Laurel's face fell. Her hutches were full of animals again, and I knew she was worrying about where they would all live. "But what about the rabbit and the baby squirrel and—"

"We'll have to find other homes for them," Mom told Laurel. "I'll go over to the Wildlife Rescue Center with you and see if they can help."

"Do I have to get rid of Henry, too?" Laurel's voice was small.

"We can't have any pets at all," Mom said. "I'm sorry, sweetheart."

I'd always detested Laurel's furry friends, but now I couldn't help feeling sorry for her. Then something else occurred to me. "The apartment has only three bedrooms?" I asked Mom. "You mean, we'll have to share?"

Mom looked at me over Lily's head, her eyes pleading for

support. "I know you're used to privacy, but if we save money on rent, we'll have more left for extras."

Immediately I felt bad that I'd sounded selfish. I'd grown up a lot since my sixteenth birthday, when I'd pouted about having to give up camp in order to get a summer job. We were a family, and we had to stick together through thick and thin. I was Mom's oldest daughter—I should back her up, not criticize her.

"An apartment sounds cozy," I said with as much false cheer as I could muster. "It might even be fun sharing a room." I turned to Daisy. "Like a slumber party, right?"

Daisy nodded, but her eyes were swimming with tears. "Yeah," she said, and her voice was strained and reedy. "It'll be great."

Laurel sniffled loudly. Lily buried her face in Mom's neck and began to sob. Daisy was still struggling to hold back tears, and so was I. Reaching out, I took Daisy's hand and gave it a firm squeeze. "We'll be together," I said. "That's what matters most."

"Isn't there anything we can do?" Daisy begged. "I'll get a job."

"And I promise to help out more around the house . . . ," Lily added.

Mom held my gaze as she hugged Lily tight. "I know we'll all be sad to leave this house, but Rose is right."

Lily nodded, her face smudged with tears. Laurel hugged herself, her feet tucked up and her arms wrapped around her knees. Daisy and I continued to hold hands, giving each other strength. We sat quietly like that for a long time, each lost in her own thoughts about what it would mean to say good-bye to the only home we'd ever known.

CHRISTMAS WASN'T LIKE any other we'd celebrated before. We were all missing Dad even more than usual. And there weren't very many packages under the tree. But that's okay, I told myself, trying not to feel sad about it. There are more important things than gifts.

"When can we open our presents?" Lily asked, hopping up and down impatiently.

Mom curled up on the living room sofa, a mug of hot coffee in her hand. "I'm ready," she said. "Why don't you start?"

Daisy took over Dad's job of handing out the presents. She found a box with Lily's name on it. "Here's one," she said.

Lily read the tag. "It's from Rose," she said. It took her about a millisecond to tear the paper off. "A new notebook, and Rose decorated it!"

"If you're going to be a famous writer, you might as well have the right materials," I told her.

"Here's one for you, Laurel," Daisy said. "From Lily."

"It's an envelope," Laurel said, tilting her head. "What is it?"

"Look inside and see!" Lily urged.

Laurel opened the envelope and pulled out a single sheet of paper decorated with animal stickers. Her eyes began to sparkle. "Lily wrote a poem for me."

"Read it out loud," I said.

"'Nearest in age, we fight the most, too,'" Laurel read. "'Sometimes I wish there wasn't any you. But deep inside, I know you really care. I'd be sad if you weren't always there.'"

"Do you like it?" Lily asked anxiously.

Laurel nodded. "It's a great present. Thanks, Lily."

"I wrote a poem for everybody," Lily said, blushing with pride.

"That was a wonderful idea," Mom said.

We continued opening our gifts. Mom had sewn a dozen headbands out of pretty scraps of fabric—three for each of us, including Daisy, whose hair was long enough to pull back again. "Look!" Daisy said, holding up a shoe box Laurel had covered in a collage of sports pictures. "This will be perfect for storing my baseball cards. Thanks!"

There was one more present for Laurel. I handed her a bulky, heavy package. "Wow. What is it?" she asked.

"Open it and see," I told her.

Laurel ripped off the paper. Inside was a brand-new hamster-size cage with a sliding tray at the bottom. I'd gotten an extra-special deal on it at Appleby's Hardware. "What's this for?" Laurel wondered.

"It's for Henry," I explained. "I talked Mom into asking the landlord if you could keep one of your animals, and it's okay as long as Henry stays in his cage."

"Oh, Rose." Laurel's smile was brighter than the lights on the Christmas tree. "Thank you so, so much!"

There was only one gift left under the tree. "It's for Rose," Daisy announced.

I took the small, flat box. "Feels like a CD," I said. "But who . . ." Then I read the tag. "From Stephen? How did this get here?"

"He left it on the porch," Mom said. "Actually, I invited him in for a cup of cocoa. He's very nice."

"Yes," I agreed softly. "He is." Stephen was here? I thought. Drinking cocoa with my mother—and I didn't even know it?

I looked at the tag: *To Rose*, it read. *We aren't as different as you think. Yours always, Stephen.* My mother didn't say anything else, and neither did I. I opened the present. I can't say that I was surprised to find it was a Sheryl Crowe CD. "I can't believe he did that," I said, swallowing tears.

"He must still like you," Lily said.

"Do you still like him?" asked Laurel.

I nodded. "Yeah. Isn't that dumb?"

"I don't think it's dumb," Daisy said. "I mean, I'm not ever going to have a boyfriend, but I think Stephen is great."

I put the CD with my other presents. He was great, but I'd blown it. And my pride was still in the way—I couldn't go after him now, and he probably wouldn't take me back even if I did. "It doesn't matter. It's ancient history," I said, drying my eyes.

We all looked at the Christmas tree. There were no more packages. Lily's lower lip pushed out in a pout. "It used to take *forever* for us to open all our presents," she recalled sadly.

"I know what we can do," Mom said. "Let's all give one more gift to the person sitting to our left."

"How?" asked Laurel. "There aren't any more presents."

"A gift of service or of time or talent," Mom explained. "There are lots of nice things we can do for each other. You start, Rose."

"Well, I'm sitting next to you, Mom," I said, smiling at her. "You work so hard, I should think of a way to make your life easier. How about . . . taking over one of your chores? I'll take out the garbage every week."

"That would be tremendous," Mom said. "Thanks, honey."

"My turn!" Lily said. "I have Rose. From now on, I'll bring you your laundry on time *and* I'll sort it and put it away for you."

"Good deal," I said. "Thanks, Lil."

Mom was gazing at Daisy, her cheek propped thoughtfully on her fingertips. "I have Daisy. Hmmm," she murmured. "How do I help my best helper?"

"Cook her something, Mom," Lily suggested.

"That's a good idea. I'll bake a care package for Daisy's whole team every time there's an away game."

"That would be great, Mom," said Daisy. "We're always starving on the bus ride home. Okay, I have Laurel. I know. When we get to the new apartment, since the only real pet you can have is Henry, I'll help you set up a fish tank."

Laurel's eyes brightened. "You're the best, Daze." She was the last to go. "I have Lily," she said, eyeing her younger sister. "We're going to share a room in the new place, which means we might fight more than ever. So my present to you is that I promise I won't pick any fights with you even if you do something that really, really annoys me. And if we do start arguing, I'll say that you were right and stop. For a month," she added.

"And maybe a month will be all it takes for you two to get along better," said Mom.

"That was fun," Lily said. "Now I feel like I got everything I wanted for Christmas."

Judging from everybody's faces, we all felt that way. I gave Lily a hug. "Me too."

THREE LARGE BOXES, totally full," Daisy declared, huffing and puffing. "And that was just the coat closet!"

It was January 1, and we were ringing in the New Year by packing boxes. "It's amazing how much stuff we've accumulated over the years, isn't it?" Mom agreed as she rolled up the hall carpet.

Laurel thundered down the stairs. "I've finished packing my room," she reported. "Now what should I do?"

"You and Daisy could tackle the garage," Mom suggested. "But don't strain yourselves. Leave the heavy stuff for Stan and Mr. Smith."

Our neighbor and his son were going to help us move our furniture and boxes over to the new apartment tomorrow. One more day, I thought as I placed volumes of the *Encyclopedia Britannica* in a box, and then we'll all walk out of this house for the very last time.

When the box was full, I taped it shut and labeled it. Then I threw on a parka and headed out to the garage to see if Daisy and Laurel needed help.

I found Laurel standing by her empty animal hutches. "Are you okay?" I asked.

I'd assumed she was crying, but instead she turned to me with a smile. "I'll really miss the yard and the barn and our trees," she said, "and the crocuses in the spring and the fox we sometimes see at the edge of the woods and the robin's nest and our view of the ocean."

"I will, too," I agreed, wondering why she didn't seem sadder about it.

"I'll be glad to have a fish tank, though," she added. "And Henry, of course."

I smiled at her and headed toward the garage. Daisy was inside, a half-packed cardboard box in front of her. She was standing very still, lost in thought. "What's that?" I asked her.

She held up the baseball mitt she was holding. "Dad's old mitt, from when he was in high school. The one he used to wear when we played catch, back when he taught me how to throw."

I smiled sadly, but Daisy didn't seem that upset. "It's all Dad's stuff in here," she observed as she dropped the mitt in the box. "Fishing gear, tools, car parts."

"We probably don't need most of it," I remarked.

"Probably not, but I'm packing it, anyway," she said cheerfully. "Well . . . maybe not the car parts."

I decided to finish packing my own stuff. Back inside the house, I walked down the hall to the staircase. Just as I passed the storage cupboard under the stairs, its door popped open and Lily crawled out. "What on earth were you doing in there?" I asked, raising my eyebrows.

Lily brushed the dust from her hands. "I'm saying good-bye to all my old secret hiding places," she explained matter-of-factly. "I'm sure the new apartment will have some good ones, but it might take me a while to sniff them out."

"There's bound to be a closet or two," I replied.

Lily trotted off toward the kitchen, probably to say good-bye to the pantry. Upstairs, I paused in the hall near my bedroom door. Bending forward, I squinted at some faint pencil marks on the wall. I smiled, remembering the last time Dad had lined us up to see how tall we were. It was years ago, but I could almost see the ghosts of the little girls we were.

My bedroom was a mess of half-packed suitcases and boxes. Paperback books spilled out of a plastic milk crate, and another crate was stuffed with shoes. Instead of resuming the task of emptying dresser drawers, though, I went over to the window and leaned my arms on the sill. I followed Lighthouse Road with my eyes, tracing it to its end, where the pines and rocks tumbled into the sea. This had been my window, my view, through all the seasons, year in and year out, ever since I was a little girl.

And I'm sad to be leaving, I thought, blinking back a tear. How come no one else is?

It was dusk when the doorbell rang. When I opened the door, I saw Cath, Mita, and Rox standing on the porch. "Hi," I said, surprised. "Are you guys here to help me pack?"

"No, we're here to get you to go out with us tonight," said Rox.

"You need a break from all this work," Cath agreed.

"We were thinking about the Rusty Nail," Mita put in. "What do you say?"

"Thanks, you guys," I said, and gave a sentimental sniffle, "but it's our last night in the old house, you know? I think my sisters and Mom and I will want to just be together and—"

"Speak for yourself," Laurel said, coming up behind me. "I'm going over to Jack's tonight."

"I'm going to the movies with some friends," said Daisy, appearing in the hall.

"Vera Schenkel invited us to come by for supper," Mom announced, emerging from the family room. "I'll take Lily. Why don't you go out with your friends, Rose?"

"Well," I mumbled. If I didn't go to the Rusty Nail, it looked like I'd be sitting home alone. Thanks a lot! I thought, feeling left out. "I guess I'll go with you. Since no one else wants to hang out with me," I added, whining a little.

"Great," said Daisy.

"Here's your coat," Laurel said, tossing it to me.

"Have a good time!" Mom called.

The four of us squeezed into the cab of Mr. Appleby's pickup truck. Cath drove, Mita sat in the middle, and I sat on Rox's lap. "So, am I a sappy fool?" I asked my friends. "How come nobody else in my family seems bummed about moving? It's like they know something they're not telling me."

Cath and Mita exchanged a meaningful glance. "Maybe they've just decided that moving's not so bad," Cath suggested.

"Maybe," I said, unconvinced.

I was still feeling a little put out when we parked at the Rusty Nail, but as soon as I got inside I was glad I'd gone out. As usual, the music was great. Cath's and Rox's boyfriends, Tony and Kurt, were there, and we took turns dancing with them. We played a game of pool—Kurt and I beat Mita and Rox—then danced some more. I was having a good time when suddenly I spotted a familiar-looking blond woman across the room.

"Whoa, Mita!" I said, grabbing her arm and making her spill her soda. "I think that's my mom. It *is* my mom! What's she doing here?"

Before I could charge over and ask Mom why on earth she was hanging out at the Rusty Nail on a Saturday night when she was supposed to be having dinner at the Schenkels', Bruno, the deejay, stopped the dance music. "It's open mike night, folks," he announced, "and for starters tonight, we have something a little different. Our first performer is here all the way from Seagate Academy. He's singing this song for someone in the audience, and I think she knows who she is. Everybody give a big hand to—"

"Stephen!" I gasped.

My eyes bulged in surprise, and I stared at Cath. She grinned and gave me a shrug. Stephen hopped onstage and took the microphone from Bruno, then beckoned to someone down in the crowd. To my amazement, three other people joined him onstage: Daisy, Laurel, and Lily!

"'If I fell in love with you, would you promise to be true

and help me understand,'" Stephen began singing. It was "If I Fell."

As Stephen sang my favorite Beatles song, with my sisters providing the background vocals, I started to cry. They were terrible—Stephen's voice kept cracking on the high notes, and my sisters are all tone-deaf—but everyone was clapping wildly, anyway. "I can't believe this," I said to Cath, Mita, and Rox, sniffling. "This is absolutely the craziest, sweetest thing anyone's ever done for me."

As he sang, Stephen stared straight down into my eyes. "'Cause I couldn't stand the pain. And I would be sad if our new love was in vain . . .'" My heart brimmed with happiness because I knew what he was trying to tell me. In this crazy way he was showing me that he *could* fit into my world, and I could fit into his, if we both were willing to make the effort. That's what love is all about.

When the song ended, Stephen and my sisters got the loudest round of applause I've ever heard at the Rusty Nail. My friends cheered wildly, and so did my mom, and so did I. Stephen jumped down from the stage and made his way toward me. "Rose," he said, taking both my hands in his. "I know a song can't say everything, but do you think we could—"

"Oh, shut up and kiss me, Stephen Mathias," I said, pulling him to me. And as everyone cheered even louder, that's exactly what he did.

Fifteen

I WAS WONDERING why everyone was in such a good mood, considering we're about to leave our home," I told Stephen later as we sat alone in my living room, surrounded by boxes. "I can't believe you planned that!"

"When I told your family what I had in mind, they were all for it," Stephen said. "I guess they think I'm okay."

"They think you're the greatest," I said, "and so do my friends. They all thought I was nuts to break up with you."

"You were nuts," Stephen said.

We wrapped our arms around each other, and Stephen kissed me. With a happy sigh I rested my head on his shoulder. "I was so stupid and proud," I reflected.

"No, it was my fault," Stephen said, stroking my hair. "I wanted to do something nice for you—the voice lessons—but I didn't think about how it might make you feel."

"I was just so insecure because of what happened with Parker," I told him. "I judged you based on how he treated me. It wasn't fair."

"Do you think we can start over?"

"I'd like that," I said, looking up at him with shining eyes. "But only if you promise you'll shake me if I ever jump to conclusions about someone based on superficial things like how much money they have or what school they go to."

"It's a deal," Stephen said, "if you promise not to make me go skinny-dipping in the Atlantic."

"Okay, if you promise we'll never double-date with Val and Parker."

"Okay, if you promise I don't have to sing at open mike night again."

"Are you kidding? The Rusty Nail wants to sign you up for a regular gig!"

We kissed again, and then I said softly, "Thanks for giving me a second chance, Stephen."

"I knew I'd never meet anyone as special as you ever again." His brown eyes twinkled. "Anyway, you *had* to take me back. Who else would put up with Henry?"

THERE SHOULD BE thunder and lightning and wind and hail," Lily said in a melodramatic tone. The next morning we were watching Stan Smith and his father carry the living room couch—the same one Stephen and I had been kissing on the night before—up the ramp into the rented moving truck. "Or maybe an earthquake or a volcano erupting."

"A volcano in Maine?" I said with a laugh.

It was a beautiful winter day—crisp and sunny. And it was hard to be too down because moving had turned into a neighborhood block party. Mrs. Smith had brought us a basket of home-baked muffins for breakfast, and the Comiskeys delivered pizzas for lunch. People stopped by to wish us luck and stayed to help carry a box or two. Stephen was there, too, helping Mr. Smith and Stan with the heavy stuff. Somehow Stephen managed to make moving heavy boxes look really cute.

Finally the truck was loaded, and I made plans to see Stephen later, after my sisters and I were somewhat settled in the apartment. My sisters were already in the station wagon, with the windows rolled down so they could say good-bye to their friends. I walked through the house one last time with Mom. "Doesn't look like we missed anything," she said, glancing into the empty hall closet. "I guess it's time to go."

We stepped out the door, and then she turned to lock it with her key. We both knew it was the last time we'd stand on the front porch, the last time we'd walk down the flagstone path to the driveway. We'd already sold the house, and in just a week a new family would be moving in. Mom's eyes were moist, but she held her shoulders square and managed to give me a brave smile. "Don't look back," she advised.

And I didn't.

L OOK. WE HAVE a view!" Lily and Laurel chorused.

Daisy and I had been debating how to arrange the furniture in our new bedroom. It was going to be cramped, with two twin beds, two dressers, and two desks. Glad to have a distraction, we jogged down the hall to Lily and Laurel's room.

We joined our younger sisters at the window. Sure enough, it looked out over the small town park, beyond which there were storefronts, a church steeple, and a glimpse of the harbor.

"This place isn't half bad," Daisy said.

"I like the way the roof slopes down under the eaves," I said.

"And the smell from Wissinger's Bakery downstairs," Lily said.

Just then the doorbell rang. All four of us raced into the front hall. "I bet it's Stephen," I said.

"Or Jack," Laurel said.

"Maybe it's Kyle," Lily said, poking Daisy in the ribs.

"Shut up, Lily," Daisy said.

Mom answered the door. A man I'd never seen before, thin and tall with glasses and brown, receding hair, stood in the doorway. "Hello," he said, sticking out his hand. He had a nice voice, deep and warm. "I'm Hal Leverett, your new neighbor. Just thought I'd introduce myself and see if you needed any help carting boxes or moving furniture."

"Why, that's nice of you," Mom said, smiling. "Come on in. I was just thinking that I'd like to slide the china cabinet to the other side of the dining room. If it's not too heavy for you . . ."

It wasn't too heavy. After Mr. Leverett had moved the china cabinet, Mom invited him to sit down while she made a pot of tea. Meanwhile Daisy and I unpacked a box of tablecloths and place mats. "Why is he sticking around?" Daisy hissed under her breath.

"Why shouldn't he?" I asked.

"He's flirting with Mom!"

"No, he's not," I said. "He's just being nice."

Her forehead furrowed, Daisy dug into another box labeled Pictures. Locating a framed photo of Dad, she marched across the living room and propped it on the center of the mantel. "Our father," she announced, to no one in particular but loud enough so that Mr. Leverett, sitting in the dining room with Mom, could hear.

I smiled to myself. Suspicious, protective Daisy. As I stored some linens in the buffet, though, I shot a glance at Mom and Mr. Leverett. They did seem to be having a lively conversation. Mr. Leverett made a remark about the bakery downstairs, and Mom laughed. They chatted about their work, and he made her laugh again, drawing comparisons between her catering and his accounting business. "More tea?" she offered.

"Please," he said.

I watched Mom's face as she refilled Mr. Leverett's cup. It's like the clock's been turned back, like she's a year younger, I thought. For a moment I glimpsed the Maggie Walker of old: lighthearted, funny, pretty—all qualities that had been buried under sorrow and worry since Dad died. Mom had been under such a strain for so long; now it was as if winter were ending early. She was ready to bloom, to be herself again.

Suddenly this moving day took on a completely different meaning for me. I realized that for Mom, selling the old house didn't represent failure. The opposite, in fact. It was a triumph—she'd held her family together, and she was going to support us, and she'd done it all on her own. And maybe, as much as we'd all loved the old house, it was better for us to start over someplace fresh. We'd never forget Dad, but here his absence would be less of a presence. We would have a little distance. Perspective.

When I went back to unpacking, I discovered Lily perched on an ottoman in the living room, the notebook I'd given her for Christmas on her knee. "What are you writing?" I asked her.

"A new story," she replied.

"Of course," I said. That's what all of us were doing. One chapter of our lives had ended, but another was beginning.

A WEEK AFTER we moved, Stephen came by to take me out. It was Saturday afternoon and a mild winter day, the kind that smells like thawing earth, like spring. "Your apartment is great," he said as we strolled down the sidewalk, holding hands. "We can walk to just about everything from here."

I knew Stephen was sincere. Besides, I wasn't insecure about this kind of thing anymore. "It's really convenient," I agreed.

"Do you miss your old house?" he asked.

I thought about it. Did I miss it? The big yard, where my sisters and I had chased fireflies on summer nights; the garage, where Dad had repaired his fishing gear and tinkered on various home improvement projects; the swing on the porch, where I'd gotten my first real kiss (from Sully in eighth grade); the bow window in the living room, where we put the Christmas tree so its lights would shine out on the snow in the front yard; the old stove in the kitchen, where Mom baked our birthday cakes.

"I'm glad I'll turn seventeen in the new apartment," I told Stephen, answering his question indirectly. "Because I'm a different person than I was a year ago." I squeezed his hand. "Do you know what I mean?"

He squeezed my hand back. "Yeah, I know what you mean."

We continued to walk along Main Street, past Cecilia's, which was closed for the rest of the winter, and Appleby's Hardware and the Village Market and the Corner Ice Cream Shoppe. The year I turned sixteen had had so many ups and downs, but I knew now that I'd gained more than I'd lost. It wasn't always easy being an adult, and it wasn't always fun, but I was getting the hang of it. I was growing up. And the year I turned sixteen, I'd fallen in love. Twice. This time, with Stephen, I knew it was for real.

"How does chili at Patsy's sound?" my boyfriend asked me.

"Spicy," I replied. "Last one to the corner buys!"

We raced toward the setting sun together.

Daisy

For Josh
and Evan

One

"CATCH THIS ONE, Daze!" My older sister, Rose, pulled back her arm and tossed the Frisbee as far as she could. The bright orange disk sailed in my direction . . . sort of. Sprinting across the sand, I splashed into the water and jumped into the air, snagging the Frisbee before it could slice into the waves. Back on the beach Rose and her boyfriend, Stephen Mathias, clapped and whistled. "Nice catch!" Stephen yelled. I grinned at them and took a deep bow.

Just then my mother called out, "Food's ready." I lobbed the Frisbee to Stephen and jogged over to join my family. It was a warm August evening, and we were having a clambake at Kettle Cove, a little beach on the edge of town, to celebrate my sixteenth birthday. Balloons were tied to the picnic table, and lobsters, steamers, and ears of sweet corn had been roasting over a fire in a pit in the sand. Living in Maine is the best.

We started with paper plates piled high with steamers. I watched Rose take a ton of them. She has long blond hair and blue eyes, and she looked incredibly pretty in a lace-trimmed tank top and gauzy flowered skirt. No one looks glamorous eating steamers, though. "Yum," she said, dipping a clam in melted butter and then popping it into her mouth.

My mom, Maggie Walker, tossed the salad while her friend Hal Leverett, our neighbor, filled plastic glasses with lemonade. Mom has short blond hair that she pushes behind her ears—she's forty now, and she's still the most beautiful woman I know.

We were all gobbling steamers—Mom too. Stephen watched my family eat, his arms folded across his chest, his own plate empty. "I still haven't gotten over the way you natives put away clams," he admitted, his brown eyes twinkling. "By the *pound.* And I bet you'll devour a couple of lobsters apiece when you're finished."

Rose laughed. "It's a Maine thing. You wouldn't understand."

Stephen turned to my twelve-year-old sister, Laurel, whose gold-streaked brown hair was pulled back in a ponytail. She had a lobster bib on over her usual grass-stained overalls. "How do *you* do it, Toad?" Stephen asked, using the nickname Rose gave Laurel a few years ago. "Clams and lobsters are your friends."

Laurel considered this question thoughtfully as she wiped some butter off her lips with a paper napkin. She's the animal lover in the family, but when it comes to clambakes, she's as carnivorous as the rest of us. "It's a food chain thing," she explained to Stephen, "and we're at the top."

"Right," I said. "Eating shellfish is our destiny."

Mom passed out claw crackers for the lobsters. "They eat seafood in Boston, too," she pointed out to Stephen, whose family moved up to Maine when he started high school at nearby Seagate Academy.

"In restaurants, mostly," replied Stephen. "I never met a lobster in person before it ended up in a pot."

Rose rested her head on Stephen's shoulder, her blondness a contrast to his dark brown hair. "Aren't we uncivilized?" she said happily.

My youngest sister, ten-year-old Lily, was buttering a hot ear of corn. "This is the best, Mom," she said. "I'm going to eat until I burst."

"Everything's great," I agreed. "Thanks, Mom."

"A clambake cooks itself," she said, brushing aside our praise with typical modesty.

"Hey, we almost forgot to toast the birthday girl." Rose raised her glass. "I can't believe you're sixteen, Daisy. That means I'm *really* old!"

Rose graduated from South Regional High School last June—she's eighteen. "Right, you're ancient," I kidded.

"No, but seriously," said Rose. "It seems like just yesterday *I* was turning sixteen." A shadow crossed her face, dimming her hundred-watt smile for a second. Rose's sixteenth birthday hadn't been such a happy occasion. Our father had died in a boating accident just a few months before the birthday.

We were all silent for a moment, thinking the same thoughts, I guess. Then Rose's face brightened again. "Remember back when Daisy liked baseball better than boys?"

Everybody laughed. I rolled my eyes. Just a few days ago my first boyfriend, Jay McGuigan, and I had broken up. I'd gone down to Boston for a Red Sox doubleheader with Tommy Bradford, this guy in my class whose dad coaches at the high school, and it was absolutely *not* a date, but Jay got absurdly jealous and we had a huge fight and that was that. "Last week I liked boys better," I told Rose with a grin. "This week I'm back to baseball."

"Let's all tell one thing we like about Daisy," Lily piped up suddenly, waving a lobster claw for attention.

"Oh, please," I groaned.

"That's a nice idea," Mom said, smiling at Lily. "You want to start?"

Lily nodded, her short blond hair bouncing. By the way, I should note here that my youngest sister was wearing a satin, twenties-era flapper dress topped off with a feather boa. To a beach party. That's Lily in a nutshell. "What *I* like about Daisy," Lily informed the group, "is that she hardly ever gets mad at me even when I really bug her."

"Except that time you lost my autographed David Ortiz baseball mitt," I reminded her.

"I said *hardly* ever," Lily said.

"I like Daisy because she's always in a sunny mood," Rose contributed. "Of course, that's also what I *don't* like about her because whenever I'm trying to enjoy a good sulk, Daisy always talks me out of it. How about you, Mom?"

Mom shook her head, smiling. "How can I pick just one thing?"

"You have to," Lily pressed.

"Okay. I like the way Daisy picks up around the house without being asked."

"Mo-o-om!" Lily complained. "That's a boring thing to like."

"Well, it's true," Mom replied, winking at me.

"My turn," said Stephen. "I like how even when she was a kid, Daisy could beat me at hoops. She taught me humility."

"How about you, Laurel?" Rose prompted.

Laurel gazed at me with shining eyes. "I like how Daisy is good at everything she tries. How she gets all A's at school and is the star of the soccer team, and how she's so pretty but she isn't at all vain. I want to be just like her," she finished softly.

"Kiss up," muttered Lily.

Laurel scowled at Lily. I reached across the picnic table and punched Laurel lightly on the arm. "Thanks, Toad," I said.

Just then Mr. Leverett cleared his throat. "Well, I—," he began.

Before he could continue, I jumped to my feet. "Anyone for more lemonade?" I asked.

As I circled the table refilling glasses my mom threw me a questioning glance, but I ignored it. Maybe I'd been rude, cutting Hal off. But what's he doing here, anyway? I asked myself.

All at once my throat tightened with unexpected tears. I'd spent the picnic trying not to think about my father, but now

I couldn't help it. If Dad were still alive, Mom wouldn't be bringing Hal to family parties, I thought. I didn't care if he *was* just a friend—if any man was going to be at my birthday party, I wanted it to be Dad.

I'm not the gooey sentimental type, but I know when I'm about to burst into tears. "Be right back," I muttered, depositing the lemonade jug on the table with a thud. Turning away from the others, I strode off across the sand.

I hadn't gone ten yards when I heard a voice behind me. "Daze, wait for me."

I stopped. Rose jogged after me, her skirt fluttering and her expression worried. "Are you okay?" she asked. I shrugged wordlessly, my hands stuck deep in the pockets of my shorts. "Thinking about Dad?" Rose guessed.

I hate falling apart—I almost never cry—but my voice cracked with emotion. "He should be here today."

"I know," Rose agreed.

Side by side, we walked along the water's edge. For a few minutes neither of us spoke. I knew we were both remembering the day two and a half years ago when we learned that Dad's fishing boat had been lost in a sudden storm at sea.

"I think you miss Dad the most," Rose ventured at last. "I mean, I miss him, too, but you and he were the closest. You were his favorite."

"Dad didn't play favorites," I said, but in a way I knew what she said was true. Dad had loved us all, but I was the one who'd liked going out on the boat with him. Back on land, I'd help him mend his nets and then we'd play catch on the lawn for hours until Dad was satisfied that I could throw as far and straight as a big leaguer. I look like him, too—I have his eyes and his height and his smile.

And his upbeat attitude . . . usually. Now I struggled to get back in a positive frame of mind. "Dad would be proud of how well we're doing on our own," I said as Rose and I hit the end of the beach and turned around.

"We've gotten our lives together," Rose agreed. She laughed dryly. "Not that it wasn't an uphill fight. Remember how mad I was two summers ago when Mom made me get a job? And when we had to use food stamps for a while—that freaked me out."

But things had changed. These days Rose was acting in summer stock theater—musicals mostly, because she loves to sing. In the fall she would start classes at the local community college and continue working part-time at Cecilia's, a boutique in downtown Hawk Harbor. That was the first job Rose got, back when she was sixteen. Mom had started a catering business about a year after Dad died and she was doing well, but money was still a little tight, so we'd all found ways to pitch in this summer vacation. I baby-sat and did yard work. Laurel ran a dog wash with her friend Jack Harrison in Jack's backyard. "We're a lot more independent than we used to be," I concluded.

"You were always that way, though," Rose said. "You didn't whine, like me and Laurel and Lily." She laughed again. "It used to drive me crazy!"

I shrugged. "I just felt like I had to do whatever it took to hold our family together."

We were back at the picnic table. "Just in time, Daisy Claire Walker," Mom called. "We can't cut the cake without you!"

Mom had baked a triple-layer carrot cake piled high with cream cheese frosting—my favorite. As she lit the candles everyone began singing "Happy Birthday to You." Rose snapped her fingers and threw in a bluesy harmony—she has a great voice.

"Make a wish, Daisy," Lily shouted when the song was over.

I closed my eyes. What should I wish for? A million dollars? A new car? An unbeaten season this fall with the South Regional High varsity girls' soccer team?

I want us all to be safe, I wished silently. Just the way we are right now. No more changes.

I opened my eyes again, and as my sisters cheered I blew out all sixteen candles on my cake.

HAWK HARBOR IS a small town on the coast of southern Maine. I was born here and so were all my sisters—our parents grew up here, too. When I was younger, we lived in a big Victorian house on Lighthouse Road that had been in the family for generations, but after Dad died, we had to sell it. Now we rent a two-floor apartment in an old brick building on Main Street above Wissinger's Bakery.

A week after my birthday I spent the afternoon babysitting: Then I stopped at our old neighbors, the Schenkels, to mow their lawn and clip their hedges. By the end of the day I was pretty tired, so I pedaled home more slowly than usual. Going through the center of town, I waved to Mr. Appleby, who was out in front of his hardware store, putting sale tags on a display of plastic lawn furniture—his daughter, Cath, is one of Rose's best friends. Half a block farther along I hopped the bike onto the sidewalk so I could shout hello through the open door of Cecilia's to my sister, who was behind the cash register.

Reaching the bakery, I squeezed the hand brakes. Before pushing my bike into the storage room in the back of the building, though, I stood for a minute, looking toward the sea. Old fishing boats and sleek yachts motored in and out of the busy harbor, summing up my town: part blue-collar New England town, part upscale summer resort.

Mom was in the kitchen when I went in, slicing vegetables. "Something smells good," I said as I rummaged in the fridge for a snack.

Mom nodded in the direction of the industrial-size oven she'd installed when she quit her old job to cater full-time. "Appetizers for the Nickersons' anniversary party tomorrow night."

I pulled up a stool and another cutting board so I could help her chop. As I took a seat Mom looked at my necklace. "That looks nice," she said.

I put my hand to my throat. I was wearing my sixteenth-birthday present, a gold chain and an antique charm from my great-grandmother's bracelet. The charm was shaped like a seashell—Rose got one that's a rosebud for her sixteenth birthday. "A little fancy with a T-shirt and cutoffs, huh?"

She smiled. "I think it's the first jewelry I've ever seen you wear."

"I like it."

"So, how are Vera and Gil?"

I filled her in on the neighborhood gossip I'd heard from Mrs. Schenkel and told Mom that the weeds were really high in front of our old house. "Whoever bought it isn't living there."

"Probably someone planning to fix it up for a summer house," Mom speculated.

"An inn," a voice called from the living room. "The owners want to open an inn."

Hal's here again, I thought. For some reason my mood turned instantly grouchy. Lately he'd become a fixture at our dinner table. Couldn't he ever cook for himself?

"An inn," Mom mused. "Well, it's a big enough house, I suppose. And they could renovate the barn. . . ."

"So, Mom," I said, changing the subject, "I started looking for a part-time job today."

She stopped slicing mushrooms. "What?"

"Now that I'm sixteen, I want to make more money than I can from baby-sitting," I explained. "That way I could help with some of our expenses."

Mom shook her head. "You don't need to do that. And with school starting soon, you won't have time."

"But Rose got a job when she turned sixteen."

"Our situation was different then. You shouldn't be worrying about money, Daisy."

"I'm not worried. I just want to start saving for college, like Rose."

Mom resumed slicing, the knife blade knocking rhythmically on the wooden cutting board. "Aren't you already stretched too thin, honey? With soccer practice every day and games on weekends. You said you were thinking about running for student council, too. I'd hate to see your grades drop. You're headed for class valedictorian when you graduate."

"Just a few hours a week, Mom," I said. "I promise I'll quit if it gets to be too much."

Hal chose that moment to come into the kitchen. He had a legal pad under his arm and a pencil tucked behind his ear. He's tall and wears glasses—he's an accountant, in his late forties, who got divorced a few years ago, right before we moved in next door to him. "Couldn't help overhearing," he began in a friendly manner. "You know, my office could use some phone and filing help. It might be just what you're looking for, Daisy. If you want to come in and fill out an application, I could put in a good—"

"Thanks, anyway, but that's not really the kind of job I had in mind." I hopped down from the stool, avoiding my mom's gaze. "I'll be in my room," I said over my shoulder as I left the kitchen. "Call me if you need me, okay?"

As I went upstairs I wasn't sure why I'd responded the way I had to Hal's offer. Answering phones would be fine, and Hal is a nice enough guy. He's always been a good neighbor—he really comes through for us whenever there's a clogged drain or a disgusting bug to kill. My sisters and I are always psyched when his cute college-age sons, Kevin and Connor, visit;

they're really nice. It just wasn't his business, I decided. I was talking to Mom, not him.

I wouldn't have held a grudge about it, but Hal just had to butt into every single conversation at dinner, too. I was still gritting my teeth at nine o'clock when Rose got home from her date with Stephen.

She and I share a bedroom, as do Lily and Laurel. Our room has tall, old-fashioned windows that make it seem bigger than it is. With two of everything in it—twin beds, dressers, night tables, and desks—it's pretty cramped. We've each given it our own sense of style, though. Rose has put up posters of her favorite singers and actors, and she's into incense and tapestries and flowering plants. My shelves are crowded with sports trophies, my baseball card collection, and odds and ends I saved when we moved out of our old house: some of Dad's fishing tackle, a plaque the chamber of commerce gave him one year, his toolbox.

I was sitting on my bed reading *Sports Illustrated* when Rose flopped down on her bed with a sigh. "I'm going to wither and die when Stephen leaves for Harvard," she moaned, flinging a hand to her forehead.

Rose can be pretty theatrical. "Are you doing Juliet?" I guessed. "Or Ophelia?"

"Seriously, Daze." She sat up. "It stinks."

Rose is always open with her feelings, and she'd been fretting for weeks over her upcoming separation from Stephen. He'd graduated from Seagate a year earlier, but since then he'd been in Hawk Harbor, working as a volunteer for county social services. He wants to be a lawyer someday, the kind who represents poor people for free. "He'll come home for vacations," I said.

"But it won't be the same," Rose despaired. "I mean, we've been like *this*"—she held up her hand with the index and middle fingers crossed—"for two whole *years.*" Rose quickly changed the subject. "So, Hal was over for dinner again, huh?"

"Yeah." I frowned. "What's *with* that, anyway? He's, like, *omnipresent* these days. I mean, our *other* neighbors don't come over every night."

"I sense romance blossoming," Rose said knowingly.

I blinked. "Mom? A romance with *Hal?* Are you kidding?"

"Why not?" she asked. "He and Mom have gotten to be pretty tight these past couple of years. Going out to lunch, lending each other books, that sort of thing."

"Yeah, but—"

"He has a great sense of humor for an accountant, don't you think? Nobody makes Mom laugh that hard. I think they make a cute couple."

"A *couple?*" I stared at my sister in disbelief. "You mean like . . ."

"Like who knows?" said Rose. "Maybe Mom's ready for a boyfriend. Maybe she'll even get married again someday."

I shook my head emphatically. "Mom does *not* need a boyfriend."

"Why not?"

"It's only been two and a half years since—"

"*Only* two and a half years?" Rose broke in. "What, you don't think that's long enough to grieve? Mom should join a convent or something? She deserves to have a life of her own that's not just work and kids."

I fell back on, "Yeah, but . . ."

"But *what?*" Rose said. "Don't you want Mom to be happy?"

Of course I wanted my mother to be happy—that wasn't the point. Turning my head away from Rose, I looked at the framed picture on my night table. My father smiled up at me from under the bill of a Boston Red Sox cap, his face tanned from spending his days on the water, his light blue eyes crinkled against the sun. I remembered that day as if it were yesterday. We'd all gone down to Boston, and he'd taken me to the game while Mom, Rose, Lily, and Laurel hit the aquarium and museum. Just him and me. We'd eaten three Fenway franks apiece. The Red Sox won in extra innings.

In the picture Dad looked so alive, and that was how I wanted to remember him. Am I the only person who's still loyal to you, Dad? I wondered. "But nothing," I said quietly.

Two

"COME ON, GIRLS. *Push* it!" Coach Wheeler roared.

I sprinted across the playing field, arms and legs pumping, sucking air into my lungs as deeply as I could. Out of the corner of my eye I could see Jamila Wade and Kristin McIntyre also running their hearts out. They were my teammates and my best friends, but I didn't intend to let them catch me. My muscles burned—I was going my fastest—but I made myself go faster still.

I didn't slow down until I reached the end of the field. One by one the rest of the soccer team crossed the line behind me and collapsed, panting. Hands on my hips, I walked back toward Larry Wheeler. He coaches girls' soccer *and* softball—two of my three sports—so he and I are pretty tight. He's stocky, with sun-bleached hair and light blue eyes—he reminds me a little of my dad, especially the "push it" part. It was Dad who taught me to give a hundred and ten percent to everything I do.

Which doesn't mean I don't whine sometimes. Coach Wheeler can be a slave driver. "Tell me that's the last wind sprint of the day," I begged, pushing a sweaty lock of hair off my forehead.

"That's it, Daiserooni." He can be goofy, too, which also reminds me of Dad. "Hey, when do you start the job?"

"Tonight," I told him.

"Good luck," he said, patting me on the shoulder. Then he shouted so everyone could hear, "Nice practice. See you tomorrow morning."

Jamila and Kristin fell into step beside me, and we headed to the South Regional High gym. When we walk in a row, Coach Wheeler says we look like a flag because we all have long hair and it's like stripes: Jamila's black braids, my bright blond ponytail, and Kristin's deep red hair. The flag was drooping a little today, though.

"Wheeler's more of a sadist than ever," Jamila observed, wiping her face on the sleeve of her T shirt. "Double session preseason practices—does he think we're bionic or something?"

"I didn't work out all summer," Kristin admitted, rubbing her quads. "Man, I'm hurting."

I was hurting, too, but in a good way. "I like double sessions," I confessed.

Jamila shook her head. "Are you crazy?"

"She's crazy," Kristin confirmed, her green eyes twinkling. "But we knew that."

I grinned. "Come on. Doesn't it feel good afterward?"

"Maybe a *week* afterward," said Jamila, holding open the door to the gym.

"You forget Daisy thrives on pain," Kristin kidded.

"And she doesn't need sleep like the rest of us mortals," Jamila added.

Inside the girls' locker room we kicked off our cleats and stripped out of our grubby shorts and T-shirts, then hit the showers. "I'm not a masochist—I just like to win," I reminded my friends as hot water ran down my body.

"It's that simple, huh?" asked Kristin, her voice echoing in the shower stalls.

"Yep," I replied.

I thought about the conversation later, though, as I strolled into the lobby of the community hospital to start my new part-time job as a receptionist. It had been Coach Wheeler's idea—his wife, Nan, is an administrator there. I'd be working three nights a week plus Sundays, and what with school, soccer, homework, and chores at home, every minute of every day would be filled. And that's the way I like it, I realized. I don't thrive on pain, but I *do* like to be challenged. I like being tired at the end of the day, bone tired, so tired I drop right off to sleep. Too tired to think. Too tired to dream.

I T'S KIND OF cool to be a junior," I said to some of my friends on the first day of school in September. Jamila, Kristin, and I were heading to third-period gym class. "You know, upperclassmen."

"Upperclass*women,*" Jamila corrected.

"Hey, look." Kristin pointed. "They put the spring team pictures up."

We stopped to look at a row of framed photographs on the wall outside the gym. There I was as a sophomore, with the varsity girls' softball squad. "You're all over this wall, Walker," Jamila said to me.

I was—I play three sports, and I'd been on varsity even as a freshman. "Yeah, but so are you." Jamila does three sports, too, although she'll probably still be JV in basketball this year.

"Daisy. I was hoping I'd run into you."

I turned around. "Hi, Mel."

Melissa Hannaway was a senior. She played softball with me, and she was president of her class last year. "I wanted to talk to you about student council elections," she said. "You're running, right?"

"I haven't made up my mind yet," I told her. "I've got so much other stuff going on, you know?"

"You should run, Daze," Kristin put in. "You'd be a great class rep."

"I'm running," Mel said. "It would be a blast if you were on the council, too."

"I'll think about it some more," I promised.

"Just let me know so I can get your name on the ballot," Mel said as she headed off.

"You'd be a shoo-in," Jamila said as we changed for gym class in the locker room.

"Maybe," I said. "It *would* be fun. How many more things can I pack into my schedule, though?"

"You can handle it," Kristin said.

"You're Supergirl," Jamila agreed.

"Super*woman,*" I corrected her.

We all laughed. I *am* kind of a classic overachiever. But I couldn't help wondering whether student council might be too much for me to handle. Is there such a thing as "too much"? I thought.

T HAT'S NOT THE way you're supposed to do it, Laurel," Lily declared. "Daisy, she's doing it wrong!"

The following Saturday my sisters and I were sitting around the kitchen table, gluing tiny pinecones and fall leaves to paper that looked like tree bark. Mom was catering a dinner party that night, and she'd given us the job of making place cards.

I inspected Laurel's handiwork. "Looks all right to me," I told Lily.

Lily pushed out her lower lip. "No, it doesn't. She's just *cramming* the leaves on instead of *arranging* them artistically."

"And I suppose you're Picasso," Laurel retorted.

They launched into one of their trademark spats. Rose looked at me. I knew she wanted me to stop them, but for once I didn't have the energy to play umpire. I'd stayed up late doing homework the night before and had gone for a five-mile run that morning.

The telephone rang. Rose practically hurdled over the table to answer it on the second ring. "Hello?" she said. "Oh, Mita, hi! How are you?"

Rose and her friend Sumita Ghosh, who had left last week for Colby College, gabbed for about fifteen minutes. While they were talking, Rose was animated, but as soon as she hung up, her expression grew gloomy. "College sounds like so much fun," she said, dropping back into her chair with a sigh. "Parties practically every night, tailgates at the football game, handsome upperclassmen . . ."

"You're going to college, too," Laurel said.

"*Community* college." Rose sniffed. "I'm still living at *home.*"

"How does Stephen like Harvard, anyway?" I asked.

Rose's gloom deepened. "He loves it," she answered, slumping down with her arms folded on the table. "The campus is beautiful, his roommates are cool, his classes are great, yada yada yada."

"Isn't that good?" I wondered.

"No. He isn't homesick at all! He's supposed to be *pining.*"

"I'm sure he misses you," I said.

"Maybe." Rose dabbed some glue onto a pinecone and stuck it haphazardly to a place card. "But face it. He was ready to get out into the real world. While I'll probably be stuck here for the rest of my life."

"At least Rox is still around," I pointed out.

Roxanne Beale, one of Rose's closest friends, was going to the community college, too. "Yeah," conceded Rose with a sigh. "Misery loves company."

"I'm done," announced Lily, pushing back her chair. "Rose, can I borrow your curling iron?"

"Sure—but what for?" Rose asked.

"To curl my hair," Lily said.

"I figured that part out. But why?"

"Because Lindsey, Talia, Kendall, and Kimberly curl *their* hair," interjected Laurel in a disdainful tone.

"Shut up, ugly" was Lily's parting shot to Laurel.

"Who are Lindsey, Talia, Kendall, and Kimberly?" I asked Laurel after Lily had flounced from the room.

"Lily's new friends from Mr. Cabot's sixth-grade class," Laurel answered. "They formed this instant clique. I see them at recess—they're like one creature with five heads."

Rose appeared as mystified as I was. "Lily's in a clique?" she said. "Isn't that one of those oxy-what-do-you-call-its?"

"Oxymorons," I supplied.

"Yeah, right," said Rose. "I mean, Lily. She's always been so . . . *different.*"

"Not anymore," said Laurel. "You should see them. They dress alike, talk alike, eat the same thing for lunch, carry the same kind of notebook, use the same shampoo."

"That's right," I said. "She wasn't wearing one of her wacky costumes just now. She was in jeans and a white T-shirt."

"New jeans," said Laurel. "Mom had to buy them for her because she wouldn't wear the old ones. They weren't the right brand."

"Sixth grade," Rose said thoughtfully. "Yeah, you know, I think that's when it starts."

"What?" I asked.

"Peer pressure."

"Speaking of which . . . ," Laurel began.

She didn't finish the sentence. "Yeah?" Rose said after a minute had passed.

"Well, do you guys remember things . . . *changing* when you got into eighth grade?"

"In what way?" Rose asked.

"Like socially. Boys."

Rose blew out a sigh of relief. "Oh, *that.*"

"All of a sudden everyone's pairing up," Laurel explained. "You're not cool if you don't have a boyfriend. So yesterday in the bus line after school, Jack asked me to go out with him!"

"What did you say?" Rose asked.

"'No way,' of course." Laurel shuddered. "I mean, he's my *friend.* I don't want to be like *that* with him."

"Are you sure? Jack's pretty cute," said Rose, wiggling her eyebrows.

Laurel's face flushed hot pink. "Beyond sure. We've always been just friends. He shouldn't have pulled that on me. It made me so mad!"

I dimly remembered having the same reaction a long, long time ago when my old neighbor Kyle Cooper flirted with me. I could have commiserated with Laurel, but once again I didn't have the energy.

"Was Jack mad at you for turning him down?" Rose wanted to know.

"Maybe," said Laurel. She chewed her lip, looking worried. "Probably. Oh, I don't care!"

"Men," said Rose, clearly thinking about Stephen selfishly having fun at his new college. "Can't live with 'em, can't live without 'em. Don't you agree, Daze?"

I wasn't so sure about the "can't live without 'em" part. I hadn't missed having a boyfriend since Jay and I broke up. But who had the energy to explain? "You bet," I said.

T HE NEXT TUESDAY night I got home from the hospital at ten. Lily and Laurel's room was dark; Rose was in our room, whispering on the phone to Stephen. To give her some privacy, I retreated to the kitchen for a snack. I was buttering a piece of toast when the front door to the apartment rattled open. "Is that you, Mom?" I called out.

Mom came into the kitchen. She was wearing a dress and heels. "Hi, Daisy," she said. "You're up late."

"I thought you were in bed," I told her. "Did you have a catering job tonight?"

Mom slipped off her jacket and slung it over the back of a chair. "No," she replied as she put the kettle on the stove and turned on the burner. "I went to a movie. With Hal," she added, blushing ever so slightly.

"A movie?" I repeated.

"A dumb action film," she elaborated. "There's not much choice in Kent."

Mom and Mr. Leverett had driven all the way to Kent to see a movie. This was a switch from their casual lunches and the meals he ate with us. "Was it a *date?*" I asked, choking on the word.

Mom took a tea bag from the stainless steel canister next to the stove and dropped it in a mug. "That makes it sound like we're in high school," she said, laughing a little. "But I suppose it was."

Her cheeks grew even pinker, and she smiled in a funny way, a secretive, inward smile that somehow didn't include me. "Is that okay?" she asked, pouring hot water into her mug.

I stared down at the now cold toast. "Sure," I said, not meeting her eyes. "Uh, I'm going to hit the sack—my first soccer game's tomorrow. Good night."

"Sweet dreams, hon."

I washed up, undressed, and climbed quietly into bed so I wouldn't wake Rose, who'd fallen asleep with a picture of Stephen beside her on the pillow. I was unbelievably tired and needed a good night's rest to be in top form for my game, but for some reason I couldn't doze off. My eyes stayed open, fixed on the harvest moon shining through a gap in the curtains. It's just nerves, I decided. I was the starting varsity forward this year, and I really wanted to win our first game. That's all it is, I told myself. Nerves.

WHEN I'M ON the athletic field, I don't think about anything but the game. My eyes are everywhere at once: on the ball, on my teammates in their blue-and-gray uniforms, on my opponents, on the goal. Soccer isn't like football or baseball—it's nonstop action, and you can't afford to be distracted even for a second or you'll lose the ball, or miss a chance to pass or tackle or shoot on goal. That's why I'm good—because I can focus one hundred percent. I inherited that from Dad.

At the end of the third quarter we were tied 3–3 with the Kent High Hurricanes. Coach Wheeler called us over to the sideline for a pep talk, and as he outlined a strategy for getting around the Hurricane defense my gaze wandered to the bleachers. Mom and Lily were sitting in the front row and had been doing more than their share of shouting. Right next to Mom, also wearing a Go, Sharks! button, was . . . Mr. Leverett.

Weird—he must've taken time off from work for this, I thought. A memory came to me—uninvited and painfully fresh despite the passage of time. Dad had been at every single one of my games back in junior high.

"And pass back to Daisy," Coach Wheeler was saying, "who will have dodged number fourteen to position herself in front of the goal. Got that, Wade? Walker?"

I felt Jamila's elbow in my ribs. I'd tuned Coach Wheeler out for the first time in my life. "Sorry," I said. "Could you repeat that?"

He flashed me a funny look, then ran over the play again. I nodded briskly and the team huddled, our arms around one another and our heads close together. "Go, fight, win!" we shouted. Clapping in unison, we jogged back out on the field.

We played aggressively right off the bat, and within thirty

seconds I was dribbling the ball down the field and then slicing a pass to Kristin, my arms extended for balance. A few seconds later the ball came back to me, courtesy of Jamila, and there was no one between me and the Hurricane goalie. I nailed the net, top left-hand corner.

My teammates dashed over to congratulate me, and the home bleachers erupted in cheers. I hugged Jamila, grinning. That's all there is to it, I thought. *Go, fight, win.* If I kept that in mind and nothing else, I'd be fine.

Three

"D IDN'T WE HAVE pot roast a couple of days ago?" Rose asked as we set the table a week later.

She was moving clockwise, putting a napkin in front of each chair. I walked counterclockwise, laying out the silverware. "Hal's coming over for dinner, and he loves Mom's pot roast," I told Rose.

Rose smiled knowingly. "Love is in the air," she sang, and whistled the tune to some awful seventies song.

I had to admit, she seemed to be right. Hal had dropped in while Mom was making the gravy. He'd poured two glasses of red wine and was standing close to her as she cooked. I had to go in the kitchen once or twice to get the salt and pepper shakers and salad bowls, and I couldn't help noticing how giggly they were with each other. What did Mom say the other night about dates sounding like high school? I thought. Who's acting like she's in high school now?

At least we got to have pot roast twice in one week. I sighed. Mom's pot roast is awesome.

As soon as everyone was seated Rose reached for the gravy boat. "Where's Lily?" she asked.

"She went to Lindsey's after school," Mom replied. "Mrs. Underwood offered to drive her home. They were going out for pizza."

"Daisy," said Hal conversationally. "How was the game against Marshfield today?"

"We won," I answered.

"Your record's two and oh?"

Usually, I'm happy for a chance to talk about sports, but I didn't feel like it right then. I speared a carrot with my fork. "Yep."

Hal lifted his wineglass. "Well, cheers."

"Yes, cheers." Mom raised her glass, too.

I looked at Mom, not at Hal. "Thanks."

"Hal, I have a question for you," Rose said. "I'm taking an economics class, and I was wondering if you could go over one chapter with me. I absolutely do *not* understand this supply-side stuff."

Hal launched into an economics lecture, which Rose and Mom both listened to as if it were Nobel Prize material. I ate as fast as I could, figuring that the sooner I was excused from the table, the better. As I took one last bite Lily waltzed into the room. "Hi, I'm home," she sang, scooting into a chair. "Any dessert left?"

Mom was gaping. "Lily, what is that on your face?"

We all turned to look at Lily, who blinked innocently at Mom with jet black eyelashes that were about three inches long. Lily's cheeks were unnaturally pink, and I thought I detected lip gloss and eye shadow, too. "Nothing?" Lily answered, but without much conviction.

"March right to the bathroom and wash that off," Mom ordered.

"But Lindsey and Talia and Kendall and Kimberly's moms let them—," Lily began to protest.

"In our house no one under the age of fourteen wears makeup," Mom declared firmly. "To the bathroom. *Now.*"

Lily slid off her chair, her starlet's eyes sullen. As she stomped from the kitchen we could hear her muttering to herself, "I guess you want me to be a loser. . . ."

Mom gave Hal a helpless look. Hal smiled. "I'm glad I had boys," he said.

Mom was scraping plates and I was rinsing them and putting them in the dishwasher when Lily reappeared, her face scrubbed pink and her eyelashes blond once more. "I hope you're satisfied, Mom," she grumbled.

"I'll be satisfied when you promise you won't put on makeup until you're fourteen," Mom replied.

"I promise," Lily said, still pouting.

Mom hugged her.

"You don't need makeup, Lily," Hal said gallantly,

carrying a platter over to the counter. "You're pretty as a peach without it."

For a moment Lily looked somewhat mollified. Then her expressive mouth turned upside down again. "Mom, will you help me with my math homework? Mr. Cabot gave us ten absolutely impossible word problems."

"I'll help you," Hal offered. "I'm a whiz at word problems."

I finished scrubbing the roast pan and dried my hands on a dish towel. "I'll be home from the hospital around ten, Mom," I said.

"Drive carefully," she advised, as she'd done every time I'd taken the car since I'd gotten my driver's license two weeks before.

I went upstairs to my room to grab my book bag. On my way out I passed by the living room. There was classical music on the stereo, and Hal and Lily were sitting on the sofa. Hal leaned toward the coffee table and scribbled something on a piece of paper. "You need to turn the word problem into an equation," he told Lily. "Cartoons help."

Lily giggled at whatever Hal was drawing. Mom looked up from the cookbook she was reading to smile at them. Laurel was feeding her goldfish, whose bowl sits on top of an end table—she has hamsters, too, and a turtle. Rose was doing her economics homework. It was a cozy domestic scene . . . and I couldn't wait to get away from it.

NOT THAT I couldn't have used a night off from my job. I was yawning when I checked in with my boss, Jody, the head nurse in the pediatric wing. "Need a cup of coffee?" she offered, looking up from her clipboard as I dumped my book bag on the reception desk.

I shook my head. Mom and Rose both love coffee, but I don't drink much—caffeine's not good for athletes. "Thanks, anyway," I told Jody.

The pediatric wing is lively. Sick kids and their families are always going in and out, the doctors and nurses are so cheerful it hurts, and the phone rings constantly. Usually I don't mind that, but tonight I was trying to study my trigonometry in between calls. I'd gotten a B-minus on Ms. Stern's first quiz, not a good performance by my usual straight-A standards. Plus the material wasn't even that hard. I just didn't have enough time to study.

The phone buzzed. Pushing aside my math book, I punched line two, lifting the receiver. "Hello? Room three-ten? I'll connect you." It rang again before I'd hung up. I punched line one. "Good evening, Community Hospital Pediatrics. No, Doctor Dimarco isn't on call this evening. Can I transfer you to the head nurse?"

It went on like that for an hour or so. I gave up on math and opened my English assignment. That's when I heard someone ask, "What are you reading?"

I looked up from my book to see a thin teenage boy in sweats smiling down at me. He had on a baseball cap, but it didn't really hide the fact that he was bald.

"F. Scott Fitzgerald," I told him, smiling back. *The Great Gatsby.* Have you read it?"

"Sure. Since I got sick, I've read just about every book that's ever been written. There's nothing else to do sometimes. I'm Ben," he added, sticking out his hand. "Ben Compton."

"Daisy Walker," I replied as we shook.

Ben pulled up a chair, straddling it backward. "You just started working here, right?"

"Right."

"I noticed because I'm here a lot," he said. "Chemotherapy."

"Oh. So you have . . ."

"Yep, the *C* word." Ben grinned. "Cancer—a brain tumor."

I raised my eyebrows. "This is funny?"

"Sure." He laughed at my shocked expression. "A cosmic joke. You've got to see it that way, or else it's too depressing."

"Well, you look . . ."

"Hairless?"

Now I laughed. "I was just going to say you look good. For someone who's sick," I added.

We smiled at each other. "Okay, so, Daisy, do you go to South Regional?"

"I'm a junior."

"I go to Kent."

"A junior?"

"Sophomore. But thanks."

"It must be tough," I said, "having to miss so much school. Are you keeping up with the work?"

"I'm managing," Ben replied. "The worst part is not being able to do sports."

"What do you play?"

"Soccer and lacrosse."

"Me too," I said. "Soccer, I mean."

"I can't wait to play again. I will, one of these days."

I looked at him, wondering. A brain tumor . . . that was serious. "Yeah?"

"Yeah." He lifted up one skinny arm. "See this?" A frown darkened his face momentarily. "I can't even do one push-up." His expression brightened again. "But in a couple of months I'll be working out again. I'll be arm wrestling every-one on this ward, so watch out."

The phone lit up.

"Excuse me," I said.

"That's okay—I'd better get back to my room, anyway. Don't want them to give my bed away," he joked.

"See you around, Ben."

"You will," he said.

As I picked up the phone I followed Ben with my eyes. From the back he looked like a beanpole, and he shuffled his feet like an old man. He's optimistic if he thinks he'll be working out anytime soon, I thought, an unexpected ache in my heart. But I hope he makes it. I really hope he makes it.

When I'd finished my *Great Gatsby* chapters, I went back to trig, but I didn't make much progress. I would read a line or two, scrawl a couple of figures in my notebook, and then I'd field three calls in a row. Around nine-thirty, though, things quieted down. The pediatric patients were tucked into bed, their relatives had gone home, and the staff settled into night mode:

fewer people running around, voices lowered, lights dimmed.

I transferred a call to the nurses' station and then looked back down at my trig book. I flipped back to the previous page, rubbing my eyes. I don't even remember reading this stuff, I thought dismally. If Ms. Stern gave one of her pop quizzes the next day, I was sunk.

I stared at the book, pencil in hand, ready to copy out a problem. Blinking, I tried to focus on the tiny print. A minute or two later I woke up with a start because the phone buzzed right next to my ear. I'd dozed off, my head dropping onto the open book. "Community Hospital Pediatrics," I mumbled into the receiver. "How may I direct your call?"

After I hung up the phone, I glanced hopefully at the clock on the wall, but its hands were moving with discouraging slowness. Twenty minutes to go, and I wasn't sure I could keep my eyes open that long. Maybe Mom was right, I thought. Maybe I don't really need this job. If I'm already feeling stressed out after just two weeks . . .

No way am I quitting, though, I decided a split second later. The money would really help. Besides, my life had always been a juggling act—I just had one more ball to keep in the air now. I could do it.

I sat up straighter in my chair, stretching my arms over my head. Then I hopped to my feet and did a couple of jumping jacks. I waved to Jody at the nurses' station. "I'll take that cup of coffee after all," I called.

"Black or with cream and sugar?" she asked.

"Black," I replied.

* * *

B Y THE TIME I got home, the caffeine had really kicked in and I was feeling a little jittery. I had a sinking feeling the coffee strategy was going to backfire and that I'd have trouble falling asleep. Well, if that were the case, I could put my insomnia to good use and finish my trig assignment, maybe even get a jump on my homework. I was only a third of the way through *The Great Gatsby*, with my first English paper due in less than a week.

"Good, Daisy, you're home," Mom said as soon as I stepped through the door.

"What's up?" I asked, hanging my denim jacket on the coatrack in the front hall.

"Come into the kitchen—I want to show you something," she replied.

I followed her into the kitchen. Mom waved at the table. My eyes widened. "A computer," I exclaimed. "Wow! Where'd that come from?"

"It was Hal's. He bought a new laptop and says he never uses this one anymore. It's for all of us," Mom explained. "I'm going to put my business records on it, and you girls can use it for homework. It has a wireless airport, too, so we can hook up to the Internet. Isn't that great?"

I nodded wordlessly.

"So, Hal gave me this manual," Mom said, lifting a glossy-covered notebook, "but I'm having a hard time understanding it. You took that computer course in school last year. Do you think you could help me figure out—"

"It's Hal's computer and Hal's manual," I snapped. "Why don't you ask *him* to help you?"

Mom stared at me in surprise. I was instantly overcome with shame. I never talked back to her, never used a snotty tone like that, and I hated myself for doing it. What is it about Hal that's driving me crazy? I wondered. The computer was a generous gift. "Mom, I'm sorry," I said. "I'm just tired. And I had a cup of coffee at work and I just feel . . . tired," I said again. "I'm sorry."

"It's okay." Her eyebrows pulled together in a frown. "I'm worried about you, Daisy. You need to get more sleep."

"I'm going to bed right now," I told her, crossing the room to give her a quick hug. "Unless you want to look over the computer manual together."

"No, go to bed," she insisted, giving me a gentle push toward the door. "We can work on it tomorrow."

"Right," I said. "There'll be time tomorrow."

THERE WASN'T TIME tomorrow, or the next day, or the next. Days used to be so long, I thought one afternoon as I dressed for soccer practice. Was it something about turning sixteen? All of a sudden there weren't enough hours in the day for all the things I needed to do. I felt like I was constantly rushing from one activity to the next, shortchanging all of them. "My paper on *The Great Gatsby* stunk," I told Kristin and Jamila as we walked out to the field.

"It had to have been better than mine," said Kristin, her arms lifted to weave her long red hair into a braid. She's in Mrs. Rogowski's section. "I got a B."

"I got a C," I said, grimacing.

"*You* got a C? You always ace your English papers," Jamila said.

"Not this one. It was supposed to be five pages long, right? I only turned in three and a half. And almost half of that was my topic sentence, which just rambled on and on because I had no idea what I was trying to say. Mr. Kamin nailed me on it."

"At least he lets you do rewrites," Kristin said. "Mrs. Rogowski doesn't." She tipped her face to the sky. "Hey, isn't it a great day for soccer practice?"

It was the first day of October. The sky was a soft blue, and a warm Indian summer breeze stirred the leaves on the trees bordering the field, leaves just beginning to turn yellow and orange.

"Yeah, the weather's nice, but Wheeler's going to work our butts off," said Jamila. "Eastport's the toughest game of the season."

We had an away game the next day at a high school half an hour up the coast. Eastport always had a strong team, and the captain of their team, the Chiefs, was a senior named Lisa Levison, who had been an All New England forward for two years in a row. "We can beat them, though," Kristin declared with confidence. "They have Lisa Levison, but we have Daisy Walker."

"Our not so secret weapon," Jamila agreed, flashing me a smile.

Usually I like a little pressure—the higher people's expectations, the better I perform. But right then it was as if I had two left feet. Jamila beat me in the wind sprints, and I missed four out of five shots on goal during the scoring drill. Every other ball I touched ended up out-of-bounds. After forty-five minutes we took a water break and Coach Wheeler took me aside. "Hey, Daisy, what's up?"

"I'm thirsty," I said.

He handed me a bottle, and I squirted some sports drink into my mouth. "That's all?" he asked.

"A little tired, too," I admitted, although exhausted would have been a more accurate term. "I stayed up late studying."

"Don't do that tonight," he counseled, "or Levison will be all over you tomorrow."

"Don't worry," I replied. "I'll be hot. You can count on me."

"I know I can," he said, giving me a swat on the back.

"I'll outscore Levison two to one," I vowed.

"That's the spirit."

We rejoined the rest of the team, and practice resumed. For some reason I felt sort of let down. It had been too easy to reassure Coach Wheeler. Why hadn't he pressed me a little harder? But even if he had, could I have told him what was really bothering me since I don't know myself? I wondered.

No, I'd given him the right answer. My coach and team could depend on me. I never let them down. I never let anyone down.

O KAY, THE CHIEFS are on top but only by one goal," Coach Wheeler said the following day as our team huddled during halftime. "I know the weather isn't helping, but we can turn things around if you put your hearts into it. Play the way you played against Kent and Marshfield. Uh, Walker."

He turned to me, his expression solemn. Rain dripped from the bill of his baseball cap. I was leaning against Jamila, both of us shivering under one raincoat. Overnight, Indian summer had fled, and the drizzle was icy but not bad enough to call the game.

"Yes?" I answered.

"I'm putting Maria in."

Maria Galdamez is the second-string forward, my backup. Maria blinked at me in surprise; I blinked at Coach Wheeler. "You're benching me?" I asked in disbelief.

"Resting you," he corrected. "I think you need it."

My face flooded with color. I hadn't had the best first half, it was true. The night before, I'd worked at the hospital until ten, then stayed up late rewriting my *Great Gatsby* paper. "Give me five minutes," I begged Coach Wheeler. "If I don't score, you can take me out."

"This isn't just about goals, Daisy." He shook his head. "It's about knowing when one of my players needs a break."

"I'm fine," I insisted. "I just needed to warm up. Please, Coach. Five minutes."

He frowned, looking me up and down. "Well . . . ," he said finally. "Okay. You've got five minutes to show me that all you need to do is warm up, but that's it."

The referee blew her whistle. It was time to start the third quarter. As I trotted back onto the field I heard Coach Wheeler say to Maria, "Stretch out a little—do a few sprints. I want you to be ready, okay?"

I gritted my teeth. I had nothing against Maria. She was a nice kid, and with more experience she'd be a good player. She can have my position, I thought, *after* I graduate.

In the center of the field I stood face-to-face with Lisa Levison. Neither of us smiled. The ball was set down on the wet grass, and our bodies tensed with readiness. Then the whistle blew.

What had Coach Wheeler said? We could win if we put our hearts into it? I put my heart into it, and my bones and muscles and guts. I wasn't playing smart—I was too tired for that. I was playing mad.

The ball bounced wildly around the field. First Eastport had possession, then we did, then Eastport again. Then Jamila dove into the action, tackled the ball away from the Chiefs' left wing, and kicked it sharply in my direction. This was my chance.

I sprinted toward the goal, pushing the ball just ahead of me as I ran. I zigzagged past the Eastport defense, dodging and pivoting, the ball glued to my cleats. I wasn't going to lose it, not on my life. I heard Kristin shout to me, "I'm open!" It was a good chance to pass, but I didn't take it. I kept the ball even though there were two Eastport defensive players between me and the goal. I feinted left, then sprinted to the right and went for the shot.

The angle was crazy. As I kicked the ball I had to twist my body to face the goal, and my left foot skidded on the wet grass. The ball flew wide, and I fell hard to the ground.

The pain in my left knee was so intense that for a few seconds I had to lie with my eyes closed. Then Coach Wheeler's voice penetrated the buzzing in my ears. "Take it easy," he said as I struggled to sit up. "What is it, your knee?"

I nodded, biting my lip.

"Yeah, look at that," he said. "It's as big as a cantaloupe already." He turned to yell over his shoulder to the Eastport coach. "Hey, let's get a trainer out here!"

"I'm okay," I lied. "Help me, you guys." Jamila and Kristin knelt down next to me, and I wrapped my arms around their shoulders. They lifted me up and I stood, balancing on my right foot. "See?" I said, my face pale from the pain. "No sweat." When I tried to take a step, though, tears rushed into my eyes. I couldn't bear any weight on my left leg.

Coach Wheeler helped Jamila and Kristin carry me over to the bench, and the Eastport trainer wrapped my knee in ice. While the game started up again, with Maria taking my place, Coach Wheeler called the hospital on his cell phone. I could hear him mumbling. "Possibly ligament damage. An MRI? Take a look at her first. No, I'm not sure about insurance. Okay. We'll be there in thirty minutes."

Coach Wheeler sat down next to me on the bench. "I'm going to call your mom and have her meet us at the emergency room."

"It's not that bad," I said, but I couldn't keep the tears from spilling down my cheeks.

Coach Wheeler put an arm around my shoulders, giving me a silent hug.

We'd all driven up on a school bus, so Coach Wheeler and

I had to borrow a van from the Eastport athletic department in order to get me to the community hospital. I went there all the time for my job, but it was different being the injured person lying on a gurney in the ER. Scarier.

A couple of nurses—no one I knew—were wheeling me into an examining room when Coach Wheeler got a call on his cell phone. "Uh-huh, uh-huh," he mumbled.

He clicked off the phone. "The team lost," he reported to me. "Five—four."

An ER resident in powder blue scrubs started asking me and Coach Wheeler questions about how I'd hurt my knee. I let my coach answer—I could hardly speak because my throat was choked up with pain and frustration. How could I have been such a klutz? I thought bitterly. I should have stayed on my feet and scored that goal. If I'd been out there till the end, we'd have won.

But I couldn't rewind the tape. The game was over.

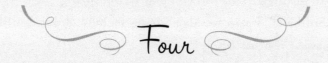

Four

T HREE *MONTHS?"* I practically shouted the words, my voice shrill with disbelief. The day after I'd fallen during the soccer game against Eastport, I was back at the hospital, sitting on an examining table in Dr. Thigpen's office, with my injured leg stretched out in front of me. Mom was there, too, and we'd just finished looking at my MRI.

"You'll need crutches for a few weeks," Dr. Thigpen said, his tone soothing. "But torn ligaments take a while to heal. Here's the bright side—you'll probably want to do some physical therapy down the road, but you don't need surgery."

Mom squeezed my hand. "That's good news," she said.

I shook my head. "But three months. That means . . . I'm out for the rest of the soccer season."

Dr. Thigpen nodded. "I'm afraid so."

I'd suspected this but hadn't wanted to believe it. "What about basketball this winter?"

Dr. Thigpen looked down at my swollen knee. "You'll be getting around a lot more easily in a few months, but you probably won't be in shape for basketball. That's one of the toughest sports on knees. By spring, though, you should be back in business. What do you play in the spring?"

"Softball," I said weakly. Spring seemed about a million years away. "Shortstop."

"Hey, I played shortstop for *my* high school baseball team," Dr. Thigpen told me with a chummy smile.

"No kidding," I said.

We talked for a few more minutes about icing my knee and stuff like that, then made an appointment for me to come back in two weeks. Dr. Thigpen sent me off with a pair of crutches and a pat on the back.

As we were leaving the hospital we bumped into Jody, the head nurse on the ward where I worked. "Daisy, what *happened?*" she exclaimed.

I told her the whole gruesome story. Jody gave me a hug. "We like you so much, we were hoping we could find a way to get you to spend more time here, but this isn't what I had in mind," she said with a rueful smile. "Take care of yourself, Daisy, okay?"

Mom was chatty and upbeat as we made our way slowly to the parking lot, but I wasn't really listening to what she was saying. Dr. Thigpen's words were still echoing in my head. *Three months, three months, three months . . .*

* * *

I CALLED JAMILA as soon as I got home from the doctor's. "That's terrible," she groaned when she heard the verdict. "What are we going to do without you?"

"You guys'll be fine." I sniffled, feeling very sorry for myself. "You and Kristen have always been the backbone of the team, anyway. And Maria will learn fast. She has a lot of talent."

"She's not in your league," Jamila said. "Besides, it's not just about how good you are. You're our best bud. I miss you already!"

I let Jamila say some more nice things about me because it made me feel less depressed, and then I hung up and limped on my crutches down the hall. I headed for the kitchen, figuring I'd see if I could set the table hopping on one foot, but when I heard Mom and Hal's voices, I detoured into the living room instead. "It's going to be rough on her," Hal was saying about somebody. *Me,* I guessed.

"I know," Mom agreed. There was a brief whirring noise—the food processor. "Sports are a big part of who she is," Mom went on. Something sizzled in a skillet. Chopped onions? "But if it had to happen to any of the girls—of course I wish that it *hadn't* happened—but if it had to happen, Daisy's the one who can handle it. She's got the right attitude. Nothing ever gets her down. Even when Jim died, she kept her chin up. I've often wished I had some of her optimism!"

I decided to let someone else set the table and hopped quietly back to my room. So that's what other people thought of me. "Daisy can handle it. . . . The right attitude . . . Nothing ever gets her down. . . ." Is that really how I seemed to the world? Tears stung my eyes. Didn't Mom know how hard it was to be strong and cheerful sometimes? *Acting* happy and *feeling* happy are two totally different things.

By the time I got back to my room, I was out of breath from the effort of using the crutches. Tossing them on the floor, I flopped on my bed, my knee throbbing painfully. Maybe I'm tired of keeping my chin up, I thought, closing my eyes.

T HE NEXT DAY after school I sat slumped forward on the bleachers, watching my soccer teammates practice. It was weird to be wearing jeans and a sweater instead of cleats and sweats. I kept wanting to run down and jump into the drills, but then I'd remember my knee. Not that I could really forget it. I was taking painkillers, but it still ached.

I'd thought sitting in on practice would make me feel like I was still part of things, and everybody did come over to talk to me and ask how I felt, which was nice. But when Kristin dropped me off at home later, I felt even more depressed than before. I dragged myself into the apartment and collapsed in a kitchen chair, groaning out loud.

Rose was eating a container of yogurt and reading her sociology textbook. "You look like death," she observed.

"Thanks for the moral support," I said dryly.

Rose put down her book. "I know exactly how you feel," she said. "Remember last May, when I got laryngitis and couldn't be in the spring musical?"

"Yeah, but it didn't take you three *months* to get better," I pointed out.

"True," she admitted. "Cheer up, though, okay? I mean, what will happen to this family if Susie Sunshine turns into Susie Storm Cloud?"

Rose was trying to get me to smile, but I didn't have anything to smile about. Not today, anyway. Susie Sunshine? I thought. Make that Susie Sidelined.

WELCOME TO THE club," Ben Compton said when I hobbled over to his hospital room to say hi my first day back on the job.

He and I had been talking a bunch of times, and I was starting to really like him. Ben knew some hilarious jokes because he surfed the Net a lot. We found out that we both collected baseball cards, so we'd done some trading—in spite of the fact that he always tried to swindle me.

"What club?" I asked him now.

"The club of ex-soccer players," Ben replied.

I was standing at the door to his room, which was in a separate oncology section of the pediatric wing. He was in the midst of heavy-duty chemotherapy and his immune system was suppressed, so he wasn't supposed to have visitors other than his family. To be perfectly honest, he looked pretty bad. "I can't come in, huh?"

"Unless you want to put on a mask and gown."

"It's just kind of hard to hear you from over here," I told him.

Ben cleared his throat. "Better?"

His voice was still kind of faint and scratchy, but I said, "Yes."

"It stinks, doesn't it?" he remarked. His eyes were half closed, and his skin was yellowish and blotchy. "But at least you know you'll be back to normal. I'll never get out of this damned bed."

Ben's condition definitely put my relatively minor problem in perspective. He was usually cheerful, though, and I had never heard him sound so negative. For a moment I didn't know what to say.

I fell back on this joke about the self-pity police. "Here they come," I said, certain he'd know what I was talking about. "They're going to arrest you."

Ben cracked a weak smile. "Couldn't you be a little nicer to a dying man?"

My stomach gave an involuntary lurch at the word *dying*, but I tried not to show it. "No way, José. Snap out of it."

"All right, all right." He smiled weakly.

A nurse appeared at my shoulder. "Ben needs to rest," she advised me.

I didn't really want to go, but it didn't look like I had much choice. "Okay. Bye, Ben. Hang in there."

I waved, and he managed to lift a hand from the sheet in response. "Like I have an alternative."

I HAD TO watch out for the self-pity police myself a day later. For the first time in memory, I didn't have anything to do after school. I had decided not to watch the team practice anymore—it made me too sad. On Friday afternoon I rode the school bus home, but the apartment was empty. Mom was out, Laurel and Lily both had after-school activities, and Rose had gone to the Greyhound station, duffel in hand, to catch a bus to Boston—she was visiting Stephen at Harvard for the weekend. I didn't feel like sitting around by myself, even though I had a ton of homework, so I headed back out on my crutches.

It was a gray October day, and the low, dark sky matched my mood. Leaning heavily on my crutches, I limped along the sidewalk, window shopping. Did I feel like a cookie from Wissinger's Bakery? Nah, I wasn't hungry, and besides, now that I couldn't exercise much, I'd have to watch my weight. There was a sale at Harrington's Department Store and also at Cecilia's, but I didn't need new clothes and couldn't afford them anyhow. I hobbled past Appleby's Hardware Store and the Down East News and Drugstore and Patsy's Diner and the Corner Ice Cream Shoppe. When I got to the end of the commercial part of town, I stopped.

For a few minutes I just stood on one foot at the corner of Main Street and Lighthouse Road. I didn't have a destination. I felt adrift, and that scared me. It was like something at the center of my life had been torn away, something that held the rest together.

A nursery rhyme popped into my head. *Humpty-Dumpty sat on a wall, Humpty-Dumpty had a great fall. All the king's horses and all the king's men . . .*

Who's going to put *me* back together? I wondered as I turned around and limped back toward home.

Five

"I'M NOT TOTALLY helpless," I told Mom a week later. "The car's an automatic, and it's my left leg that's hurt—I can still drive. Besides, it would give me something to do."

Mom studied me, arms folded. "Are you sure?"

I nodded. "I'm sure."

"Well, it would be a big help," she admitted, fishing in her purse for her keys. "I need to get started on this wedding cake because I'm catering the cocktail party, too, and that noisy muffler's been driving me crazy. And tell them the engine light's blinking on and off and have them change the oil, too, okay?"

Mom called ahead to Dave's Fuel 'n' Fix to tell them I was bringing the car in. They told her they could look at it right away, so I took along my backpack—I figured I'd do some homework while I was waiting.

The station wasn't busy, and the mechanic, a burly middle-aged guy named Ralph, had the car up on blocks in no time. I settled down on a bench in front of the service station, my crutches propped against the wall, and pulled my history book out of my pack. I didn't open it right away, though; I just held it on my lap while I tipped my face to the sky, the autumn sun warm on my skin.

I think I was starting to snore when an amused voice jolted me from my daydreams. "Hey, Sleeping Beauty."

I opened my eyes and blinked. A tall, thin guy about my age stood in front of me, blocking the sunlight. He was wearing a shirt with the name Peter embroidered over the chest pocket. His sandy hair was longish—he had a couple of dreadlocks on one side and a pierced ear with a little silver hoop in it. That kind of alterna-look wasn't usually my thing, but his sharp-featured face was handsome, and for some reason I found myself blushing. "Um, are you talking to me?" I asked.

"Do you see anyone else here?" he asked, smiling. He put one foot up on my bench and leaned his crossed forearms on his knee, gazing down at me. His eyes were intensely blue. "You're Daisy, right? Ralph just sent me to tell you that the car'll be about forty-five more minutes."

"Oh. Okay," I said, adding, "um, yeah, I'm Daisy. And you're . . . Peter."

"My friends call me Paco."

"How come?"

"I have no idea."

We both laughed. "You, uh, work here?" I asked. I don't

usually come up with such dumb questions, but this guy was so cute, he was affecting my brain.

"Just since last week." A smile lingered in his eyes. "In case you were wondering why you hadn't noticed me before."

Dave's was the only gas station in Hawk Harbor, and I *had* been wondering that. I blushed again. "Pumping gas?" I asked lamely.

"Pumping gas," he confirmed. "Lucky for me, Hawk Harbor still hasn't heard of self-serve."

Just then a red pickup truck pulled up to the pump. "Back in a minute," Peter said, and walked over to it. "Fill 'er with regular," I heard the driver say.

I watched as Peter moved around the truck, cleaning the windows with the squeegee. He had the easy stride of an athlete, and that got me wondering again. When the pickup drove off, he took the ten-dollar bill inside to the cash register, then rejoined me on the bench. "You don't go to South Regional," I guessed.

Peter shook his head. "Nah. I went to Kent High for a while, but I got kicked out."

I was intrigued. "Really?"

"It wasn't my scene," he said with a careless shrug.

"Does your family live in Kent?"

"We used to, but now we're bunking with my aunt in Hawk Harbor. It's just me and my mom. My dad bailed when I was in kindergarten."

"Wow. That's awful."

"Yeah, apparently he was a bum," Peter said. "I don't remember him, to tell you the truth."

I thought about my own lost father. I remembered every single thing about him. "That must've been rough on your mother."

"Sure, and now she has MS—multiple sclerosis. So she's sick on and off, can't hold down a job. That's why we're freeloading off Aunt Trish."

"Wow," I said again. "That must be really hard."

"Life deals some people a lousy hand," Peter agreed.

Another car pulled in and he hopped up. After he'd tallied up the sale, he came back outside again. This time he was carrying a guitar. Without speaking, he sat down next to me and started strumming. "What's that?" I asked, pointing to something on his finger that looked like a glass thimble.

"A slide. So you can get sounds like this." He played a quick riff.

The notes were liquid and beautiful. "It sounds like a voice," I told him. "Like singing."

"It does, doesn't it?"

Bending his head, he played for a minute. Then he stopped abruptly, clapping his hand against the strings to silence them, and looked straight at me. "What were you playing?" I asked.

"Don't know. Haven't given it a name yet."

My eyes widened. "You *wrote* that?"

"Yeah," he said dismissively. "It's nothing."

"I thought it was really pretty."

"Well." He smiled slowly. "Then maybe I'll call it 'Daisy's Song.'"

I blushed yet again. Peter put the guitar down. He stretched his arms over his head, yawning, and his shirt lifted up a little, exposing a narrow strip of flat, sun-browned abdominals. I shifted my eyes away, wondering if it were possible for my face to get any pinker.

"Kind of slow right now, huh?" Peter observed, gazing at the vacant gas pumps. "And Ralph's still working on your car. How about you and me"—he paused suggestively as my throat tightened—"play a game of chess?"

"Chess?" I laughed. "Are you joking?"

"Nope. Got a portable set inside. You wait right here."

When Peter brought the chess set out and opened up the board, I confessed that I'd never played. He explained the rules to me, and we played a couple of short games. Needless to say, it didn't take him many moves to trounce me. "I'll never get the hang of this," I said with a laugh as he seized my queen.

"Sure, you will," Peter said. "You play soccer, right?" I'd told him how I hurt my leg. "It's the same kind of thing. You have to think ahead, visualize how the game will unfold, how the players will move. Let your brain roam over the possibilities."

I shook my head, smiling. "I think that might be harder than it sounds."

Inside the garage I saw Ralph waving at me. It looked like my car was done, but I wasn't in a rush to leave. When will I see this guy again? I wondered with a strange urgency. My family didn't do that much driving—we wouldn't need another fill-up for a week or so. "So, since you live in Hawk Harbor now, do you think you'll enroll at school?" I asked Peter.

Peter packed away the chess pieces. "Doubtful. I'd just get kicked out again. I have, like, every learning disability in the book, supposedly. You know, lots of 'potential,' but I could never quite follow the rules. Anyhow," he added, his eyes glued to mine, "there are better ways to learn what the world has to teach."

"Oh. Right. I know what you mean," I said, even though I didn't.

I paid for the car repair with the blank check Mom had given me, and then Peter helped me into the driver's seat. It was a little awkward—I couldn't bend my left leg all the way because of the brace.

I rolled down the window. "See you around . . . uh . . . Paco," I said, trying not to sound too hopeful.

"You bet," he replied.

As I pulled onto the road I glanced in my rearview mirror. Peter was watching me drive away. He lifted a hand in a casual wave, and I hit the horn.

I don't usually spend that much time thinking about the opposite sex—I'm not boy crazy like Rose, or like she was before she settled down with Stephen. But I thought about Peter all the way home . . . and until dinner . . . and after dinner until I went to bed. Then, even though I usually sleep like a log, I saw him in my dreams.

THE NEXT SUNDAY morning Mom dragged us all out of bed to go to church. I have to admit that during Reverend Beecher's sermon, I was still picturing Peter, playing the slide guitar and stretching his arms over his head in a yawn.

When we got home, my sisters and I crowded into the kitchen to make brunch—since Mom cooks for a living, we give her a break whenever we can. Lily mixed the waffle batter while Laurel haphazardly sliced apples into a saucepan for applesauce. Rose threw in a load of laundry—the washer and dryer are in a closet off the kitchen—and I set the table, hopping on one foot.

"It's eleven. Do you think it's too early to call Stephen at school?" Rose asked me as she sorted the lights from the darks. She answered her own question before I could. "Yeah, I'm sure he's sleeping in—there was probably a party last night. Or two or three parties."

She sounded disapproving. "Didn't you go to a bunch of parties last weekend when you were down there?" I asked. "I thought you said it was a blast."

"It was." Rose twisted the dial on the washing machine. "But I'm not there this weekend. You know?"

"Maybe you should just tell Stephen you expect him to stay in his room with his nose in a book when you're not there," I said.

"I don't think he'd go for it." She sighed. "You should see that campus. It's incredibly gorgeous and crawling with pretty girls. Pretty *and* brainy."

"No one's smarter or prettier than you," I reminded her.

"Yeah," said Lily. "Remember what it said in the yearbook last year? You got 'Best Smile' and 'Most Talented.'"

Rose frowned. "Anyone can be a big fish in a small pond. South Regional's not exactly Harvard."

"I still wouldn't worry," I said. "When's Stephen going to come home for a visit?"

"Probably never," Rose said, obviously determined not to

be cheered up. "Why would he, when he's having so much fun at school?"

I finished setting the table and retrieved my crutches. "Need help?" I asked my younger sisters.

"Would you get me the cinnamon?" Laurel replied.

I grabbed a jar from the spice rack. "Is Jack coming over?" I asked her.

Laurel sprinkled some cinnamon on the apples. "I doubt it."

"How come? He never misses waffles."

Laurel gave the applesauce an impatient stir. "Since I said no, he asked another girl in our class to go out with him. Tammy Nickerson," she added with a sniff.

"The one who started wearing a bra in, like, third grade?" Rose asked.

Laurel nodded grimly. "Yep."

"Couldn't you still invite him over for brunch?" I wondered.

Laurel shook her head. "You can't hang out with another girl when you're going out with someone," she informed me in a duh-don't-you-know-anything? tone. "He's probably having brunch with Tammy."

"You sound like you're sorry you turned him down when he asked *you* to go out with him," Rose remarked.

"I am not," Laurel declared. "Absolutely, totally not!"

I raised my eyebrows at Rose. "Oh," Rose said to Laurel. "I see."

JACK DIDN'T MAKE it to brunch, but Hal did. "Great waffles," he said, piling his plate high. "You made these, Lily?"

Lily nodded, pleased. "Yep. Cooking talent runs in the family."

Hal chuckled. I tried not to gag. For once Mom wasn't smiling, either. Leaning her elbows on the table, she looked at Lily. "Lily, were you using the computer last night?"

Lily blinked at Mom's tone. I could almost see her thinking, Is this a trick question? "Um . . ."

"Because someone erased one of my files—my budget for the catering business."

Lily's face turned a guilty red. "Oh. I didn't mean to—"

"You know you're not supposed to go into my files," Mom said.

"Well, I was on the Internet," Lily explained. "You know, in that chat room? And then it started to get really stupid, so I decided to write a story, and I accidentally clicked on your file instead, and I don't know how it happened, but—"

"You better not have been snooping in *my* files," Rose cut in.

"You mean the one with the letters you write to Stephen?" Lily asked. "No, I'd never—"

"And that's another thing," Mom said. "This chat room business." She looked at Hal. "Lily and her friends spend an awful lot of time that way, on weeknights, too, when they should be doing homework."

"Well, if you're worried about it," said Hal, "maybe you should consider limiting the time Lily spends in chat rooms to, say, twenty minutes a night." Mom nodded, and Hal went on, "And maybe she should forfeit her computer privileges for a while if she can't learn to respect privacy."

I couldn't believe Hal—who did he think he was? "Didn't you hear her say it was an accident?" I spoke up, my eyes flashing. "And *Mom* makes the rules around here!"

"Daisy!" Mom said, surprised.

"Well, I just think . . ." I swallowed the rest of the angry words that threatened to spill out. What was the matter with me? Dad would have been furious at rude behavior like that. "I think I'll have another waffle," I finished.

Mom didn't let it go at that. When brunch was over, Hal went to see if he could recover Mom's lost computer file. My sisters took off, leaving me with the dishes. As I rinsed off the plates and put them in the dishwasher, balancing awkwardly on my good leg, Mom poured another cup of coffee and gave me a little lecture. "I didn't like your manners when you were talking to Hal," she told me. "You spoke out of turn."

Even though I knew she had a point, I couldn't stand to talk about it. "*I* spoke out of turn?" I countered. "I thought Hal did. It's not his place to tell us how to act. He's not our father."

Mom didn't respond. For a minute she sipped her coffee, her eyebrows furrowed and her jaw tense. Then she left the kitchen.

I WORKED AT the hospital from 2 until 8 P.M. on Sunday. It was a good shift. Ben was doing better, and I spent a good chunk of time chatting with him.

Heading home, I found myself taking a detour. I was feeling so good, I felt like having an adventure. Instead of driving straight back to the apartment on Main Street, I turned down the Old Boston Post Road and pulled into Dave's Fuel 'n' Fix.

I didn't really need gas—I still had half a tank. And he might not even be working tonight.

When I spotted Peter, my heart rate doubled. What if he doesn't remember me? I thought as I rolled down the window.

He remembered me. "Fill 'er up, Sleeping Beauty?" he asked, giving me a slow smile.

"Yes. Thanks," I said somewhat breathlessly.

Peter filled up the tank—I only needed three gallons—and I paid him. I hesitated with my right hand on the key in the ignition. I couldn't just drive away. I wanted something to happen. My tongue was tied in a knot, though. How do you make the first move? I wondered, wishing for the first time in my life that I knew how to flirt.

As it turned out, I didn't need to make the first move. Opening the door on the other side of my car, Peter climbed into the passenger seat. "I'm off work as of now," he told me. "Want to go to a party?"

"It's a school night," I pointed out.

He grinned. "So?"

"So . . ." I thought about all the homework I still had to do. I thought about Mom waiting for me at home. Mom . . . and Hal. "So nothing," I said. "Let's go."

THE PARTY WAS at Peter's friend Zeke's house on Forest Road, on the inland edge of town. The music was so loud that we could hear it as we parked the car by the curb. "I guess Zeke's parents aren't home," I said.

"Zeke's parents are out of it," Peter answered. "We could tear the whole house down and they probably wouldn't notice."

I leaned on my crutches and hopped toward the house. Peter went right in without knocking, and I followed him.

The living room was cloudy with smoke. Kids were flopped on the furniture, some with cigarettes in their hands, others holding plastic cups. Beer? I wondered. "Paco!" someone shouted.

"Hey," he yelled back. "This is Daisy."

A couple of people waved; one guy lifted his cup. A girl with short blue hair standing near the stereo turned the volume even louder. "My favorite song," she screamed in explanation.

Peter introduced me around, but I couldn't hear any of the names over the screeching music. I made some mental notes, though. The girl with the blue hair is with the guy in the tie-dyed shirt, I decided. And the guy with the tattoos must be Zeke.

Peter put his arm around me and steered me into the kitchen. The music wasn't as loud there—we could actually hear each other. "How about a beer?" he asked.

"I don't really drink," I told him.

"Really?" His sandy eyebrows shot up. "Well, that's cool, I guess. Is it, like, a health thing?"

None of my friends drink—we're underage. But then, so was Peter. I didn't want to sound like a loser, so I said, "Yeah."

"How about food, then? Are you hungry?" Peter opened the refrigerator and bent over to peer inside.

"I'm not really—"

Peter was already slapping together a couple of ham-and-cheese sandwiches. "Let's find someplace we can talk," he suggested.

I nodded. "Okay."

We ended up sitting in the upstairs hall with two boys and a girl whom I recognized from South Regional. Although needless to say, we didn't usually hang out in the same crowd. "Daisy's a jock," Peter reported, biting into his sandwich.

"It sure looks like you got over it," the girl named Amy remarked, pointing at my crutches.

Everybody laughed. "I kind of wrecked my knee," I explained.

"It's just as well because exercise is, like, really bad for you," said a guy named Marcus. "I read that somewhere."

"It's much better to exercise your brain," the other guy, Kirk, agreed.

"Like in this fascinating conversation we're having?" Peter asked. Everyone laughed again.

I slumped against the wall, my injured leg stretched out in front of me. We talked about music for a while, then switched to TV shows and movies. Kirk, Marcus, and Amy were funny—they didn't take anything seriously. At one point I said to Amy, "You're in Mr. Kamin's English class, right? Have you started that Mark Twain paper yet?"

"Are you kidding?" Amy laughed. "It's not even on my radar screen. It's due, when, Thursday? I *might* read the book Wednesday night. Or at least the back cover."

Peter disappeared for a minute. When he came back, he had a guitar. I guessed it was Zeke's. For half an hour we played Name That Tune—he'd pick out a few notes, and we'd shout out the song title. Then I happened to get a look at my watch. Ten forty-five! "I have to get home," I told Peter, struggling to my feet. "Do you need a ride anywhere?"

"I think I'll hang out here," he replied, putting down the guitar, "but I'll walk you to your car."

Outside, we stood for a moment next to the car. I jingled the keys nervously, not sure what to do or say. I didn't have that much dating experience . . . and had this even been a date?

"Thanks for inviting me to the party," I said at last, immediately wanting to kick myself for sounding like such a priss.

"Glad you could join me," Peter replied, smiling at our formality.

I hesitated before getting into the car. Peter lifted a hand, lightly touching my hair. "This is really cool hair," he said. "And it's real."

I laughed. "Believe it or not."

"It was good to see you, Sleeping Beauty." Bending forward, he kissed my cheek.

"Um, yeah," I said. "Bye."

"Bye."

I was lucky I didn't run into a police car, or I definitely would have gotten pulled over. I was weaving a little—I kept wandering over the yellow centerline. Peter's kiss had made me dizzy—and it wasn't even on the lips!

At home I crutched into the front hall, heading straight

for my room. Mom's voice stopped me before I got to the stairs. "Daisy, is that you?"

I backtracked to the kitchen. Mom was sitting at the table in her bathrobe and slippers. "I was worried about you," she told me, frowning. "I expected you home at eight."

"I know," I mumbled. "I went out after work."

"You should have called."

"I know," I said again.

"Either way, it's almost eleven and your weeknight curfew is ten."

"Sorry."

"Where were you?"

"Just at this guy's house, with someone I met the other day." I yawned. "I'm going to bed. See you tomorrow."

I could tell Mom didn't like my evasiveness—she was still frowning—but I left before she could ask more questions. In my room I dropped my crutches on the floor, then hopped around on one foot, getting ready for bed.

Crawling under the covers, I thought about the evening. Usually I'm careful not to make Mom mad—she has enough to worry about without that hassle. And usually she and I talk about pretty much everything. We've always gotten along really well. But for some reason I didn't feel like talking to her about Peter. Maybe it's because I'm sixteen now, I thought sleepily. Things are going to change. I put a hand to my face, where Peter had kissed me. At least, I hoped so.

Six

WHEN MELISSA CAME up to me on Wednesday, I was in the cafeteria. Waiting for Jamila and Kristin, I'd bumped into Amy, the girl I'd met at Zeke's party, and we got in the lunch line together. Melissa gave Amy a funny look, and I could tell she was wondering why I was talking to someone with a butterfly tattoo on her forearm, a pack of cigarettes in her pocket, and six pierces in her ear.

"Daisy, hi," Melissa said. "You haven't stopped by the student council office yet. You're going to run, aren't you?"

Amy cocked one eyebrow. "You're thinking about joining the Establishment?" she asked sardonically.

Suddenly it occurred to me that Amy might tell Peter about this conversation. He didn't even *go* to school—would he think running for student council was totally dorky? "Just thinking about it," I said to Amy with studied nonchalance.

"I still haven't made up my mind, Mel. How much more time do I have?"

"We're printing the ballots next Monday," Mel answered. "I really hope you run, Daisy."

"I'll sleep on it, okay?" I told Mel.

"Okay." She gave Amy a polite smile. "See you around."

Amy and I moved up in the lunch line. Jamila and Kristin still hadn't appeared—sometimes Coach Wheeler called a short team meeting during lunch, and I figured that was where they were—so Amy helped me with my tray since I was using crutches. We both took sloppy joes and french fries. "Are you really going to run for class president?" Amy asked, laughing. She reached for an orange. "So you can, like, pick the theme for the prom and other important stuff?"

I laughed, too, to show that I didn't take myself too seriously. "I probably won't bother," I said.

"Yeah, because what's the point?" Amy asked.

"Right," I agreed. "What's the point?"

WEDNESDAY AFTER SCHOOL I went to a girls' varsity soccer home game against Lewisborough. I'd been to all the games, and sometimes I watched part of practice, too—just to stay in touch. Today, though, I wasn't really paying attention to the action on the field even though Jamila scored a hat trick—three goals—and the Sharks won 5–4.

After the game the team took showers and then went to Cap'n Jack's, a burger place, to celebrate the victory. Jamila,

Kristin, and I ended up in our own booth, and as soon as we were alone I leaned forward with my elbows on the table and said, "Guess what?"

Kristin was chugging a glass of water. "What?" Jamila asked, opening her menu.

"I met a guy," I announced.

Kristin put down her empty glass. "A guy? You're kidding! Who?"

"His name is Peter," I told them. "He has a nickname—Paco."

Kristin shook her head. "I don't think I know him. Is he a senior?"

"He doesn't go to South Regional," I said. "He works at Dave's."

Jamila's eyebrows drew together. "The gas station?"

"No, the jewelry store," I kidded. "Yeah, the gas station," I added in an anything-wrong-with-that? tone.

Kristin's eyes lit up. "The blond dreadlocks guy, right? He's *cute.*"

"The blond dreadlocks guy? You're kidding! How did this happen?" Jamila wanted to know.

While we waited for our burgers and fries, I told them about the first time I'd bumped into Peter and the second time, including the party at Zeke's. "Did you kiss?" Kristin asked.

A giveaway blush stole up my face. "Sort of," I confessed.

"This is wild," Jamila said. "Straight-arrow Daisy and the funky guy from the gas station."

"I'm not a straight arrow," I protested.

Kristin laughed. "It's okay. We like you that way. And obviously Peter does, too."

The waitress had brought our food. "I would never have picked him for your type, though," Jamila admitted as she poured ketchup on her burger.

"He's different from anyone I've ever known," I agreed. "But that's what's cool about him. He's a nonconformist, and so are his friends. Getting good grades, being popular—they're not hung up on that stuff."

"Hmmm," said Kristin thoughtfully, munching a french fry.

"When are you going to see him again?" Jamila wondered.

"I don't know," I answered. I tried to sound casual, but inside, I had the same fluttery feeling I got every time I thought about Peter. Soon, I thought. I hope it's soon.

YOU HAVE TO go already?" Rose said into the phone. "But it's only been five minutes!"

It was late Friday afternoon, and Rose was talking to Stephen. I was sitting at my desk, getting some books together to take to the hospital—I was working the six-to-ten shift.

"Well, okay. You can call me back tomorrow," Rose said. "I love you. Bye."

She hung up the phone, then folded her arms across her chest, scowling. "That was weird," she muttered.

"What?" I asked.

She turned to look at me. "Well, when I called Stephen last night, he was on his way to the library, you know? So he told me to call him today before dinner. And now he's on his way out the door again!"

"He's busy."

"Yeah, but doing what? There were all these voices in the background, like there were people in his room."

"He has two roommates," I reminded her.

"But there were *lots* of voices," Rose said. "Male *and* female."

"Stephen has friends," I concluded. "That's a crime?"

Rose sighed. "I'm being paranoid, aren't I?"

"Yep."

"I just feel so left out," she confessed. "Everything in his life is new and exciting. Meanwhile I'm getting more boring by the minute."

I had to laugh. Rose is anything but boring. "Right."

"But Daze, seriously," Rose said. "What if—"

Just then the telephone on the night table rang. Rose grabbed it. "Hello, Stephen?" Her hopeful smile faded. "Oh, sorry. Yes, just a second, she's right here," she said, handing the receiver to me.

"This is Daisy," I said.

"Daisy, it's Peter."

His voice was deep and a little bit raspy—it sent a shiver down my spine. "Hi," I squeaked. "What's up?"

"I was just thinking about the other night," Peter said. "I want to see you again."

His bluntness made me blush. "Oh, well, y-yeah," I stammered. "Umm . . . me too."

"Is tonight okay?"

"Tonight?" I repeated.

I glanced at Rose, who was walking toward the door. Turning back, she mouthed, "I'm leaving."

When the door shut behind her, I said to Peter, "Yes, tonight's okay. Why don't I meet you at Dave's?"

WHEN I PULLED into the gas station, I still couldn't believe I'd done it—called in sick at the hospital and then pretended to my family that I was heading off to my job. For an instant I *did* feel sick. What if Mom found out?

When Peter tossed his guitar in the back and then climbed into the passenger seat, though, I was glad I was there. I wanted something and I went for it, I thought, secretly pleased with myself.

"Where to?" I asked him.

"You're in the driver's seat," he pointed out. "You decide."

"Well . . . there's always good music at the Rusty Nail," I said. Rose goes there a lot with her friends. "Or we could get a pizza or see a movie."

"How about the beach?" Peter suggested.

"There's going to be a frost tonight. And I won't be able to handle the sand on crutches."

"Let's try it, anyway," he said, his eyes on my face. "The moonlight'll keep us warm."

The parking lot at the main town beach, south of Kettle Cove, was empty. We walked over to a bench with a view of the water. "In the summer the beach is so tame and touristy," Peter said. "Off-season, it gets wild again."

"Yeah," I agreed, my eyes on the black waves.

"Do you like storms?" he asked.

My father's fishing boat sank in a nor'easter. I shook my head. "No, I don't like storms."

"You like sunny weather." Peter took my hand and pulled me closer to him.

"I guess I do," I said softly.

"There's something I've wanted to do all week." He held both my hands now, his grip tight. "Kiss you."

I looked into his eyes, my own widening. "You do?"

His laugh was low and husky. "Don't you want me to?"

Suddenly my shyness disappeared. I answered him by leaning close, my face lifted to his.

The kiss was electrifying. I was glad I was sitting down— both my knees would have given out on me, the bad one *and* the good one. Peter had put both his arms around me, and mine had gone around him, and we were holding each other for the first time and it made my mind go blank.

We kissed again—less rushed, more thrilling. I hoped Peter couldn't tell that I hadn't done this much before. One thing was for sure, making out with Jay hadn't prepared me for how it would feel kissing Peter.

"You're not cold now, are you?" Peter asked when we drew apart a little.

I laughed breathlessly. "Hardly."

He slumped back on the bench, reaching for his guitar. "Yeah, if we heated up any more, we might melt." He started playing. "Listen, I worked some more on that song from the other day. Your song."

I closed my eyes and let the music wash over me.

"I like it," I told him when he finished. "I can't believe you wrote that yourself."

"I didn't actually *write* it," he said. "I don't read music—this isn't on paper anywhere. I just play for myself, you know? I don't care if anyone else listens. Unless it's you."

He put the guitar away. For a few minutes we sat side by side, looking out at the ocean. Then I turned to face him. Lifting a hand, I touched the hoop in his right earlobe. "I like this," I told him.

He gave me a crooked smile. "I'm getting another pierce next week—lost a bet with Amy. Will you like that, too?"

My cheeks felt warm in the frosty air. "Sure," I said.

Peter was looking at me with a funny expression in his eyes. "Wow, are you beautiful," he said at last.

I tucked my chin into my coat collar. "Uh, thanks."

"And sweet, too." He shook his head. "Man, it's just as well."

"What's just as well?"

"I was just thinking you'd be really hot if you loosened up a little," he said. "But maybe I couldn't handle it."

What was he saying? That I was a nerd? I didn't want him to think that. "I'm not totally wholesome," I told him.

He grinned. "I know. I could tell by that kiss. But I mean *wild*, Daisy. Do you want to be wild?"

At that question a jumble of emotions ran through me. On the one hand, I was a little afraid. I'd spent my life playing by the rules. Could I even function without them? But as I stared into Peter's blue eyes I felt all the pressures I'd been under for so many months—for years even, ever since Dad died—fade away. The fear suddenly vanished. I was still in Hawk Harbor, but I felt as if I'd walked out of my life. I'd escaped.

Wild, I thought. Why shouldn't I be?

"Yes," I whispered to Peter as our lips met again.

Seven

"YOU'RE COMING TO the game at St. Joseph's today, right?"
Jamila asked me at school on Thursday.

The final bell had rung, and we were at our lockers. "I
don't think so," I answered.

"You have to," Kristin urged. "You're our good luck
mascot."

"Are you working?" Jamila guessed.

"Not today," I replied, sticking a textbook into my backpack.

"Well, if you're worried about the trig test, you could study
on the bus," Kristin suggested. "I promise we won't bug you."

I was *not* worried about the trig test. "I'm seeing Peter," I
told them.

"Wow," said Kristin. "You two have been spending a lot of
time together."

"Yeah," I admitted. Peter and I had seen each other every day since our first real date the other night.

"When do we get to meet him?" Jamila asked.

I pictured clean-cut Kristin and Jamila hanging out with Peter's crowd. Kristin is allergic to cigarette smoke, and Jamila can't stand people who aren't in shape. Neither one of them drinks. "One of these days," I answered vaguely.

"Daze, I was talking to Mel during study hall, and she said you decided not to run for student council after all," Kristin said. "How come?"

I shrugged. "It just didn't seem like it was going to be cool. Every other junior running is a loser."

Kristin raised her eyebrows. "Matt Daly? Heather Holmes?"

Matt and Heather hung out with us sometimes. I shrugged again. "I guess I just didn't feel like it."

"You would have been great," Jamila said. "But it's your choice."

I turned to leave. "Good luck in the game."

"Thanks," Kristin said.

My friends seemed disappointed, but I didn't spend much time dwelling on that. I was too eager to get to Dave's Fuel 'n' Fix.

But when I hobbled outside, I found Peter waiting for me in front of the high school. "Hi!" I said, surprised.

He slipped an arm around my neck, pulling my face to his for a kiss. "Got my mom's car today," he said. "Come on."

When we were in his mother's old station wagon, I asked, "Don't you have to work today?"

"Nope. I quit."

"You *quit*? How come?"

"Dave. I'm telling you, that guy's a—" Peter broke off and slammed his palm against the steering wheel. "There was some money missing from the cash register last weekend, right? And he asked me about it in this way, like, forget about innocent until proven guilty, you know?"

I stared at Peter, confused. "You mean, Dave accused you of taking the money?"

"Not in so many words, but obviously he thinks it was me." Peter steered the Ford onto the street. "Supposedly someone had been rigging the receipts, like ringing up sales for a smaller amount and pocketing the extra cash, and he asked me did I know anything about it, and I just blew up, you know?"

"And you quit." I realized I sounded stupid, but I couldn't help it. I was stunned. I wasn't sure what part of the story was more upsetting—the fact that Peter had bagged his job or that his boss had accused him of stealing. I didn't have any experience with a situation like this. It threw me off balance.

"I'm not going to work for someone who doesn't trust me," Peter declared. "I don't need that kind of grief."

"Of course not," I said, suddenly feeling protective. I put a hand on Peter's arm and massaged his bicep. "Dave's a jerk."

"Hey, it's just a job." Peter punched the button on the radio, and the music started blasting. "I can find another one."

He was driving toward Kent—probably to the mall, where there's a movie theater and video arcade plus lots of cheap fast food. "I wonder who stole it?" I said. "If it wasn't you."

Peter yanked on the steering wheel, abruptly pulling over onto the shoulder. "It wasn't me, okay?" he insisted.

"I know it wasn't you," I said, but the way he'd snapped at me seemed strange. For a split second I had a terrible thought. What if Peter *did* steal the money? He was smart enough to figure out a way to do it without leaving behind any evidence.

I squashed the suspicion fast. Peter had dropped out of school, and he had kind of a cynical attitude, but that didn't mean he'd do something illegal. Society always trashes people like Peter. Caring about him meant loyalty, and that's something I'm good at. "I know it wasn't you," I repeated with conviction.

Peter looked into my eyes. "Thanks for believing in me, Daisy."

MY FAMILY LIKES rituals: cutting down our own Christmas tree, having an egg hunt on Easter, the Fourth of July parade and fireworks in town, birthday parties. Every fall we go to McCloskey's Farm to pick apples and buy a pumpkin for Halloween. This year we went on a sunny Saturday afternoon in October. It was my first day without crutches—I limped along pretty slowly, but at least I was on both feet again.

Hal came along, too . . . unfortunately. "Let's pick some Northern Spies," Mom told him, pointing to the far side of the orchard. "They're the best for pies."

"Sure thing," said Hal, grabbing a bushel basket in one hand and taking Mom's hand with his other. "Northern Spies for pies—hey, that rhymes. Ha, ha."

Laurel laughed, too, as if Hal had said something that was actually funny. Mom smiled at Hal in a sappy way. Plucking an apple from a tree as we walked by, Lily announced, "Mom, I want to get my ears pierced. At the Piercing Pavilion at the mall it only costs—"

"No," said Mom.

"But I have to have pierced ears," Lily informed her. "This is *important*, Mom."

"Let me guess." Hal winked at Mom. "Your friends at school have pierced ears."

"They do, Mr. Leverett, and they all have the same gold heart earrings, and—"

"You know the rule, Lily," Mom cut in. "When you're thirteen, you can have your ears pierced, but not before."

"But Mom!" wailed Lily, stamping her foot on the fallen leaves. "Without pierced ears I'll—"

"Next subject," Mom suggested, watching as Laurel hitched herself up onto a low branch to reach a couple of particularly big red apples. "What's happening at school for you these days, Laurel?"

I lifted my basket so Laurel could drop the apples into it. "Nothing much," she answered. "Oh, Nathan Green asked me to go out with him. I said yes," she added without much enthusiasm.

"That's nice," said Mom.

"Nathan's brother, Adam, was in my class," Rose reported. "If Nathan looks anything like him, he's a hunk."

"He's pretty cute," Laurel admitted with a melancholy sigh.

"Then why aren't you psyched?" Lily asked. "You are *so* strange."

"I don't know." Laurel jumped down from the tree, dusting off her hands on her jeans. "I thought maybe I should just do it—if everyone else is—have a boyfriend, I mean."

"Speaking of boyfriends," Rose said. "Daisy's been spending a lot of time with the mysterious Peter lately."

"That's right," said Mom.

"Yes, when are we going to meet this fellow?" asked Hal.

"I don't need your permission to date him," I snapped at Hal.

Everyone stopped walking and turned to stare at me. "I don't think that's what Hal meant, Daisy," Mom said, her forehead wrinkled.

"Sorry," I said, although I wasn't. "My mistake."

"We're just eager to meet your new friend, that's all," she went on. "Maybe you could invite him over for brunch or dinner tomorrow."

"Sure," I mumbled, kicking at a rotten windfall apple.

We wandered on through the orchard. Mom and Hal and Rose started gabbing about menu possibilities for a party Mom was catering in Portland the following weekend. Lily complained to Laurel about the injustice of not being allowed to have pierced ears; Laurel, tracking a family of pheasants through the underbrush, ignored her.

I trailed behind everyone else. My knee was killing me, and that wasn't all. I'd always enjoyed these outings, but not today. All at once apple picking seemed like a waste of time, and on top of that, my mom and my sisters and Hal most of all were getting on my nerves in a major way.

I picked a Macintosh apple and bit into it. "Yuck," I said, tossing it aside. "Worms."

So much for family rituals, I decided. From now on, count me out.

Y OU REALLY WANT to have dinner with my family?" I asked Peter when we went out that night.

"Sure," he said. "What time should I be there?"

Dinnertime on Sunday rolled around, and I started to get nervous. I told myself to chill—it didn't really matter if Peter and my family hit it off. But when he rang the doorbell and I saw him standing there—wearing khakis and a pullover sweater like some prep from Seagate Academy—I couldn't help hoping. I was crazy about him, and I wanted Mom and Rose and Laurel and Lily to like him, too.

The evening started off pretty well, despite the fact that Hal was there as usual. Mom had made steak and twice-baked potatoes—she didn't go to that much trouble for just anybody. It means she's psyched about meeting Peter, I thought. And Peter's manners were great. "It's nice to meet you, Mrs. Walker," he said politely, shaking Mom's hand. He turned to Hal. "And you must be Mr. Leverett."

Hal shook Peter's hand, but I could see him checking out Peter's long hair and double-pierced ear.

We all sat down at the dining room table. Peter was across from me and next to Mom. "So, Peter," Mom said while Hal passed around the steak. "Are you in Daisy's class at school?"

I tensed up. Mom didn't know that Peter had dropped out . . . somehow I'd forgotten to mention it. Oh, God, she's going to freak, I thought.

"I'm not in school currently," Peter answered, not in the least bit thrown by the question. "I decided to take some time off from academics and acquire some real-world experience."

"Oh," said Mom. "Then you haven't graduated from high school yet?"

"I can always get my GED," Peter said offhandedly.

"I hope so," Mom said. "It's hard to have a career nowadays without a *college* degree, and I speak from experience."

"I'm not worried," he replied. "If I decide there's really a point in going back, I will. Right now I just don't see it."

Hal opened his mouth, probably to make a speech about the importance of education for people who want to have fascinating careers as accountants. Luckily Lily spoke up first. "I can't eat this, Mom," she said, pushing her plate away.

"Why not?" asked Mom.

"Because it's animal flesh," Lily explained. "Kendall, Kimberly, Talia, and Lindsey and me are on this vegan diet. That's strict vegetarian—no dairy, no eggs, no animal products at all, not even honey. It's really cleansing."

"I see," said Mom.

Rose laughed. "This will last about three hours, I bet," she predicted.

Lily frowned. "It will not. I'm committed."

"To giving up cheeseburgers and pizza and ice cream and Mom's chicken pie and lobster and fried clams?" Rose asked. "Have you ever actually *tasted* tofu, Lily?"

"Pass the carrots, please," Lily said, ignoring Rose.

Lily had provided a momentary distraction, but it didn't last. Mom put down her fork and turned back to Peter. "Since you're not a student right now, are you working, then, Peter?" she asked.

"I was working at Dave's Fuel 'n' Fix," he answered.

I prayed Mom wouldn't notice the past tense, but she doesn't miss a trick. "Was?"

"It didn't really turn me on," he told her. "Not enough intellectual stimulation. I mean, physical labor's cool, but I'd like to balance the brain and the body, you know?"

"Are you looking for another job?" she asked.

Peter nudged my foot under the table and smiled at me. I happened to know he was just hanging out. "Yeah, I'm polishing up my résumé," he said.

I shot a desperate, please-change-the-subject glance at Rose.

"Did I tell you guys about the acting class I'm going to take next semester at the community college?" she asked brightly.

The rest of the meal went okay once Mom and Hal stopped grilling Peter. I only managed to eat a few bites, though. Not because I'm becoming a vegetarian like Lily but because my stomach had tied itself into an anxious knot. I know my mom really well, and even though she was smiling, I could tell she wasn't all that thrilled by Peter. I don't care what she thinks, I told myself. I don't care what any of them think! But if that was true, how come I felt like crying?

W HEN PETER WAS ready to go, I walked him out to the street. "I think that went okay," he said, putting his arms around me as we stood on the sidewalk near his car.

"Yeah," I lied.

"Your family's not bad. A little uptight, but I've seen worse. And your sisters are babes."

He tickled my waist a little, and I snuggled close for a kiss. "When will I meet *your* family?" I asked. "Your mom and aunt Trish?"

"No rush," Peter said. "I did this for you tonight, but in general I'm not into the meeting-the-family routine. I don't have anything to say to Mom and Aunt Trish, you know? Just because we share the same genetic material doesn't mean we click."

"Oh," I said. "Right." I've always thought family was really important, but maybe Peter had a point. Being related didn't necessarily mean you got along. "See you tomorrow?" I asked.

"Absolutely," he replied.

"Love you," I said. I caught my breath a little as the words left my lips. I hadn't said them to him before. Please let him say it back, I thought. Please let him feel the same way I do.

Peter smiled and then he kissed me again. "Love you, too, Sleeping Beauty."

S O, WHAT DID you think of Peter?" I asked Rose later after Peter had left and she and I were alone in our room, listening to music and doing homework. I was still flying from telling Peter I loved him.

Rose turned her desk chair to face me, flipping her long hair back over her shoulder. "You really want to know?"

Now I regretted asking the question, but it was already out there. "Sure."

"Well, he seems bright. And he's cute," Rose said. "But . . ."

"But what?"

"Don't take this the wrong way, okay?" she advised. "But he's not in school, he doesn't do sports or anything like that. He's not ambitious the way you are. Are you sure he's the right boy for you?"

"So what if he's not going to Harvard like Stephen?" I countered angrily. "Maybe if he'd had Stephen's advantages, he'd be on that track, but his life's been really hard."

"I didn't say he had to go to Harvard," Rose replied. "Look, you asked my opinion. I just think you haven't dated that much, and maybe you don't know what you're looking—"

"I love Peter and he loves me and that's all there is to it," I declared.

Rose's eyes widened. "Well, okay. If that's how it is, Daze, you know I just want you to be—"

I interrupted her again. "Maybe Peter's not perfect, but neither am I. And I'm not going to break up with him just because you and Mom and Hal don't approve of him. Unlike some people in this family, I believe in loyalty."

Rose frowned. "What's *that* supposed to mean?"

"Who was that guy on the phone before?"

"You mean Craig? He's in my economics class."

"That's not the first time he's called."

"And your point is?"

"You already have a boyfriend."

"Sure, but that doesn't mean I can't make new friends," Rose said.

"I just think people should be faithful to each other," I argued.

Rose looked at me for a moment and then glanced at the picture of Dad on my night table. "Are you talking about me or about Mom?" she asked quietly.

I shook my head, confused. I didn't know *who* I was talking about or what. I just knew that tonight my knee hurt like crazy, and the pain had spread through my whole body and settled in my heart. I just knew that for whatever reason, the only thing that made me feel better anymore was being with Peter.

Eight

"FINALLY WE GET to party with Peter!" Jamila said. It was Friday night, and Jamila had invited a bunch of people over to her house. We were in the basement, listening to music and playing silly games like Ping-Pong with five people on a side. "That is, if he ever shows up," she added.

"He'll show up," I promised. Kristin, Jamila, and I were lounging on beanbag chairs, within arm's reach of a giant bowl of Cheez Doodles. "He wanted to meet me here because he has a job interview at the video store at the mall tonight."

"That's cool," Kristin remarked.

"Yeah, I hope he gets it," I said. It had seemed a *little* weird lately with Peter not in school and not working, either. Not that I would ever criticize him—I wouldn't want to sound like somebody's parent. I respected the fact that he needed time to figure out what he wanted to do with his life. "First crack at the new releases, you know?"

Just then Jamila waved to someone coming down the stairs. "Speak of the devil," said Kristin.

"Hi!" I called.

Peter crossed the room to join us. He was wearing seriously baggy jeans and a ripped T-shirt. Nice outfit for a job interview, I couldn't help thinking. His long blond hair was pulled back in a ponytail, so when he leaned in to kiss me, I noticed his gothic-style crucifix earring and also a new gold stud in his left ear. "Hey, you got pierced again," I said.

"The interview stunk, so I went over to the Piercing Pavilion to say hi to Alison, and the next thing I knew, bang." Peter grinned. "She got me with the gun."

"Peter's friend Alison works at the Piercing Pavilion," I explained to Jamila and Kristin. "For that reason Lily thinks he's a god."

"So, the interview at the video store didn't go well?" Kristin asked.

"The guy was a total jerk," Peter answered. "Making this big deal about checking my references, you know?"

"They always do that," Jamila pointed out.

"Yeah, well, I wasn't about to give him Dave's number. What, so he could call the gas station and hear about stuff I didn't even do? I just told the guy, 'Later.'"

I slipped my arm around Peter and gave him a supportive squeeze. "Too bad the guy was a jerk," I said.

Kristin and Jamila exchanged a glance. "Yeah, too bad," Kristin said.

"I think it's Twister time," Jamila announced, getting to her feet. "Want to play?"

Peter cocked one eyebrow. "Twister? You mean, that lame 'left hand on red' game?"

"It's fun," Kristin said.

"I'll pass," Peter said.

Jamila nudged me. "What about you, Daisy?"

"Um, you know, my knee's bothering me a little. I'll just hang out with Peter."

We watched Jamila and Kristin round up Phil, Raj, and Molly. In a couple of minutes bodies were tangled up all over the place. Smiling, I looked at Peter. He was yawning. "So, where's the beer?" he asked.

I couldn't tell if he was kidding or not. "My friends don't drink. Want a soda?"

"We could be at a rave in Portland—Amy and Marcus were going," Peter told me.

"A rave?"

"A *real* party."

"If you're not having fun, we can leave," I said.

"Hey, no. This is cool." Peter hugged me. "Whatever."

We didn't stay much longer, though. Peter didn't feel like talking to my friends or playing Ping-Pong, and because of my knee we couldn't dance. We ended up back at his aunt's ranch house, which is about a mile from where I live, making out on the living room couch.

"You're sure this is okay?" I whispered, wriggling away from him slightly.

"Aunt Trish is out, and Mom's asleep," Peter assured me, locking his arms around my body and pulling me close again. "She takes a ton of meds plus sleeping pills. We'd have to bang cymbals next to her ears to wake her up."

We kissed again, and I started to get a little worried. Peter had more experience with sex than I did, and I knew he wanted us to sleep together, but I wasn't even close to being ready for that. I was relieved when he got up, saying, "Want a drink? I know where my aunt keeps the good stuff." Crossing the room, he opened a cabinet. "Bourbon, scotch, vodka. Name your poison."

I sat up, gingerly flexing my sore knee. "No, thanks."

He faced me, a bottle in his hand. "One of these days you should give it a try. Good things would happen."

I shrugged. "I just don't feel like I need it."

He put the bottle back in the cupboard. "Okay, we'll do it your way." Smiling, he came over and pinned me back on the couch. "Stone-cold sober."

We kissed pretty intensely, but it was hard for me to relax. I decided I'd better distract him before things got too steamy. "Thanks for going to Jamila's party with me," I said.

"No problem."

"Did you have fun?"

"It was okay."

Just okay? I thought. Couldn't he lie to make me feel better? My disappointment only lasted an instant, though. Of course Peter wouldn't lie—that was what I liked about him, that he didn't feel like he had to impress people. He was just himself, take it or leave it.

Peter was still holding me, and now his arms tightened. "Forget the party. All I wanted all night was to be alone with you. I love you so much, Daisy."

"I love you, too," I said as our lips met in a passionate kiss. And I did. Maybe Peter didn't get along so great with my friends or with my family. Did that matter? I don't get along all that well with my family these days, either, I thought. If I had to make a choice, Peter was it.

I T DID END up turning into a choice. I wanted to spend time with Peter, so that meant I didn't have time for a lot of other things. I kept my job at the hospital because I needed the money, but I stopped going to watch my friends play soccer, and I blew off chores and homework. When my first-quarter report card came, it was a shock. "Two C's and only one A-minus," I told Peter as we sat in the Ice Cream Shoppe one afternoon in early November, eating hot fudge sundaes. "I've never gotten a C in my life. Mom's going to kill me!"

"Grades are meaningless," Peter declared. "Just some screwed-up teacher's subjective evaluation. Why should you let other people's expectations rule your life?"

I nodded. "You're right. A report card's just a stupid piece of paper. I'm not even going to show it to Mom."

Peter's aunt was working, and his mom was at the doctor's in Portland, so we spent the rest of the afternoon at his house watching soaps. He has a whole lineup that he watches since he's not working. I tried to get him to switch to the public television station—an interesting documentary about Thomas Jefferson—but he thought it was boring.

When I got home, it was dinnertime. It had been ages since I'd helped cook or set the table or anything like that, and as I came into the kitchen Mom started to lecture me, but when she saw me, the words died on her lips. "Daisy, I wish you'd come home in time to—" Her mouth dropped open. "What did you *do* to your hair?"

"Oh, my God," exclaimed Rose, almost dropping the salad bowl she was holding. "It's worse than that time in eighth grade!"

Peter and I had been bored, so he'd given me a buzz cut with an electric razor. Then I'd dyed what was left of my blond hair jet black. "You are *so* conservative," I said to Rose, my tone disdainful.

Just then Lily entered the room. "Wow, look at Daisy," she said admiringly. "Man, are you *ugly.*"

Mom glanced at Lily. "That's not very nice," she said. "I guess if Daisy wants—wait a minute." Mom narrowed her eyes. "Lily. Your *ears!*"

Lily took a step backward, as if she thought Mom was going to rip the gold studs from her earlobes. "I went to the Piercing Pavilion," she said in a rush, "and Peter's friend Alison did it for free!"

Mom turned back to me. "Did you know Lily was getting her ears pierced?" she asked.

"I didn't have anything to do with it," I said, which was true. "But what's the big deal, anyway?"

"The big deal is that I told her she had to wait until she was thirteen," Mom snapped. "And I—"

The buzzer on the stove went off. Mom shook her head, exasperated. "The casserole's ready. We might as well eat while it's hot. But I'll talk to you after dinner, young lady," she told Lily.

When dinner was over, though, Lily escaped discipline. Mom was picking on me again. "I've seen everyone else's report card," she said. "Where's yours, Daisy?"

"I think I left it in my locker," I mumbled.

"You think?"

It was still hard for me to lie to her. "Well, maybe I have it," I admitted, and walked over to the foot of the stairs, where I'd tossed my backpack. I pulled out the crumpled report card. "Here," I said defiantly, handing it to Mom.

She scanned the grades and then looked up at me. I braced myself. "Daisy, I'm . . . ," she began.

"Mad?" My tone was belligerent. "Disappointed?"

"No, I'm . . . worried. Daisy, since you met Peter, you—"

"It doesn't have anything to do with Peter," I cut in. "Those are my grades, not his."

"I know." Mom's gaze took in my haircut and the midriff T-shirt and baggy black jeans I'd just bought at the mall. "But you've had such a great academic record until now. Grades are important. When you apply to colleges next year—"

"I'll worry about next year next year," I interrupted.

"I'd appreciate being allowed to finish my sentences," Mom said sternly.

"Sorry. Please go on," I said with elaborate politeness. "I'm listening."

She frowned. "This fresh attitude is another thing I'm not too happy about."

"Look, are we done with this conversation? Because maybe I should work on my homework, right, Mom?"

"We're not quite done," she said. "One more strike and you're out, Daisy. Grounded. Do I make myself clear?"

"You're *punishing* me because you don't like my *attitude?*" I asked in disbelief.

Mom stared back at me without blinking. "If you keep performing poorly at school and missing curfew, yes, I'll punish you."

I turned away and walked upstairs without responding.

Rose had gone to a night class at the community college, so I had the bedroom all to myself. Unbelievable. Absolutely unbelievable, I thought as I walked past the mirror on my way to pick up the phone to call Peter and tell him Mom had ragged on me about the report card.

Then I stopped, surprised by my own reflection. I looked wild with my short black hair and outrageous clothes. For a split second I wondered, Who is that girl?

I smiled grimly at myself. Mom thought Peter was a bad influence on me—so what if he was? "It's my choice," I whispered to my reflection. I'd always, always done the right thing my whole life, and who'd ever appreciated it? Not Mom.

Why shouldn't I do the *wrong* thing for once?

Y OU'RE DOING A terrific job," Jody told me a couple of nights later. "Do you like the work?"

She pulled up a chair to sit next to me at the reception desk. "Sure," I said. "Hospitals are interesting."

"I'm worried that you're getting bored," Jody said. "How would you like to take on some other responsibilities?"

"Like what?"

"We need someone to organize social activities for the kids on the ward, like our Thanksgiving dinner in a couple of weeks, and to help coordinate volunteers. It would mean working more closely with patients *and* with doctors and nurses."

"Oh. Um . . ." I thought about it. I kind of liked the reception desk; it kept me at a comfortable distance from what was actually going on in the hospital. Do I *want* to get closer? I wondered. "I'm not sure, Jody."

"Well, we can talk about it some more." She patted my arm, then stood up. "Hey, Ben," she said.

I turned. "Hey, Jody," Ben said. He came up and took the seat Jody had just vacated, pulling his chair right next to mine. Talk about close, I thought. More like in your face!

"Are you trying to look like me?" he joked, pointing to my cropped hair.

"Yeah, maybe I *should* just shave it all off."

For a second he didn't say anything. "Who are you mad at?" he asked finally.

I was taken aback. "What do you mean?"

"Cutting your hair."

"I'm not mad at anybody," I told him. "I just wanted a change."

Ben was wearing a bathrobe, and he had a blanket wrapped around him as well. He's so thin, he gets cold easily. Now he pulled the edge of the blanket up over his head like a hood. "I bet your mom loves it."

"As a matter of fact, she hates it," I said. "She hates everything about me lately." I told him about our most recent blowup. "I have to get my grades back up or else."

"Well, yeah, of course," Ben commented. "What's she supposed to say, 'It's okay with me if you slack off and throw away your future'?"

"It was just a report card," I protested.

"Right. Grades are meaningless." I cringed. He couldn't know that he was echoing Peter. Of course, the difference was that Ben was being sarcastic. "They just go on your permanent transcript, which goes to the colleges you apply to, who decide whether you get in or not, which determines the rest of your life, basically." He shrugged under the blanket "No biggie."

He stood up. "Where are you going?" I asked, wondering why it didn't tick me off when Ben lectured me.

"To my room to study. Ciao."

I watched Ben make his way slowly down the corridor. I

couldn't believe he was still trying to keep up with his classes. He'd missed so much school, I'd assumed he would have to repeat the year. Or would he? People could do almost anything when they want it badly enough, and Ben wanted it. I used to be the same way, I thought. Not anymore.

O N THANKSGIVING MORNING Mom had gotten up early to stuff the turkey. The bird was already in the oven and she was having a cup of coffee with Rose when I came into the kitchen. "Good morning," Rose called from the table as I poured a bowl of cereal.

"Morning," I replied sleepily.

"You and Peter were out late last night," Mom commented.

Oh no. Here it comes, I thought. "Hmmm," I mumbled.

"Past curfew," Mom went on. "We talked about this the other night, Daisy."

"We did," I agreed, pulling a jug of milk from the fridge.

"Look at me, Daisy," Mom requested.

I looked at her, one eyebrow lifted so she wouldn't think I was intimidated.

"It was just a few minutes last night, so I'll give you one more chance, but that's all," she warned.

"You just don't like Peter," I accused. "Why don't you admit it?"

"I'm simply talking about the rules of this house," she replied. "They apply to all of you equally, and if you want to be part of this family, you can start following them."

I looked at Rose, who was eating cantaloupe at the table. She just shrugged. "Whatever," I said, opting for one of Peter's favorite expressions.

AROUND NOON I was reading a magazine on my bed when Rose came to find me. "We're making the pies," she announced.

"So?"

"So, you always slice the apples while I make the crust," she reminded me.

"Laurel can slice the apples."

"Not as well as you. Come on."

"I'm comfortable here," I told her.

Rose put her hands on her hips. "It's *Thanksgiving*, Daze," she said. "Can't you snap out of it for once?"

"Look, I don't feel like it, okay?"

Rose looked like she was going to keep arguing. Then she shook her head. "Okay, have it your way," she grumbled as she stomped off. "See if I care."

For an instant I thought about running after Rose. Laurel would probably make a mess of the apples. Halfway off the bed, though, a twinge in my bad knee made me wince. Flopping back down, I picked up the magazine again. Who needed corny pie-baking rituals, anyway?

And here's something else I don't need, I thought an hour later as my family gathered around the dining room table. Hal, the master turkey carver. I couldn't believe I'd been naive enough to think we could have a meal without him.

"I don't think I'm hungry," I announced, staying on my feet while everyone else pulled out chairs and sat down.

"Don't you feel well?" Mom asked.

"No, I'm just not . . ." I stuck my hands in the pockets of my jeans. I hadn't bothered to put on a dress like my sisters. "I think I'll go over to Peter's."

Out of the corner of my eye I saw Hal frown. "Are they having Thanksgiving dinner over there?" Rose asked.

"No. His mom and aunt went to some relative's house. Peter's just hanging out." I headed for the door. "I'll see you later."

"This is a family occasion, Daisy," Hal spoke up. "I think you'd better—"

"Let her go," Mom said. "It's her choice."

I'd been ready to talk back to Hal, but the way Mom sounded more sad than mad made me feel like a jerk. I kept going, though, because I'd made up my mind to do it and because I really *wasn't* hungry. My sisters watched me, different expressions on each of their faces: Rose looked serious, Laurel looked puzzled, and Lily looked amazed and impressed that I hadn't gotten in more trouble. None of them understands, I thought as I grabbed a coat from the hall closet. The door to the apartment banged shut behind me. They just didn't get it.

For a minute I stood on the sidewalk, looking up and down Main Street. Because of the holiday Hawk Harbor was even deader than usual. The sun was out, but it was cold. It was starting to feel like winter.

Since it was only a mile, I decided to walk to Peter's. My

knee would be killing me by the time I got there, but maybe the exercise would be good for it—and Mom would be *really* ticked if I took the car without asking. Not that I care what she thinks, I reminded myself.

As I walked along, though, past stores and restaurants closed for Thanksgiving or for the season I started to feel more and more bummed. I tried to push away the thoughts and memories of past Thanksgivings with my family. With Dad. Peter is all I need, I told myself. I hoped it was true.

Nine

THE WEEK AFTER Thanksgiving, Coach Wheeler called me to his office. I hadn't talked to him in a month, and I felt self-conscious as I knocked on his door. He's going to laugh at my hair, I thought, suddenly wishing it was still long and blond.

He didn't laugh at my hair, although he gave me a pretty good look-over. "Sit down, Daisy."

I perched on the edge of the beat-up chair across from his desk, not getting comfortable because I didn't plan to stay long. "What's up?"

"We missed you at the tournament," he said.

The girls' soccer team had made it to the county play-offs. "How'd you do?" I asked.

"You should've seen the semifinal game against the Tigers. The girls played their hearts out. We lost in overtime, but it was close."

My eyes wandered over to the door. I really wanted to get out of there. Was he trying to make me feel guilty? "There's always next year," I mumbled.

Coach Wheeler leaned forward, his elbows on his desk. "Come to the sports banquet on Saturday night," he urged. "Your name is on the tournament plaque—I'll have a varsity certificate for you."

I looked at him, my expression bitter. I hated being reminded of the season I'd lost. "I didn't earn it."

"Sure, you did. You're still part of the team, Daisy."

I shrugged, looking away again. A minute passed. Then Coach Wheeler said, "So, what have you been up to lately?"

"Not much," I replied. "Just kind of hanging out."

"How's the knee coming along?"

"Okay. Um, Coach." I stood up. "If it's all right, I've got to run. Study hall's almost over, and I still need to finish my math."

"Right." He stood up, too. "I just wanted to check in with you since it's been a while. Stay in touch, Daiserooni."

Now, instead of feeling bitter, I suddenly felt sad. The silly nickname reminded me of so many great times, and his tone had remained affectionate and fatherly despite my foul attitude. I don't know why I'd never realized before that he cared about me.

I nodded, not meeting his eyes. "Sure."

He walked me to the door. For a second I thought he was going to hug me, but instead he just gave me this little good-bye salute. Which is just as well because if he'd put a hand on my shoulder or something, I might have started to cry.

I T MUST HAVE been national Check In with Daisy Day because right after the last bell, Kristin and Jamila ambushed me at my locker. "Hey, Daisy," said Jamila. "Can you believe it? We're free women—soccer's over for the year."

"How does it feel?" I asked.

"Great," answered Kristin. "Like getting out of prison."

Jamila laughed. "It wasn't *that* bad, but it's cool having afternoons off. We're thinking about catching a five o'clock movie at the mall. Want to come?"

"I don't know," I said.

"Oh, come on," Kristin urged. "We never see you anymore!"

She didn't sound critical, but I felt guilty, anyway. It must have shown on my face because Jamila jumped in quickly. "Hey, it's okay. We're your buds—we know how it is, a serious boyfriend and all that. We just miss you, Daze."

I looked at my friends, not sure how I was feeling, whether I missed them or not. "A movie would be fun, but I'm pretty sure Peter's expecting me to stop by," I said. "Maybe some other time, okay?"

Kristin and Jamila exchanged a glance. Then Jamila smiled, but she looked sad. "Sure, Daze. Some other time."

They walked off, and I stood by my locker for another minute. I thought about calling after them, but I didn't. What would I say? They don't know me anymore, I realized. We've grown apart. Why? Was I out of the loop because I'd stopped playing sports with them? Was it because I could tell they weren't crazy about Peter? And Coach Wheeler, I thought. I used to really open up to him, but just now in his office even if I'd wanted to . . .

I slammed my locker shut. My old friends were worried about me. They thought I'd changed, and they wanted to know what was going on with me. And I can't tell them, I thought as I headed out to the line of school buses, because I don't know.

ON SATURDAY MORNING I stayed in bed until eleven. I never used to sleep in, but lately I'd been having a hard time getting started in the morning. This morning was worse than usual because I'd stayed up later than usual the night before. I'd gotten in past my curfew by a measly five minutes because Peter and I had to fix a flat tire on his car. Mom had been waiting up for me, and she'd had no mercy. I was officially grounded for the first time in my life: No going out with Peter or anyone for two whole weeks.

I was thinking about getting out of bed when I heard Rose and Laurel's voices out in the hall. "Should we see if Daisy wants to go?" Laurel asked Rose.

I sat up to listen. "Are you kidding?" Rose responded. "She never wants to do anything these days. It wouldn't fit her *image*, you know?"

Their voices receded. Where are they going? I wondered. A minute later someone rapped on my door. "Come in," I said, expecting one of my sisters.

The door swung open. Mom took a step into my room. "We're going to McCloskey's to cut down a tree," she announced, her manner stiff.

"Is that an invitation? I thought I was grounded," I replied.

"We can wait while you get dressed," Mom offered. "If you want to come."

"Don't bother. I might as well get used to being imprisoned."

Mom looked like she was about to say something else, but she didn't. She left, closing the door quietly behind her.

I sat on my bed for a few more minutes. When I heard the front door to the apartment slam, I limped into the hall—my knee is always stiff in the morning.

The apartment was quiet. "Anybody home?" I called. No one answered.

I went to the front window and leaned on the sill. Looking down at the street, I could see my family piling into the car. Hal was there, too. Before he got in the passenger seat—Mom was driving—he tossed a length of rope and a handsaw in the trunk.

Watching them, I had a pang for the old days. Cutting down a Christmas tree is a family tradition. When we lived on Lighthouse Road, we'd always picked one from our own woods. We'd do it at the beginning of December so we could enjoy it all month long.

The car drove off, and I turned away from the window. I was alone.

THAT AFTERNOON I had to answer phones at the hospital from two until six. Ben showed up before I'd even taken off my coat. "Hi," I said, sticking my book bag under the reception desk. "I thought you'd be at home by now."

"They're keeping me another week," he replied. "I'm on this new protocol, and they want to do some more radiation treatments. What's new?"

I dropped into my chair and glanced at the list of which doctors were on call. "I'm grounded for missing curfew. I can go to school and come here, but no parties or dates for two weeks. Can you believe it?"

"Uh . . . yeah. Your mom said she'd ground you, didn't she?" Ben reminded me. "You've got to respect her for sticking to her guns."

I hadn't looked at it that way, not that looking at it that way helped much. "I still think it's unfair," I said. "Has *your* mom ever grounded you?"

Ben laughed. "Are you kidding? I have *cancer*. She lets me do whatever I want."

I laughed, too. "That makes sense."

"I could get away with murder if I wanted to. But I don't want to waste my time testing limits."

"I'm not testing any limits," I said. "I'm just trying to live my life. And now I have no life."

"Well, here's a project for you," he said. "Help with the holiday party on the kids' ward. I'm going to be Santa."

I had to laugh. Ben weighs about a hundred pounds. "You?"

He grinned. "So I'll need major padding. Will you?"

"What?"

"Help."

I pointed to my spiky black hair. "I don't know. I'd make a pretty scary elf."

"None of us is winning any beauty contests these days," Ben reminded me.

I shook my head. "It wouldn't be my thing. Why are *you* doing it, anyway?"

"You mean, why put on a stupid Santa suit and act like there's a reason to be jolly when we're all sick and some of us will probably die?"

"That's not what I meant," I protested softly, although it was, sort of.

Ben gets tired really easily. Now he pulled up a chair and slumped forward with his arms folded on the desk, his chin propped on one hand. His eyes stayed on mine, though, and his gaze was intense. "Well, what's the alternative?" he asked. "I got dealt a rotten hand with this brain tumor. So what? I should just roll over and die? Just give up on myself . . . and those other kids?"

I stared at Ben. For some reason I thought about Peter. Hadn't he said something like that once, about getting a bad deal? I tried to picture my boyfriend dressing up as Santa Claus for a bunch of sick children but couldn't. He'd think it was so lame, I thought.

"Maybe you're right," Ben said, and he looked like he was about to cry.

"No," I said quietly. I put out my hand and touched his. "No, Ben, I'm not right. *You* are."

* * *

PETER PICKED ME up in his aunt's car at eight. Mom had given me a night off from being grounded to go to the sports banquet. Marcus and Amy were already in the backseat. "Paco told us you're blowing off some sports banquet," Amy remarked as I climbed into the car. "Smart."

Jamila and Kristin had both tried to talk me into going, but at the last minute I'd decided to go out with Peter instead. "I didn't even finish the season," I said, buckling my seat belt.

"Just a bunch of dumb jocks, anyway," Marcus commented. "Talk about boring, right?"

Those "dumb jocks" were some of my closest friends, or they had been, anyway, but I didn't say so. "Where are we going?" I asked Peter as he hit the gas.

He shot me a glance, smiling mischievously. "Are you in the mood for some fun?"

"Sure," I said. Marcus and Amy both laughed. "I guess," I added, wondering what the joke was.

Marcus and Amy laughed again, and so did Peter. Then Peter cranked the radio, thumping out the beat on the steering wheel with his hands and rocking in his seat as he drove. "Where are we going?" I asked again.

"You'll see," he said, grinning at Marcus and Amy in the rearview mirror.

Five minutes later he pulled into the parking lot of the Liquor Locker on the Old Boston Post Road. I turned to Peter. "They won't sell to us," I said.

"Just watch a couple of experts at work," Peter advised.

He and Marcus got out of the car and strode into the liquor store. Amy crawled into the driver's seat. "They are so cool," she said.

We watched the guys through the store window. Peter had wandered out of sight. Marcus was at the cash register, talking to the clerk. Marcus must have cracked a joke. The clerk laughed. Then Marcus pointed, and the clerk turned to look at the shelf behind him.

That's when Peter reappeared . . . walking straight toward the door with a case of beer tucked under his arm, as calm as if he did this sort of thing every day of his life.

Amy started the engine, and Peter jumped into the backseat. When Marcus had hopped in, too, Amy peeled out of the parking lot. The three of them were laughing so hard, I thought Amy was going to drive off the road. For a minute I was too shocked to speak. Then Amy said, "Where do you want to party, Paco?"

"You need to take me home," I blurted suddenly.

Peter leaned forward, his hands gripping my shoulders. "But the party's just getting started."

"I feel sick," I said, and it was true. "I think I'm going to throw up or something."

"You'll feel better after a beer or two," Peter promised, massaging my shoulders.

"I don't think so," I said.

"Give it a try."

"Could you just take me home, please?"

Amy looked at Peter for guidance. He nodded.

When we got to my building, Peter walked me to the door. "You're sure you don't want to go out?" he asked.

I shook my head. "I probably just need a good night's sleep." I thought about leaving it at that, but I would have hated myself for being such a wimp. Underage drinking was one thing; petty theft was another. "Peter, did you have to do that? Steal the beer?"

He laughed. "It's just a case of cheap stuff. It won't hurt their profit margins."

Suddenly I recalled the gas station theft. Had that been Peter after all? "Maybe not, but if everybody took whatever they felt like—"

Peter struck his forehead with the palm of his hand, speaking to the sky. "I'm trying to impress the girl, and she reads me the riot act!"

I stared at him. This baffled me more than anything else that had happened tonight. Didn't Peter know me at all? "You thought that would *impress* me?"

"I thought we could have a good time, that's all," he said. He kissed me on the lips. "I'll talk to you tomorrow."

I kissed him back and then ducked into the building. In our apartment I went straight to my room so no one could ask me any questions. For a long time I lay on my bed in the dark, too wired to close my eyes. I thought about Peter and the liquor store, Jamila and Kristin at the sports banquet, my knee injury, Ben Compton's cancer, Mom and Hal, Dad. Nothing seemed to fit anymore or to make sense. I was mad at Peter for stealing the beer . . . or was I mad at myself? Am

I just too uptight? I wondered. So what if Peter wanted to get trashed with his friends?

That wasn't all there was to it, though, and I knew it. It wasn't about having fun—it was about right and wrong. Was it possible that Peter genuinely didn't know the difference?

Since I loved him, should I try to teach him? Would he even let me?

It was hours later when I finally fell asleep.

Ten

MERRY CHRISTMAS, DAISY!" Lily yelled into the bedroom. I glanced at the clock on my night table and then rolled over, burying my face in my pillow. My family had gone to Christmas Eve services at church the night before, and I'd gone out with Peter. I wasn't grounded anymore, but Mom was still breathing down my neck and being totally judgmental about everything I did. I had a new, ridiculously early curfew that Peter and I had gotten around by coming back to my house and watching DVDs on the family room couch until three in the morning.

Now it was Laurel's turn to shout. "Get out of bed, Daze, or we're going to start opening presents without you!"

"I'm coming, I'm coming," I mumbled.

I put a sweatshirt on over my pajamas and stuck my feet in some slippers. Shuffling downstairs, I joined everybody

around the tree. Mom was sipping coffee; Rose was loading
film in her camera; Lily and Laurel were on hands and knees,
checking out the packages under the tree. "Wow, here's a big
one for you, Daze," Lily announced.

"Yeah?" I said, surprised. I hadn't expected much—I
hadn't been too "good" lately.

"Can we start opening, Mom?" Laurel asked eagerly.

Mom gave Laurel the green light, and the wrapping paper
began to fly. Christmas has gotten simpler in our family
since Dad died. To save money, there are a lot of homemade
presents, and it's a tradition to give each other favors, like
making your sister's bed for a week—stuff like that. The holiday still means a lot, though, and as I saw Lily and Laurel's
bright eyes and smiles as they opened their presents, I felt
guilty that I hadn't put more thought into my gifts. I'd tried
to get Peter to go Christmas shopping at the mall with me,
but he refused and went on some tirade about "commercial-
ism," so I'd just bought a few bottles of bubble bath at the
drugstore in town. "Yum, this smells good," said Rose when
she opened her bubble bath.

"Big deal, huh?" I mumbled.

"I like it," she assured me. "I can't wait to take a bath
tonight."

"You'll smell pretty for Stephen," Lily said.

Rose frowned. "For what it's worth—he's going back to
school the day after tomorrow."

"Isn't he on vacation?" Laurel asked.

"Yes, but he says he has some independent study project

he's working on." Rose bit her lip. "I can't help thinking there must be some other reason. . . . Anyway." She forced a smile. "Who's next?"

"Speaking of smelling pretty," said Mom, "whose perfume is in the air?"

Laurel, sitting next to Mom, blushed slightly. "It's me," she admitted. "'Windswept.' Nathan gave it to me for Christmas."

"How *romantic*," teased Rose.

Laurel rolled her eyes. "Yeah."

At that moment the doorbell rang. Lily ran to get it. When she came back into the living room, Laurel's friend Jack Harrison was with her, wearing a blue blazer and tie under his parka. "Merry Christmas," he greeted us.

Laurel's face was now as red as Santa's suit. "What are *you* doing here?" she asked, none too graciously.

"We're on our way down to Boston for Christmas dinner with my cousins," he explained, "and my parents had something for you." He handed Mom a basket of fruit tied with a big green velvet bow.

Mom kissed Jack on the cheek. "Take this down to them," she said, giving him a tin of homemade Christmas cookies, "and tell them we'll see them at the New Year's Eve party."

Mr. and Mrs. Harrison were parked on the street below, but Jack didn't seem in a huge hurry to leave. "Are you and Nathan coming to the party?" he asked Laurel politely.

Jack's parents give a big New Year's Eve party every year, and they invite everybody—grown-ups and kids. "I don't know," Laurel said.

Jack put a hand to his tie. "Tammy gave me this," he reported. "Her mom helped her pick it out."

Laurel eyed the tie with distaste. "Great."

"Well, have a fun day," Jack said.

"Come by again soon, Jack," Mom told him.

When Jack was gone, Lily declared, "Well, it's obvious he's still into you, although who knows why."

"Let's get back to presents," said Rose. She handed me the large package Lily had noticed before.

I read the tag. "It's from all of you," I said. "What is it?"

"Open it and find out," Laurel suggested.

I tore off the paper. Inside was a box. "Richardson's Sports," I said. "A softball glove!"

"I bumped into Larry Wheeler in town last week," Rose explained, "and we were talking about spring and how you'd probably be ready to play, and I thought—"

"No, it was my idea," Lily cut in. "Your old one is so beat up, and I talked to the guy at the store and he said this was the best glove they carry and—"

Laurel cut to the chase. "Do you like it?"

I stared down at the new glove. I hadn't done anything athletic in months. It was so hard to imagine running and throwing and sliding again. "I don't know if I'll play softball in the spring, but . . . yeah, sure. It's a great glove. Thanks."

Rose said, "You could always trade it for something else like . . ."

"A tennis racket," said Lily.

"Golf clubs!" said Laurel.

Everyone laughed. I cracked a smile, too, despite myself. "Right, and which package has the country club membership?" I joked.

I THOUGHT ABOUT blowing off Christmas dinner the way I did Thanksgiving—Peter had been talking about going to the movies—but since Hal was skiing in Colorado with Kevin and Connor, I decided to stick around.

After the meal I even volunteered to wash the dishes. When the kitchen was clean, I headed upstairs to call Peter.

In our room Rose had just hung up the phone, and she looked like she was about to cry. "Stephen?" I guessed.

"There's got to be another girl," Rose said. "Why else would he be in such a hurry to get back to Harvard? 'Independent study project'—yeah, right!"

"Stephen wouldn't cheat on you."

Rose was chewing on a fingernail. "I hope not. I mean, he'd tell me if he wanted to go out with someone else, wouldn't he? Of course he would. We've always been completely honest with each other." She brightened. "I could just ask him, right? If I tell him what's on my mind, maybe he'll tell me what's on his."

"In the meantime can I use the phone?" I asked.

"First look at this." Rose opened a big photo album that was lying on her bed. "I dug this out of the closet downstairs—I'm going to show Mom. Look at this picture of your very first Christmas, Daisy!"

In the photograph I was sitting on Mom's lap—she looked

so young—wearing a red-and-white-striped stretchy suit. I was as bald as an egg. "Look at my chubby cheeks," I said, laughing.

Rose flipped ahead in the album. "Look at us here. Matching velvet dresses."

"I hated those dresses. And the lace tights. Ugh!"

"This is more like it." Rose pointed to another picture of me. I was about eight, standing in front of the Christmas tree with a basketball tucked under one arm and a soccer ball under the other one.

She closed the album. The trip down memory lane seemed to be over, so I reached for the telephone. Before I could dial Peter's number, though, Rose said quietly, "You've changed so much, Daisy. Since you started dating Peter. You used to be so . . ."

"Wholesome?" I supplied sarcastically.

"That's not necessarily a bad thing, you know."

"Maybe I've just discovered that there's more to life than soccer," I told her.

"That's fine, but when you're with Peter, you—"

"Get off his case," I said. "It's not like you're such a relationship guru, anyway, Rose. You just said it yourself—things aren't so hot between you and Stephen these days."

"Yeah, okay, my relationship with Stephen isn't perfect," she admitted. "But my standards are really high. Being with Stephen has made me a better person because he respects me and expects a lot from me."

"Spare me the sermon," I said, but on some level Rose's

words hit home. I couldn't pretend that Peter brought out the best in me. I thought about the stolen case of beer. Had loving me changed *him* for the better?

"Okay, sorry," Rose said. "I shouldn't preach. I mean, I've dated some not so great guys. Remember Parker Kemp?" She laughed, then got serious again. "I thought I was in love with him, but he made me feel about two feet tall."

"My self-esteem is fine," I said.

"Is it?"

I shrugged. "Well, what if it isn't?"

Rose was looking at the photo album again. "Our first Christmas after Dad died," she said softly.

I didn't want to look at the picture. "Put that away," I told her.

"That was a hard time for me," Rose recalled. "All the adjustments. But you were always so . . . together. Happy Daisy. Responsible, unselfish, perfect."

"I was never perfect," I told her.

"Yeah, well, you *acted* like you were."

"Because you guys expected me to be that way."

Rose tilted her head thoughtfully. "Maybe. But we only *expected* it because you already *were*. Perfect," she added. "But you're showing us, huh?"

"I'm not trying to prove anything," I said.

"Good." Rose shut the photo album. "Okay, I'll get out of your hair. Make your phone call."

As Rose left the room I could hear Christmas music downstairs. Then the door closed, and it was quiet.

I started to call Peter but put the phone back down before I'd finished dialing. Rose was right about something. In the past few months, since I'd turned sixteen, I *had* made a 180-degree turn. Now I stared out the window at the winter dusk. I've stopped being perfect, I thought, but has that made me happy?

Eleven

THE SECOND HALF of my junior year started after New Year's. It was weird not having much to do. For the first time since I'd entered high school, I hadn't made honor society, and I wasn't playing basketball. People had stopped asking me to join clubs and be on committees.

Coach Wheeler hadn't given up on me, though. One Wednesday he called me to his office again, but I never got around to stopping by. I was on my way out the door after school when he came running after me. "Got a minute, Daisy?" he asked.

I shrugged. "Sure."

"What do you think about going to Patsy's with me? I skipped lunch today."

I shrugged again. "Yeah, okay."

We drove into town in Coach Wheeler's red Honda Civic.

At the diner we picked a booth by a sunny window and both ordered clam chowder. "How's the knee?" Coach Wheeler asked me as he dumped a packet of oyster crackers in his soup.

"Still a little stiff," I answered.

"So, I was thinking about spring," he said. "If you start a conditioning regimen now, you'll be in shape for softball, and it's going to be a fun season—we're planning a trip to Florida during spring vacation. I have a friend who's a physical therapist—a trainer at the state university gym—and he'd work with you for free. Then maybe a couple of slow, easy jogs a week or the Exercycle in the school weight room. How does that sound?"

I took a sip of my soda, not sure how to answer. I'd pulled so far away from that world. Did I want to go back? "It sounds like a lot of work," I said at last.

"Absolutely," he conceded. "You're starting over, basically. But you'll probably be voted cocaptain this year. The team needs you. And I think you need the team."

"Believe it or not, I've been doing okay without sports," I said dryly.

Coach Wheeler looked at me. "Have you?"

Dropping my eyes, I fidgeted with my spoon. Then I opened a packet of crackers and started crumbling them. "I'll think about it," I said after a minute, still not meeting his gaze. "About the conditioning thing."

He nodded. "Good enough. You know, I don't mean to hound you, Walker, but I miss you. You never come to see me anymore. How's stuff at home?"

"Okay," I said.

"Your mom's business is good?"

"Yeah, she's really busy. It's cool—she has to turn down jobs sometimes now, she has so much stuff on the calendar. But the thing that really bugs me—" I stopped abruptly.

"What?" he prompted.

I hadn't intended to blab about my personal life, but since I'd started, I decided to finish. "It's Mom's boyfriend. Hal. They're really getting serious, and he's *always* at our house, and it drives me crazy because it's like he thinks he's already our stepfather or something. You know, helping us with our homework, telling us what to do."

"You used to let *me* boss you around and give you advice," Coach Wheeler said.

"Yeah, but you're not dating my mom," I pointed out.

He didn't reply, but he gave me this look he has—in fact, on the soccer team we always called it The Look, as in, "I'm getting The Look." It's this coach thing, and it kind of means, "What do *you* think you should do?" as in, figure it out yourself.

So I thought about it, and it started to seem pretty obvious. I'd liked Hal before he started dating my mom. And now I hated his guts because I didn't want him to marry my mother and become my stepfather. I didn't want *anyone* to be my stepfather.

And I was mad at my mom for the same reason.

Coach Wheeler had polished off his chowder. "How's that boyfriend of yours?" he asked as he took a couple of bucks out of his wallet to pay the check.

It had been kind of a relief to talk about what was going on with me, and I thought about telling Coach the truth about Peter, too—that things weren't so hot in some ways. What would I say, though? I wondered. I don't even know where to begin.

"My boyfriend's great," I answered.

AT THE HOSPITAL on Saturday, I looked for Ben first thing. When I found out he was with his doctor and couldn't see me, I was surprised at how disappointed I felt. I'd been counting on him to cheer me up. Isn't it crazy that the most optimistic person in my life right now is a fifteen-year-old kid with a brain tumor? I thought.

I answered the phones for an hour and in between calls sorted mail for the doctors. Then Jody trotted over. "I need a favor from you," she said. "Melody, our candy striper, called in sick. I'm going to have the nurses take turns picking up the phone, and I want you to take over for Melody."

She pulled me to my feet before I could answer. Not that there was a question involved—she was giving orders. "What does Melody do?"

Jody smiled. "She assists me. She delivers meals, changes sheets, reads books, you name it. Ready?"

"Sure," I said.

As we passed the supply closet Jody tossed me a pink smock. I made a face. "Pink?" I said distastefully.

She laughed. "What were you hoping for, a Red Sox jersey?"

She gave me a list of tasks and basically threw me into the deep end. I put clean sheets on the beds in rooms 303 and 310. I brought a pitcher of fresh water to the boy in room 317 and read two chapters of *The Hobbit* to the girl in room 301. I played cards with a couple of kids in the patients' lounge and then had to run down the hall to help one of the nurses calm a crying child. "I hate getting my temperature taken, too," I commiserated with the little boy. "And that medicine really does look yucky. Let's pretend it's a chocolate milkshake. No, make that a superdouble chocolate fudge M&M's whipped cream vanilla strawberry baseball football basketball milkshake."

The kid took his medicine and actually smiled. Becky, the nurse, shook her head. "Want to deliver the rest of the meds for me?" she joked.

I rejoined Jody at the nurses' station. "There you are," she said. "Dr. Dimarco's in room three-eleven. Would you take these charts to her?"

Jody handed me a clipboard. I carried it down the hall to room 311. Dr. Dimarco was inside, examining a girl who looked about Lily's age.

"Is it tender here?" she asked, gently palpating the girl's abdomen. "Or here?"

"Ouch," the girl said.

I handed the clipboard to Dr. Dimarco, watching her make some notes. Despite the white lab coat and stethoscope, she looked too young to be a doctor—she had a long blond ponytail and freckles and she was wearing high-tops.

"We're going to run some more tests," Dr. Dimarco told

the girl in the bed. "It might be your appendix. Let's bring your folks in here and talk to them, too." She turned to me. "You're Daisy?" I nodded. "Would you run to the family lounge and bring Mr. and Mrs. Seaver in here?"

I escorted the Seavers to their daughter's room, and then Jody nabbed me. "Lunchtime." She pointed to a cart. "All the trays have cards on them saying where they go. Can you manage?"

"No problem," I assured her.

I delivered the meals to the entire ward, taking a minute to chat with each kid. I'm good at this, I realized as I plumped pillows and poured juice. "Your head really hurts, huh?" I said to a ten-year-old boy. "I'll tell the nurse, and we'll get you something to take care of that." There was a note in my voice that I hadn't heard for a while: energetic, efficient, enthusiastic. I'd forgotten how much I liked feeling busy and useful.

Pushing the empty cart toward the elevator, I bumped into Dr. Dimarco. "Are you premed, Daisy?" she asked.

"I'm still in high school," I told her, kind of flattered that she'd mistaken me for a college student.

"Thinking about going into medicine?"

Having seen Dr. Dimarco with her freckles and sneakers, it was easier than I would have thought to picture myself in a white coat with a stethoscope. And what better work could there be than making sick people well again? "Yes," I said. "I am."

H ow do i look?" Rose asked me the following Friday. "I borrowed the dress from Rox. How about perfume—should I borrow Laurel's Windswept?"

We were in our bedroom, and Rose was turning around in front of the mirror, tugging on the hem of the black dress and fluffing her hair like some crazed beauty pageant contestant. "Let me guess," I said. "Stephen's coming home."

"I haven't seen him since Christmas." Rose put on some lipstick and smiled at her reflection so she could see if she'd gotten any on her teeth. "This dress had better light some sparks."

The dress was short and close fitting with a scooped-out neckline. Rose has a great figure, and with her long blond hair cascading over her shoulders she looked like a cover girl. "If it were any hotter, you'd catch on fire," I said.

Rose smiled again, this time for real. "Good, because I—"

Just then the phone rang. Rose grabbed it. "Hello?" she asked. "Oh, Stephen. It's you!"

I flopped down on my bed, thinking I'd take a little nap before I went out with Peter. I assumed Rose would just confirm her plans with Stephen and hang up. Instead she sat down on the edge of her bed. "You're not coming?" I heard her say.

For a couple of minutes it was quiet. Then Rose said, her voice trembling a little, "There's someone else, isn't there?"

I sat up. Rose had her back to me, and as she listened to Stephen she hunched her shoulders forward in a self-protective way. She was whispering, but I could still hear. "I know the long-distance thing is hard, Stephen, but . . . well, what am I supposed to feel? . . . I guess if you want to try it that way, it *might* end up making our relationship stronger. . . ."

I fiddled around at my desk. Finally Rose hung up the

phone. I turned around. She looked at me, tears brimming in her eyes. "He broke up with me, Daze." She snapped her fingers. "After two whole years, just like that!"

"What happened?"

"He started off by canceling the weekend. He's still in Cambridge, and something came up at the last minute, yada yada yada. So then I just came right out and asked him if there was another girl. And he said . . . he said . . ." She sniffled loudly. "There *is* someone. Hayley. Can you believe it? Hayley! I even met her while I was visiting! I should have known. . . ."

Rose started to cry in earnest. I'd never seen her so upset . . . not since Dad died, at least.

"He swore nothing had happened between them yet," Rose went on. "He says he wouldn't cheat on me. But he wants to ask her out. He wants us to 'see other people.' Of course, that's just another way of saying it's over."

Rose covered her face with her hands, her shoulders shaking. I felt helpless. What should I do? I wondered. It really was a shock. Rose and Stephen had been together for ages—I always figured they'd get married someday.

Sitting down next to her on the bed, I patted her back. "Maybe he just needs some space," I said.

"Maybe. I tried to be mature, you know? I said, 'Okay, let's try it this way for a while.' But what if . . ." Her voice dropped to an anguished whisper. "What if I never see him again? He's my best friend, Daze. What will I do without him?"

I didn't know the answer, so I just hugged her. It was

strange. My heart ached for my sister, but the ache also felt good. Rose needed me.

"It'll be okay," I told her, my chin on her hair. "It'll be okay."

I ENDED UP staying home on Friday night to keep Rose company so she wouldn't be too depressed. We made brownie sundaes with tons of whipped cream and watched videos until past midnight. Peter and I got together the next day instead. He picked me up around lunchtime. "Is the mall okay?" he asked as I buckled myself into the passenger seat.

"It's such a nice day," I replied, "and my knee's feeling a lot better. How about going for a walk or something? You know, just to be outside?"

"Too cold," Peter said. "Let's just go to the arcade."

"If that's what you want." Peter popped in a CD. As we drove along I twisted in my seat to take a good look at him. I knew his face so well now, and I still found him incredibly handsome. But *is he my best friend?* I thought, remembering what Rose had said the night before about Stephen. *Do Peter and I have a foundation like that?*

We bought tokens at the arcade, or rather I did—Peter doesn't have a lot of money, and I usually have some from my job, so I don't mind spotting him sometimes. We started to play this game called Annihilation. Video games are pretty antisocial—Peter doesn't like to be distracted, so we don't usually talk—but today I decided to break the rules. Best friends are supposed to share their feelings. "I saw my coach the other day," I told him. "You know, Larry Wheeler? He coaches softball, too. Anyway, he's after me to get back in shape, and I think I might do it. I mean, see this trainer he knows."

Peter shrugged one shoulder, his eyes glued to the screen. "Huh," he grunted.

I decided to take that as a display of interest. "Yeah," I went on. "Maybe it's something about spring. I feel like I want to try stuff. Like this job at the hospital. I might branch out from just answering phones. Being around all those doctors— maybe I'll be premed in college, you know? If I take AP biology next year, I could place out of freshman science."

Peter shot me a surprised glance. "You're not gonna get nerdy on me, are you?" he kidded.

"I used to be a good student," I reminded him.

"Until you found better things to do with your time," he said. "Think you'd even get into AP bio?"

That was a good question. I wasn't having the best year academically. "I don't know, but it won't hurt to try."

"Whatever," said Peter, turning his focus back on Annihilation.

I'd already lost my game, but he kept racking up the points. For a while I watched him play. His hands were so quick, and his eyes blazed with energy. What would happen if he ever put his energy into something productive? I wondered.

"So, we got this flyer in the mail the other day," I said conversationally. "From the continuing education program at the community college where Rose goes. They have all these cool-sounding courses for people who want to get their high school equivalency—computers, literature. . . ."

I paused. Peter shot up a few more bad guys before saying, "And?"

"And I thought about you. That's all," I said. "You have so much potential, like the way you're so good at chess. You could study math and—"

"You sound like my aunt." Peter flicked his wrist, then cursed and slammed a hand on the machine. "Lost the game."

"Sorry," I said, flinching a little.

"Hey." Peter turned to me and lifted a hand to touch my face. "I shouldn't have yelled. I didn't mean to hurt your feelings. It's just . . . me and school. I've told you how it is. It's not a good combination."

"These classes might be different, though," I said. "More informal. You could study whatever you wanted."

"Maybe I'll give it a try." He put his arms around me. "If it'll make you happy."

I nodded, even though I wasn't sure it *would* make me happy. He'd gone along with me but not necessarily for the right reason. "Should we play another game, or do you want to get something to eat?" Peter asked.

"I'm hungry," I answered.

We headed out to the food court. "Amy's having a party tonight," Peter said. "I'll pick you up at eight, all right?"

Suddenly I had a really odd feeling. It was like the walls of the mall were closing in on me. I didn't want to go to Amy's party. Everybody would be drinking and smoking and having the usual unofficial competition to see who could be the crudest and most sarcastic, and that didn't seem particularly entertaining anymore.

"Actually, I'm helping my mom at a party she's catering," I fibbed. "Passing appetizers and stuff."

"Too bad," Peter said.

Waiting for our order at the pizza place, I wondered why I'd made up that story. I don't feel like going out tonight, I decided. It doesn't mean I don't love Peter.

As we picked a table and sat down to eat, though, I knew I couldn't just brush aside those feelings. Peter was part of that scene. It was where he wanted to be, and for months now I'd been willing to follow him there. Now it was as if I'd come to the end of a road and found out it was a dead end. I was ready to turn around and head back. What I didn't know yet, though, was whether Peter would follow *me*.

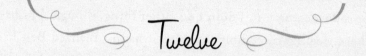

Twelve

I ALMOST CALLED Peter back that evening and told him I could go out after all, but I didn't. I didn't want to go out. I needed to talk—really talk to someone—but who?

Jamila? I considered, sitting at my desk with the phone in my hand. Kristin? I was so out of touch with them these days. They'd probably be shocked if I called up just to chat.

Instead I dialed a familiar number—the pediatric ward at the hospital. "Is this Maxine?" I asked. Maxine and I sometimes see each other when we're changing shifts at the reception desk. "It's Daisy."

"What's up?" she asked.

"Can you connect me to Ben Compton's room?"

"Ben is no longer with us," Maxine answered.

My heart stopped beating. No, I thought. Not Ben. He can't be dead. "Oh, my God," I whispered. "He was my friend."

"Oh, honey, I'm sorry. I should have phrased that differently—I didn't mean to give you a scare. He's gone home for a while. Do you have that number?"

I was so relieved, I almost slid off my chair. "Yes, I have it. Thanks, Maxine."

I hung up the phone, but I was still shaking a little. I didn't actually have Ben's home number. I could look it up, I thought, or call information. I didn't do either thing, though. I just sat there, feeling incredibly thankful. I hadn't realized Ben had come to mean so much to me, but for a few seconds there I'd stared into a frightening void. Everything had looked black. Now the world had color again, rich colors I hadn't noticed before: the pale coral paint of my bedroom walls, the aqua and lavender of the twilit sky out my window, the warm pink-gold hues of my own skin. I exhaled the breath I hadn't realized I'd been holding. Thank you, God, I thought.

I NEED DOUGHNUTS," Rose declared the next morning.
Mom had just left for church with Laurel and Lily; Rose and I had stayed home. "Like, now?" I asked. Wissinger's Bakery was right downstairs, but we were still in our pajamas.

"Chocolate glazed," she said.

I knew she was still bummed about what had happened with Stephen, so I decided to be a good sister. "Give me two minutes to throw on some clothes."

"You're an angel, Daze."

It's amazing we all haven't gained a hundred pounds since we moved into this apartment—Wissinger's always smells so good, and it's tempting when you're on your way home to just grab a giant M&M's cookie or a piece of carrot cake. Today I had to wait in line for a few minutes—Mr. Schenkel, our old neighbor, was buying doughnuts, and so were a few other people. When it was my turn, I said hi to the girl behind the counter. "How's it going, Gabby?"

Gabrielle's a classmate of mine at South Regional. "Busy," she replied. "Doughnuts?"

"A half dozen. Three chocolate glazed and three jelly."

Gabby stuck the doughnuts in a white bag. "It must have been a wild night, huh?"

I pulled a couple of dollars out of my coat pocket. "What?"

"Aren't you still going out with that Paco guy?"

"Yes," I told her, "but I didn't see him last night."

Gabby's eyes brightened. Her name fits—she's a gossip.

"So you don't know."

"I guess not," I said.

Gabby leaned on her elbows on top of the glass display case. "He and Marcus were picked up by the cops."

"You're kidding!" I was shocked. I hated hearing about this from someone like Gabby, but I had to find out what had happened. "What for?"

"Someone robbed the convenience store on the Old Boston Post Road. A couple of guys in ski masks."

My eyes widened. "And they picked up Peter and Marcus?"

"Just for questioning," said Gabby. "I guess they let them go. There wasn't enough evidence to arrest them or anything like that. I heard about it from Amy—she was here ten minutes ago, but she didn't know all the details."

"Wow," I said, a little bit dazed. "Peter would never do anything like that, but . . . I suppose he'll tell me what happened. Um, thanks. For the doughnuts."

"Sure. See you around," Gabby said.

Back upstairs Rose and I polished off five of the six doughnuts and two cups of coffee apiece, which I'd gotten totally addicted to in the past couple of months. I didn't tell Rose about my conversation with Gabby, obviously, because for all I knew, it was just a rumor, and the last thing I needed was for my family to have a worse opinion of Peter than they already had.

The story got out, though, and fast. Rose and I were still hanging out in the kitchen when Mom, Lily, and Laurel got home. "How was church?" Rose asked.

Mom didn't answer Rose's question. Instead she looked at me with a troubled expression. "I heard something disturbing at coffee hour after the service," she began.

"What?" asked Rose.

Right away I knew what Mom was going to say. "There was a robbery at Reiser's Store," she said, "and apparently Daisy's boyfriend was questioned about it."

"Questioned," I emphasized. "That's all."

"I'm upset about this," Mom continued.

"Why?" I asked, my tone confrontational. "Peter didn't have anything to do with it. They released him, didn't they?"

Mom was chewing her lip in this way she has when she's thinking really hard about something. "You're old enough to choose your own companions, Daisy. I can't forbid you to go out with Peter, but—"

"Don't even try, Mom," I cut in. I shoved away the plate with the last doughnut on it and jumped to my feet. "You have no right. And whatever happened to 'innocent until proven guilty'?"

"Daisy, I'd like to give Peter the benefit of the doubt, but according to Joe Devon's wife, Chrissy—Joe was the officer who questioned Peter and his friend—the boys were—"

"I can't believe it," I shouted. "This is what you talk about at church? How Christian of you!"

"Take it easy, Daisy," Rose advised.

"No, I won't take it easy," I said. "She's been out to get Peter from the beginning. I'm sick of your interfering and judging me, Mom. Stay out of my life, okay?"

"How dare you talk to me like that when I'm trying to help you?" Mom asked, her voice shaking.

"You call this *helping?*" I shook my head. "I wish I were eighteen instead of sixteen—I'd be out of here so fast."

Mom drew in a deep breath. "Go to your room, Daisy. Let's both take a break before we say more things we'll regret. We can talk later."

"There's nothing to talk about," I declared as I ran from the room. "Peter's innocent, and I'll prove it!"

J UST GO AHEAD and ask him, I counseled myself. He'll set the story straight, and then I can tell everyone to leave us alone.

It was Sunday afternoon, and Peter and I had met at the

mall to see a movie. We bought some popcorn and slid into a couple of seats in the second-to-last row. "Uh, Peter," I said, grabbing a handful of popcorn, "I saw Gabby St. James at the bakery this morning, and she told me that last night you and Marcus—"

"Man, those dumb cops," Peter broke in. "We just happened to be driving by Reiser's, but they kept us at the station for an hour. Like they needed some Saturday night entertainment and we were it."

"You mean you didn't—"

"In a small town the police have nothing better to do than harass you," Peter said. "Supposedly it was just fifty bucks, anyway. Big deal, you know?"

I looked at him, but the lights in the movie theater were dimming—it was coming attractions time—so I couldn't read his expression. Did you do it, though? I wondered, remembering how coolly he'd walked out of the liquor store with the case of stolen beer. I struggled with my feelings. Ask him, part of me urged. Let it drop, another inner voice said.

Just then Peter leaned close to me, showing me something he'd pulled out of his pocket. "I picked up a course catalog at the continuing ed place," he whispered. "After the movie you gotta tell me what to take."

At that moment the movie screen lit up with flashing, colorful images and sound boomed from the speakers. Peter took my hand, and I held on tight. I wanted so much to believe that he was a good person who'd gotten some bad breaks, that underneath his tough attitude he had a gentle heart. He'll take some classes, I thought hopefully. We'll study together. Our relationship will grow.

If I didn't ask about the robbery, I wouldn't find out. Maybe that was the way to go.

WHEN I GOT home, Mom was in the kitchen. She called after me as I headed for the stairs, but I didn't stop.

She followed me up to my room. She was wearing an apron, and her arms were white with flour. She's baking, I thought. Pie crusts. "Daisy, I'm sorry we had a fight," she said.

I shrugged.

"Let's make a date to sit down and—"

"Peter didn't rob Reiser's," I told her, turning away, "and that's all I have to say. Excuse me, I want to be by myself."

After about ten seconds I heard my door shut. I glanced over my shoulder. Mom was gone.

I stared at the closed door. I had a feeling things between me and my mother would never be the same again.

Thirteen

A WEEK PASSED, and then another. There was a short
article in the local paper about the convenience store
robbery, in which it said there were "no suspects." No suspects,
I thought on Saturday afternoon as I stuck the newspaper
in the recycling bin. That's as good a motto as any, I guess.

Mom was catering a brunch in Portland, and she wasn't
back yet, but my sisters were home. Rose was playing the piano
and talking on the cordless phone at the same time. Lily was
watching TV in the next room. Laurel had emptied the living
room bookshelves of about a thousand back issues of *National
Geographic* and was cutting them up with scissors. "Did Mom say
that was okay?" I asked Laurel.

"I checked with her," Laurel answered.

"What are you doing, anyway?" asked Rose, clicking off the
phone and wandering over.

"Making a collage," Laurel explained.

"For Nathan?" Rose's tone was teasing.

Laurel grimaced. "Definitely not. We broke up."

"You did?" Rose said. "How come?"

Laurel was wearing grubby overalls, and her tangled hair looked as if it hadn't been brushed in days. I didn't smell Windswept. "I just decided I don't care if everybody else is a couple—it's just not me."

"Good for you. There's nothing wrong with being single," Rose said with feeling.

"I thought you went out with that guy from your econ class last night," I said.

Rose shrugged. "Craig? Yeah, we had an okay time. But it's not going anywhere." For a second her face looked inexpressibly sad—I knew she was thinking about Stephen. "Which is okay because I think it's going to be cool not having a boyfriend for a while. Who needs the distraction, you know? This way I can study all the time and get my grade point up so I can transfer to a better college someday. I can work more hours at Cecilia's and save money for acting lessons. I won't have time for dates."

It sounded like a good argument, but she wasn't convincing— she turned away to wipe a tear from her eye. Before I could say anything, Lily bounced into the room. "Come watch this cool TV show about haunted houses with me." The rest of us stared at her. "What are you looking at?" she asked.

"You. What are you *wearing?*" Rose asked.

Lily looked down at her outfit, which consisted of a

Japanese kimono, metallic gold high heels, and about fifty bangle bracelets. "Nothing much."

"What happened to the uniform?" Laurel wondered.

"What uniform?" asked Lily.

"The Lindsey, Talia, Kendall, and Kimberly uniform."

"I'm not hanging around with those guys anymore, if that's what you mean," Lily informed us.

"Why not?" Rose asked.

"Because all they ever wanted to do was make lists of the boys they like and fill out surveys in *Seventeen* magazine about what's your favorite color of lipstick. They had no *imagination*," she concluded with an expressive roll of her eyes.

It's nice to see my sisters back to normal, I decided a few minutes later as I went up to my room. Well, Laurel and Lily, anyway. Rose was down about Stephen, but knowing her, she'd bounce back fast. She had a lot of self-confidence, and her life was full of friends and activities. That leaves me, I thought, walking over to the window and staring out at the gray winter sky. Wasn't I kind of wearing a uniform, too? The spiky dyed hair, the baggy black clothes. I'd done it to fit in with Peter and his crew. I'd never thought about the fact that they made such a point of not conforming that they were conformists in their own way.

I traded the window for the mirror over my dresser. I'm not the vain type, but now, looking at my reflection, I was almost overcome by a wave of nostalgia and regret. I missed my long blond hair and healthy glow. Even my eyes didn't look familiar anymore. The detached, cynical expression that I'd adopted since I'd started hanging out with Peter was like a mask.

I turned away from the mirror. This is me now, I told myself. Peter and I had a date that night, and for once I wasn't looking forward to it.

I WAS ON my way out the door—Peter doesn't come in, we always meet down on the street—when Mom got home. She was lugging a bunch of stuff from the party she'd catered, so I took one of the platters and a bag of dirty table linens to help her out. It was kind of awkward because I've been avoiding her as much as possible lately, but I couldn't just stand there and watch her struggle.

We dumped everything on the kitchen table, and Mom let out a big sigh. "What would I do without Sarah Cavanaugh?" she asked, kind of talking to herself. "I think I'd better ask her to be my permanent assistant." Just then Mom noticed my jacket and gloves. "You're going out?"

"Yeah."

"With Peter?"

"Yeah."

"I wish—," she began.

"I'm sorry you don't like Peter, Mom. But it just so happens that I do."

"I don't not like Peter," Mom protested.

"But you wish I wasn't going out with him," I said.

"I think you'd be happier with a different boyfriend," Mom admitted. "But it's your decision. Hal said that when Kevin and Connor were your age, they—"

Anger bubbled up in me. "Who cares about Hal?" I burst

out. "What does he have to do with anything? We were doing just fine without him. We don't need him."

For a minute Mom stared at me, her brows lifted and her eyes wide. Then she said quietly, "Maybe *you* don't need him, Daisy, but I do."

I stared back at her, not knowing how to respond. What could I say? You're a mother—you're not supposed to have needs. And if you fall in love with another man, what will that do to our memories of Dad?

Mom seemed to be waiting for something. "I'm going out," I managed to mutter as I walked fast to the door. "Don't wait up."

I hurried down the stairs as fast as my stiff knee would let me and out to the sidewalk. The February night was overcast, and I could see snowflakes beginning to fall in the circles of light cast by the streetlamps. Peter wasn't there yet, so I stood on the curb, bouncing up and down a little to keep warm while I waited for him.

When the car pulled up, I knew right away that something was weird. The headlights bobbled, as if Peter had hit a pothole or something. When he stopped, he hit the curb—I had to jump back. "Hey, watch it!" I yelled.

Peter leaned over to open the passenger side door. "Hi, Sleeping Beauty," he said, grinning up at me.

I started to climb in, then stopped. Glancing over the back of the seat, I saw a pile of empty beer bottles on the floor. "Have you been drinking?" I asked suspiciously.

Peter looked at me with innocent eyes. "Who, me?"

"Look, I'm not driving with you if—"

Peter grabbed my arm and pulled me into the car. "Come on, Daisy. Don't be a drag." He gave me a sloppy kiss that tasted disgustingly of alcohol. "Anyhow, I'm a better driver drunk than most people are sober."

"I still don't think—"

He stepped on the gas, and the car lurched away from the curb. I had no choice but to slam my door. "I'll be careful," he promised. "Have a beer. It'll put you in a better mood."

I buckled my seat belt. "No, thanks," I said stiffly.

Peter cranked some tunes as we headed out of town. "Is there a party?" I asked, thinking that I could bum a ride home with someone else, or if worse came to worst, call home and ask Rose to come get me.

"I thought it could just be us tonight," Peter answered, slipping his right arm around me. "Maybe we'll get past second base for once, huh?" He grinned. "Like that baseball metaphor, Miss Jock?"

All of a sudden the boy sitting next to me seemed like a stranger. I was almost scared to be alone with him. "Sure," I said, though I didn't mean it.

We were on the Old Boston Post Road. As we cruised by the convenience store that had been robbed a few weeks ago Peter laughed. "Ol' man Reiser bought himself a guard dog," he said. "Guess we scared him, huh?"

I turned in my seat to stare at him. "What?"

He shot me a wry glance. "It was just fifty bucks, Daze. And for a good cause. I gave twenty of it to my aunt for the rent."

I gripped my hands together to keep them from shaking. "It *was* you and Marcus?"

"I never pretended to be a saint," Peter said.

"But Peter, robbing someone—"

"I mean, the man charges a fortune for a quart of milk," Peter rationalized. "He drives a brand-new Dodge Dakota. He's not hurting."

I stared at Peter, trying as hard as I could to see his point of view. Maybe it was just a prank, I thought. No one got hurt, and Mr. Reiser doesn't really need the money. But it didn't work. What Peter had done wasn't cool; it was wrong. I couldn't laugh it off. "Peter, I think we should go someplace where we can talk. Let's go to Patsy's—I'll buy you some coffee."

"Not if you're going to lecture me," Peter said. "I get enough of that at home."

But he flipped a U-turn, heading back to town. Before we got to Patsy's, though, he pulled abruptly into the parking lot of a dark building—the community center. "Why are you stopping here?" I asked.

"I started my continuing ed class," he told me. "Astronomy. I thought it would be cool, looking at the stars. But the instructor slammed us with a quiz right off the bat, and she had the nerve to fail me. Can you believe it?"

"Did you talk to her about it?" I asked. "Maybe she'll let you take it over if you—"

"Forget that." Peter slammed his fist on the steering wheel and then swung open his door. "Continuing ed's a crock." Now he was out of the car, fumbling in the backseat for something. "Is that your window, Ms. Turner?" he shouted into the night. "Here, I've got something for you!"

Peter pulled back his arm and threw something. A second later I heard the sound of breaking glass. "Peter, stop!" I yelled. Ignoring me, he hurled another empty bottle at the community center's windows. More glass shattered, and an alarm went off in the building. I was crying now. "Peter, *please!*"

He just went for another beer bottle—he'd lost all control. I thought about grabbing his arm to keep him from throwing it, but I was afraid to touch him. He was acting so crazy. How did I know he wouldn't hurt me?

Another window shattered. Was he going to break every single one?

I didn't stick around to find out. Peter wasn't even looking at me—he didn't see me turn and run away from him and from the sound of breaking glass, away from the police siren in the distance. I ran as fast as I could. My lungs burned from the cold air, and my knee hurt because I hadn't used the muscles in so long, but it was a good hurt. For the first time in ages I was moving.

I ran all the way home.

Fourteen

WHEN THE SUN came up in the east the next morning, turning the ocean silver, I was sitting at my window in my desk chair, watching it. I was still in my clothes—I hadn't been able to sleep.

I tried to be quiet as I walked back across the room to my bed, but I tripped over a shoe. Rose rolled over in her bed, her down comforter rustling. "Is that you, Daze?" she mumbled sleepily.

I dropped down on my mattress. "Yeah."

Rose sat up. "Why are you up so early?"

"Never went to bed," I admitted.

She blinked. "You're kidding."

"No."

"How come?"

I hadn't planned to tell anyone about Peter breaking the

windows, especially not my family. Lily was the only one who'd ever really liked him, and she did only because of his pierced ear. Why make them think worse of him than they already did? But suddenly I was tired of being alone with what I was feeling. "Rose, it was awful," I began, my voice shaky. "He'd been drinking, and I didn't want to drive with him, but he . . ."

She listened to the whole story without interrupting. When I got to the part about the robbery at Reiser's Store, she bit her lip, but she still didn't say anything. When I was done spilling my guts, I just sat on the edge of my bed, my back hunched and my eyes on the floor. I felt completely drained and as empty as one of Peter's beer bottles.

I waited for Rose to say, "I told you so; he was never any good." Instead she got out of bed and came over and put her arms around me. "I'm sorry, Daze," she said softly. "I'm really sorry."

I didn't want to cry, but tears spilled from my eyes, anyway. "Why does it have to be like this?" I asked.

Rose sighed. "Loving someone can be *so* hard."

My head on my sister's shoulder, I nodded, more tears sliding down my face.

L ATER THAT MORNING the doorbell rang. I was doing sit-ups in the family room, watching TV. "Can you get that?" I shouted to whoever might happen to be in the apartment. A minute later the bell jingled again. Grumbling, I got to my feet and went to the door.

Peter was standing in the hall. His guitar was slung over

one shoulder, and he was holding a bunch of flowers. Daisies. "Can I come in?" he asked, shifting his weight awkwardly from one foot to the other.

I nodded, pulling the door wider. "Sure."

No one seemed to be around, so I led him into the kitchen. We sat down at the table, facing each other. I looked at Peter, waiting for him to speak. His eyes were a little bit bloodshot, and there was stubble on his chin. "Daisy, I'm sorry," he said finally.

I didn't say anything. "I don't know what came over me last night," he went on. "I just kind of lost it, I guess. I didn't mean to scare you. I swear."

I still didn't say anything. Peter shoved the bouquet across the table toward me. "It was just a couple of windows," he said, smiling crookedly.

"Peter, it's more than that," I said, choking a little. "You know it is."

He dropped his head. "Yeah, well . . . So, I wrote you another song. Listen."

He pushed his chair back so he could cradle the guitar on his lap. Then he bent his head, his hair falling forward, and picked out a sweet, sad tune. "There are words, too," he told me, "but I'm still working on them. How about . . ." He began to sing, his voice low and raspy. "Sleeping Beauty in the night, breaks away, takes my light." He looked up at me, flashing the crooked smile again. "Crummy, huh?"

I'm really not the crying type—I'm not emotional and dramatic like Rose. But something about the song Peter had written for me, or maybe it was his smile or the way he held the guitar in a kind of embrace, made my eyes brim with tears. "Peter, I—"

"Say it's okay, okay?" he said. Then he laughed at himself. "Say it's okay, okay," he repeated. "Now, that could be in a song."

"Peter . . . it's not."

"It's not what?"

"Okay," I said. "It's not."

A shadow flickered across his thin, handsome face. "What are you saying? You don't mean it's over just because I got a little wild last night . . . do you?"

"I've been thinking about it for a while," I confessed. "About us. And I just think . . ."

I couldn't finish the sentence. In my heart I knew it was time for us to go our separate ways. I knew it was for the best. But I also knew it was going to hurt a hundred times more than tearing the ligaments in my knee.

"We could still be cool together," Peter said when I stayed quiet. "I love you, Daisy."

His voice was rough—I'd never heard him speak with so much emotion. I believed he was telling the truth. He did love me, in his own way. When I looked in his eyes, I felt the same attraction that had been there the very first day we met. But it's still not right, I thought.

"I'm sorry, Peter," I whispered.

"So, that's it?" he said in disbelief. "I should just leave?"

Not looking at him, I nodded.

I heard his chair scrape along the floor. His guitar bumped the table, the strings reverberating with a discordant sound. There were footsteps, and a door closing, and then nothing.

I slumped in my chair, my head dropping onto my folded arms, and began to cry. When I felt a hand on my hair a minute later, I jumped.

"Are you all right?" Rose asked.

I shook my head, sniffling. "No."

She knelt on the kitchen floor so she could give me a hug. "Believe it or not, the world will keep turning," she said. "You'll get over this."

I knew she was speaking from experience, but it didn't help. The first boy I'd ever really loved had just walked out of my life . . . because I'd told him to.

M OM HAD GONE to the mall with Lily and Laurel, so for a while longer the apartment was quiet, which was a plus since I didn't feel like explaining why I was bawling my eyes out. By the time they got home, I'd stopped crying. Mom went right back out again with Hal, and Laurel headed over to Jack's—he'd broken up with Tammy, and they were friends again. I hid out in front of the TV. I never used to watch much before I met Peter—I used to be too busy—but he was a dedicated channel surfer, and now I clicked the remote, sniffling when I came across a commercial he and I had laughed over together or a music video he'd liked.

When the doorbell rang, I went to get it, bumping into Lily at the door. "Rose said you and Peter broke up," Lily whispered. "Do you think that's him, coming back to make up with you?"

I was wondering the same thing. "Oh, Lily, I hope not." But when I opened the door, it wasn't Peter. "Stephen!" Lily and I exclaimed together.

Rose had come downstairs just in time to hear us. She appeared in the front hall, her face pale and her eyes wide. "Stephen!" she said, sounding even more surprised than we were.

"Sorry to just drop in on you this way," he said, "but I was really hoping . . ." He glanced at me and Lily. "Um, do you think we could talk someplace private?"

"Sure," said Rose. "Let's go in the family room."

They walked off, and I heard Rose turn off the TV. Lily and I loitered in the hall, drifting casually toward the family room. Rose had closed the door but not all the way.

"I was going to call you, but then I thought, this is too important," Stephen was saying. "I had to see you. I want us to be together again, Rose."

"What about Hayley?" Rose asked, her tone cool.

"We went on a couple of dates," Stephen admitted, "and I like her, but it just didn't click. Whenever I was out with her, I'd spend the whole time thinking about you. It just made me realize how much I love you."

"Really?" Rose said, not sounding quite as frosty as before.

"Really." There was a brief pause, and I guessed he was putting his arms around her. "I hope I didn't hurt you, Rose.

I mean, I think I needed some time to test this out. Thanks for giving me the space."

"I needed to experiment, too," she said. "I went out with this guy from school. But it was the same thing—you were on my mind all the time."

"God, I've missed you so much."

"Me too."

There was another pause—a long one. They're kissing, I thought happily. I looked at Lily. She mimed clapping and mouthed, "Yay!"

Just then Rose peeked around the door and saw us standing there. She didn't get mad, though—she was too blissed out. Smiling, she shut the door in our faces.

"And they lived happily ever after," Lily declared with satisfaction.

I nodded. It sure looked that way.

STEPHEN STAYED FOR dinner, and it was like a holiday. Mom whipped up an incredible meal. Everyone was so glad to have him back in the family, it was almost sickening. He and Rose were completely moony—they were sitting next to each other at the table, and Stephen's a lefty, so they kept bumping elbows and giggling.

After dinner the lovebirds went for a drive. Lily and Laurel did their homework at the kitchen table while Mom and Hal watched *Masterpiece Theater* in the family room. I went up to my room, thinking I'd read my English assignment, but I couldn't concentrate. I kept picturing Peter's face and hearing his voice in my mind, singing the song he'd written for me.

What a day, I thought with a sigh as I sat on my bed, my back propped against the pillows. Peter and I break up, and Rose and Stephen get back together. I was glad for my sister, but her joy made me wistful—it was such a contrast to my own misery. But it was my idea to end things with Peter, I reminded myself. We could never have had the kind of solid relationship Rose and Stephen had.

Shifting on the bed, I reached over for the two small wooden picture frames on my night table. One held a photo of my father and the other one a photo of Peter.

As I stared at their faces my vision blurred with tears and my heart ached with a sense of loss so intense, I thought it would tear me in half. I'd kept my grief about Dad's death buried deep inside me for three whole years; now there was no holding it back.

Clutching the picture of my father, I rocked back and forth on the bed, sobbing. "I got to say good-bye to Peter, but I didn't get to say good-bye to you, Dad," I whispered. "You went out on the boat, and we never saw you again. We didn't even have a body to bury—just a stone at the cemetery with your name on it. Oh, Dad."

I continued weeping silently. Gradually my body stopped shaking. Sniffling, I wiped my wet eyes on the sleeve of my shirt. I drew in a deep, uneven breath, then let out a sigh that seemed to hold a lifetime's worth of emotions.

A weird feeling of peace settled over me. I put the pictures of Dad and Peter back on my night table. I knew I'd never completely get over the pain of losing my father—there would always be things I wanted to share with him, questions I needed to ask him. Memories were thin compared to the real thing, but memories were going to have to be enough.

Poor Mom, I thought suddenly. Trying to be a mother *and* a father to the four of us. Dad didn't beat around the bush—if he'd still been around, he'd probably have come down a lot harder on me than she did.

My eyes grew misty again, but I smiled. "You'd have set me straight, wouldn't you, Dad?" I said aloud.

Instead I was going to have to do it on my own.

Fifteen

"ONE MORE LAP," Kristin panted as we rounded the far turn on the high school track.

"Think you can make it?" Jamila asked me.

"Yeah," I huffed. "No sweat."

It was an afternoon in early April, and we were working out to get in shape for the spring sports season. Jamila runs track and Kristin plays tennis, and they'd both slacked off over the winter—I wasn't the only one making up for lost time.

We'd started out just jogging, but now, as we headed into our final lap, we all pushed a little harder. Kristin sped up, so Jamila and I did, too. Then I gave it a little more gas, and they kept pace with me. We're all supercompetitive—no way did any of us plan to lag behind.

As we entered the home stretch we were sprinting full

out, staying exactly abreast of one another. At the finish line, though, I'm pretty sure I was ahead by an inch or two.

We collapsed on the infield grass, laughing and groaning. "You guys are killing me," I said breathlessly.

"That's what Coach Wheeler told us to do," Jamila huffed.

She and I flopped on our backs. We were wearing sweats, but the grass was cold and damp. "Come on, get up," Kristin ordered, "or your muscles'll tighten up."

She gave me a hand and hauled me back onto my feet. We walked a brisk lap of the track, then did some stretching. "I almost forgot I *had* muscles," I said as I leaned against a bench to stretch my calves and Achilles tendons.

Kristin was bending sideways to stretch her waist, her long red braid hanging almost to the grass. "Do you hear from Peter?" she asked.

It had been over a month since we'd broken up. "No," I admitted.

"That must hurt," Jamila said.

I nodded. It hurt a lot.

My friends were quiet for a few minutes. I was glad they didn't ask any more questions about Peter or about everything else that had gone on with me the past few months. Maybe at some point I'd feel like talking about it, but not right now, and they seemed to sense that.

We finished our cooldown and walked back to the gym. I took deep breaths of the fresh air. The trees were still bare, but the days were getting longer and a little warmer. Last fall when I'd hurt my knee, I'd thought spring would never come, but here it was.

"Just like the good old days," Kristin said.

"I was just thinking that," Jamila agreed.

I smiled at them. "Thanks for letting me back in the club."

"Are you kidding?" said Kristin. "It wasn't right with only the two of us."

"We were lazy without you," Jamila confirmed. "Extra butter on our popcorn at the movies and zero exercise."

I slung one arm around Jamila's shoulders and the other around Kristin, leaning my weight on them. I remembered how they'd helped me off the field after I injured my knee. They were still holding me up. "Well, from now on," I said, "we're hard-core."

"Super-hard-core," said Kristin.

"You better believe it," said Jamila.

"Although you guys still have to buy a bunch of the candy bars I'm selling to raise money for the softball trip to Florida," I reminded them.

"Put me down for five," Kristin said. "I swear I'll give them to my brothers."

We were almost to the gym. Suddenly I felt like running again. I took off at a dead sprint, with Jamila and Kristin tearing after me. "Last one to the showers is a smelly old jockstrap!" I shouted back to them.

A COUPLE OF nights later I was working at the hospital. Whenever nurses and doctors stopped by the reception desk, I hit them up to buy candy bars for the softball team fund-raiser. An hour into my shift a call came in for me. "Ben!" I said cheerfully.

"Just thought you might be bored," he said.

"You can't fool me," I teased. "You miss this place."

"No way," he said with feeling. "It's a zillion times better being an outpatient."

Another call came in and I put him on hold. "Don't you have anything better to do?" I asked when I punched his line again.

"Nope," he said.

"So, tell me what you think. Jody mentioned the job again, you know, organizing activities for the ward, and I think I might do it. Do you think kids would like puppet shows?"

Ben and I chatted about the possibilities. Then we talked about opening day in the major leagues and school—I was studying my brains out these days, trying to pull my grades back up. Ben thought he might want to do premed, too. "Maybe I'll do research," he said. "Find a cure for cancer."

"Why not?" I said.

"Well, I'll let you do your homework. I just wanted to make sure you weren't too bummed about Peter."

"Yeah, well . . ."

"I'm not going to get mushy on you," he swore. "Don't get the wrong idea here. But you are possibly the most beautiful, coolest, nicest, smartest girl I've ever met, Daisy. Okay? Bye now."

Ben hung up fast. Blushing a little and smiling also, I

replaced the receiver. "What's so funny?" Jody asked as she stepped up to get her phone messages.

"Life," I replied.

Driving home later that night, I found myself detouring way out of the way toward the mall in Kent. I don't know why—maybe because the song on the radio reminded me of Peter. I hadn't planned this, but as I parked and walked inside to the video arcade I really hoped I'd find him there. I needed to see him one more time.

There was a guy playing Annihilation, but at first I didn't think it was Peter because he had a crew cut. Then I got closer and recognized my ex-boyfriend. "Hey," I said, suddenly feeling shy.

Peter glanced at me, then back at the game, and then did a double take. "Daisy! Hey."

He hit pause and turned to face me. He slouched against the machine; we didn't touch. "What are *you* doing here?"

"I was heading home from the hospital, and I had this craving for a strawberry-banana smoothie from Juice Junction," I fibbed. "I'm working out a lot for softball, and I get starving."

"You look good," he said.

"So do you." I smiled. "I almost didn't recognize you, though."

Peter put a hand to his chin. Along with the crew cut, he was working on a scraggly goatee. "Yeah, it's my new look for spring. And you're blond again."

"Yeah," I said. My hair was growing out, and I'd had the dyed part trimmed off. It was kind of nice not to jump every time I looked in the mirror anymore. "It matches my eyebrows—that's a plus. So, what are you up to these days?"

"Mom's on this new medication and she feels really good, so she's been on me to look for a job. I just found something—riding around on a recycling truck. I start tomorrow."

"Cool," I said in an encouraging tone.

He shrugged. "Yeah, well, we'll see. It's a paycheck. I've been thinking about getting out of here, though, you know? Maybe move to Portland or Boston. Someplace where there's a little more action."

"Yeah?"

"Yeah." Another shrug. "But whatever."

I nodded. "Well."

"Well," Peter echoed.

For a minute we just looked at each other. We'd run out of things to talk about. "I guess I'll go grab that smoothie," I said at last.

"Okay," he replied. "Take it easy."

"You too."

I lingered a few seconds longer. Shouldn't we be crying or fighting or hugging or something? I wondered. But I couldn't think of anything else to say. The emotion just didn't seem to be there for either of us.

That's what made the tears jump into my eyes. Not that Peter and I had broken up but that I didn't miss him nearly so much as I'd thought I would. That my first love could die so quickly.

I turned away before he could see that I was crying and jump to the wrong conclusion. "See ya," I said as casually as I could manage.

He'd already turned back to his video game. "Yep."

As I left the arcade, though, with my shoulders square and my chin up, I had a feeling I wouldn't ever see Peter again.

THE FIRST SOUTH Regional High girls' softball game was held on a damp April Wednesday after school. Thanks to the misty, cold weather the home bleachers were nearly empty, which is why I couldn't help noticing the woman with the yellow umbrella.

Mom.

She cheered right until the last inning, when I batted a triple to bring in the winning run. My teammates and I hopped all over one another, congratulating ourselves on our first victory of the season, and then lined up to shake hands with the Eastport team, who weren't quite so happy about how things had turned out. Then while we all pulled on sweatshirts and slickers, Mom came up with a big Tupperware container full of oatmeal-raisin cookies.

The team descended on the cookies as if they hadn't eaten in a week. Coach Wheeler grabbed one, too. "Thanks, Mrs. Walker," everybody said.

I didn't take a cookie, and I didn't say anything. I felt pretty awkward, in fact. Mom had shown up at the game as if there weren't any tension between us—as if we were some totally tight mother-daughter act, when in fact we'd hardly talked in months.

The rest of the team was starting to drift toward the gym and a hot shower. I got ready to bolt, too, but before I could take a step, Coach Wheeler grabbed my arm. "What?" I asked. He didn't explain himself. He just kept shoving me . . . in Mom's direction.

Coach Wheeler and the softball team disappeared. Mom and I were suddenly alone on the deserted field. The drizzle had stopped, so she folded up her umbrella. "Great game," she said.

"Yeah."

There had been a question in Mom's voice. I'm not sure what she was asking, but I guess she got the right answer. One of us took a step, anyway, and then we were hugging. "I've missed you, Daisy," she whispered.

"I know. I'm sorry," I whispered back.

We hugged a little more, both of us sniffling, and then we started laughing. Mom's umbrella was between us and it was practically stabbing me. "Let's sit in the bleachers," she suggested. "It's not too wet."

We found a dry spot—the sun was actually peeking out from behind a cloud. Mom put the Tupperware on the bench between us, and we each munched a cookie. "I haven't had a chance to tell you that I'm sorry things didn't work out with Peter," Mom said.

"It's probably for the best," I told her. "We didn't have that much in common. And anyhow, you can't *really* be sorry."

"It was a tough position to be in for me as a parent," she said. "I wish I'd handled things differently. I shouldn't have alienated you like that."

"I did a pretty good job of alienating myself," I assured her.

"Well, sometimes I thought you were only dating Peter to punish me," Mom confessed. "How self-centered could I get!"

"Why would I want to punish you?" I asked.

Mom reached for another cookie and broke it in two. "Because of Hal."

"Well, you didn't like Peter, and I'm not crazy about Hal," I said. She offered me half of the cookie, and I took it. "That makes us even."

"Why don't you like Hal, though?" Mom asked. "He's trying so hard with you girls."

"Maybe he's trying *too* hard."

Mom was silent for a moment. Then she said quietly, "Being in a relationship with another man doesn't mean I've forgotten your father. I loved Jim. I'll always love him, and he'll always live for me in my daughters. Especially you."

I had to fight through my tears to get the words out. "I hate it, though. That Dad's just a memory. Every day I want him back with us."

"I know," Mom said.

"I don't want him to live in me," I went on. "I want him to live."

"I know," Mom said again, and reached for my hand. Tears were streaming down my face. I took a deep breath. "Well," I said shakily, "I'm sorry I've been giving you a hard time about having a boyfriend. It just takes some getting used to."

"Sure. I understand."

We finished the last couple of oatmeal cookies. "I can't believe I ate that," Mom said with a laugh. "That's my cardinal rule—don't eat what you cook. If I tasted everything, I'd be a blimp."

I smiled at her. "You're not a blimp, you're a babe," I told her. "No wonder Hal couldn't resist you."

Mom stood up. "I don't know about that, but I'll tell you, I *do* feel young sometimes. Like I've had a chance to start my life over."

"What do you mean?"

"Well, things couldn't have seemed worse to me after your dad died. But that chapter ended, and another one began. I've decided that's what life is like—a book," Mom said. "And every time we start a different chapter, we get to be a different person, too. I used to be a housewife and a mom, and now I have my own business. The other day I officially hired Sarah—I'm an employer! Who'd have thought it?"

"It's pretty amazing," I agreed. I thought about how *I'd* tried being a different person for a while.

"Anyway," Mom concluded as we walked to her parked car, "I guess the important thing is to be who *you* want to be and not who other people want you to be."

"You mean, like peer pressure?" I asked.

"Or like what your parents might expect," she said. "I know sometimes I asked too much of you, and I'm sorry for that."

"It's all right," I said. "I liked feeling needed."

"Of course I need you," Mom said. "That's not going to change. But let's find a happy medium, okay?"

We climbed into the car. Mom tossed her umbrella and the Tupperware in the backseat—I fiddled with the radio. "Hey, what happened to my station?" Mom protested as rock music blasted from the speakers.

"That boring classical stuff?"

"Come on." She laughed. "There's got to be a—"

"Happy medium?" I finished. I grinned. "Okay, I'll settle for oldies."

We drove home, both of us humming to the Beach Boys, and I realized for the first time in ages that my knee didn't hurt. I'd finally healed.

Sixteen

THE DAY BEFORE Easter my sisters and I gathered in the kitchen to color eggs, as we do every year. We each had half a dozen, and we took turns sticking them in cups of vinegar with purple, pink, green, blue, yellow, and orange dye.

"You've got to leave it in for longer or it's too pale," Laurel advised Lily as Lily scooped an egg out of the pink dye.

"I like it this way," Lily insisted, placing her egg carefully in the egg carton and then dropping another one in the blue cup. "It's understated."

"It's *white*," said Laurel.

"Just because you leave your eggs in for an *hour*," Lily said.

"Time out," I told them. "Can't we have a little harmony here?"

Rose got up from the table to open the window over the sink. "Doesn't it smell like spring?" she asked happily.

It *was* a beautiful April day. Crocuses were blooming in the park, and the ocean was a softer blue. "And I heard you and Jack have spring fever," she added, looking at Laurel as she sat back down at the table.

"What did you hear?" Laurel asked, blushing fiercely.

"Well, Rox's cousin Rachel was at that party with you guys last night, and Rachel told Rox that you and Jack spent a *long* time in the kissing closet. And Rox told me, naturally."

"We were playing spin the bottle," Laurel said defensively. "We *had* to go in the closet—that's the rule."

"And?" Rose pressed.

Laurel dumped an egg in the green cup, splashing dye all over the newspaper covering the table. "Well, we were just going to sit in there and count to fifty," she said, "but then we thought we should just kiss fast because that way we wouldn't have to lie about it, but then he, like, kissed me for *real*."

Laurel looked disgusted. I tried to hide my smile as I remembered how *I* felt about the opposite sex back in eighth grade. "Was it awful?" I asked sympathetically.

"It was totally gross," Laurel confirmed.

"Jack's so cute, though," Rose said. "I'd think he'd be a great—"

"We're just friends, okay?" Laurel said.

"The kiss didn't chase you off?" I asked.

"I made him promise he'd never ask me out again," Laurel explained. "Well, at least not for a few years."

"In a few years you might change your mind about kissing," Rose predicted in a knowing tone.

"I doubt it," Laurel declared.

We finished coloring the eggs, leaving them to dry in the egg cartons. "Who's up for a game of catch in the park?" I asked.

It turned out that everyone was. We grabbed a bunch of mitts and a softball and headed outside.

"What's happening with that spring break trip, anyway?" Rose called as she lobbed the ball to me.

"The team's going to a tournament in Florida," I answered, tossing the ball to Lily. "We've raised some money selling candy bars and doing car washes, but everybody has to pitch in three hundred bucks. I'd like to go, you know? Now that I'm back into the sports thing. Bonding with the team and all that. But I haven't saved up enough. I have, maybe, one-fifty." I was disappointed but not *really* disappointed. There would be other trips, and it wouldn't be a bad thing for me to spend spring vacation studying.

"Hmmm," said Rose. "That's too bad."

"Yeah, well, maybe next year," I said.

We played catch for fifteen minutes and then headed back inside, discussing what we were going to wear to church the next morning. "Stephen's coming to the service with us, so I think I'll wear my light blue dress since it's his favorite," Rose said.

"I'm going to wear my light yellow dress with the white collar," I said.

"It's so good to see you abandoning black," Rose exclaimed.

"Don't you want to hear what I'm going to wear?" Lily asked.

"Of course," I said.

"I sewed the lace back on that old-fashioned pink dress we found in Great-grandma's trunk," Lily began. "And I'm going to wear white gloves and a straw hat with a long pink ribbon."

"You'll look like Little Bo Peep," I predicted.

Lily ignored me. "And I have a little pink beaded purse to carry my offering in and a white velvet cape the lady at Second Time Around sold me for only three dollars, and I'm going to pin a sprig of lily of the valley to the breast of my gown as an emblem of spring."

"You'll be a vision," Rose said, winking at me.

I smiled. Lily's outfit sounded ridiculous, but I felt like hugging her. It was just so good to be back to normal—all four of us. I was kind of bummed that I wouldn't be able to go on the softball trip, but in the grand scheme of things, that was pretty minor.

Life was as it should be.

L EG OF LAMB with rosemary and mint jelly," Rose gushed. "And scalloped potatoes," Laurel said. "My absolute favorite."

"The asparagus is what I'm looking forward to," Hal said. "Your mother cooks it perfectly."

We were home from church, and Mom was making a special midday Easter dinner because later we were all going to the hospital to help with the Easter egg hunt I'd organized for the children's ward.

"Lily, would you set the table?" Mom asked. "Use the good china."

"How about flowers and candles?" Lily asked.

"The candles are in the pantry," Mom replied, "and the flowers . . ." She put a hand to her forehead. "I knew I forgot something when I was shopping yesterday. Flowers!"

"There are a ton of daffodils growing at the edge of the park," I said. "Do you think anyone would care if we picked a few?"

"Maybe just a handful," Mom said. "It *would* brighten up the table."

I started toward the door. Before I could leave, Hal joined me. "I'll walk to the park with Daisy," he announced. "Then I can grab that bottle of wine from my fridge on the way back."

He and Mom exchanged a significant glance. "You don't have to," I told Hal, not exactly psyched at the prospect of a chat with him.

"No, it's okay," he assured me. "While you're picking daffodils, I'll stand guard in case any local law enforcement passes by."

It looked like I was stuck with Hal, so instead of arguing, I jogged down the stairs and then hurried along the sidewalk with brisk strides. Hal practically had to run to keep up with me.

"Daisy, I'd like to talk to you," he said as we got to the park.

"No kidding," I replied with a trace of my old Peter-style sarcasm.

Hal grinned. He's geeky looking, with his glasses and

receding hairline, but for the first time I noticed that he had a nice smile. I could *almost* imagine what Mom sees in him. "I'm not Mr. Subtle," he acknowledged. "It's just, you and I . . . we haven't had an easy time of it since your mother and I started dating."

"She's the one who's going out with you, not me," I pointed out as I bent over to pick some daffodils.

"Right." Hal stood off to the side, his hands stuck in the pockets of his gray flannel trousers. "But it's important to me to have a good relationship with you and your sisters."

Well, then you shouldn't always butt into our lives and tell us what to do, I thought. I didn't say anything out loud, though. I knew he wanted some encouragement, but I couldn't bring myself to say, "We're all wild about you, especially me."

Hal broke the silence. "The thing is, Daisy, I know how hard it's been for you to lose your dad. My father died from a heart attack when I was in college."

I straightened up, clutching a handful of daffodils. How did Hal know that had been bothering me? I wondered. But I still didn't say anything.

"I missed him for a long time," Hal went on. "Still do every now and then. Kevin and Connor never got to know him."

I nodded.

"I guess I just want you to know that whatever happens between me and your mom—if we really start getting serious, and I hope we do—I don't aim to take your dad's place. No one can do that."

I cleared my throat. "Well . . . thanks," I said lamely.

"And if I ever seemed kind of high-handed, I'm sorry," he concluded. "It's just that I had a houseful of boys, and I'm used to bossing people around."

"It's okay," I said, and suddenly, it was. Hal glanced around "I don't see any cops."

Bending, he plucked a flower. "Happy spring, Daisy," he said, holding it out to me.

I took the daffodil and smiled at him. "Same to you."

EASTER DINNER WAS delicious, naturally. "I ate so much, I don't have room for dessert," Lily complained at the end of the meal.

"Not even cheesecake with fresh strawberries?" Mom asked.

"Well . . . maybe a *little* piece," Lily said.

"Aren't you glad you're not still a vegan?" Rose asked her.

Lily laughed. "Am I ever."

Mom served dessert and hot tea. When everyone had a slice of cheesecake, Rose clinked a spoon against her water glass. "Attention, please," she said. "I have an announcement."

"What is it?" asked Stephen, who was sitting to her left.

She bumped him with her elbow. "*You* know, but no one else does." She turned to Mom. "Okay, guess what I did a couple of months ago?"

Mom gave Rose a bemused smile. "I have no idea, but you've got me curious."

Rose leaned over to Stephen so she could hook her arm

through his. "You know how hard I've been working in my classes. I got all A's last semester."

"I know, and I'm very proud of you," Mom said.

"Well, I applied for a scholarship." Rose paused dramatically. "At Boston University. And . . . they invited me for an audition in the music and drama department. And . . ." She paused again.

"What happened, Rose?" Lily squeaked excitedly. "Did you get it?"

Rose broke into a smile. "I got it. I got the scholarship! I'm transferring to BU in the fall!"

We all cheered loudly. "Yahoo!" I yelled.

"Rose, that's wonderful!" Mom exclaimed.

"Isn't it great?" Stephen was beaming. "Boston University. Right across the Charles River from Harvard!"

"What a coincidence," Hal said, grinning.

"So, that's not all," Rose said when we'd quieted down.

"What else?" Mom wondered.

"Well, you know how I've been saving money for acting lessons," Rose said. "I have enough now, and I'm taking lessons in Portland starting next week."

"Congratulations," Mom said. I was sitting on Rose's other side, and I high-fived her.

"That's not all, though," Rose told us. She looked at me. "I have some money left over. A hundred dollars. I want you to have it, Daze. For the Florida trip."

"You're kidding," I said.

"No. And Hal has something to add," she said.

"Fifty dollars," Hal said. "Rose told me that would be enough to make up the total, along with your own savings."

"What?" I looked from Rose to Hal and back again. They were smiling. "I can't believe you guys."

"You've always done so much for me and for the whole family," Rose said. "It's the least I can do."

I blinked back a tear. "Thanks," I told her. I turned to Hal. "Thank you so much."

"You're welcome," he said.

Mom lifted her wineglass. "I think this is a good time for a toast." Hal raised his wineglass, too, and my sisters and I lifted our water glasses. Mom looked at me and then at Rose. "Here's to softball trips and scholarships." Her gaze moved to Lily and Laurel. "And Easter bonnets and kissing closets."

"Hey, who told?" Laurel yelped indignantly.

"Here's to my family," Mom concluded, smiling. Her eyes were on Hal's now. "And to the future."

"Here, here," said Hal.

I clinked my glass with Rose's. "Cheers," I said.

AFTER DINNER WE washed the dishes and then packed up the car with food Mom had made for the party at the hospital, along with bags of Easter candy and stuffed rabbits donated by people from church. When we got to the hospital, Laurel and I set up the Easter egg hunt while Mom put out the food and Rose and Lily did face painting for the little kids. It turned out to be a pretty fun party—the kids had a great time hunting for candy and eggs.

At one point Ben joined me. Rose had painted a rainbow across his cheeks and nose. "Nice face," I commented.

"Where's *your* paint?" he asked.

I laughed. "I've gotten the urge to dye myself strange colors out of my system."

Ben pulled up a chair so he could help me pour jelly beans into bowls. "Guess what?"

"What?"

"I'm better."

I tilted my head to one side. Ben had been sick the whole time I'd known him. "What do you mean?"

"Better," he repeated. "As in 'full remission.' As in I'm finishing up this round of outpatient treatment and then I'm done. For good."

"Ben, that's the best news I ever heard!" I threw my arms around him, tears sparkling in my eyes. "I'm so glad!"

"So, what do you say?" Ben wriggled away from me. He's not the touchy-feely type. "It'll take me a couple of months to get back in shape, but this summer I should be biking and stuff again. I'll race you up Mountain Road—how does that sound?"

I pictured Ben healthy again, with color in his face and meat on his bones and hair on his head. I thought about the year I turned sixteen and all the things I'd learned working at the hospital. I thought about how I'd said good-bye to Peter, my first real love, but at the same time I'd made a friend like Ben. I thought about my fights with Mom and how we were getting along better than ever. I thought about Dad and how I'd always, always miss him.

What a wonderful world it was. I couldn't wait for the softball trip to Florida. And next year I'd visit Rose at BU and apply to colleges myself. Maybe I'd get an athletic scholarship. I'm going to go for it, I thought. No more pretending to be someone I'm not.

"It sounds great," I told Ben as we helped ourselves to handfuls of jelly beans. Remembering Mom's toast, I added, "Here's to the future."

Laurel

For my parents

One

YOU REALLY DON'T have to give me a party, Mom," I told my mother, Maggie Walker, the day before my sixteenth birthday. I meant it, too. Birthday parties aren't exactly my favorite things.

"Should I just throw away the cake, then?" she teased.

We were in the kitchen. Mom had just baked a triple-layer lemon cake with raspberry filling, and now she was using a tiny spatula to etch a basket-weave pattern in the white butter cream frosting.

It looked delicious, and I was sure, knowing Mom—she's a caterer—it would taste even better than it looked. "Of course I want the cake!" I said, smiling. I pushed the long, gold-brown hair out of my eyes, then stuck my hands deep into the side pockets of my faded denim overalls. "I just don't like people making a fuss over me."

"It'll just be us," Mom assured me, "and Hal. And I invited Jack. That's okay with you, right?"

"Sure." Hal Leverett is our neighbor. He's divorced, and Mom is a widow, and they've been dating for a couple of years now. As for Jack Harrison, he's been my closest friend since we were ten. Jack and Hal are both like family.

Mom finished frosting the cake. She offered me the beaters from the electric mixer. "Do you want these, Laurel?"

Of course I did. I grinned and leaned back against the counter and licked the frosting off one of the beaters. The kitchen window was open, letting in a warm Indian summer breeze. "Remember how I used to practically beat Lily up to get the beaters after you baked a cake?" I asked Mom.

Mom laughed. "Poor Lily."

"Poor Lily—yeah, right." Lily is my younger sister. She's thirteen now, and I've been waiting for her to outgrow her "brat" stage for the past thirteen years.

The phone rang; I had to put down the beater to answer it. "Hello?"

"Hi. It's me," said my nineteen-year-old sister, Daisy.

A warm feeling settled over me. "Daze! What's up?" My mom smiled at me, and I smiled back as I pointed to the phone excitedly. "It's Daisy," I mouthed, and Mom nodded.

"Just wanted to wish you a happy day before your birthday, Toad."

"Daisy! Haven't I outgrown that ridiculous nickname yet?"

"Have you outgrown your roomful of animals yet?" she shot back.

I laughed. Back when my dad died, we had to move out of our huge house and into a two-floor apartment on Main Street in Hawk Harbor, the small town on the coast of southern Maine where I've lived all my life. At first the landlord told us no pets. Since then Mr. Wissinger, who also owns the bakery downstairs, has relaxed his policy a little, so I've adopted as many animals as I could squeeze into my bedroom.

"Anyway," she went on, "I'll be home tomorrow afternoon." She's a freshman at Dartmouth. "I have a soccer game in the morning, but if I leave Hanover by noon, I should be in Hawk Harbor around three-thirty."

"How are you getting here?" I asked. "Bus?"

"I'm borrowing Annie's car," Daisy replied. "What a great roommate."

"I can't wait to see you!"

"I'll drive as fast as I can. Don't start the party without me."

"Are you kidding? Of course we won't. Bye, Daze."

Hal walked in as I hung up the phone. He doesn't bother knocking anymore—he and Mom are always running back and forth between each other's places.

At first it was weird, Mom having a boyfriend. Daisy especially freaked out about it, maybe because she was the one who'd been closest to Dad. Now we're all pretty used to it, and Hal's about the nicest man on earth.

He greeted Mom with a kiss on the cheek, then set a paper bag on the counter. "Party decorations," he explained. "Streamers, balloons, hats, noisemakers."

I rolled my eyes. "Noisemakers?"

Hal took a party hat out of the bag and stuck it on his head. He's an accountant, with brown-gray hair and wire-rimmed glasses and he's at least fifty, but when he smiles, he looks like a kid. "Come on, Laurel. Live it up!"

"Why don't we start decorating?" Mom said to Hal as she wiped her hands clean on a dish towel. "We're going out tonight and we won't have time in the morning because I'm catering that bridal shower brunch."

I thought about making one more plea for a low-key celebration but decided not to. It wasn't that I didn't appreciate them going to so much trouble. It's just that I don't like being the center of attention. When I was thirteen, Jack threw a surprise party for me and invited practically everyone in our class. Even though I knew he had the best intentions in the world, I hated every minute of it.

Now I trailed my mother and Hal into the living room. I tried to reach for a roll of crepe paper, but my mother told me to sit down and relax. So I propped my scuffed sneakers up on the equally scuffed coffee table. We have a lot of really old furniture that Mom says is too beat-up to qualify as antique.

Mom draped crepe paper streamers around the room while Hal blew up balloons that said Sweet 16. "It'll be good to have your big sisters home, won't it?" Hal observed.

I nodded. Daisy was coming home for my birthday, and so was Rose—she's twenty-one, the oldest in the family, and a senior at Boston University.

"Is Rose bringing Stephen?" Hal asked, pausing in between balloons to catch his breath.

"She sure is," Mom answered. Rose's boyfriend, Stephen, goes to Harvard. They've been dating forever. They met in Hawk Harbor when they were about my age, they broke up once or twice, but they always got back together. "Those two don't do anything without each other."

"Quiet around here, isn't it," Hal said to Mom, "now that two of your four girls are away at college."

Mom sighed. "I'm still trying to get used to it." She tossed me a smile. "Not that Lily doesn't make enough noise for four girls sometimes!"

"At least we had an extra year with Daisy," I said. I gave a little sigh; I couldn't help it.

Daisy graduated from high school a year ago, but she put off starting college until this fall so she could work full-time and help out the family. Our father died six years back—his fishing boat was lost in a storm at sea—and Mom's gotten a catering business off the ground now, but money is still tight sometimes. We all pitch in however we can.

Mom gazed at me, her expression thoughtful. "You and Daisy got to be good friends this past year, didn't you?"

I nodded. I missed Rose, but she had already been away at college for three years. I was used to seeing her only on holidays. Daisy had just left, and I still wasn't used to the fact that she was gone. I missed her. A lot.

Hal stopped blowing up balloons. He thumped his chest with one hand. "The old man's lungs aren't what they used to be," he said, chuckling. "Think I'll take a break."

"Let's start dinner, then," Mom suggested.

They went back into the kitchen, and I walked upstairs to my room to feed my pets. I was still thinking about Daisy. She and Rose are both amazing people. Rose is a very good singer and actress. Daisy's a star, too. She was captain of three different sports teams in high school, and she's on a scholarship at Dartmouth. Plus she's an A student, plus she's beautiful, plus funny, plus kind, plus plus plus.

My lab partner, Ellen Adams, who's the middle of five kids, has asked if it bugs me having a big sister like Daisy who's such an achiever. It doesn't. I don't feel like I have to follow in her footsteps. I couldn't even if I wanted to!

After Alfalfa, my rabbit, was taken care of, I fed my iguana, my turtles, and my tropical fish. As I was pouring birdseed into Lewis and Clark's bowl—they're parakeets—the door to my room banged open. "Where's my iPod?" Lily demanded.

As I mentioned before, my younger sister is a brat with a capital *B*. Sometimes I can't believe we share the same DNA. "I don't know," I replied, "and did you ever hear of knocking?"

"You borrowed it yesterday and I haven't seen it since," she shot back in an accusing tone, hands on her hips.

I gave her a cold stare. She had on a white ruffled shirt with a black bow tie and vest—Lily's into putting together funky outfits. Today she looked like a waiter, but I didn't say so. She's always antagonizing me, but I try not to pick fights unless she forces me to. "I left it in your room," I told her.

"Then why can't I find it?"

I shrugged. "It's kind of a pigsty in there."

"*My* room's a pigsty?" Lily wrinkled her nose and took a sniff. "It smells like cow manure in here. Or is that your hair, which you probably haven't washed in a month?"

I'd washed my hair that morning, but I decided not to dignify her question with a reply. For about the millionth time, I silently thanked heaven that Lily and I weren't sharing a room anymore, like we had to before Daisy and Rose moved out. "Close the door behind you," I suggested.

Lily didn't just close the door—she slammed it. Turning to the parakeets, I sighed. "Sorry, guys. It's not true about the cow manure. You smell fine."

When everyone was fed, I lifted Alfalfa from his cage. Walking over to my bedroom window, I looked out at the boats in the harbor.

I've got a great view, which makes up for the fact that the room is small. That was the only good thing about Daisy's going off to college: inheriting her bedroom. I can decorate it however I want without having to argue with Lily, whose clothes used to take up our whole closet. There's space for all my animals, and I salvaged an old rocking chair that Mom wanted to give to charity—it's the chair she rocked us in when we were babies.

I sat there now with the bunny on my lap. I *did* like having my own room; still, I'd rather have had Daisy back. It was lonely sometimes. Lily and I were the only sisters left. And we'll never be friends, I thought.

*   *   *

I T'S COLD," JACK said.

   "No, it's not," I replied.

"Feels like a frost." He turned up the collar of his denim jacket.

I took a deep breath of woodsy October air. "I think it's nice. Perfect, in fact."

"My battery's dying." Jack's flashlight flickered and went out. A second later I heard him stumble on a tree root. "Ouch!"

I had to laugh. Moonlit expeditions with Jack are always like this. He moans and groans, pretending I'm dragging him out against his will, but then ends up having as much fun as I do.

Tonight we were hiking up a path not far from his house. When we got to the top, we were in Meredith's Meadow, one of the highest spots in town. Jack spread an old quilt on the dewy grass while I pulled out my binoculars. "There's Jupiter," I said, pointing the binoculars skyward. "Just above the horizon. See?"

Jack took the binoculars and looked through them. "Doesn't it have a bunch of moons?"

"Yeah, but we'd need a telescope to see them."

We lay back on the blanket, the binoculars and an open bag of potato chips between us. Looking up at the sky, we took turns naming the constellations. Perseus and Andromeda, Aries the ram, Cepheus and Cassiopeia.

"Even with the moon almost full, there are still so many stars," Jack said after a minute.

"That's what's good about living in the country instead of the city. No lights from buildings and stuff to dim the stars."

"There are other solar systems besides ours, right? Do you think somewhere out there a couple of kids are lying in a field looking through binoculars at us?"

I laughed. "Maybe."

I sat up and wrapped my arms around my knees. Jack was munching potato chips. Without speaking, he stuck the bag out and I took a handful.

Jack and I have known each other almost forever, since the summer before sixth grade, when he moved to Maine with his parents. He was sort of a prissy little kid back then—his clothes were always spotless and pressed. Meanwhile, I was usually covered with grass stains and mosquito bites. For some reason, though, we hit it off. Maybe because we were both a little lonely. My father had just died and Jack didn't know anyone else in town yet, and since he's an only child he didn't have brothers or sisters to play with.

We're still best buddies even though we've changed over the years. Now I turned to look at him in the moonlight. He has thick, straight brown hair and green eyes. According to the majority of the female population at South Regional High School, he's gotten pretty cute. He's popular, too. Sometimes I think that if we hadn't been friends forever, Jack would never want to hang out with someone like me.

Jack noticed me staring at him. "Your hair's frizzing out."

I lifted a hand. My long hair was going wild—the damp sea air does that to me. "Yeah, I forgot a ponytail holder."

"I bet that's what Meredith looked like," Jack speculated.

Meredith's Meadow is named for a colonial girl who sup-posedly came up here to look at the ocean and wait for her seafaring lover to return. I laughed. "If I look like Meredith, then no wonder that guy never came back!"

Jack just looked at me.

I gazed back up at the sky.

We sat quietly for a couple more minutes. I was think-ing about how maybe I wasn't that different from eighteenth-century Meredith. We both loved this high, wild meadow. Both of us knew how to wait for people we loved to return.

"What's that smell? Flowers or something?" Jack asked.

I breathed in deeply. The meadow had a faded, autum-nal sweetness. I didn't need to turn on my flashlight to iden-tify the plants and grasses that surrounded us. "Meadowsweet and oxeye daisy," I told Jack. "Calico aster, burdock, nodding thistle. And smell the licorice? We must have put our blanket down on the last of the sweet goldenrod."

"Everything's dying, huh?"

"Yeah, but that's when the fields are the prettiest, I think. The bunchgrass is turning red now—we should come back in daylight."

"That would be great."

We packed up our stuff and headed back down the dark trail. At the road we said good-bye. "See you tomorrow at your birthday party," Jack said.

"Don't bring a gift, okay? I don't need anything."

Jack's smile was bright in the moonlight. "Are you kidding? I already got you a present. I know you're going to love it."

"Really?" I was curious in spite of myself. "What is it?"

"Nice try, Walker. Catch you later."

"Bye."

We walked off in opposite directions. All the way home I wondered what Jack was going to give me for my birthday. I've always hated getting presents. Everyone gathers around and stares as you open them—it's so embarrassing. That's the problem with birthday parties in general. But still, even though I don't usually like parties, I had to admit that I was starting to get a little excited about this one.

Two

THE NEXT MORNING was Saturday, so I rode my bike to the Wildlife Rescue Center, where I volunteer. Pedaling through town, I thought how nice Hawk Harbor looks in the fall. Pretty soon a lot of stores and restaurants would close for the winter, but during foliage season we still get tourists.

The shop windows held displays of pumpkins and wheat sheaves, and Indian corn was on all the doors. Flags fluttered in front of the town hall. Everyone was outside enjoying the sunny, mild weather. Mr. Appleby stood in front of his hardware store, talking to Patsy, who runs the local diner. Mrs. King, who owns Cecilia's, a boutique where Rose worked for a long time, was setting up sale racks on the sidewalk. The town veterinarian waved to me as he got out of his pickup truck in front of the animal clinic.

"How's the bunny?" he called.

Alfalfa was taking antibiotics for the snuffles. "Much better," I called back as I sped by. "Thanks, Dr. Grady."

I followed the coast for a mile and then turned inland.
The Wildlife Rescue Center is in a renovated barn near Goose
Creek. I've been volunteering there for a couple of years, and
today, if I could get up my nerve, I wanted to talk to the director about becoming a regular part-time staffer now that I was
sixteen.

Inside, I peeked into the office. Griffin, the guy who runs
the center, was reading e-mail and drinking chai tea. Just ask
him, I told myself. But another inner voice was louder. Why
would he want to pay you? It's not like you do anything someone else couldn't do just as well or better. You're lucky they let
you stick around at all.

I started to walk away from him, but Griffin had spotted
me. "Greetings," he called.

I doubled back to the office doorway. "Hi."

Griffin was a hippie when he was young, and he still wears
beat-up sandals, old blue jeans embroidered with peace signs,
and a ponytail. He waved at the battered lawn chair across from
his desk that's reserved for guests. The WRC is nonprofit, and
the facilities aren't fancy. "Have a seat, Laurel," he invited
sociably. "What's new?"

I sat down, folding my hands on my knees. "Not much.
Today's my birthday."

"Cheers." He lifted his mug of tea in a salute. "Sixteen,
right?" I nodded. "Gonna look for a real job?" he asked.

This was my opening, but, predictably, my mouth went

dry and I couldn't get my tongue to work properly. "Um . . . uh . . . yeah," I stammered. "But, you know, well . . ."

"Do you like working here?" Griffin asked.

I managed to spit out the words. "Yes, very much. I was actually wondering if I might . . . you might . . . we might . . ."

"Do you want a job? You're hired," Griffin cut in. "I can only pay you minimum wage, but fill out a couple of forms and it'll be official. Okay?"

I could feel my mouth drop open a little. That was so easy! I thought. "Thanks, Griff." I know my eyes were glowing. "I promise I'll work really hard."

"I know you will. I wouldn't want you on the staff if I thought you were a slouch," he said.

I stood up shakily and practically floated back to the wild animal infirmary. My first real job! I thought. I practiced telling people about it in my head: "I work at the Wildlife Rescue Center. Yeah, it's really good experience. I'm going to be a wildlife biologist or else a vet like Dr. Grady."

Carlos Alvarez was mopping the floor of the operating room. Carlos is nineteen—he's studying environmental science at the state university. He worked at the WRC full-time over the summer, and since the school year started, he comes in every Saturday.

He and I don't usually talk a whole lot. I'm shy around everybody, but especially around guys (except Jack) and *especially* older guys (except Stephen). Plus Carlos is really cute, which makes me even more self-conscious. Today, though, I was bursting with my news. "Guess what?" I said. "I'm not a volunteer anymore—Griffin just hired me!"

Carlos has dark eyes and short black hair. He's quiet, but when he smiles, which he did now, it lights up the room. "Excellent!"

"It's the best birthday present I can imagine," I confided.

"It's your birthday?"

Suddenly I felt a little stupid. I didn't want him to think all I did was talk about myself. "It's no big deal," I said quickly.

"Sure it is. How are you going to celebrate?"

"My big sisters are visiting. I'm psyched about that."

"Sisters, huh?" He smiled again. "There are more like you at home?"

"They're not like me at all," I assured him. "They're beautiful and smart and popular."

"Well, I bet they don't know the difference between a duck and a grebe," Carlos said. "And could they pull porcupine quills from a bear cub's nose?"

I laughed. "They wouldn't want to!"

Carlos leaned on the handle of the mop. "What I'm trying to say is, I'm glad Griff hired you. I was going to tell him he should. You're really good with the animals."

I blushed. "Thanks," I said shyly. I hadn't realized he thought I was doing such a good job. In fact, I hadn't realized that Carlos had noticed me at all.

"I'm still your boss, though," he reminded me.

"Okay, boss. What do you want me to do today?"

He reeled off a list of chores: feeding animals, cleaning

cages, giving medicine. I got busy, but I didn't stop smiling. What a great day—I got hired for my dream job and Carlos said he thought I was a good worker! I couldn't wait to tell my family, especially Daisy. She and I always talk about how maybe someday she'll be a doctor and I'll be a vet and we'll both move back to Hawk Harbor. I'll take care of the sick animals, and she'll take care of the sick people—we'll have the whole town covered. My first job, I thought. My first job!

H APPY BIRTHDAY, LAUREL!" seven voices shouted loudly as Mom carried the cake, sparkling with sixteen candles, to the table.

We'd just stuffed ourselves with Mexican food because it's my favorite. Now everyone waited for me to blow out the candles so we could start in on the cake. "Time's a wastin'," Lily pointed out. She'd already told me ten times that we needed to hurry up because she had a date to go to the mall with her friends.

"Okay, here goes."

I blew out the candles with one breath. Daisy clapped and Jack whistled. "What did you wish for?" asked Rose's boyfriend, Stephen Mathias.

I put my hand over my mouth. "I forgot to make a wish!"

"Too bad," Rose said. "Sixteenth birthday wishes come only once in a lifetime."

"Did *yours* come true?" Lily asked her.

Rose thought back for a moment and then grinned. "No, thank goodness. I wished I'd marry Parker Kemp!"

We all laughed, including Stephen. Parker was the rich,

snobby boy Rose had dated before she met Stephen. "You can still make a wish, Toad," Daisy decided. "There must be a statute of limitations. If you make it within three and a half minutes of blowing out the candles, it's still valid."

I thought about it, then shook my head. "I have everything I want already." I smiled at Daisy. "Who needs wishes?"

I cut the cake and passed out slices. As everyone prepared to dig in, Rose said, "This seems like a good moment. Are you all listening?"

"What's up, Rose?" Jack asked.

Rose glanced at Stephen. Then she looked at me, a big smile on her face. Rose is incredibly pretty—she has long blond hair and big blue eyes and a perfect smile—but right then she looked even more beautiful than usual. Her eyes were sparkling, and her cheeks were pink. "Stephen and I have decided"—she paused for dramatic effect—"that after we graduate next spring . . . we're going to get married!"

Rose's announcement was met with shouts of joy. A couple of chairs toppled over as we all jumped up to hug her and Stephen. "This is wonderful," Mom said, embracing Rose. She had tears in her eyes.

Jack high-fived Stephen. "Nice going, man."

Rose turned to me. "I'm sorry to do this at your birthday party, Laurel, but Stephen and I are leaving tomorrow, and everyone is here tonight, and we just couldn't wait to—"

"Please!" I interrupted, laughing. "You're apologizing for the best news I could have possibly hoped for? I'm counting this as one of my birthday presents."

Rose grinned and I grinned back. I don't think I'd ever seen her look so happy.

"A wedding. Great!" Lily clapped. "Can I wear my purple flapper dress and a feather boa?"

Rose laughed. "You're going to be a bridesmaid, silly. I'll pick out special dresses for you and Daisy and Laurel to wear. You will, won't you?" Rose turned to me and Daisy. "Be my bridesmaids? And of course I want you to be my maid of honor, Daze."

A bridesmaid? I thought. That means walking down the aisle in front of a whole church full of people, right? Before I could start worrying about it, though, Daisy said, "Of course we will." She gave Rose a big hug. "I can't think of anything more fun."

After the birthday cake we went into the living room, still talking about Rose and Stephen's plans. "I'm applying to law schools," Stephen said. "Harvard's my first choice, so keep your fingers crossed."

"There are more acting and music opportunities in New York, but we'll probably stay in Boston," Rose added. "There are some good theater companies there. I'm sure I'll find work—I'll get an agent."

"It sounds so exciting and grown-up," Lily commented with a sigh of envy.

Rose grinned. "Doesn't it? I feel like I'm talking about someone else's life—like how can this be happening to me? I'm still in college! Stephen and I *did* talk about putting off the wedding for a year, but . . ."

Stephen put his arm around her and pulled her close. "We can't live without each other. So why wait?"

"You know, the wedding will be great and all, but it's months and months from now," Daisy broke in, carrying a stack of gift-wrapped packages over to my chair. "Meanwhile it's still Toad's birthday."

I flushed pink, but I settled down to open the presents. Rose and Stephen gave me a book of wildlife photographs. In a surprisingly thoughtful gesture, Lily had decorated a spiral notebook to make a bird-watching journal. There was a hand-knit sweater and a sweet card with a seashell on it from Gram and Grandpa—they live in Florida.

The box from Mom was small. "I think I know what this is," I said, smiling at her.

She smiled back at me. "That's the problem with being the third sister."

When Rose and Daisy turned sixteen, Mom gave them each a charm from our great-grandmother's charm brace-let. The gold rosebud went to Rose, naturally—Daisy's was a seashell.

I opened the little box. Inside, suspended from a delicate gold necklace, was a charm shaped like a tiny maple leaf. "It's beautiful," I murmured.

"I thought it was just right for you," Mom said. "It will look natural even with overalls."

Daisy helped me put on the necklace. "I love it, Mom," I said.

Mom kissed my cheek. "I'm glad, sweetheart."

"Thanks, everybody," I said. "You're all so thoughtful."

"Hey, there's one more." Jack jumped to his feet. "I left it in Hal's apartment. Be right back."

Hal and Jack disappeared. I remembered what Jack had said the night before, about having gotten me a special present. "What do you think it is?" I asked.

Mom and my sisters pretended they had no idea, but I got the definite impression they knew something I didn't—they were trying not to smile.

Hal came back in, carrying a grocery bag. "This stuff is from me," he explained. "Accessories."

"Accessories? What for?" Then I saw Jack. He walked into the room, holding one end of a bright red leash . . . on the other end of which was a roly-poly brown puppy with a big bow around its neck.

"Oh," I gasped. "Is that for *me?*"

"Only if you like her," Jack said. The puppy jumped up on my lap as if she knew she was mine. "I can take her back to the pound if—"

"Of course I like her," I interrupted, laughing as the puppy slobbered all over my face. "Don't you dare take her back to the pound!"

"What are you going to name her?" Daisy asked me.

I held the puppy up, looking into her chocolate brown eyes. "What breed is she?"

"Part poodle, part collie, part retriever," Jack said. "A little of everything."

"Name her after Henry," Stephen suggested, referring

to a pet mouse I had a long time ago. Henry was famous for running across the dinner table the first time Rose invited Stephen over for dinner to meet the family.

"She's a girl, though," I pointed out.

"Henrietta," Rose said.

I kissed the puppy's nose. "Are you a Henrietta? Nah."

"She's the color of a chocolate bar," Daisy pointed out. "Maybe you should give her a name that has to do with candy."

I smiled. "She's sweet, too. Well, then, how about Snickers?" The puppy licked my face again. "She likes it!"

Hal dumped out the contents of the grocery bag. There were food and water bowls, a brush, a bag of puppy kibble, and some dog toys. Right away Snickers started chewing on a rubber bone.

"Isn't she smart?" I asked proudly.

"A genius," Jack agreed.

"Like Stephen," Daisy put in. "With these new additions we're going to be the smartest family in Hawk Harbor!"

Everyone laughed and I looked over at Rose, who gave Stephen an impulsive embrace. Daisy leaned in and turned it into a group hug. I gazed at my older sisters—they both looked so beautiful and happy, they were practically glowing. My heart was filled with a sudden ache. I wished they didn't live so far away. And now Rose was going to be in Boston for another few years. I guess I should be grateful, I thought. It could be farther.

My gaze shifted. Jack was staring at me with a funny look

on his face. I smiled at him as I stroked the puppy's silky fur. "She's so wonderful," I whispered. "Thanks."

He gave me a grin. "Happy birthday," he whispered back.

THERE WERE STILL a couple of hours of daylight left after the party, so Jack and I took Snickers for a hike in the town forest. "Remember the time you brought me on a walk here to look for owls?" Jack said.

Snickers stopped on the trail to bark at a squirrel. "With all that noise, we won't see any today," I said, laughing.

We walked deeper into the woods. Snickers gave up on the squirrel and started chasing windblown leaves. "I can't get over it," I told Jack. "A dog! I've been begging for one *forever.* How did you get Mom to go along with this?"

"I begged for a month."

I had to laugh at that. "Well I have to say that it was worth it, as far as I'm concerned," I told him. "What an incredible day. Can you believe that Rose and Stephen are getting *married?*"

"Well, when you find true love . . . ," Jack began.

Just then Snickers galloped over with a stick in her mouth. Jack picked her up and plopped her into my arms. "You know, she's not your only present," he said.

"She's not?"

"Check her collar."

I dug my fingers into the thick fluff on the puppy's neck, feeling for her leather collar. There was something silver twined around it. "What . . . ?" I looked at Jack in surprise.

It was a bracelet. "They're dolphins," he said, indicating the links of the delicate chain.

I unclasped the bracelet, then dropped Snickers back onto the path. She promptly took off after another squirrel. "It's so pretty. Why didn't you give it to me before?"

Jack shrugged, his hands in the pockets of his khakis. "I guess I felt funny in front of your family. Like, you know, Stephen might give me a hard time."

"You shouldn't have," I told him.

"Why not?"

"Because . . ." My words trailed off as a blush stole up my neck to my face.

My mind flashed back on a memory of eighth grade. For some reason, Jack had asked me to go steady with him. I'd said no way, of course. One night at a party, playing spin the bottle, though, we ended up kissing. It was totally awkward, so after that we both agreed we weren't meant to be a couple. Jack knows I have absolutely no interest in him and me *ever* getting romantic. In fact, I have no interest in romance *period*. But this bracelet seemed like . . . well . . . a "romantic" kind of gift.

"Um, I was hoping that . . ." Jack studied my beet red face. "You know, that you might . . ."

I turned away from him. "Snickers!" I called, clapping.

"Uh, hoping that you'd like the dolphins," Jack finished. "Don't worry. It doesn't mean I'm secretly in love with you or anything."

"Oh!" I gave a little laugh that I hoped sounded perfectly relaxed. "I'd never think anything like that." The truth was,

I was relieved. I'd really hate for anything to jeopardize my friendship with Jack, and if he liked me more than I liked him, it would just be too strange.

I stuck the bracelet in my pocket and grabbed Snickers so I could clip her leash back on. "Don't know about you, but I'm ready for another piece of birthday cake."

"Me too," Jack said.

THE NEXT MORNING Rose and Stephen went out to brunch with Rose's high school friend Roxanne Beale. Rose was planning to ask Rox and two other old friends, Cath Appleby and Sumita Ghosh, to do readings and sing in the wedding. Daisy set out on a long run, and Mom and Lily went to church. I sat on the curb out front of Wissinger's Bakery, my bicycle leaning against the brick building, and waited for Jack. After our hike the night before, we'd made a date to ride out to McCloskey's Farm to pick apples.

At ten-thirty Jack pulled up, but not on his bike. "Wow!" I said when he climbed out of the blue Mustang. "Nice wheels!"

"Dad bought it used," Jack said with a proud grin, "so we have an extra car now that I have my license."

I stood up and walked around the car, wishing my family had enough money to get an extra car. And such a nice one, too! I'm not really into cars, but this one looked like it would be really fun to cruise around in. I looked up at Jack, suddenly excited. "Should we drive to McCloskey's, then? Let me just put my bike back inside."

"Actually . . . I have to cancel."

I felt my smile slide off my face. "What's up?" I asked him.

"Well, Ashley Esposito just called. We're going to Patsy's for waffles."

"Oh?" I folded my arms across my chest, frowning. Ashley Esposito is a cheerleader. She has big hair, and other parts of her anatomy are prominent, too. "So you drop everything for waffles?"

Jack shrugged. "Sorry it's so last minute."

"But . . . ?"

"But I thought you'd understand. I mean, you and I are just friends, right?"

"What does *that* have to do with anything?"

"Look, I'm sorry about canceling plans with you. I am. But I think I might want to ask Ashley out. Is that a problem?"

Jack waited for me to answer him, a funny, watchful look in his eyes. Usually I can read his mind, but right then I didn't have a clue what he was thinking. *Is* it a problem? I wondered. It was, kind of. I was mad—my feelings were hurt that he was blowing me off. And for Ashley! I have to admit, on some level I felt betrayed. But I didn't want to make a scene. I didn't want him to get the wrong idea and think I was jealous because he had a date with another girl.

I still hadn't spoken, so Jack said, "Laurel, I won't go out with her if you—"

"No, no," I said quickly. "You should go. It's fine. I was psyched for a bike ride, that's all."

Jack looked a little disappointed that I hadn't put up more of a fight. "We could always take a ride later."

"Okay," I agreed. "Well, have fun."

"So long."

He climbed behind the wheel of the Mustang and started the engine. Watching him, I had a feeling of déjà vu. It's like eighth grade, I thought, when he asked Tammy Nickerson to go out with him after I said no. But I hadn't been jealous then, and I wasn't jealous now.

As Jack drove off, though, rolling down his window to give me a good-bye wave, I was surprised at how abandoned I felt. The car made him look so grown-up, and there I stood in my old overalls with my bicycle, as if I were ten years old. I couldn't help wondering whether he was leaving me behind.

L OOK, THEY PUT up a new sign," Daisy said, pointing. She and I were walking with Snickers down Lighthouse Road to the beach. Our old house had been painted white with pale purple trim. It was a bed-and-breakfast now: the Lilac Inn.

"Isn't it weird?" I asked, tugging Snickers away from some brambles along the side of the road. "People pay money to stay in our old rooms."

Daisy laughed. "I hope they cleaned them up a little."

"Mom went in there once. She said it was totally redecorated. Remember how saggy the porch used to be? They fixed that and all this other stuff we could never afford to."

"Then it's for the best," Daisy said, but she cast a longing look back at the house, and I knew she missed it as much as I did.

We walked fast, a strong wind pushing along behind us. Clouds raced across the sky. "Why didn't you and Jack go to the orchard this morning?" Daisy asked as we cut across the dunes to the beach.

I told her about Jack's brunch date with Ashley. "I can't believe he'd want to go out with her," I said. "I mean, she's pretty, but she doesn't have the greatest personality."

"You're pretty, too, you know," Daisy said.

I knew she was only trying to make me feel better, so I didn't bother replying.

"Does it bum you out that Jack's interested in someone else?" she asked a minute later.

"No," I said firmly. "Definitely not."

"Hmmm," Daisy murmured thoughtfully.

We didn't stay long at the beach because huge waves were kicking up a cold spray. Back on the road, we cut inland to a tree-lined lane that was more sheltered from the wind. "I miss these walks," Daisy said. She gestured to the maples and oaks. "The trees, the rocky beach . . ."

"Dartmouth's nice, too."

She nodded, her blond ponytail bobbing. "The mountains are beautiful. You'll have to come visit me some weekend, Toad."

"I'd love to," I said.

As we passed under a sugar maple tree a gust of wind shook a shower of orange and red leaves down on our heads. We both laughed. "Remember how we'd rake up huge piles of leaves at the old house and then jump in them?" Daisy asked.

"Yeah. And remember the winter it snowed, like, five feet, and you jumped off the barn roof into a big drift?"

"Mom saw me from the kitchen window and nearly had a heart attack. And then she almost *killed* me," Daisy said.

"I built a snow igloo that time and Lily wrecked it," I recalled.

"Because you put up a sign that said No Little Sisters Allowed," Daisy reminded me.

"She's still a snoop," I complained. "That's one thing that will never change."

Daisy bent to pick up an acorn. She tossed it, and it bounced off an aluminum mailbox with a ping. "When you're the youngest in a family, people are always doing stuff and going places without you. Lily just wants to be part of things."

"She's not a baby anymore, though," I pointed out. "She has her own life and her own friends."

"Yeah, but you're her sister," Daisy said.

"She doesn't even like me! We have nothing in common."

"Maybe someday you'll find you're not as different as you think," Daisy predicted.

We continued along the road. For a second I had a pang. It was so great to spend time with Daisy again. I could be myself with her. She made me forget I was shy—we could talk about anything. I missed her so much when she was gone.

We were almost back to Main Street. As we'd walked, the

sky had darkened and now raindrops started to fall along with the autumn leaves. Laughing, Daisy and I ran the last block home.

A COUPLE OF hours later, Daisy had packed up her stuff and was putting on her coat. Rose and Stephen had already left for Boston in Stephen's car. "This was such a short visit," I said sadly as Mom, Lily, Snickers, and I walked Daisy downstairs.

"It'll be Thanksgiving before you know it," Daisy replied, putting her duffel bag down in the entryway so she could give us all hugs. When it was my turn, we hugged for an extra minute. "It was great to be with you on your birthday, Laurel," she said softly. I pressed my cheek against her sweet-smelling hair. "This is going to be your year. I just know it."

Daisy gave me one more squeeze and then we stepped apart. Mom, Lily, and I crowded around the door to watch her sprint out to Annie's little white Toyota. It was dusk and still drizzling. Daisy opened the hatch to toss in the duffel bag and then jumped into the driver's seat. Her blond hair was bright against the rainy darkness. "Bye!" Lily and I called after her.

"Drive safely!" Mom added.

Daisy started the engine and switched on the windshield wipers just as the rain began to fall in earnest. Then she drove off, with us waving until she was out of sight.

Mom, Lily, and I were quiet as we climbed the stairs

back up to the apartment. Even Snickers seemed a little subdued.

Just us three again, I thought with a sigh.

I WENT TO bed, but I didn't fall asleep right away. Usually I like rain, but tonight for some reason the steady drumming on the roof sounded bleak and foreboding. No matter how hard I tried, I couldn't doze off. When the telephone rang, I sat up abruptly. Who could be calling so late?

A minute later I snuggled back under my comforter. A wrong number, I thought.

Then the door to my bedroom swung open, banging loudly against the wall. Mom stood there in her long white nightgown, silhouetted by the light from the hall. "What is it, Mom?" I asked.

I couldn't see her expression, but the instant she spoke, I knew something was horribly wrong. "That was the New Hampshire state police," she told me, her voice shrill with fear. "There was an accident."

"Daisy," I gasped.

Three

DAWN ON MONDAY was dark and cold. The rain had ended, but the air was still heavy with moisture. Sitting by the front window, Lily and I heard the foghorn moaning off Rocky Point. It was an eerie sound.

"When do you think they'll get home?" Lily asked. After the phone call Mom had dressed and then gone over to get Hal. The two of them had driven together to the hospital in New Hampshire where Daisy had been taken by ambulance. Unable to go back to sleep, Lily and I had stayed up all night. We were both still in our nightgowns—she was wrapped in a crocheted afghan with just her face peeking out.

"I don't know." I pulled my flannel bathrobe up to my chin, "I'm sure Mom will call if Daisy can't leave the hospital right away and she needs to stay with her."

We continued to stare out the window. "Maybe we should

call the hospital and find out what's going on," Lily suggested.

"We don't even know what hospital it is," I reminded her.

"We could call New Hampshire information," Lily said. "Or the state police. Maybe they could—"

Just then the headlights of a car sliced through the fog on Main Street. Hal's new Subaru pulled up to the curb. Lily and I watched Hal help Mom out of the car. Daisy wasn't with them.

"She must still be in the hospital," Lily said, chewing her lip anxiously.

"I hope she didn't break her leg or something," I said. "Remember how awful it was when she tore her ligaments junior year in high school and couldn't play sports?"

"What if its worse than that, though?" Lily's face was pale. "Like a coma?"

"It isn't," I said softly. "Daisy will be fine."

We went into the front hall. A key rattled in the lock. The door swung open. Instead of coming in, though, Mom paused in the doorway. Hal was behind her, his hand resting protectively on her shoulder.

The moment I saw her face, I knew the news wasn't good. Her eyes were red, and her skin was blotchy. She'd been crying. "Mom?" Lily said, her voice trembling with the question we were both suddenly afraid to ask.

"Girls," Mom began. "Your sister is . . . Daisy is . . ."

Mom covered her face with her hands. Hal put his arms around her.

"No," I whispered. My whole body went cold with dread. *No no no no no no no . . .*

The words tore themselves from Mom's throat in a raw, heartbroken sob. "Daisy is dead."

I'M NOT SURE how long Mom, Lily, and I stood there, hugging one another and crying. At some point Mom collected herself enough to call Rose. While Hal made breakfast, Lily and I managed to get dressed, but then the four of us just sat at the table with plates of eggs and bacon and toast sitting untouched in front of us. No one could eat.

I kept my head down and hoped no one noticed the tears that were falling on my omelet. I took a sip of orange juice but choked on it. I spent the next few minutes taking deep breaths and collecting myself.

Rose and Stephen left Boston the minute they got Mom's call—they reached Hawk Harbor around eleven. When they burst into the apartment and I saw my big sister's grief-stricken face, my own tears began to flow again. "Oh, Mommy," Rose cried, flinging her arms around Mom. They stood that way for a long time, rocking back and forth and sobbing. Stephen looked sort of lost, standing next to her, so I walked over to him and squeezed his hand. He looked down at me gratefully, and I gave him a shaky smile through my tears.

When Rose noticed us standing there, she walked over and hugged me. We were both crying. "What are we going to do without her?" Rose whispered.

"I don't know," I whispered back. And I didn't.

* * *

JACK CAME OVER at lunchtime and helped my mother make the funeral arrangements. He was very calm, and I was so grateful to have him there that I kept bringing him cups of tea, even though I know he doesn't like tea. I didn't know what else to do. He must have understood why I was doing it, though, because he thanked me every time I brought him one and drank them all.

Somehow we got through the grim, gray day. At dinnertime Daisy's high school coach, Larry Wheeler, came over with his wife—they brought some food. Coach Wheeler and Mom hugged and cried while Mrs. Wheeler preheated the oven for the casserole. I lurked in the background because I didn't know how to act around people who were trying to cheer us up.

"Here's some dressing for the salad," Mrs. Wheeler told Rose, "and a loaf of Italian bread. If you need anything else, you just call us."

Her eyes brimming with tears, Rose hugged Mrs. Wheeler.

The casserole smelled good, but it had the same fate as the bacon and eggs at breakfast. Around the table nobody knew what to say to one another. I racked my brain for a topic of conversation to break the silence but couldn't come up with anything—my social skills aren't that good at the best of times. After a bite or two I pushed my plate away. "Mom, can I be excused?" I asked.

She nodded without speaking.

I went into the living room, but I didn't sit down. For

some reason, being still made me feel panicky. I paced up and down in front of the fireplace, my arms folded tightly across my chest.

A minute later Rose and Lily joined me. "I need to do something or I'll go crazy," I told them.

"Throw another log on the fire," Rose suggested.

I picked up a long cast-iron fork and turned the half-burned logs. The embers flickered as I put a fresh piece of wood on top of the pile.

"I'm cold," Lily said, huddling close to the hearth.

"The heat's up to seventy." Rose touched Lily's hand. "You *are* icy, though."

Rose wrapped her arms around Lily, resting her chin on Lily's head. For a minute the three of us stared at the fire in silence. I started pacing again. "It's not fair," I exclaimed suddenly.

"I know," Rose agreed.

"Isn't it enough that Dad died?" I went on.

"Maybe it wasn't Daisy in the car." Lily's voice was small. "Maybe it's a mistake."

"Mom saw her," Rose said gently.

Suddenly I was overcome by a feeling of helpless fury. "If that crummy car had had better tires, Daisy wouldn't have driven off the road," I cried. "Annie shouldn't have let Daisy borrow it!"

Rose looked at me for a moment. "I want to blame someone, too," she said finally, "but it was an accident, Toad. Annie cared for Daisy, too. It's nobody's fault."

"It still shouldn't have happened." My voice cracked with anguish. "We need her. She's our *sister.*"

Lily's face crumpled, tears slipped from Rose's eyes. Neither of them spoke, and my words seemed to echo in the silent room. *Our sister, our sister, our sister . . .*

Unbidden, a memory popped into my mind. Lily, at age six, was crying over a broken doll. When Daisy figured out what was the matter, she helped Lily bandage up the poor thing. Then she had helped Lily set up an entire doll hospital with a few of Rose's old castoffs. By the end of the day Lily had completely forgotten to be sad over her doll—she was too busy scouring the house for other "patients" who needed help.

Who could stop Lily from crying now? I wondered. My heart ached unbearably.

All at once everything felt wrong to me. It was as if the earth had tipped on its axis or stopped turning. As if the sun hadn't come up and never would again.

"Daisy," I whispered, the name like a prayer on my lips. A prayer that couldn't be answered.

D AISY'S FUNERAL WAS set for Wednesday. Tuesday afternoon, I wandered into the living room and found Rose sitting at the piano. Her hands rested on the keys, but she wasn't playing. "What are you doing?" I asked.

She closed the piano lid with a sigh. "Mom asked me to choose the hymns for the church service," she explained, "and I remember some of Daisy's favorites, but I can't bring myself to play them."

She got up, and we went over to sit on the couch. "I'm supposed to give a eulogy, too," Rose said. "Do you want to hear what I've written so far?"

I nodded. Lily planned to read at the funeral, too—she was writing a poem—but I'd told Mom I didn't want to. I don't write well, and I turn red and stammer when I have to speak in front of people. I'd have to find another way, a private way, to show my love and respect for Daisy. I knew she would understand.

Rose took a piece of notebook paper from the pocket of her jeans. She unfolded it and cleared her throat. "We're all here because we loved Daisy," she began, "and we loved Daisy because she brought sunshine into our lives. Today let's remember her warmth, her strength, her humor, and her generosity, and hold those memories close."

Rose paused. She closed her eyes for a few seconds, her jaw clenched. She started reading again. "Daisy wasn't only my sister. She was my best friend." Once more Rose had to stop, and this time she lifted the piece of paper, hiding her face. "I can't do it," she whispered.

I put a hand on her arm. "Yes, you can."

Rose shook her head, sniffling. "I thought I'd tell a couple of stories about Daisy, but even the funny ones make me cry."

"No one will care. We'll all be crying, too."

Rose didn't answer. We sat side by side on the couch, our arms around each other and tears on our faces, staring at the mute piano and listening to the silence that seemed to have enveloped the world.

I WAS UP early the morning of the funeral because I hadn't
been able to sleep the night before. Every time I'd dozed
off, the same terrible dream woke me up. In it, Daisy was leaving for New Hampshire the rainy day after my party. Over and
over I watched her climb into Annie's car. Over and over I
tried to warn her about the slippery roads, but when I opened
my mouth to speak, no words came out. Over and over she
drove blithely away, never to come back.

I was putting on a dark plaid dress with a black velvet collar
when Lily barged into my room without knocking, as usual.
"What do you want?" I asked.

"I don't know what to wear."

My horrible dreams had worn me out and had left me with
a feeling of helplessness and an edge of anger. I was about to
make a sarcastic comment about how she, of all people, should
have just the right outfit for a funeral in her overstuffed closet,
but then I took a closer look at her. In her pink terry cloth
robe and teddy bear slippers, Lily looked about five years old,
and sad, and scared.

"Come on," I said, softening. "I'll help you."

She shuffled down the hall with me. "It's supposed to be
something dark, but it doesn't have to be black," I told her as
we inspected her wardrobe. I pulled out a navy blue dress with
red piping at the neck and sleeves—pretty much the most conservative thing she owned. "This would work."

"Yeah?" Lily asked.

"Yeah."

"Th-thanks, Laurel," she whispered.

Tears welled in her eyes. Her nose was runny, too. I grabbed a tissue from the box on top of her dresser. "Here," I said.

Lily blew her nose.

"Are you going to be okay?" I asked.

She nodded.

I went back to my own room. It was strangely quiet. Alfalfa stopped eating his hay and looked up at me, his head tilted and both ears flopped over to one side. The parakeets weren't chattering the way they usually did. Even the turtles and fish seemed to be mourning along with me.

I gazed out the window at the heavy, dark clouds. Then, leaning my forehead against the glass, I closed my eyes, a feeling of dread weighing heavily on me. A moment later I heard Rose's voice behind me. "Laurel," she said quietly. "It's time to go."

OUR LITTLE CHURCH was packed. Mom's parents, Gram and Grandpa Sturdevant, had flown up from Florida the night before. Daisy's college roommates, Annie and Meghan, and her soccer teammates had driven over from Dartmouth. I spotted her high school friends Jamila and Kristin, and Coach Wheeler, and some of her old teachers from South Regional, and her friend Ben Compton, who'd survived a brain tumor. The Schenkels, the Comiskeys, the Applebys, the Beales, and the Mathiases filled a couple of pews, and Jack was sitting right behind me with my friend Ellen Adams.

The organist played some hymns that made my eyes well

up. Then Rose read her eulogy. It was very moving, and as she'd predicted, she cried, and as I'd predicted, everyone else in the church did, too.

When it was her turn to speak, Lily looked at me with wide eyes. "I'm scared," she whispered.

"You'll do fine," I whispered back.

Her shoulders rigid, Lily walked slowly to the front of the church. Reverend Beecher gave her an encouraging smile. Clutching a piece of paper in her trembling hands, she turned to face the congregation. She didn't look at the paper, though. She'd memorized her poem.

"Daisy's hands could throw a strike," Lily began in a small but lilting voice. "Or mend a doll, or fix a bike. / They were gentle, they were strong; / Her fingernails were never long— / That would have gotten in the way / Of making dinner, of work, of play. / Her hands were beautiful to me, but she was never vain." She stopped and took a deep breath. "I'll never hold those hands again. / The lonely wind sighs out her name."

Lily ducked her head, hiding her face behind a curtain of blond hair, and hurried back to the pew. Reverend Beecher resumed his homily. I took Lily's hand and held it tight.

The service concluded with a final hymn: "Amazing Grace." The melody is solemn, but I usually find it uplifting. Still, my heart felt as heavy as a stone inside my chest. I knew that the hardest part of the morning was still to come.

The last notes of the hymn died away. Reverend Beecher gave the benediction. For a minute the church was silent. Then the pallbearers—Hal, Stephen, Grandpa, and Coach

Wheeler—carried the coffin outdoors to the cemetery next to the church.

The day had turned cold and drizzly, but Reverend Beecher stood by the new grave with a bare head, his Bible open in his hand. "'The Lord is my shepherd, I shall not want,'" he read. "'He maketh me to lie down in green pastures: he leadeth me beside the still waters.'"

Jack stood next to me, gripping my hand in one of his and holding an umbrella over our heads. I listened to the words of the Twenty-third Psalm, but they didn't comfort me. I felt as if I were standing on a precipice, about to fall. Trying to hold myself onto the earth, I looked at Mom, her face pale against the black of her dress, and Rose clutching Stephen's hand, and Lily standing between Gram and Grandpa with her little bouquet of daisies.

"'Yea, though I walk through the valley of the shadow of death, I will fear no evil: for thou art with me.'"

Lily's face was streaked with tears. So was mine.

"'Surely goodness and mercy shall follow me all the days of my life: and I will dwell in the house of the Lord forever.' Amen." Reverend Beecher closed the book. He looked at Lily, and she stepped forward to place her flowers on top of the coffin. Then slowly the coffin was lowered into the grave.

I wanted to run forward and stop them from putting my sister's body in the ground. I couldn't stand to think of the weight of all that earth on her coffin—Daisy hated to be closed in, she liked the outdoors. . . . A ragged sob caught in my throat.

Jack squeezed my hand in silent sympathy. Mom was standing tall, but Rose and Stephen were both weeping. Meanwhile Lily had not stepped back. Her body small and hunched and her hair hanging down, she knelt on the wet grass at the edge of the grave, as if she could somehow get close enough to say good-bye.

A few minutes later people began to walk away across the damp grass to the cemetery gate. Ellen came over to pat my shoulder awkwardly before leaving. Jack and I were the last ones left. "Laurel?" he asked.

"Go on," I said. "I'll be right there."

He offered me the umbrella, but I didn't take it. I didn't care about the rain. Just a few days ago Daisy and I were together, I thought. Remembering our walk to the beach last Sunday and our talk, I realized that I'd never again hear the sound of her voice.

My tears fell with the raindrops onto the fresh dirt of the grave. I'd always depended on Daisy's love and advice. "Who will I talk to now?" I whispered.

There was, of course, no answer.

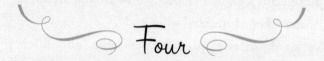

Four

I WENT TO school on Friday because I knew I would have to sooner or later, anyway. The minute I got there, though, I wished I'd stayed home. Everyone at South Regional had heard about Daisy, and people I didn't even know came up to me to tell me they were sorry. I didn't know what to say in return, so I just mumbled, "Thanks," my face red and my eyes stinging with unshed tears.

Somehow I made it through my morning classes. At lunch I hesitated outside the cafeteria. It was such a public place. Everyone will stare at me, I thought, cringing at the prospect.

I was about to turn away when Ellen appeared at my elbow. She has straight red hair and glasses and freckles, and she wears big sweaters that hang down to her knees. She's only about five feet tall. We're lab partners in physics, and she's about the closest girlfriend I have at South Regional.

Now she smiled tentatively up at me. "Hi. Want to have lunch?"

"I—I'm not that hungry," I said.

"You should eat, though." She gave me a friendly push. "Come on. I'll buy."

We got in the lunch line. Ellen slid my tray along for me and picked out a grilled cheese sandwich and an apple. "This okay?" she asked. I nodded wordlessly.

We sat down at a quiet corner table, and Ellen pulled something out of her backpack. "Physics notes from the days you missed," she explained.

I took the sheets of paper, touched by her thoughtfulness. "Thanks, Ellen."

"Just let me know if there's anything else I can do," she said.

The physics notes made me a little sniffly. As I was struggling to keep the tears away I spotted Jack. He'd come into the cafeteria with Ashley and Liz, one of Ashley's cheerleader friends. I could tell they were discussing where to sit. Jack glanced my way, but Ashley deftly steered him to another table.

He put his tray down with hers, then headed over to Ellen and me. Girls at neighboring tables checked him out as he walked past, but he didn't even notice.

I hope he's coming over to tell me a joke, I thought. I needed a laugh. Instead he placed his hands flat on the table and looked down into my eyes. "How're you doing?" he asked, his voice low and full of concern.

Something about the way he said it . . . I don't know, for some reason, his voice made me lose it. "Excuse me," I choked out, pushing back my chair.

I bolted out of the cafeteria, my braid flapping behind me. Jack ran after me. "I need a ride," I told him when we were out in the hall.

Jack didn't ask any questions. He just nodded.

We stopped at the principal's office so I could get excused from my afternoon classes and Jack could get permission to leave school. Then he drove me home.

Inside the apartment it was quiet. All week long there'd been nonstop activity as friends and neighbors dropped by with casseroles and condolences. This morning, though, my grandparents had flown home to Florida and Rose and Stephen had headed back to Boston because Stephen had a meeting with his thesis adviser that he couldn't postpone and Rose had a weekend performance with her a cappella singing group.

I felt dumb for making such a scene at school, so I tried to cover it up with talk. "I wonder where Mom is?" I said as Jack and I went into the kitchen. "Working or doing errands, I guess, but usually she leaves a note, you know?"

Jack bent to open the door to the puppy's crate, which is in the corner next to the refrigerator. Snickers catapulted out and started jumping on him. "She's working this week?"

"Yeah, everybody's trying to throw themselves right back into normal life, I guess. Mom has a couple of parties this week-end. Her assistant, Sarah, offered to take over the catering stuff for a while to give her some time off, but Mom didn't want to. Do you want something to eat?" I asked, turning to look in the fridge. "You didn't get to have lunch. I could make a sandwich. There's leftover roast chicken."

"No, thanks. I think I'll just head back to school."

I whirled to face him. I don't know why, but suddenly I was terrified of being alone, and I'm sure it showed on my face.

"Unless you want me to stick around," Jack added. "I'll stay if you want, Laurel."

"N-No. That's all right," I stammered, embarrassed that my feelings were so transparent. "You might get in trouble."

"I'm sure I could get an excuse. I'm not worried about it."

"No, I'm okay," I said, even though I wasn't.

We were on opposite sides of the kitchen island. Now Jack walked around to stand next to me. "Laurel," he said softly. "You know I'm always here for you if you need me."

"I—I know," I said, dropping my eyes.

"Like after school or tonight, if you want company. We could go for a hike or see a movie."

I was about to say that I did want him to stay with me. Instead, for some mysterious reason, I found myself asking in an accusatory tone, "Don't you and Ashley have a date tonight?"

At this point I wasn't sure what, if anything, was going on between Jack and Ashley. It seemed like a year since the waffles incident last Sunday morning. They were about to eat lunch together today, though, I recalled.

"We don't really have a date," Jack answered, "I mean, we talked about maybe doing something, but it's not definite."

"Well, don't change your plans on my behalf," I said testily. I don't know why I was feeling so furious. "You don't need to sit around holding my hand."

"All right," Jack said, his expression puzzled.

I turned away so he wouldn't see that once again, I was about to start crying. "I'm really all right," I repeated. I grabbed a loaf of bread and a jar of peanut butter and got busy making a sandwich. "Thanks for the ride." Please say that you know I'm not all right, I thought. Please give me a hug.

"I'll call you tomorrow, okay?"

"Okay."

He waited a minute. I knew he was watching me, but I kept my back stubbornly turned. I certainly wasn't about to beg him to comfort me. "Adios, amiga," he said at last.

Jack's footsteps receded. I heard the front door squeak open and then thump shut. Looking out the kitchen window a few seconds later, I saw him get in his car and drive off. Then, even though peanut butter probably isn't good for puppies, I tore the sandwich into bits and fed it to Snickers.

AN HOUR LATER I decided that coming home early from school hadn't been the greatest idea. I didn't have anything to do, and I needed a distraction—something more stimulating than homework—to take my mind off Daisy. There's no point in going outside, I decided. Bright bolts of lightning illuminated the dark sky, and rain pelted the windows. I knew better than to walk in the woods or on the beach in weather like that.

I considered my other options. The library? The mall? I called the WRC, but the machine picked up. "We're closed right now. If this is an emergency, contact County Animal Control. Otherwise call back tomorrow," Griffin's raspy voice advised.

I wandered aimlessly around the apartment, Snickers tagging along at my heels. In the family room I put away some CDs that were lying on top of the stereo and straightened the couch pillows. Mom had left a grocery bag of canned goods on the floor outside the pantry, and I stacked them on the shelves, taking extra time to separate the vegetables from the fruits and the soups. Then I had a brainstorm. Laundry! It had been piling up all week. It was all downstairs already; I just needed to throw it in the washing machine.

I started a load and sorted the rest of the dirty clothes into three baskets: lights, darks, and in-betweens. When that was done, I headed upstairs to my bedroom. I'll change my sheets, I thought, and dust the bookshelves and clean Alfalfa's cage and . . .

I reached my room, but I didn't step through the door. Someone was sitting in my rocking chair.

Mom.

My room used to be Daisy's room before she left for college, and some of Daisy's stuff was still in the closet. Mom had gotten out a box full of sports gear. A softball mitt lay on her lap, and she was clutching one of Daisy's old South Regional High soccer jerseys, the faded cloth held up to her cheek. She was sobbing.

I stood in the doorway, paralyzed. Mom hadn't noticed me yet, and I didn't know what to do. I wanted to comfort her, but I didn't know how.

Just then Snickers bounded into the room, heading straight for the rocking chair. Mom looked up, startled. "Oh, Laurel, I'm sorry." She dabbed at her wet eyes with the shirt. "I didn't know you were—I just—I just—"

The tears started again. Mom bent and picked up Snickers and hugged her as she'd hugged the soccer jersey, grief flowing from her like a river.

I crossed the room and crouched beside the rocking chair. My own loss was unbearable; I could only imagine Mom's. What could I say to make her feel better? Words seemed so inadequate.

I ended up not saying anything. I put my arms around my mother and she rested her head on top of mine while Snickers licked the tears from both of our faces.

O N SATURDAY MORNING I woke up at dawn and couldn't go back to sleep. After showering and eating breakfast, I stuck a banana and a couple of books in my backpack. Dressed in a turtleneck and overalls with an anorak on top, I headed outside into the misty fall morning.

I still didn't have my driver's license—I was going to take the test in another week—and I had lots of time to kill, so instead of biking I decided to walk the three miles to the WRC.

I set out down Lighthouse Road, then cut across a field to the woods that ran behind the Lilac Inn. I followed a path that hopped the creek and emerged from the trees by the Schen-kels' driveway. After another half mile I reached the rocky beach at Kettle Cove.

I sat down on a big, flat boulder and ate my banana, listen-ing to the water rolling and hissing up to the seaweed-covered shore. Past the neck of the cove, fishing boats chugged out to check the lobster pots. My father and his father before him were fishermen, and whenever I'm near the ocean, I think about Dad. This morning, with the newly risen sun shining in my eyes, I tried to picture his face, and for the first time since he died, I couldn't. It had been too long. Will I forget Daisy's face? I wondered, my heart aching at the thought.

Griffin was at his desk doing paperwork when I got to the WRC around eight-thirty. "Didn't think you'd make it this morning," he called out as I hung my backpack on a peg in the hall. He walked out and stood near me, his hands in the pock-ets of his jeans. "I'm sorry about your sister, Laurel."

"Thanks." I shrugged, trying to look tough. It didn't work. I'm not going to cry, I thought, but it was too late. A tear slid down my cheek.

Under his scruffy exterior, Griffin is a warm and gentle person. He folded his arms around me in a bear hug. "It'll be okay."

"Thanks," I said again, whispering this time.

I cut through the building to the infirmary, where I found Carlos sitting on a table with something round and fuzzy and brown cradled in his arms. "What have you got?" I asked him.

Carlos was trying to stick a baby bottle in the animal's mouth, but it kept wriggling. "Harbor seal," he grunted. "A couple of months old. His mom got killed by a boat propeller." Carlos frowned down at the seal. "He won't take the formula."

We haven't had a seal the whole time I'd worked at the WRC. They don't hang out in the waters of Hawk Harbor anymore. "Want me to do some research and find out what they like to eat?" I offered.

"I already put a call in to the aquarium guy down in the city, but yeah. See what you come up with. Jeez." Carlos's voice cracked. He shook his head. "He's dropped a lot of weight already, you know? I don't want to lose the little guy."

I put out a hand to touch the seal's sleek fur. "We won't lose him," I declared. "I'll look on the Internet right now."

Carlos met my eyes. For a second he looked young and a little scared—as young and scared as me. Then he managed to smile. "Right. You're right, Laurel. I don't know why I even said that. Just because I haven't cared for a seal before doesn't mean I should panic."

"You'll figure it out."

"We'll figure it out."

I turned to head back to the office and Griffin's computer. Carlos's voice stopped me at the door. "I should've said this sooner, Laurel. I'm sorry . . . about Daisy."

It was the same thing people had been saying to me for days, but somehow I knew Carlos really meant it. "Thanks," I told him softly. I hoped he knew I meant it, too.

* * *

WHEN I GOT home, I called Jack from the family room phone. "I was wondering when I'd hear from you," he said. "I called this morning, but you'd already left for work. How are you holding up?"

"Not bad," I lied. "It felt good to be busy, anyway."

"Well, I thought about you all day."

My throat got tight. I decided to get right to the point to minimize the possibility that I'd end up crying. "I just wanted to thank you for bringing me home yesterday," I said. "That was nice of you."

"The least I could do, Walker."

"So, do you want to go canoeing on the river tomorrow? We won't have many more decent days—pretty soon it'll be too cold."

"Actually . . ." He hesitated. "I might be going to the outlets in Kittery with Ashley."

"So you two are really a couple, huh?" I asked, my voice a little shaky.

"I guess."

"You *guess?*"

"It's kind of heading in that direction, yeah. But Laurel, you know, you're—" He stopped and sighed. "Look, I'll call you tomorrow, okay?"

"Don't bother if you're busy." I didn't know why I was acting so sulky, but I couldn't seem to control it.

"I'll call you," Jack repeated.

I hung up the phone, and once again the tears began to fall. How many could a single person shed?

* * *

AT DINNERTIME MOM put a meat loaf in the oven for me and Lily and then dashed off to a wedding cake workshop in Portland. When the timer went off, I called upstairs, "Lily, supper."

Five minutes later I'd made a salad, set the table, and poured a couple of glasses of milk, but Lily still hadn't appeared. With a sigh, I stomped upstairs to get her.

Her door was ajar, so I walked in. The room was dim. Lily's desk lamp was on, but she'd draped a towel over the shade. Lily herself was lying facedown on the bed with her face buried in the pillow.

She looked asleep. I won't wake her up, I decided, turning to leave. She can microwave her dinner later. Then I heard a sniffle.

I took a step toward the bed and then hesitated. Maybe Lily wanted to be left alone . . . then again, maybe she didn't. I didn't know what to do. How could I comfort her? I guessed I could say, "I know how you're feeling," but did I? Was our sorrow the same? I don't know how to talk to my own sister, I realized. Not unless we're fighting.

I knelt beside the bed, the same way I'd knelt next to Mom in the rocking chair, and touched Lily's back so lightly, she probably didn't even feel it. At any rate, she gave no sign. I waited a minute, listening to her ragged breathing, and then stood up and tiptoed out of the room.

I didn't go back down to the kitchen and the lukewarm meat loaf. Instead I retreated to my own room, feeling sick to my stomach.

What was wrong with me? I took Lewis from the birdcage, then paused in front of the mirror to study my reflection. My brown hair had come loose from its braid and looked a little wild; my green eyes were big in my pale face. I hugged my parakeet. Why did I know the right thing to do around animals but never around people?

Lewis started pecking at the buckle on my overall strap. I turned away from the mirror to stick him back in the cage, tossing in a handful of seed before I latched the door. Around me, the stillness of the house felt heavy and oppressive, like the air before a storm. The only sounds I heard were Alfalfa munching his hay and my own heart beating in a lost, erratic way.

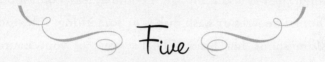

Five

FALL DARKENED INTO early winter, and I alternated between feeling numb and being overwhelmed by uncontrollable emotions. One Monday afternoon there was a special ceremony at the South Regional gym—a plaque was put up in Daisy's memory. Mom and Lily both cried when Coach Wheeler made the dedication, but I sat stiff and dry eyed, as if I were carved of granite. The next day, though, heading to gym class, I spotted Daisy's face in one of the team pictures on the wall outside the locker rooms and I burst into tears.

"I'm not going to be around the next few nights," Mom told me when I got home from school that afternoon.

She was in the kitchen, sifting flour into a gigantic mixing bowl. "What's up?" I asked.

"I'm catering a preconcert event at the Portland Symphony tomorrow," she answered, "and then I'm taking a class at the culinary institute, and I have a cocktail party in Kent on Friday."

"You're so busy! Do you need any help?"

"I think Sarah and I can handle it," Mom replied.

"I'm around, though, you know." I hitched myself onto a stool at the counter. "I mean, Daisy used to help you with parties when she was about my age. I could at least come along to pass hors d'oeuvres or wash dishes or something. Lily, too."

Mom shook her head. "That's sweet of you, Laurel. I absolutely don't want to burden you two girls, though. No. But thanks, hon."

She patted me on the cheek with a floury hand and then turned back to her work.

Since she didn't need me, I went into the family room, planning to turn on the computer to type up an English paper that was due the next day. Lily was already sitting in front of it, though, as usual. She surfs the net twenty-four hours a day. "I need to use the computer," I told her.

"So do I," she countered, not turning away from the screen.

"You're only supposed to use it for an hour at a time, and only for homework," I reminded Lily. I crossed the room to look over her shoulder. As I suspected, she was in a chat room. "That doesn't look like homework."

Lily hit exit, but not before I saw the last few words she'd typed. "Who's 'lilli'?" I asked her.

She raised one eyebrow at me.

"What's with the lowercase *l?*" I pressed.

"I just felt like a change, okay?" she said defensively.

I took her place in front of the computer. "What were you and Mom talking about just now?" she asked.

Typical Lily—always putting her nose in everyone's business. "Catering," I said. I couldn't hold back a troubled sigh. "Mom won't let me help her."

"Of course not," Lily said offhandedly. "You'd just screw up."

I frowned. I knew I wasn't as capable as Daisy had been, but it didn't help to hear Lily say so. "Thanks for the moral support," I said dryly.

"Anytime," she shot back on her way out of the room.

I clicked the mouse on my homework folder and propped up my spiral notebook so I could read the notes I'd scribbled for my English paper. At least Lily's back to normal, I thought. For a while there, it had almost looked as if Daisy's death might draw us closer together. That didn't seem too likely anymore.

T HE FOLLOWING SATURDAY morning I beat Carlos to the WRC. When he arrived, I was already in the infirmary, feeding the baby seal, whom we'd named Lefty because he liked to wave his left flipper. "He took twelve ounces!" I announced proudly.

"No kidding!" Carlos joined us. "What's the trick?"

"A new bottle," I said. "I bought a bunch of different styles at the drugstore. Lefty likes this one the best."

The seal was still guzzling formula. Carlos laughed. "I'll say."

"Plus I added some pureed anchovies. First I soaked them to get the salt off. I read about that on the Net."

"Must be the biggest meal he's had yet," Carlos said.

I nodded.

I started to hand Lefty over to Carlos, but Carlos shook his head. "No, you're doing great. Stick with it."

Carlos went over to the counter to read my notes about the formula. He tapped a pencil on the page. "The expert from the aquarium, Fred, is coming up on Monday," he told me. "He's going to talk to us about how we should handle Lefty so that he'll be ready to be re-released into the wild next summer."

I ran a fingertip along the glossy fur on Lefty's brow. It was hard to believe he'd ever be big enough to fend for himself in the ocean. "Oh."

"Why don't you put together a short presentation for Fred to fill him in on what we've been doing so far? That is, if you don't have anything else going on after school on Monday."

I glanced quickly up at Carlos, momentarily panicked. "No, I can't. I'm really not good at—" Thankfully, I remembered something. "I have a science club meeting on Monday. I shouldn't miss it."

"Are you sure? This would be good experience for you."

"You should give the presentation," I insisted. "You're in charge. You know more than I do."

Carlos leaned back against the counter, his arms folded across his chest, and studied me. "Okay," he said finally. "I don't want to pressure you."

I dropped my eyes and pretended to be busy rearranging Lefty and his bottle.

Did I look like a total wimp? I wondered. Carlos was trying to teach me, to give me more responsibility. "Well, maybe I should give it a try," I started to say. But when I looked up, he was gone. It was just as well. If I tried to give the presentation, I'd only get tongue-tied and humiliate myself in front of Carlos. It was best for me to stay behind the scenes, where I belonged.

R OSE AND STEPHEN came home that weekend to help Mr. and Mrs. Mathias look for a place to hold the rehearsal dinner. The wedding date had been set for early June. "I'm stuffed," Rose groaned on Sunday afternoon. "We ate lunch at three different restaurants!"

Stephen had popped over to his parents' house. Rose and I were in the family room, channel surfing. It was raining, for a change.

"I'm glad I caught you before you headed off to the WRC again," Rose said. I'd been running over there a lot lately, even when I wasn't working, to check on Lefty. "I want to talk to you about something." She clicked off the TV.

"What is it?" I asked.

"It's about the wedding," Rose said. "I want you to be my maid of honor, Laurel."

I stared at her in surprise. I have to admit, I had barely thought about the wedding at all lately. It was the furthest thing from my mind. "You mean, because Daisy . . . But why me?"

"You're my next oldest sister," Rose explained. "You're the one I want standing next to me when I take my vows with Stephen."

I knew this was a big honor, but I didn't squeal with delight. The whole idea of taking Daisy's place, of doing her job . . . it didn't appeal to me on a lot of levels. "Wh-what else does a maid of honor do?" I asked nervously.

"Well, usually the maid of honor plans the bridal shower," Rose told me, "and in general helps the bride with stuff, especially on the day of the wedding. You're basically the head bridesmaid. Chairwoman of the board."

Plan a bridal shower? This was getting worse and worse. All of that was the kind of stuff Daisy would have been great at. And it was the kind of stuff that I would totally screw up. "Val's older than me," I pointed out. "She'd probably do a better job."

Valerie is Stephen's twenty-one-year-old sister. She and Rose didn't get along back in high school, but now they're friends. Stephen's younger sister, Elizabeth, who is my age, was going to be a bridesmaid, too.

"It has to be you, Toad," Rose insisted with a smile. She looked a little sad, though. "Val doesn't even come close to meaning as much to me as you do." I thought about how Rose had said in her eulogy that Daisy was her best friend. It must be really hard for her to ask anyone to stand in for Daisy, I realized. I can't make her ask Val.

"I'll do it," I told her, reaching for her hand.

She smiled and I smiled, too, and that was the end of the

conversation. I consoled myself with the thought that the wedding was more than six months off. I didn't have to worry about it . . . yet.

Afternoon on Monday, before the science club meeting started, Ellen and I went to the cafeteria to buy snacks at the vending machine, and we ran into Jack and Ashley. "Hi," Jack said.

Ashley flashed me an insincere smile. I can tell it bugs her that Jack's best friend is a girl. Not that I'm much of a threat.

"Hi," I replied.

I feel uncomfortable around Ashley, so I gave Ellen a let's-get-out-of-here look. Before we could take off, though, Jack said to me, "Science club, right? I'm walking Ash to cheerleading practice, and then I have a wrestling team meeting. We're going the same way."

He was right—unfortunately. The four of us fell into step together. "Science club?" Ashley asked, lifting one blond eyebrow. "How intellectual!"

"We're planning the spring science fair," Ellen told her.

"Think you'll enter this year?" Jack asked me.

I shrugged. I like science—that's why I'm in the club. But I'm not competitive. "Maybe."

"We should do a project together," Ellen suggested.

"You should, Laurel," Jack declared. "Maybe you'd win a prize."

The science talk must have bored Ashley because she changed the subject. "We were just talking about ski season," she said, giving Jack's arm a possessive hug. "I bought a new ski outfit in Kittery the other day, and I can't wait for the snow. Do you ski, Laurel?"

"A little. I'm not very good."

"She likes to do other things," Jack put in loyally. "Canoeing, bird-watching . . ."

Ashley laughed. "You'd rather look at birds than ski?"

Luckily we'd reached the room where the science club meets, so I didn't have to answer her. "So long," Jack said as he and Ashley continued on toward the gym.

Ellen and I sat down. "Ashley's something else," she commented.

"You're not kidding."

"Jack must have a split personality. He's best friends with you, and he's dating her. You two are like different species. What's the common denominator?"

Personally, I thought that Jack going out with Ashley Esposito was pretty depressing, but Ellen's expression was so genuinely baffled, I had to laugh. "Beats me."

NOVEMBER DAYS ARE short. It was already dusk when I got home from the science club meeting. Still in my parka and mittens, I let Snickers out of her crate, clipped her leash to her collar, and took her outside for a walk.

This was my favorite part of the day. It's hard to explain, but I always feel really connected to animals, and that was especially true with Snickers. Walking with her was my time to just be.

As we crossed the street to the park it started to snow—big fat flakes that made Snickers bark and jump. It was the first snow of the year.

"What do you think?" I asked as she snapped at a snowflake, trying to eat it. "Cold, huh?"

I let her off the leash so she could romp a little. The snow was falling faster. I tilted back my head. Flakes stung my cheeks and nose—I opened my mouth to get a taste.

As snowflakes tickled my tongue I almost smiled. Then I remembered . . . not that I could ever forget. One month since she died, I thought. A month that had felt like a year, each hour heavy and dark.

I clapped my mittened hands together, whistling for Snickers, but she was busy digging a hole and didn't pay attention to me. The snow swirled around us, and suddenly I was bombarded by the kinds of memories I'd been trying hard lately to suppress. Daisy had loved winter. We'd always had so much fun playing in the snow! She made the goofiest snowmen—there'd been one with a baseball mitt and Boston Red Sox cap. And she never got tired of towing me and Lily on the sled up the hill in our old backyard on Lighthouse Road. Then there was that big neighborhood snowball fight when I was about seven. Kyle Cooper had nailed me in the nose. Daisy made sure I was okay and then carried me home piggyback.

Tears streamed down my face, mingling with melted snowflakes. "Snickers, come on," I shouted hoarsely.

I started walking home. Then the walk turned into a run. I could hardly see where I was going, and I didn't even care if

Snickers was following me, which luckily she was. I ran blindly down Main Street, back to my building and up the stairs, with Snickers barking at my heels because she thought this was some sort of new game.

"Hello?" I cried out when I entered the apartment. Silence answered me. "Mom?"

No one was home.

At that moment I would have welcomed even Lily's company. Where are they? I wondered, shivering uncontrollably.

I stood in the kitchen, still bundled in my parka. My frantic gaze came to rest on the telephone. Quickly I grabbed the handset and punched in a well-known telephone number. "You're home from wrestling," I exclaimed with relief when I heard Jack's voice.

"What's wrong, Laurel?"

"Oh, Jack." A sob caught in my throat.

I started to cry. "Are you at home?" he asked.

"Yes."

"I'll be right over."

Five minutes later car tires screeched to a stop in front of the bakery. Jack's feet pounded on the stairs and he pushed through the front door, which I'd left ajar. "Oh, Laurel," he said. I was too sad to be embarrassed about bawling in front of him—not that I could have stopped. "Here, let's get you out of that coat."

He unzipped my parka and pulled it off, draping it over a chair. I'd hoped that seeing him would cheer me up, but somehow his tenderness only made me cry harder. "Jack, I can't stand it anymore," I sobbed, flinging myself into his arms.

"I know," he said, hugging me.

"Why did it have to happen to *her*, when so many people loved her?"

"It doesn't seem fair."

"I want her back."

"I know."

Jack kept murmuring comforting things as he stroked my hair.

I clung to him tightly. I knew that if I let go, I'd start to fall over that cliff that always seemed to be right in front of me these days. "Oh, Jack," I whispered. "What would I do without you?"

I lifted my tear-streaked face to his. In my grief, I hadn't really noticed how close we were, but now I grew aware of the warmth of his body against mine. I stared into the green eyes I knew so well. "Jack," I whispered again.

I'm not sure if I made the first move or if he did, but suddenly my mouth touched his and we were kissing. It was galaxies apart from our awkward spin-the-bottle kiss back in eighth grade. It was an adult kiss—deep, searching, passionate.

I wanted it to last forever.

Six

"YOU MIGHT AS well just shoot me," I told Ellen as we huddled by my locker the next morning, "before I die of embarrassment."

"I can't believe you guys *kissed.*" Ellen grabbed my arm and gave it a shake. "After knowing each other for, like, a hundred *years!* And when he's dating *Ashley!* What happened after that?"

I filled Ellen in on the rest of the episode, including Lily's timely arrival. Jack and I hadn't gotten a chance to talk about the kiss, and when he called later, I instructed Lily to tell him I was asleep.

Now I considered climbing into my locker and locking the door behind me. "I only told you because we might need to make a speedy getaway," I explained. "In case we see—"

At that moment I spotted Jack striding purposefully toward me. Slamming my locker, I bolted in the opposite direction,

Ellen hurrying after me. At the end of the corridor I ducked into the girls' room. "How long do you think you can keep this up?" she panted.

"Indefinitely," I replied.

Avoiding Jack was a challenge, though. We usually sat next to each other in the second-to-last row in English. Today I slipped into class just as the bell was ringing, snagging the last empty seat in the front row. I could feel Jack's eyes on the back of my head for the whole hour, but when the bell rang at the end of class, I sprinted out of the room before he could catch me.

I knew I'd be a sitting duck in the cafeteria, so I decided to spend lunch period in the library. I took a roundabout route, steering way clear of Jack's locker. Just when I thought I was safe, though, I rounded a corner and bumped right into him.

"Whoa." Before I could try the girls' room trick again, Jack grabbed my arm. "Hold on."

"I have to go. There's a book in the library I really—"

"We need to talk," he cut in.

My face was burning. When I saw that Jack's was pink, too, I blushed even harder. "What if we just pretend this whole thing—"

Still holding my arm, he dragged me over to the stairwell door. "No."

I was trapped, so as soon as we were alone in the stairwell, I launched into the speech I'd been rehearsing in my head all morning. "About yesterday," I began. "I was just upset. It was a mistake. Ashley doesn't have to know anything about it. I'm really sorry—"

"I'm not," Jack interrupted.

I blinked at him. "You're not?"

He shook his head, smiling wryly. "Are you kidding? That was a great kiss."

My blush had started to fade, but now my cheeks flamed again. It *was* a great kiss, I had to admit. Not that I had much to compare it to, but still, I'd read enough books and seen enough movies. "But Jack. You and me. We're friends."

"We're friends," he agreed. His eyes were shining with a bright, hungry light. "But that's not all, at least, not for me. I've been in love with you a long time, Laurel."

In *love?* "B-But in j-junior high, w-we—"

"That going-steady fiasco—yeah, I remember. You wanted to be just friends after that, so I hid my feelings. But they didn't change."

I was speechless. Not that Jack's words should have totally surprised me—on some level, deep inside, I could have guessed how he felt about me. "But what about Ashley?" I asked.

"Forget Ashley," Jack said gruffly.

"But you're a couple."

He shrugged. "We're not serious."

I didn't get it. Ashley was gorgeous—half the boys in our class had a crush on her. "How *come* you're not serious?"

"I don't love her. I love *you,* and I always have."

Jack stepped over and slipped his arms around my waist, pulling me close. "She's so pretty, though," I said, resisting the hug a little.

"Not where it counts."

"She's a cheerleader! Everybody wants to go out with a cheerleader."

"Yeah, but she doesn't know the names of the constellations and she can't climb a tree and she couldn't tell bear tracks from coyote tracks. She doesn't think about things the way you do. She doesn't *care* about things the way you do."

Relaxing a little, I allowed Jack to hold me. I still felt self-conscious, but it was passing. This feels okay, I thought. "I still don't understand. If you don't like Ashley, why have you been hanging out with her?"

"I don't know. I was a little mad at you, I guess. I felt like you took me for granted. Okay, I'm not proud of this, but I wanted to make you jealous."

"I *was* jealous," I admitted. It was true, even though the jealousy hadn't felt romantic. Or had it? I was confused.

"But then, after Daisy died, spending time with Ashley started to feel wrong. I was thinking about breaking up with her. Not that you gave me any encouragement in that direction." He gave me a squeeze. "That is, until yesterday."

"You're going to break up?"

"Yes."

I didn't try to talk him out of it. Let's face it, I wanted Jack all to myself. "What do we do now?" I asked.

"I have a proposal," Jack said.

"What?"

"We could kiss again. Then if it *was* a mistake, like back in eighth grade, we'll know. Right?"

It sounded logical. I smiled. "Right."

"All right. So, um . . ." He put his hand under my chin, tipping my face upward. "Is this . . . okay?"

I didn't answer. I didn't have to. We kissed for a long time, and it wasn't like eighth grade at all. It was awesome—even better than the day before.

There was something else about this kiss. This time it wasn't an accident. We knew what we were doing, so it felt like a promise. Like the start of something.

Me and Jack, I thought dizzily. Me and Jack!

Y OU AND JACK. Cool," said Karlee Kennedy, who's in my homeroom.

That pretty much seemed to be everyone's opinion. By lunchtime on Wednesday the whole school knew that Jack and Ashley had broken up and that Ashley was now going out with Reeve Shipley, cocaptain of the South Regional varsity ice hockey team, and that Jack and I were a couple. In some ways being a couple was totally weird, but in other ways it felt completely normal. It was distracting, anyhow. It gave me something to think about besides Daisy.

"I saw you holding hands in the hall!" Ellen hissed in my ear as we walked into physics.

She and I had gotten pretty tight lately. It was kind of fun to have a girlfriend to gossip with. "So?" I hissed back, only blushing a little.

"So, I still can't believe it."

I shrugged. I'd never had a boyfriend to hold hands with in the hall, unless you counted my brief nonrelationship with

Nathan Green in eighth grade, but now that I did, it really didn't seem like that big a deal. "It's just Jack," I reminded Ellen.

"Yeah, but things are different now," she pointed out.

Maybe that was true, but in some ways nothing had changed. Jack was still my best friend. It was kind of convenient, really. "I always thought I'd be nervous about going out with somebody," I confided. "I wouldn't know what to say or how to act. But it's not like that at all with Jack."

"I'm psyched for you guys," Ellen said. "I always thought you'd make a great couple."

"You did? You could have predicted this?"

Ellen nodded wisely. "Of *course*. It was *inevitable*."

I bounced Ellen's theory off Jack as we waited for the movie to start at the cinema in Kent on Friday night. "Do you think this was inevitable?" I asked, reaching over for a handful of popcorn.

Jack slid an arm across the back of my seat. "Yep."

"You mean, like, destiny?"

He flashed me a grin. "Definitely. Destiny. Meant to be. I didn't even mind having to wait for you. Like Meredith in the meadow."

The lights dimmed and the previews started. We finished the popcorn, and Jack put the empty box on the floor so he could take my hand. He leaned over to whisper in my ear, "You're not getting cold feet, are you?"

My feet were pretty warm, and so was the rest of me. "I don't think so," I whispered back.

We didn't get home until almost midnight. "This is the first time I've stayed out until my curfew," I told Jack as he parked in front of Wissinger's Bakery. "I wonder if Mom's waiting up for me?"

"She knows you're in good hands," Jack said.

We unbuckled our seat belts and then sat there. Time to make out, I thought nervously. "Um, do you want to . . ."

"Yes," said Jack.

"Okay. So . . . how?"

"Like this," he suggested, pulling me close.

I was halfway on his lap, with the gearshift poking me in the waist. I felt pretty ridiculous. After kissing for a minute I pulled back. "Does this seem kind of . . . um . . . *physical* to you?" I asked, figuring Jack might as well know what was on my mind. "Since this is only our first real date?"

"You mean, maybe we shouldn't be kissing when we hardly know each other?" he joked.

"Seriously," I said. "Maybe it was inevitable and all that, but that doesn't mean we have to go so fast."

"I won't pressure you about sex," he promised. "I'd never be like that, especially not with you."

"Good. But Jack . . ."

His eyes twinkled in the darkness. "Unless you *want* me to pressure you about sex."

"No!" Just the mention of the word *sex* made me blush furiously. "What I'm trying to say is . . ." I hesitated. What *was* I trying to say? How *did* I feel about all of this? "It's me, Jack. Laurel Walker, the girl who used to make you roll up your nice pants and wade around in mud puddles collecting tadpoles. Is this really what you're looking for?"

Jack's arms tightened around me. "Didn't I tell you that I've always been crazy about you?"

I squirmed a little. "Yeah, but—"

"I'm not going back to before," he said suddenly.

"You're not?"

"We're not," he corrected himself. "This is better. Isn't it?"

I gazed into his eyes. They were so warm and loving. Just then I realized something. I hadn't cried once today, and it was thanks to Jack. Who could ask for a more perfect boyfriend? He knew me better than anyone else. He knew what I was going through. And he'd help me deal with it. Maybe I'd be okay after all. "Yes," I said softly. "It's better."

We kissed again. Jack was a great kisser—a lot better than me, I'm sure. His kisses made me feel as if we were the only two people on the planet.

"I adore you," he whispered in my ear.

I snuggled into the curve of Jack's arm. No one had ever said that to me, and if I'd thought about it, I might have been embarrassed. But I didn't think about it. It was easier just to feel, and at that moment I felt better than I had in a long time.

Seven

THE NEXT MORNING Lily talked Mom into taking us to a wedding reception she was catering at an oceanfront mansion a few miles up the coast. Mom didn't have much choice—the night before, Sarah had come down with a bad case of the flu. I was pretty sure Lily didn't actually plan to work—she probably just wanted to mingle with the guests and pretend she was someone she's not—but I intended to be as helpful as possible. Who knows? I thought, not quite daring to hope. Maybe I'd do a great job! Anyway, some experience with wedding stuff would probably be good for me—I could use a little maid of honor practice.

The first hour Lily and I set tables on the veranda. Then, while Mom consulted with the florist and the bartender, we started warming up hors d'oeuvres—the huge kitchen had four ovens. Mom always made giant batches of appetizers ahead of time and kept them frozen until the day of the party.

We could hear the guests beginning to arrive. Mom stuck her head in the kitchen. "When the first tray is ready, bring it out," she told me before disappearing again.

"I can't believe *you're* going out with Jack Harrison," Lily remarked, using a hot mitt to pull a baking sheet from the oven. "He's so cool and you're so . . . not."

"What do you know about anything?" I retorted. I started arranging the little shrimp and goat cheese tarts on a silver platter. "Here." I tossed Lily a dish towel. "Wash those other platters—they got dusty in the car. I'm going to pass out the hors d'oeuvres."

"Why should *I* wash the platters?" Lily protested. "I want to pass hors d'oeuvres."

I was trying to be patient with her but having a hard time. "Because I'm the oldest and Mom wants me to do it." I picked up the tray.

"You are the least coordinated and graceful person in the entire world," Lily declared. "I'm going to pass the hors d'oeuvres. I'll do a much better job." She tried to take the tray from me.

I pulled it back. "No, you're not."

"Yes, I am."

She gave the tray a yank and it slipped out of my hands. The next thing we knew, the tray flew into the air and suddenly it was raining shrimp tarts! "Now look what you did!" I cried.

Of course Mom had to pick that moment to come back

into the kitchen with a tray of empty champagne glasses. When she saw hors d'oeuvres all over the floor, she flushed angrily. "What's going on here?"

"I'm sorry, Mom," I whispered.

"It was Laurel's fault," Lily said. "She's making me do all the grunt work."

Mom swept the ruined food into a garbage bag. "You're lucky I brought extra appetizers," she snapped. "There's a Ziploc bag with mushroom toasts in the freezer, Laurel. And if there's any more fighting between the two of you, you're both going home. Do you understand me?"

"Yes," Lily and I mumbled.

Mom went back out to the party. I scowled at Lily and she scowled back at me. "I can't believe you did that," I said. I was so mad and ashamed, I felt like crying. "You messed up my chance to do a good job for Mom."

"*I* messed up your chance?" Lily scoffed. "You're lucky I saved you from spilling those appetizers all over the wedding guests."

"Oh, just wash the platters," I said. "I'll put the mushroom toasts in the oven. You can pass them out when they're warm."

Lily ended up passing out appetizers the whole time while I worked in the kitchen. She had a blast. I was miserable. Driving home after the reception, Mom pulled the car over to the side of the road and apologized. "Accidents happen," she said. "I shouldn't have come down so hard on you two. I was just feeling stressed. Will you forgive me?"

"Of course, Mom," I said.

"Don't worry about it," Lily agreed.

Mom didn't bring it up again. She also didn't ask me to help her with the next party she catered or the one after that. Big surprise.

When I mentioned it, she said it was only because she didn't want to put pressure on me. "This family's going through a hard time," she said. "Let's not rock the boat, okay? Just have fun with Jack."

"Sure, Mom." I knew what she was really thinking, though. Come out of your shell, people are always urging me. Don't be so shy. Well, I'd had a chance to follow in Daisy's footsteps and I'd tripped all over myself. I belonged in my shell, where I wouldn't look like a fool.

I T ALMOST DIDN'T matter that Mom didn't want me to help at her parties because being part of a couple was starting to take up all my free time. Jack and I had always hung out together a lot, but now we were inseparable. During the week we met at my locker in the morning, walked each other to class, and sat together at lunch. In the evening we had study dates. Then every Friday and Saturday night we went out. Jack had lots of friends, so there was almost always a party to go to. Before we started dating, I never went to parties—I could never think of anything to say to people I didn't know well. Even after we started going out and I kind of became a regular on the junior class party scene, I always stuck close to Jack and let him do most of the talking.

"What's up tonight?" I asked him one Friday morning in December as we walked to homeroom. We'd been dating for three weeks. "We don't have to go out if there's nothing special going on."

"I kind of assumed we would." Jack looked hurt that I'd even suggested otherwise. "Don't you want to?"

"I didn't say I didn't want to. I just meant, you know, we don't *have* to just because it's Friday." I skipped a beat. "Or do we?"

Jack draped an arm around my shoulders. "Of course we don't *have* to. There's no law. Like I said, it's only if you want to. You do, don't you?"

"Sure," I said.

"Maybe we can double with Eric and Monica," Jack suggested. Eric was his best wrestling team buddy; Monica was Eric's girlfriend.

"Okay," I said.

And that was that. We had another date. I couldn't exactly complain about it even though the plan didn't thrill me. After Jack kissed me good-bye outside my homeroom, I glimpsed a bunch of freshman girls ogling me enviously. They started to whisper, and I knew what they were saying. "She's so lucky to be Jack Harrison's girlfriend!"

I *am* lucky, I thought. Not only was Jack cute, he was thoughtful, chivalrous, funny, and sweet. He dressed nicely and got good grades. He drove a funky car. He lived in a beautiful house with really cool parents. Best of all, he loved me.

When we first got together, Jack had said that I used to take him for granted. I knew I'd never do that again.

W E HAD A pretty good time at the movies with Eric and Monica on Friday. Saturday morning I found a message from Mom—Ellen had called the night before. I decided to call her back before having breakfast and heading to the WRC. Maybe she'd want to meet me at the center for lunch—we needed to talk about possible science fair projects.

I was about to pick up the receiver when it rang right under my hand. "Hello?" I said.

"Hi, Laurel," Jack said.

"Hi. What's up?"

"I just wanted to touch base with you about the skating party this afternoon," he told me. "It turns out it's at four, not three. I guess Karlee's family has floodlights at their pond."

"See you at four, then."

"And I was thinking about something else," Jack went on. "You know the science fair at school?"

"Ellen and I have been total slouches," I confessed. "We haven't even started yet."

"Good, because I want to be your partner," Jack said.

"What?"

"Your partner," he repeated. "Wouldn't that be fun?"

I sat down at the kitchen table, the phone cradled between my shoulder and ear, and adjusted one of the straps on my overalls. "Well . . ."

"I already have an idea. Tell me how this sounds."

He described a software program he wanted to write—a cross between a science tutorial and an adventure game. "Computers aren't my thing," I reminded him.

"Well, I'll do whatever you want to do, then," Jack replied. "You're the science whiz. All I want to do is find a way for us to spend more time together."

Personally, I didn't see how that would be possible, but I didn't say so. "The thing is, I already told Ellen I'd work with her," I told him.

"She won't mind if you work with me instead."

"I'm just not sure I want to—"

"I'll ask her, then," he said. "Call you right back."

He hung up. I dialed Ellen's number. It was busy. I have to admit that I was somewhat relieved that Ellen didn't have call waiting. I wasn't sure how I felt about the whole situation—angry that Jack was being so presumptuous or flattered that he liked me so much?

Three minutes later, as I was pouring milk on my cornflakes, the phone rang again. "It's all set," Jack announced. "You and I can be partners—Ellen said she doesn't mind flying solo."

"But what about what *I* want?" I asked.

"What do you mean? We want the same thing, right?"

I wasn't really sure *what* I wanted, so I tried another angle. "Are you sure you have time for it? You've already got wrestling, and I thought you wanted to get a weekend job at the realtor's or the travel agency."

"I've changed my mind about that," Jack told me. "I'd rather spend time with you."

I wrinkled my forehead. "Really?"

"Really. I love you, Laurel."

I hesitated for a second. Jack's voice was full of emotion. I wasn't sure I entirely understood.

"Laurel?"

"Uh, I love you, too," I said quickly. "I do," I added, in case I hadn't sounded convincing enough the first time.

"Good. See you at four."

"Bye."

I hung up the receiver and stared at my soggy cornflakes. My head was spinning a little. I guess it's good that Jack knows more about this relationship stuff than I do, I thought, so he can tell me how things are supposed to work.

I felt as if I didn't have a clue.

I LEFT WORK at the WRC a little early so I'd have time to change before the skating party. Overalls and a turtleneck or jeans and a sweater? I wondered, staring into my closet.

Lily broke into my train of thought. "It's a good day for it," she announced, sticking her head into my bedroom.

"A good day for what?" I asked.

"For cutting down a Christmas tree," she answered. "Mom's got a job in Portland, but Hal said he'd drive us to McCloskey's in the Subaru to pick one out."

Maybe the other girls at the party would be wearing perky skating outfits, but I decided to stick with overalls since I was already wearing them. "I don't think so," I said to my sister.

"What don't you think?"

I turned around to look at her. "I don't think it's a good day to get a tree."

She strolled into the room and stuck a finger between the bars of the birdcage to stroke Clark's feathers. "When do you want to go, then?"

"Maybe I don't. Not this year."

I didn't explain myself further, but it had to be obvious what I meant. *Not this year, without Daisy.*

"But I want to cut down a tree the way we always have," Lily whined.

"Go with Hal, then. I don't have time."

Clark gave Lily's finger a peck. She jumped away from the cage, tears springing into her eyes. "Did he hurt you?" I asked worriedly.

She shook her head. "No."

"Then why are you—" I sighed. Clearly this meant a lot to Lily. Still, the idea of going to get a tree without Daisy . . . Get over it, I told myself sternly. You'll have to get a tree sooner or later. "Okay," I said, relenting. "I only have half an hour, though, so let's get going."

As it turned out, Hal didn't have time to take us after all. He'd gotten called into the office to do some work for a client who was being audited by the IRS—he was on his way out the door. "Take the car," he said, tossing me the keys. I had my license by then.

"Are you sure you don't need it?"

He nodded, smiling. "The office is only a block away. I think I can walk."

With Lily in the passenger seat I drove slowly out the Old Boston Post Road to McCloskey's Farm. "You're a good driver," Lily ventured after a minute. "You know, always using your turn signals and stuff."

I still didn't have that much experience behind the wheel, so I was cautious. "Mom hardly ever lets me drive," I remarked.

"Because of Daisy's accident," Lily said simply.

"Oh." I hadn't really thought about it. "Right."

We were quiet the rest of the way to McCloskey's. Since we didn't have much time, we decided to take a ready-cut tree instead of cutting one down ourselves the way we always did in the old days. It wouldn't have been any fun, anyway, without Rose and Mom singing Christmas carols, and without Daisy. She'd always been the one who spotted the perfect tree.

Mr. McCloskey helped us tie the tree to the roof of the Subaru with twine. I was climbing into the driver's seat when Lily trotted back to the farm stand. "One more thing," she called.

When she got in the car, she was holding two small evergreen wreaths decorated with berries and ribbon. "What are those for?" I asked.

"You'll see," she replied.

Driving back to town, we passed the cemetery. "Stop," Lily commanded.

"Here?"

"Yeah. Park by the church."

I guessed what she had in mind. I followed her into the cemetery and watched as she laid one wreath on Daisy's grave and the other by Dad's headstone. "I know you're in a hurry," she said, glancing at me over her shoulder. "Can we just take a minute?"

"Sure," I said. Suddenly I didn't care about getting to the skating party on time. "As long as you want."

She sat down on the dry brown grass. "I come here a lot," she confessed.

"Really?"

She nodded. "I talk to Dad and Daisy." Lily cast me a sideways glance. "I guess that sounds kind of weird."

I shrugged. "I don't know. Do they . . . do they talk back?"

"No. But sometimes I feel like they're close by."

We both fell silent. The wind whispered in the pines, reminding me of Lily's funeral poem.

Finally Lily sighed long and deep. "Let's go," she said.

When we got home, I parked Hal's car in front of our building. "We can take the tree off later. Would you drop the keys through Hal's mail slot?" I asked Lily. "I'm going to wait down here for Jack."

Lilly lingered on the sidewalk with me. "You're going to a skating party, huh?"

"Yep."

"I love skating."

"I know."

"I just bought this vintage velvet skating skirt at Second Time Around. It's really cute and swirly."

"Hmmm."

"Can I come with you?"

I shook my head. "It's going to be all juniors. You wouldn't know anyone."

Lily clasped her hands. "Please?"

Was she kidding? "It's a *date*, Lil. Two's company, you know?"

Lily didn't get a chance to beg further because Jack pulled up. I hopped into the Mustang and waved good-bye. I know it sounds awful, but I couldn't wait to get away from her suddenly. The whole Christmas tree excursion had made me so . . . sad. Skating with Jack would take my mind off all that. "See you later," I told her.

As we drove off, I looked in the side mirror. Lily was still standing on the sidewalk, watching us go. Maybe Lily's like me, I thought, beginning to feel bad about leaving her behind. She just doesn't like to be alone these days.

We were too far away now for me to see the expression in my sister's eyes, though. And when Jack turned the corner, Lily disappeared from sight.

I FORGOT ALL about Lily when we got to Karlee's house. Jack is Mr. Winter Sports, but I'm not a good skater, and even with him holding my hand, I had to struggle to stay upright on the frozen pond in the Kennedys' backyard. "This isn't natural," I said. "Balancing on these skinny blades. I like having my feet flat on the ground."

Jack swept me in a circle, then twirled me—shrieking—under his arm, Ice Capades style. "You don't give yourself enough credit."

I collapsed against him. "I'm a menace to the safety of others. Can we stop, please?"

It was getting dark and cold. We weren't the only ones who'd given up on the ice—in Karlee's basement rec room a bunch of people were drinking hot chocolate and eating sugar cookies. Jack went upstairs to the bathroom, and I had a moment of panic. Who was I going to talk to? Then I spotted Jon Rotner, a guy I knew from science club. He was standing in the corner, looking as out of place as I felt. "Hi, Jon," I said, joining him.

"Hi, Laurel," he replied with obvious relief. "Hey, I've been meaning to ask you. You work at the Wildlife Rescue Center, right? Are they looking for any volunteers these days?"

I started telling Jon about how Griffin wanted the center to get involved in more educational outreach programs. I was really pleased that Jon wanted to help out—we could definitely use it. Our conversation got pretty intense, so when someone hugged me from behind, I jumped. Of course it was Jack, but for a second I must have forgotten we were a couple. I almost shouted, "What do you think you're *doing?*" Luckily I remembered in time and smiled at him instead.

"Laurel, can you move over a little?" Jack requested politely but mysteriously. "Take, like, three steps sideways?"

I raised my eyebrows. "Why?"

"Just do it," he said, grinning.

I took a couple of steps with Jack hovering over me. When I stopped, he leaned in and gave me a big kiss on the lips. "Jack!" I exclaimed, blushing.

He pointed upward. "Mistletoe."

I twisted around to apologize to Jon for ditching him, but he'd already melted back into the crowd. Meanwhile Jack started to kiss me again. Suddenly I felt claustrophobic. "Let's go back outside," I said abruptly.

"I thought you weren't into skating."

"I feel like some fresh air. Okay?"

"Sure." Jack slid his hands up my arms and playfully flicked the straps on my overalls. For some reason, it made me want to smack him. "No problem."

We bundled up again and went outside, and Jack immediately got pulled into a twilight game of touch football. I sat down on a nearby tree stump, pushing my hands deep into the pockets of my parka. Jack was good at running and passing and being part of a team. There was a lot of laughter and high-fiving. Gradually the closed-in feeling I'd had inside Karlee's house faded. The evening air smelled like pine needles and wood smoke and snow. I like being by myself like this, I realized, more than I like being at parties.

Immediately I felt disloyal. It wasn't that I didn't like having a boyfriend and a social life, I told myself. I did, and I figured I'd get better at it as time passed. I just needed my own space. I'd always been that way. That was why I'd liked Jack so much when we first met when we were ten. I was this shy, odd kid who liked to mess around in the woods or sit in a hammock with a book, and he didn't seem to mind that we didn't talk that much. He hadn't had so many friends back then.

"Touchdown!" Jack shouted, doing a little dance on the far side of the yard. He looked over at me for approval.

I remembered to act like a girlfriend. "Way to go!" I yelled, clapping.

Eight

"THE HOUSE LOOKS beautiful," Rose told Mom on Christmas Eve.

"We threw the decorations up at the last minute," Mom confessed.

Rose had gotten home from Boston just that day, after finishing her finals at BU. The four of us were in the living room now, dressed for church despite the fact that it was snowing like crazy outside and the roads would be terrible. Snickers, who was four months old now, was on the couch with me, her head on my lap.

Rose, Lily, and I watched as Mom unpacked the Christmas stockings and hung them from hooks on the mantel. "Rose's stocking is bigger than mine," Lily pouted.

I rolled my eyes. "You say that every year."

"And then you count your stocking presents to make sure you didn't get shortchanged," Rose put in.

"So?" Lily asked. "Why shouldn't I?"

Usually when Lily says something like that, Mom tells her not to be so greedy. Now, though, Mom remained quiet. She was standing by the fireplace, her head bent, holding something. Daisy's Christmas stocking, I realized, my heart swelling with sorrow.

Rose went over to Mom and put an arm around her. "Are you okay?" she asked softly.

Mom nodded. Bending, she laid the stocking carefully back in the box, covering it with tissue paper. "Every now and then something takes me by surprise," she said in a small voice. "I have some piece of her in my hand and I simply can't believe she's gone."

We were all quiet for a minute. I scratched Snickers's silky ears, my eyes on the snow whirling beyond the windowpanes. Lily sniffled. Sadness filled the room, but before the real tears could start, the colored lights on the Christmas tree flickered and then the room went dark.

"The power's out!" Lily exclaimed.

This kind of thing happens a couple of times a year, and we jumped into action. Rose got out the candles while I hunted for matches. Flashlight in hand, Mom went into the kitchen to check that the gas stove was still working—she was toasting bread cubes for the turkey stuffing. "Should I put another log on the fire so the room stays warm?" Lily asked.

"Not if we're still going to church," Rose replied. "Are we, Mom?"

"I think we should," Mom answered.

"But won't the power be out there, too?" I asked.

"Maybe," Mom said. "But it's Christmas Eve. Reverend Beecher would hardly cancel services."

Mom was right, of course. The little church was packed, and people kept their coats on and sang carols by candlelight. "I really feel the Christmas spirit," Rose whispered to me after the congregation sang "Silent Night." "Don't you, Laurel?"

I nodded.

I did feel the Christmas spirit, although it was more solemn than joyful.

The next morning the electricity came back on, and the sun sparkled on new snow. Delicious smells drifted from the kitchen, and there were plenty of presents to open— homemade gifts, mostly, because that became our tradition after Dad died. But when Rose tried to snap some pictures with the new camera Stephen had given her, it was hard for any of us to smile. Memories of Daisy were too vivid.

When Christmas dinner was ready, we gathered in the dining room. Mom stood behind her chair at the foot of the table, with Hal at the head. Even with Stephen there, one spot was empty. I tried not to look at it, but I saw Lily's eyes dart in that direction. "Why don't you say grace?" Mom asked Hal.

We stood around the table, holding one another's hands, our heads bowed. "Gracious God, help us be thankful for our many blessings," Hal began.

Before he could continue, Lily burst into tears. "Excuse me," she sobbed, running from the room.

Rose and Mom went after Lily. Unsure what to do, I turned to look at Stephen. He was standing to my right, and our hands were still clasped. He gave mine a squeeze. "It's tough, isn't it?" he said simply. I nodded, not trusting myself to speak. I didn't let go of his hand.

Mom and Rose returned. Hal walked over and rested a comforting hand on Mom's shoulder. "Let's eat," she said quietly. "Lily said she'd join us in a few minutes."

Lily didn't come back to the table, though, and the rest of us ate in silence. Gracious God, I found myself praying, help us be thankful for our many blessings. Even with Daisy gone, I knew I *did* have a lot to be thankful for. My family was loving and strong. I still had two sisters and the world's best mother. Hal was really supportive to all of us. And I had Jack.

A strange longing washed over me. Jack was coming over with his parents for dessert, and suddenly I couldn't wait to see him. There were some aspects of being in a relationship that I still hadn't adjusted to, but I knew one thing for sure. When my grief over Daisy was the worst, being with Jack was the only thing that seemed to help.

"WE'RE DOING THE rehearsal dinner at the Harborside, and Stephen's parents have offered to have the reception at their house," Rose said to Mom. It was the morning after Christmas, and they were discussing wedding plans over coffee in the kitchen. "They have that big backyard with the gardens—we can set up a tent."

"How many people do you want to invite?" Mom asked, pouring fresh coffee into her and Rose's cups.

"Eighty or a hundred." Rose looked at me, wrinkling her nose. "Does that sound absolutely huge, Laurel?"

I sat down with a bowl of oatmeal. "I don't know."

"Because the thing is, Stephen has about a million cousins and he wants to invite them all," Rose went on. "And when we start adding up all our friends . . ."

"You only have one wedding," Lily put in. She was toasting an English muffin. "You should be able to invite everyone you want."

Mom drummed her fingers on the tabletop in a thoughtful way. "Lily's right. We'll keep costs down by doing as much as possible ourselves."

"Cath's dad told me he can get rental stuff, like tables and chairs and tents, for a discount," Rose said. "And some friends of mine from BU who are in a band will do the music."

"And I'll do the food," Mom said.

Rose raised her eyebrows. "How can you do the food? You're the mother of the bride!"

Mom laughed. "You'll pitch in, of course, and we'll have Sarah. It will be something for you to do the day before the wedding so you don't get too jittery."

"Why would I be jittery?" Rose smiled. "I'm marrying my best friend."

Mom's eyes got misty. We all cry at the drop of a hat these

days. "Oh, honey. I'm so glad. That's exactly what marriage should be about."

I finished my oatmeal as fast as I could. Mom and Rose were acting like they were in one of those corny coffee commercials. I mean, I was dating *my* best friend, but it didn't make me all dewy eyed. "Wait, Laurel," Rose said when I pushed back my chair. "I want your advice about clothes."

"Clothes?" I repeated, as surprised as if she'd said "mutual funds."

"Stephen and I aren't sure whether to go the formal route—you know, long white gown, tuxedo—or to wear something more casual. What do you think?"

"You're asking the wrong person," Lily interjected before I could answer. "Laurel has no fashion sense."

Rose shushed Lily. "I'd like Laurel's opinion."

"I don't know," I said.

"I'm just not sure," Rose confided. "I always fantasized about a lacy white princess dress with a long veil, but it could be cool to wear something more sophisticated." She gave me a hopeful smile. "What kind of bridesmaid dress do you want?"

"I'll wear whatever you want me to wear," I replied.

Rose turned to Mom. "I told Laurel about the bridal shower."

"I'll be happy to help you plan it when the time comes, Laurel," Mom offered.

"Someone else should probably be in charge," I said.

"Why?" Rose wanted to know.

"Mom can tell you about the spilled hors d'oeuvres," I explained. "If you leave it up to me, it'll be a disaster."

"What spilled hors d'oeuvres?" Rose asked.

"That was an accident," Mom remarked. "The shower will be fine."

"It's not too late to make *me* your maid of honor, Rose," Lily kidded. "Or at least your style consultant. Can we look at those bridal magazines you bought the other day?"

While Rose went for the magazines, I made my escape. I didn't feel like talking about the wedding. When Rose and Stephen had first announced their engagement back in October, I'd been really psyched. Now, for some reason, I couldn't deal with it at all.

Maybe it's because Rose expects me to take Daisy's place, I thought. And I knew I never could.

M R. AND MRS. Harrison throw a huge New Year's Eve party every year at their house, Windy Ridge. This year Lily had another party to go to, but my mother went to the Harrisons' with Hal, Rose took Stephen, and of course I was there to be with Jack.

"You look incredibly pretty," Jack told me as we stood in the front hall. Taking both my hands, he gave me a kiss on the cheek. "I like that dress."

Rose had loaned me the dress. It was a lot sexier than anything I'd ever worn before—I didn't feel totally comfortable revealing so much skin. "Thanks," I said.

The dining and living rooms were packed with adults, so

Jack and I headed back to the library, where kids our age were listening to music. "It's kind of noisy," I shouted.

"And?" he shouted back.

"Do you want to go someplace quieter?"

He wiggled his eyebrows at me. "Is this a proposition?"

"Could be."

We ended up in his bedroom. "I didn't think I'd get you up here until the end of the party," he joked.

"I'm just not crazy about crowds."

Jack sat down on his bed. He patted the mattress next to him. "Hey, Laurel."

Instead of joining him, I wandered over to his bookshelves. "Lloyd Alexander!" I exclaimed. "Remember that summer when we read all the Taran books in, like, a week?"

"The Chronicles of Narnia, too," Jack said. "Come here."

I touched the faded spine of a well-worn volume. "*The Year-ling. I *loved* this. It was so sad."

"You always cried over the animal stories. Sit down with me."

I shoved aside a pile of *Sports Illustrated*s to reach Jack's photo album. I opened it up at random. "I remember this," I said, pointing to an old picture. "Your mom and dad took us horseback riding."

"Laurel, would you come over—"

"And this one!" I tapped a page. "That Halloween when we went trick-or-treating dressed as a goalpost. Remember how hard it was to walk?"

Jack got to his feet. Taking the album from me, he tossed it on his desk and placed his hands on my shoulders.

"I don't want to look at photo albums—I want to kiss you."

His lips touched mine. After a few seconds I turned my face away. "Is something wrong?" he asked.

"No. I just . . ."

"What?"

I shook my head. I had no idea why I felt the way I did. "I forgot what I was going to say. Um, how about some music?"

Jack put a CD on the stereo, a female vocalist we both liked. Turning off the light, he came over and wrapped his arms around me. "Let's pretend it's midnight," he whispered, his lips tickling my earlobe.

He was obviously feeling a lot more in the mood than I was. I thought I should at least make an effort to be romantic, though. It *was* New Year's Eve, after all. I lifted my face to his for a kiss.

It was a wonderful kiss . . . as always. Jack's arms tightened around me; his mouth on mine was warm and insistent. This is where it gets exciting, I thought. But instead of pleasant anticipation, I felt strangely detached.

Turning my face away again, I rested my head on Jack's shoulder. As we swayed to the music, a sigh escaped me. "I hope this is okay," I whispered.

"What?"

"That I just want to be held."

I looked up and our eyes met. Jack nodded. "I want whatever you want, Laurel."

So we slow-danced in the darkness as the final minutes of the year ticked away.

Nine

IT WAS A gloomy January in Hawk Harbor—record amounts of snow and day after day of icy temperatures. By the end of the month I had a serious case of cabin fever. I took Snickers for short walks every morning, afternoon, and night—she didn't mind the cold—but that was about it.

Jack called one Saturday morning as I was wrapping a scarf around my neck. "Let's go to Kent for lunch and a matinee," he suggested.

"I have to work at the WRC," I reminded him.

"You're always over there." Jack's tone reminded me oddly of Lily. If he weren't my boyfriend, I'd have called it whining. "Can't you call in sick or something?"

"I suppose I could . . . but I don't want to. I like my job."

"Better than me?"

"Of course not! Don't be ridiculous. What are your other friends up to today?"

"Eric got tickets for a Celtics game."

I knew Jack liked basketball. "That's a hundred times better than seeing a movie in Kent," I pointed out.

"Yeah, well, I'm not going," Jack said.

"Why not?"

"I'd rather be with you."

I couldn't believe Jack would pass up live NBA in order to sit around waiting for me to get home. It was his choice, though, I supposed. "I'll see you after work, then."

"Love you, Laurel."

"Love you, too."

With a feeling of escape, I headed outside to the car. It was cold, and the engine coughed and sputtered for a few minutes before finally starting with a grouchy roar.

The snow tires made a nice, crunchy sound as I drove down Main Street, which was covered with a new layer of powder. Turning on the radio, I sang along, suddenly feeling cheerful. I *did* love my job at the WRC. It wasn't the money, although I did like watching my savings account grow. It's the one thing I have all to myself lately, I thought. Jack and I do everything else together.

"It's oppressive," I said out loud.

The words hung there in the cold air of the car. I ventured another thought out loud. "And it's driving me crazy."

It wasn't that I didn't like—rather, love—Jack, I decided as

I stamped the snow off my boots outside the WRC. It *was* possible to have too much of a good thing, that was all.

Inside, Carlos was drinking some of Griffin's chai tea. "We're on our own today," he informed me. "Griffin just called—his car battery's dead."

"Excuses, excuses," I kidded. "Couldn't he hitchhike or something?"

"Yeah, on the back of a snowplow." Carlos lifted his mug. "Want some?"

As we drank our tea and ate a couple of stale bran muffins I thought about how I used to be too shy around Carlos to do more than say hello. Now we talked and joked like real friends. He was definitely one of the things I liked best about the WRC.

We got to work feeding the animals and cleaning cages. Just before noon we met up by Lefty's pen. We'd worked hard on creating a good habitat, and now the baby seal had rocks to climb on and a small pool to splash around in. "Look at him," I said to Carlos. "He's getting so fat!"

"Can you believe it?" Carlos picked Lefty up. "Pretty soon he'll be too heavy to lift."

I'd already mixed up a bottle of formula. Carlos handed the seal to me. We grinned at each other. It almost felt like we were Lefty's parents or something. "You saved him," Carlos said. "Makes you feel good, doesn't it?"

I gave Lefty the bottle. He started sucking hungrily. "Yes," I said. "It makes me feel great."

"You did an incredible job."

Carlos crossed the room to take care of a wounded fox. I watched him out of the corner of my eye. An incredible job, I thought, feeling a tickle of pleasure at the compliment. Did he just say that to be nice? Probably. I wouldn't know what to do most of the time without him telling me. Then again, idle flattery wasn't really his style.

Carlos broke into my musings. "How's your science fair project coming along?" he asked, moving along to the raccoon cage.

Shifting my hold on Lefty, I grimaced. "It's not. We're doing this grafting experiment and our bean plants keep dying."

"How come?"

"I don't know." I did know, though. "Jack means well," I told Carlos, "but he doesn't have a green thumb. He doesn't—" I stopped. Carlos looked over at me. I shrugged. "We still have some time left. I'm sure it'll work out."

"Knowing you, it will," Carlos agreed.

"But I wish Ellen was my partner," I found myself confessing.

"Yeah. I would've said don't mix work and love, but maybe that's just me," Carlos remarked.

I ducked my head, brushing my chin against Lefty's soft, musky-smelling fur. I'd never really talked to Carlos about my personal life. "Anyway," I mumbled a little self-consciously.

Latching the door to the raccoon cage, Carlos started humming "Take Me Out to the Ball Game." All of a sudden, I thought of Daisy. Something about the quiet, efficient, cheerful

way Carlos went about doing things, and of course the tune he'd
picked, made me see Daisy out in our old backyard, mowing the
grass in the summer, her baseball cap turned backward, singing
along to her iPod. Daisy humming as she helped me with my
algebra homework, or as she polished silver for Mom, or as she
climbed a stepladder to put in the storm windows in the fall and
then again to switch the storm windows for screens in the spring.
But this time thinking about Daisy didn't make me sad, exactly.
Instead it made me want to *talk*.

The words spilled from me before I even realized I was saying them out loud. "Nothing's how it should be nowadays," I
blurted. "I feel like I don't know how to connect to my mom—
not that she's ever around. And Lily and I might as well not even
be related. All Rose thinks about is the wedding, and Jack . . . I
don't know why I do *anything* anymore," I finished.

I was pretty embarrassed by this outburst, but when Carlos
glanced at me, there was sympathy in his dark eyes.

He kept busy with the animals, though, as if sensing that
I'd be mortified if he paid me too much attention. "You're
missing Daisy, huh?" he asked.

How did he know that? I wondered, but I just nodded
wordlessly, my eyes bright with tears.

"Death changes the world for the people who are left
behind," he said after a minute. "I've been there, Laurel. I
lost a good buddy back in high school. You're going to grieve
for your sister for a long time, but eventually relationships
and stuff like that will shift into a new place that feels right.
You'll find your balance again."

"Really?"

"Yeah," Carlos said with quiet assurance. We looked at each other a moment. Finally I smiled, and a grin broke out over his face. "Hey, when you're done with Lefty, will you play the fishing game with the raccoon kits?"

I spent the next half hour coaching three orphaned raccoons on how to fish bits of food out of a pail of water. I got soaking wet, but they made me laugh, and at one point I caught Carlos looking at me, a half smile on his face. I wanted to thank him, but I figured I didn't need to—I was pretty sure my gratitude showed in my eyes.

Balance. A place that feels right, I thought. Maybe I'd found it already, right here.

I DON'T KNOW that much about relationships," Ellen admitted when I asked her advice the following week. "I mean, since I've never had a boyfriend. But maybe you and Jack are just in a rut. Why don't you put a little spice into your life? Do something different."

I decided Ellen was right. The way I'd been feeling about Jack lately—it wasn't that we didn't have a good relationship. The last thing I wanted was for things to go wrong between us—Jack meant the world to me. He was my anchor. We were just in a rut; that had to be the problem.

I came up with an idea for a fun, romantic outing, something I knew Jack would like. "Skiing?" he repeated when I mentioned it. We were eating lunch in the cafeteria at school. "I thought you didn't like it that much."

"Don't you think it would be fun to do something different for a change? We can drive to Cabot Mountain. We could go on a sleigh ride, too."

Jack reached over to hug me. "It'll be great," he agreed.

I got up early the following Sunday and put on long underwear under my clothes. Downstairs, I made some sandwiches and stuck them in my backpack along with a bottle of water and two apples. I was heading out the door to wait for Jack on the street when Lily came in the kitchen. "Where are you going?" she asked.

"Skiing at Cabot Mountain with Jack." Mom was in the family room, reading cookbooks. "Be home for dinner," I shouted so she could hear me.

"Cabot Mountain?" Lily's eyes lit up. "I'd love to go skiing. Can I come with you?"

I gave her the same answer I'd given the day of Karlee's skating party. "It's a date, remember?"

Lily's expression darkened. "I never get to go anywhere," she complained. "Just because I can't drive yet. It's not *fair.*"

Mom walked into the room in time to hear that. "Where do you want to go, Lily?"

"Skiing with Laurel and Jack," Lily said, "but Laurel said I can't. I'm sure if I asked Jack, he'd—"

"We just don't want you tagging along, okay?" I cut in. I knew I was being rude, but I really felt like I needed this date to be as romantic as possible. And having my annoying little sister come with me was hardly going to evoke the kind of mood I was looking for.

"Maybe it's not such a bad idea. Laurel," Mom remarked, looking at me significantly.

"Yeah," Lily jumped in. "I'll run and put on my ski clothes right now." Lily raced up the stairs.

"Well, this is great," I grumbled.

"Will it really be so terrible?" Mom asked. "I'm catering a party this afternoon, so Lily would be alone all day. I'll feel a lot better if I know she's having a good time with you and Jack. Consider it a favor for me, honey."

I sighed. How could I say no to that? "Well, okay, Mom. Since you put it that way." But we're ditching her as soon as we get to the mountain, I thought as I stomped downstairs to break the news to Jack.

N O SUCH LUCK. Lily stuck to us like a burr. "Maybe I'll rent a snowboard," she said as we stood in line to buy lift tickets. "I've never tried it, but it looks cool. Do you know how to snowboard, Jack?"

"Yeah, it's a blast," he told her. "You'll like it."

Jack and I waited around while Lily rented a snowboard. When it looked like she was all set, I gestured to Jack. "Come on. Let's get in the lift line."

We skied over and I thought we'd finally gotten rid of Lily, but then she shouted after us, "Hey guys, wait for me! I'll ride up with you!"

It was a quad chairlift, so we couldn't exactly blow her off, and somehow when we took our seats, she ended up in the middle. "Isn't it a beautiful day?" she asked, twisting to point at the clear blue sky and snow-dusted pine trees lining the slope. "It's not too cold. Isn't this fun?"

I rolled my eyes at Jack, but he was busy sticking his ski poles under his thigh. The whole way up the mountain Lily chattered nonstop, commenting on the outfits of the people skiing under the lift. When we dismounted at the top, Jack skied off to the right; I grabbed Lily's arm and dragged her to the left. "Look, Jack and I need to have some quality time together," I said. "We drove you here and we'll drive you home, but you can do your own thing in between, okay?"

Lily dropped onto the snow to buckle her free boot onto the board. "Fine," she agreed. "But first—"

Just then Jack skied over to us. "What's up?" he asked.

"Lily's heading over to Centennial," I said, naming a trail on the far side of the ski area where the snowboarders hang out.

"But first you have to tell me how to stay up on this thing," Lily said to Jack, balancing precariously on the snowboard with her arms held out. "What do I do next?"

For the next two hours Jack gave Lily a snow-boarding lesson while I skied along beside them, flashing my little sister dirty looks, which she cheerfully ignored. Finally Jack and I had a few minutes alone riding up on a double chairlift. "Lily can take care of herself, you know," I told him. "I think we've done our duty."

"She seems to want to hang out with us, though," Jack said. "I really don't mind."

"But this was supposed to be *romantic,*" I reminded him, leaning my head on his shoulder.

"How's *this*"—Jack pushed my goggles up so he could kiss me—"for romantic?"

From the chair behind us we heard Lily shout, "Hey, none of that!"

Jack laughed; I groaned. "Right," I muttered. "The pinnacle of romance."

There were plenty of kids Lily's age snowboarding and I kept hoping she'd hook up with some of them, but no such luck. We had the pleasure of skiing with her for the entire day. She was starting to get the hang of snowboarding by the time we took our last run—Jack was a good teacher—but then she got going a little too fast and fell. "Wow!" Jack exclaimed as we watched her belly flop into a drift. "That was some wipeout."

He and I did sharp hockey stops, sending snow flying. "Lily, are you all right?" I asked, sidestepping over to her. She didn't answer right away, and suddenly I felt a stab of fear. God, maybe she's hurt, I thought, or . . . "Lily!" I cried, my voice shrill with fear.

Lily sat up groggily. Relief flooded through me. "I . . . got . . . the . . . wind . . . knocked . . . out . . . of . . . me," she panted, flopping onto her back with her arms flung out. "Ugh."

When Lily had caught her breath, Jack helped her to her feet. She was still wobbly, so he kept his arm around her waist.

"Are you going to be okay?" I asked her. Lily nodded, but she didn't look as if she meant it. "Maybe you should sit back down," I suggested, steadying her with a gloved hand.

"I'll just take it slow," she said.

That was an understatement. Lily was so shaky, Jack had to practically carry her down the slope. Now that I was over my worry, I started to get annoyed with her again. It was truly amazing how she always managed to wedge herself into the center of every situation.

I studied the pair of them, thinking that Jack might be losing his patience with Lily, too, but his expression was good-humored. He was being a sport about the whole thing.

That's when I noticed the look on my sister's face. I blinked, wondering if I'd imagined it, but Lily was still gazing at Jack with adoration in her blue eyes. She'd be drooling soon if she didn't watch it. Lily has a crush on Jack! I realized.

I tried to remember if I'd ever seen her act moony around him before, but I didn't come up with much. Maybe she'd had a crush on him forever. And why shouldn't she? He was a cute older guy who'd always been nice to her in a big-brotherly way.

We got to the bottom of the hill without anyone falling down again. Jack was talking about where to stop for a burger on the way home, oblivious. Lily went to return her snowboard and I watched her go, my feelings muddled. My sister has a crush on my boyfriend, I thought. I decided this was harmless—I knew how much Jack cared for me; Lily couldn't really be a threat. It made me think, though. I glanced sideways at Jack as we carried our skis and poles to his car and pictured Lily's worshipful look. Do my eyes ever glow like that when I look at him? I wondered.

Somehow I doubted it.

* * *

I T DIDN'T REALLY work," I reported to Ellen the next day. Her parents were out, and I was helping her keep an eye on her kid brothers.

As Caleb and Quinn ran around the house in Superman capes, trying to karate chop each other, I told Ellen the abridged version of our trip to Cabot Mountain. She laughed. "Maybe you should stick to quiet walks in the woods."

"Maybe," I said.

"I wouldn't worry. You two are a great couple. Hey, Quinn! Caleb! Cut it out!"

We managed to keep the boys from tearing the house apart until Mr. and Mrs. Adams got back. Late in the afternoon I walked home. For no particular reason I took a roundabout route, following a back road that rolls up and down hills with an occasional view of the ocean. I wanted to be alone with my thoughts.

Not that my thoughts were so comforting. I was still wondering what I should do about Jack. Ellen said we were a great couple. Were we, really? What did that even mean?

I needed advice, and I knew who I wanted to ask. There was one person I'd always been able to go to when I had something on my mind. One person who never laughed at my questions. One person I trusted to be understanding and kind.

The road curved, and I found myself at the back of the little white church that my family attended. Beyond it was the cemetery.

I cut over to the gate and paused. I could see Daisy's and

Dad's headstones. The wreaths Lily had brought back in December were gone—I guessed the groundskeeper had eventually removed them.

If it works for Lily, I decided, pushing open the gate, maybe it will work for me.

I sat down on the cold, hard ground near Daisy's grave. For a minute I didn't speak. Even though the cemetery was deserted, so no one could see me, it seemed too silly. I ventured a single word. "Hi." I whispered.

The wind made the bare tree branches murmur.

I tried again. "I have a boyfriend, Daze," I told her. "Isn't that a riot? It's Jack. That would have made you happy, wouldn't it? You always liked him. Everybody does. He's like a son to Mom and a brother to Rose and Lily. He belongs with us. But . . ."

I stopped, hunching my neck down into the collar of my coat. A chipmunk scurried between two nearby headstones. "But it doesn't feel right, Daze. Something's missing. I don't know what it is." I paused again, searching my heart for the response Daisy might have given if she were alive. "Talk to him, right? I know I should, but I'm scared. What if he gets mad? I can't risk that."

I waited to feel Daisy's presence, but I didn't. Not really.

I sighed. "I wish I could talk to you, Daisy," I said sadly. "I could talk to Rose, I guess. She's always been a good big sister to me. But we're just not as close as you and I were. Besides, she's so busy with all of that wedding stuff. Mom? She's working constantly. We never have time to talk. Lily? I don't think so."

I got to my feet and stared at Daisy's gravestone, reading her name and the dates over and over. My eyes blurred with tears. "I miss you so much, Daze," I whispered. "I thought it would get better with time, but it doesn't. It gets worse."

When I'd cried my fill for now, I walked slowly out of the cemetery. Back on the road, it was only a quarter of a mile to Main Street. I was home. But home seemed as cold and hopeless as the graveyard. I still had questions and no answers.

Ten

"I LOOK LIKE a sofa," I declared, twisting to see my back in the mirror at the bridal shop in the mall.

Lily's voice floated over the wall between the dressing rooms. "It looks good on me."

Rose was standing outside. "Do you really think it makes you look big, Toad?" she asked. "Come out here so I can see."

Lily and I emerged from our dressing rooms. Rose inspected the bridesmaid dresses we were wearing, tugging at the necklines, adjusting the sleeves, and retying the bows at our waists. "A sofa?" she said to me.

"It's just so . . . floral," I explained. "Weren't there some plain navy blue dresses on the rack?"

"I *like* flowers, though," Rose said.

"And it's Rose's wedding," Lily piped up. "She's the bride."

Rose handed me three more flowered dresses to try on. I shuffled back into the dressing room with a sigh. "Right. It's Rose's wedding."

It was Rose's wedding, but somehow it seemed to have spiraled out of control—to me, at least. It had taken over the world, or our household, anyway. Whenever Rose came home lately, all anyone talked about was the wedding, flowers and cakes, dresses and honeymoons, guest lists and gift registries. Cath and Rox would come over to rehearse the songs they were going to sing during the ceremony and giggle about the nightgown Rose had bought for her wedding night. It never ended.

When I'd tried on six dresses, I stomped out of the dressing room in my underwear, not caring who saw me. "Can you just pick something?" I begged Rose. "We've been here all morning!"

Rose frowned as she pushed me back into the dressing room. Following me in, she yanked the curtain closed behind us. "This is important, Laurel. You can't wear your overalls, you know."

"No one's going to be looking at the bridesmaids. You're the main attraction," I pointed out as I pulled on my overalls and turtleneck. "Does it really matter what we wear?"

"Of course!" Rose clearly couldn't believe my ignorance. "Do you want me to gag every time I look at my wedding photos?"

I supposed that *would* be pretty bad. "I still think you should make up your mind. I want to get to the WRC before the sun sets."

Rose gathered up the discarded bridesmaid's dresses, acting offended. "Well, sorry I've been wasting your valuable time. I didn't realize it would kill you to show a little interest in something that means so much to me."

Immediately I felt like a jerk. "I'm sorry, Rose," I said contritely. "I *do* care about the dresses. I like . . . that one." I pointed to a dress at random.

"Really?" Rose perked up. "That's the one I was leaning toward, too."

"Me too," Lily said.

"Then let's do it," Rose declared.

The saleswoman recorded our measurements and Rose ordered the dresses, which were going to be a gift from Stephen's mother. Then we headed out into the mall. "Come with me to look at wedding rings," Rose said.

The three of us went into a jewelry store. I didn't want to hurt Rose's feelings again, so I pretended to be fascinated by the different cuts and carats and what have you.

"So, Toad," Rose said. "I've cleared a weekend in May for the bridal shower. Have you thought about where you want to have it?"

"No," I admitted. "Where do *you* want to have it?"

"You could do it at a restaurant or at home," Rose replied. "I'm sure the Applebys or the Beales would be happy to host it, too."

"So, there's a meal involved?"

"If you want. It's up to you, Toad. You're the maid of honor."

The maid of honor. I felt paralyzed. "Um . . . I'll let you know what I decide, okay?"

"Okay." Rose pointed at a gold wedding band. "What do you think about this one, Lil? Too plain?"

Lily gushed over the ring's simplicity and elegance. I felt ill. I'd been hoping I'd be able to find a way to get out of arranging the shower, but that was starting to look impossible.

I SPENT THE afternoon at the WRC, helping Carlos and Griffin lead a workshop for new volunteers, one of whom was Jon Rotner. When I came home for dinner, Rose met me at the door. "You're just in time," she announced. "Come on."

I followed her and Mom upstairs. On our way we grabbed Lily from in front of the computer. "You're on that machine night and day," Mom said.

Lily shrugged. "What are we doing?" she asked.

"Looking for Mom's wedding dress," Rose explained.

There was a small attic over our apartment that was crammed with all the stuff that used to be in our much bigger attic in the house on Lighthouse Road. When we'd all crowded up there, Mom contemplated a couple of old cedar chests. "It's in one of these," she said. "Here, help me open them."

Mom and I lifted the lid on the first chest while Rose and Lily opened the other. "It's not in here," Lily said, "but check out these cool shoes! Were they yours, Mom? Can I have them?"

She held up a pair of platforms. Mom laughed. "In a million years I would never have guessed that those would come back into fashion. Sure, you can have them. Just be careful not to fall off them and break your neck."

Inside the chest Mom and I had opened was a large, flat cardboard box. "This must be the dress," I said, opening the box.

Ivory satin peeked through layers of ancient tissue paper. "Look, it hasn't yellowed at all," Rose exclaimed. "It's still as white as snow."

As Mom carefully lifted the dress from the box my sisters oohed and aahed. Even I caught my breath. We'd all seen pictures of Mom in her dress, but it was even more glamorous in real life, with off-the-shoulder sleeves and a fitted bodice flaring out to a full skirt with a long train. "It's beautiful," Lily gushed. "Look at that tiny waist."

Mom held the dress against her body, a wistful smile on her face. "I was a size six back then."

"You're so slim—you could still fit in it," I said.

"What was *your* wedding day like, Mom?" Rose asked.

"It was June, like yours will be, Rose. A beautiful day. I had four bridesmaids, just like you, in shell pink dresses. We all wore traditional clothing—your father looked very handsome in his morning suit. But the actual ceremony was a little unconventional. The minister married us on the deck of your father's fishing boat."

"You're kidding!" Rose said. "Why didn't we know that?"

"Maybe because we had the formal portraits taken on my parents' porch," Mom replied, "and because no one ever asked me."

She held out the dress to Rose. Talking about her wedding to Dad had brought tears to her eyes. "What do you think? Too old-fashioned?"

"No, it's perfect," Rose said. "I want to wear it, Mom. Is that okay?"

"Of course it's okay." Mom hugged Rose. "Nothing would make me happier."

Now Rose started to cry, too. "What is it, honey?" Mom asked.

"I wish Daisy were here," Rose answered, sniffling. She turned to me. "That doesn't mean I don't love you, too, Toad. I'm glad you're going to be my maid of honor. But she should be here to share my wedding day with me." I nodded to show I understood. Rose didn't really need to explain it to me—I felt the same way she did. "And so should Daddy," she added in a whisper.

Mom nodded.

Everyone was quiet for a moment, and suddenly the attic felt full of ghosts. "Let's go back downstairs," I suggested quietly.

We took turns climbing down the pull-down ladder.

In my room Rose laid the dress on the bed she sleeps in when she's home. "Maybe *you'll* wear this someday, Toad," she said.

"Yeah, right," I said, still looking at the dress.

Lily, Rose, and Mom headed downstairs to start dinner. I lingered in my room for a minute. I couldn't take my eyes off the layers of white satin. I should put it in the closet, I thought. So Snickers won't get her paws on it.

I picked up the dress. The yards and yards of fabric made it heavy, and the satin was incredibly smooth. Walking across the room, I stopped halfway, Rose's words in my head. "Maybe you'll wear this someday. . . ."

I lifted up the dress, holding it against my body, and looked at myself in the mirror over my dresser. Would I ever get married? Probably not, I decided. A wildlife biologist who spent months at a time in the field wouldn't exactly have time for a husband and kids. But the dress *was* pretty. . . .

Still looking in the mirror, I tried to picture myself as a bride, wearing Mom's gown and holding a bouquet of wildflowers picked in Meredith's Meadow. I supposed I'd need a groom. Jack? My eyes grew dreamy. I had a sudden vision of myself standing at the altar, but who was that? Facing me with my hand in his and slipping a gold ring on my finger was . . . Carlos Alvarez.

Carlos? I blinked in surprise and the vision faded. Confused, I shoved the wedding dress onto a hanger in the closet and slammed the door fast.

JACK AND I had a date that night. We went to a party at Eric's and then parked at the beach to look at the stars. Even though my fantasy about marrying Carlos had been totally unintentional, not to mention ridiculous, and even though of course there was no way Jack could ever find out about it, in fact no one on the *planet* would ever know, I still felt guilty, so I tried as hard as I could to make it a romantic evening. We had a major make-out session in Jack's car. When we finally said good night, he had kind of a dazed, happy look on his face. "See you at school on Monday," he murmured, giving my neck one last nuzzle.

"Um-hm," I said.

"I love you so much, it hurts."

I never know how to respond when he says stuff like that, so I settled for, "Same here."

He walked me up to the door of the apartment. We kissed for a few more minutes. "This feels so good. Do we really have to stop?" he asked.

"I need to get to bed," I told him. I yawned, just to prove it was true.

"I wish I could come with you."

"Sorry." I laughed.

We kissed one last time, and then Jack headed reluctantly back down the stairs to the street. Inside the apartment, I went quietly to my room. Rose had fallen asleep with the light on, a copy of *Modern Bride* magazine on the bed beside her.

As I turned out the light I heard something clatter against the glass of the window. I crossed the room and looked down. Jack was standing on the sidewalk, about to toss another pebble.

I opened the window and leaned out. "What are you doing?"

"I just wanted to tell you that you mean the world to me."

What was I supposed to say to that? Sometimes Jack is a little overboard with his feelings. I ended up just saying, "Good."

We blew some kisses, and then I closed the window.

Amazingly, considering all the noise, Rose hadn't woken up. Putting on some pajamas, I climbed into my bed.

For a long time I lay with my head on the pillow, staring into the darkness. I still couldn't quite believe that I had a boyfriend who threw pebbles at my window to tell me he was crazy about me. Something bothered me, though. Whenever Jack said something like, "You mean the world to me," I could never say it back. The words stuck in my throat.

I'm just not the demonstrative type, I decided. But was that it, really? I thought back on the evening, particularly parking at the beach. I couldn't lie to myself. No matter how warm the kisses, I'd still felt cool inside.

I rolled over, my face to the wall. I'll talk to him about it soon, I decided, then started thinking about Rose's bridal shower. I finally fell asleep and dreamed about stones hitting my windowpane and cemeteries and baby seals in shell pink dresses.

Eleven

W OW. FEEL THAT wind," Ellen said.

Jack pointed to the sky. "Check out the clouds."

"A nor'easter," Eric said.

It was late Friday afternoon and a bunch of us were leaving the school building, on our way to Cap'n Jack's for burgers. The wind whipped my long hair out behind me. I shivered, and not just from the cold. A storm was definitely brewing, and weather like this always reminded me of the storm that swamped my father's fishing boat.

At Cap'n Jack's six of us squeezed into a booth: me, Jack, Ellen, Eric, Monica, and Nikolai, another buddy of Jack's. We'd gone to an after-school college fair, so naturally that was what we talked about.

"Look at all this stuff." Monica dumped the contents of her backpack on the table. About a hundred college brochures spilled out. "How are we ever supposed to decide?"

Our waitress had just delivered a big basket of french fries, and Eric reached for one. "You narrow it down," he said. "You know, big public university or small private college? What kind of major do you want, hard science or liberal arts? Stay in New England or move someplace else?"

"I really like Stanford." Nikolai picked up a brochure and held it up so we could all see the palm trees. "Palo Alto, California. It looks warm."

Monica laughed. "That's your reason?"

Nikolai grinned. "It's as good as any."

"I don't want to go that far away," Ellen remarked, pouring some soda from the pitcher into her glass.

"I go back and forth," I said, dipping a french fry into the ketchup. "Sometimes I want to stay close to home, like maybe Colby or Bates. Then I think, what about the University of Virginia or Berkeley or Northwestern?"

"I thought we were going to apply to Williams and Amherst," Jack said to me.

"I know those are your favorites," I replied, "but bigger schools have more science classes to choose from."

"But we have to go to the same place." Jack slipped an arm around my shoulders and gave me a possessive squeeze. "I would miss you too much if we were apart. Besides, a long-distance relationship is a hassle, you know?"

I started to say that in my opinion, relationships in general were a hassle, but I bit my tongue. Why do we have to do everything together? I wondered. It was the science fair all over again.

Ellen was sitting across from me, and she caught my eye. My feelings must have shown on my face because she gave me a small, sympathetic smile. I shrugged. "It's too soon to make up our minds, anyway," I concluded. "We aren't seniors yet."

We finished our burgers and headed back outside. The days were getting longer—the sun wouldn't set for another hour or so—but it was almost as dark as night. As we walked across the parking lot raindrops began to fall. Within seconds it was a downpour. "Another thing about Stanford," Nikolai shouted as we sprinted to the cars. "It hardly ever rains!"

J ACK WALKED ME to the door, holding an umbrella over my head. "See you in about an hour," he said.

We were going dancing later at the Rusty Nail—I just needed to change my clothes. I don't really like to dance, but it's the most popular place for South Regional couples to hang out, so Jack and I went there pretty often. "See you," I echoed.

Bending, Jack brushed the corner of my mouth with a kiss. While he hurried back to his car in the rain, I ducked into the building.

Inside, I found a note from Mom on the kitchen counter: *I'm working until ten or so. Chicken pie in the fridge—heat at 350 and make a salad.*

I preheated the oven, then headed upstairs. As I passed the family room I saw Lily at the computer. I almost walked past, but then I stopped and went into the room, curious. "Surfing the Net again?" I asked.

At the sound of my voice, she jumped a little. I stepped closer and she quickly hit a few keys in a secretive, I-don't-want-you-to-see-what-I'm-doing way.

"Chat room?" I guessed.

Lily swiveled in her chair. Her cheeks were pink. "Do you really care?" she challenged.

I did, a little. Lately no one had time to monitor Lily's computer use. But I didn't have time to get into some intense discussion with my sister. "I'm just changing, then I'm going out with Jack, so you're on your own for dinner," I told her. "I'll put the chicken pie in the oven and set the timer. Listen for the buzzer, okay?"

Lily's expression grew even more sulky. "Fine," she said as she turned back to the computer.

I went upstairs, wondering about Lily and the Internet. Poetry? Boys? A cult? I didn't dwell on it for long, though—I was too busy staring into my closet. I hated dressing up, but I had one skirt and a chenille top that Jack really liked. Instead I reached for a clean pair of overalls folded on the shelf. I wasn't sure why, but tonight I didn't feel like dressing to make my boyfriend happy.

As I turned back around, a gust of wind rattled the window-panes. I looked out into the grayness. Rain was falling in sheets and lightning flickered in the distance. A few seconds later thunder rumbled.

Again I shivered. It's not a good night to go out, I thought.

I remembered waving to Daisy as she drove off into the rain the day after my birthday. Storms never brought good things to my family.

What did this one hold in store?

THE PHONE RANG at seven o'clock the next morning. I sat up in bed, my heart pounding. Daisy, I thought, reliving that phone call in the middle of the night. But of course the call couldn't be about Daisy. Not anymore.

I ran out to grab the phone on the hall table, hoping it wouldn't wake up Mom. She'd been up late the night before, balancing the books for her catering business after getting home from a job. "Hello?" I said, my voice scratchy with sleep.

"Laurel?" a male voice asked.

"Speaking."

"It's Carlos."

"Carlos, hi," I said. "Why are *you* calling at the crack of dawn?"

"I'm at the center," he answered. "I came early on a hunch, and I was right. All this rain—the creek is over its banks. And it's still coming down. Another hour and it'll be flooding the paddocks and hutches. Griffin's in DC at a conference. Can you get over here and help?"

"I'll be there in ten minutes."

"I knew I could count on you."

I scribbled a note for Mom quickly, dressed quickly, and drove quickly. About a mile out of town the Old Boston Post

Road dipped to pass under a bridge. The low part of the road was flooded. Keeping my fingers crossed, I plowed through, water splashing up over the hubcaps. Nothing happened—the engine didn't stall—and I made it to the WRC in ten minutes, just as I'd promised.

But ten minutes turned out to be long enough to start having doubts. Why did Carlos call me? I wondered. I wasn't as physically strong as some of the volunteers, like Jon. What if animals drowned because I didn't work fast enough? It would be all my fault.

Throwing on my slicker as I went, I hurried around to the back of the building. Just as Carlos had said, Goose Creek had swollen into a raging river. Water was already rushing under the fences of the far paddocks, and I spotted Carlos leading a skittish yearling fawn by a halter. I ran over to him. He glanced at me briskly, his dark hair wet from the rain. "Good, you're here."

"Is Lefty all right?" I asked.

Carlos nodded. "The building's high enough. Come on."

In the urgency of the moment, my fears evaporated. Carlos and I worked together for an hour moving animals— deer, bear cubs, a coyote, an injured moose, raccoons— into the building or to higher ground. For the most part, we didn't speak. I knew what Carlos wanted me to do. It was as if there were a connection from his brain directly to mine—we didn't need words.

When we got the last animal to safety—a skunk—Carlos gave me a rain-soaked hug. "We did it," he declared.

My heart swelled with joy and relief and even a little pride. "We did it," I echoed.

We were still standing in the rain. Carlos hadn't been wearing a raincoat, and my hood had fallen back, so I was almost as drenched as he was. "Thanks, Laurel. You were great. No one knows the animals like you do."

I blinked away the raindrops, staring at him, and that was when it hit me. Rather, a couple of things hit me. One was that Carlos was right—I *had* been great. I'd totally kept my cool. I never would have thought I could handle something so difficult.

The other thing that hit me was that I was looking at Carlos in the same way I'd caught Lily looking at Jack that day on the ski slopes. Oh, my God, I realized. I'm in love with him.

"I think I'll head inside and—is there anything else you want me to—maybe I could . . . ," I stammered.

"Go on in and get dry," Carlos recommended.

I turned away, hoping he hadn't noticed my sudden blush. Despite the rain, I felt hot. Let's see, I found myself thinking. If I'm a high school junior and he's a college sophomore, that means he's three years older than I am. Nineteen. That's not too old, is it?

Inside the building, I stripped off my raincoat and threw it over the back of a chair. I put my hands to my cheeks—my face was still burning. I have a crush on Carlos, I thought dizzily.

It was crazy. He was older than me, and he'd never given the least indication that he thought of me as anything other than a friend. Still . . . three years wasn't *that* huge an age difference. There were plenty of girls at South Regional who dated older boys, college boys.

The age difference wasn't the real issue, though. I already *had* a boyfriend.

I bit my lip, thinking guiltily about Jack. Daydreaming about another guy isn't cheating, I told myself. But I couldn't ignore what was happening. The charge of intense physical attraction I'd felt for Carlos was nothing like the warm, fuzzy feelings I had for Jack. *I've never felt that way about Jack,* I thought, *and I never will.*

T HE RAIN HAD let up by the time I met Jack after work that afternoon. I had tried to push my thoughts about Carlos out of my mind, but it was difficult. As we walked along Main Street, trying to decide where to go for a bite to eat, I told him about saving the animals at the WRC. "I think it was the most important thing I've ever done," I said.

"I bet," Jack replied, but he didn't really sound interested. He didn't seem to understand what a revelation it had been for me to discover that I could rise to the occasion and be utterly competent.

"Anyway," I told him, "I had this idea on my way home. About Rose's bridal shower. I've been stressing about getting everything just right. But I'm just not a conventional maid of honor, so why should the shower be conventional? My parents got married on a fishing boat—that was totally unique. What if I held the shower at the picnic tables by the creek behind the WRC?"

Jack cocked one eyebrow. "Different," he conceded.

My doubts returned instantly. "It's too weird, isn't it? Rose would hate it."

"I didn't say that. Do whatever you want to do." He gave me a teasing look. "By the way, does all this wedding talk give you any ideas?"

I stopped in my tracks. Wedding? Jack wasn't seriously thinking along those lines, was he? Then again, the way he talked about his feelings for me, it was possible. I couldn't stand it one minute longer—I couldn't keep pretending I felt something I didn't. I couldn't mislead him anymore. It would only be worse in the end for him if I didn't say something now. "Jack, I can't do this," I told him.

He looked at me, his forehead creased. "If you're not hungry, we don't have to—"

I shook my head. "No. I can't do *this.*"

I took my hand away from his. We stood on the sidewalk, facing each other. Jack still looked puzzled, and I wished more than anything that I'd kept my mouth shut, but it was too late. The air was still wet with rain, reminding me of Carlos at the WRC that morning. I had to finish what I'd started.

"What are you talking about?" Jack asked.

I took a deep breath. "I'm talking about our relationship."

"What about it?"

"I—I don't think we should go out anymore."

He stared at me, his eyes wide with shock and disbelief. "Why? What's wrong?"

"It's not that I don't love you," I said quickly. "I do. You're my best friend. But I . . . I don't love you the way you want me to love you."

Now his expression turned stony. "What's been going on, then? Are you saying that for months you've been—"

"Maybe I should've figured this out sooner," I cut in. "But it's confusing because I do love you. I'm just not *in* love with you. I never, ever meant to do anything to hurt you. You've helped me so much, but going on like this wouldn't be fair to either of us."

"I still don't get it." Jack stuck his hands deep in the pockets of his coat. "Haven't I treated you okay?" He smiled crookedly. "I can change—just tell me what you're looking for. Different hair, different clothes, different friends . . ."

"Jack, its not about *hair.*" I lifted my hands to my face, covering my eyes. I couldn't stand seeing the pain behind his smile. "You're a great person. I don't want you to change. But—"

"But you're dumping me."

The seconds passed. I had to look at him.

My hands dropped, and I met his eyes. They were glittering with tears. "It's not dumping. It's—"

"And right in the middle of Main Street." His voice cracked. "Gee, thanks, Laurel."

Jack turned. I grabbed his arm. "Wait," I pleaded. "Can't we talk about this some more? I want us to stay friends, to go back to the way we were before we became a couple and stopped being our real selves."

"This *is* my real self, Laurel!" he said hoarsely. "What do you think I am? A machine? You can punch a button and we shift back to being platonic, like all these months meant nothing?"

"I still want to spend time with you, though. I still want—"

"It won't work. It's got to be all or nothing." Jack clenched his jaw; I could tell he was trying not to cry. "Because you might not be in love with me, Laurel, but I'm in love with you."

I couldn't think of anything else to say. Jack gave me one last look and then he turned away, and this time I let him go.

I watched him stride off down the sidewalk, and now I was crying, too. An elderly woman coming out of the Down East News and Drugstore saw the tears on my face. "Are you all right, dear?" she asked.

I nodded. "I'm all right."

I wasn't, though. Not at all.

Twelve

B OY, ARE YOU stupid."

That was Lily's comment that night after she overheard me telling Mom that I'd broken up with Jack.

We were in the upstairs hallway. "Shut up, okay?" I snapped, stomping to my room. "I never asked for your opinion."

I slammed the door, but not before she could yell after me, "He was too good for you, anyway!"

The rest of the weekend was dismal. I moped around, too depressed even to play with Snickers or Alfalfa. When Monday morning dawned, I looked unhappily out my window. The sky was blue, trees were budding, birds were singing, but it didn't mean anything to me. My canoe and paddles were practically crying out to hit the water again after a long winter in the storage room behind Wissinger's Bakery. Meredith's Meadow would be a rainbow of wildflowers. It didn't matter. For the first time in my life, I didn't want to leave the house. Most of all, I dreaded school.

I considered pretending to be sick, but I knew Mom would see right through me. Maybe Jack will stay home, I thought as I rode the school bus. If I was feeling rotten, he had to be feeling worse.

I ran into him right off the bat, naturally. We were heading in opposite directions in the main hall at South Regional, both walking to our lockers. I started to say hi, but he kept looking straight ahead, not even acknowledging me, so I swallowed the greeting.

Word gets around school fast when a couple gets together or breaks up, but not everyone had heard by lunchtime. I was sitting with Ellen when Jack walked across the cafeteria with a couple of guys from his wrestling team. None of them was his close friend—they weren't people Jack would have told about our breakup. "Should we sit there?" asked one of the guys, Luis, nodding toward my table.

Without speaking, Jack steered Luis in another direction, his face a blank mask.

"I hate this," I whispered, staring down at my sandwich. I couldn't eat a bite.

Ellen patted my hand, then offered me an Oreo. I gazed after Jack, my heart aching. Did I do the right thing? I wondered.

THERE WAS A science club meeting after school. It was one place I knew I'd be safe from bumping into Jack—even though he'd wanted to do the science fair project with me, he'd never really been into that sort of stuff.

"Speaking of which," I said to Ellen with a heavy sigh. We'd taken seats in the back of the room. "Jack and I didn't get that far on our project. There's no way I can finish it on my own in just one week."

"Tell you what." Ellen took a spiral notebook out of her backpack and opened it up. "I still have a lot to do myself." She pushed her glasses up on her freckled nose, then pointed to a page. "Three experiments. Why don't you help me?"

I looked at Ellen. "That's really nice of you."

The senior who's president of the club, Mimi Grange, called the meeting to order. The club started to discuss plans for setting up the science fair the following week.

Ellen handed me her notebook so I could read the notes she'd written on her experiments so far. We're both into environmental stuff, and her project was about how natural things like algae could purify contaminated water. I found myself nodding as I read along—she'd designed some good experiments.

I nudged her with my elbow. "Did you think about trying it on salt water, too?" I whispered.

"Salinity kills the algae," she whispered back.

"But what if you . . ."

We whispered back and forth until Mimi gave us a dirty look. Then I switched to scribbling notes. Twenty minutes later I realized that I'd temporarily forgotten how horrible everything was with Jack. My heart was still sore from losing Daisy, and now another important person had been torn from my life, in a different way, but still. It was my choice this time, I reminded myself; I did the right thing. And maybe there was life after breaking up.

I CAME HOME to a quiet house. As usual Mom had left a note on the kitchen counter: *I'm at a meeting in Portland. Be back around eight.*

I sighed deeply. I don't have a mother lately, I thought, just a pile of paper scraps. Immediately I felt bad for being so selfish. Mom was doing her best. She worked hard for all of us, not just for herself. But I'd rather have less money and see her more often, I decided.

I left the note out in case Lily hadn't seen it yet, although I assumed she was already home from school—she doesn't have extracurricular activities on Monday. Mom's note hadn't mentioned supper. "Lily?" I called, walking out into the hall. "Want to order a pizza?"

The only answer was silence. "Lily," I yelled again. I glanced into the family room. The computer was on, but Lily was nowhere in sight. I walked over. Lily was always extremely secretive about her computer habits, but for once she'd left her e-mail folder open. I couldn't resist—leaning close to the bright screen, I read the most recent message.

It was kind of shocking. *Dear Tigerlilli,* her correspondent wrote. *I could tell from your last letter that you're really sad. Your family sounds like they don't understand you at all. Why don't you just get out of there? You know you want to. I have plenty of room at my place. A double bed. : -) Write back and tell me where to meet you. XXOO, J.H.*

I whirled on my heel. "Lily!" I shouted. My gaze fell on the coffee table. Running over, I seized a brochure. "The bus schedule," I said aloud, suddenly in a panic. "Oh, my God, she ran away."

I sprinted out of the room . . . and barreled straight into Lily. We both screamed. "What's wrong?" she asked. "I thought I heard you yelling—I was in the bathroom."

"What's *wrong?*" I gasped, pointing to the computer. "That's what's wrong!"

Lily hurried over to the computer and closed her e-mail file. "You shouldn't have been reading my private stuff," she exclaimed angrily.

"Lily, what's going on?"

She turned to face me, her arms folded tightly across her chest. "Nothing."

"Come on," I pressed. "Are you thinking of running away with whoever that is? J.H.? Who is he, anyway?"

"What difference would it make to you?" she retorted. "People on the Internet care more about me than you do!"

I stared at my sister. She'd turned fourteen over the winter, and she was starting to fill out. She had a curvier figure than me now, and in some of her getups—like today's psychedelic seventies micromini—she looked precociously grown-up. I could still see the little girl under the surface, though. A little girl who needed a big sister. And with Daisy gone and Rose in college, that leaves me, I realized with a pang as I remembered all the times in the past few months that Lily had tried to get my attention and I'd told her to get lost. What had I been thinking? I couldn't stand to lose another sister.

"Lily, I'm sorry," I said. "I've been so caught up in my own life lately, I haven't kept track of what's going on with you."

Lily narrowed her eyes at me. *"Lately?* How about *forever."*

"Tell me about J.H.," I said.

Lily rolled her eyes. "We met in this chat room," she explained, "and at first I thought he was really interesting. It was his initials, partly." She blushed slightly. "I knew he wasn't Jack Harrison, obviously, but I thought maybe he was as nice as Jack."

"But that line about his double bed—"

"Can you believe that?" Lily exclaimed. "What a creep! Like I would really run off with some guy I'd never even met in person! I'm glad I didn't tell him my real name."

I was so relieved, I rushed over and gave her a hug. "Oh, Lily. You're crazy. You know that?"

"Not as crazy as you." She pushed me away. "I still can't believe you broke up with the coolest, sweetest guy in Maine."

"Here's the thing," I said, figuring I might as well confide in Lily as anyone. "He *is* the coolest, sweetest guy in Maine. But I just didn't feel . . ." I thought about the jolt I'd gotten from Carlos the other day in the rain. "Sparks."

"I don't know." Lily shook her head. "Sparks might not be all they're cracked up to be. Like, Tom Muldoone? This guy in my math class? Talk about sparks. But I happen to know he's a real jerk to the girls he goes out with. I wouldn't want to date him. I think it would be the ultimate to go out with a guy who was my best friend, like you and Jack, or Rose and Stephen."

"I thought so too at first." I sighed. "But it just wasn't right."

"I guess he'll have to wait for me to grow up, then," said Lily, smiling mischievously.

I thought about the age difference between me and Carlos. Lily and Jack? It wasn't impossible. "Maybe," I agreed, smiling back at her.

Lily and I ended up curled up on the couch, talking about boys. We had a pizza delivered and ate the whole thing, still talking. It was as if some wall that had stood between us for years and years had tumbled. Then again, maybe the wall wasn't gone altogether—we still disagreed about nearly everything—but it had some major cracks in it. It was almost like the old days, gabbing with Daisy.

When the pizza was gone and we'd polished off a pint of ice cream, too, I asked Lily, "What are you going to do about J.H.? The e-mail guy?"

"Write back and tell him I was *about* to run off with him, but my big sister wouldn't let me," she answered, her eyes twinkling, "so I decided to save myself for Mr. Right."

"I guess I'll do the same," I said.

T HE SCIENCE FAIR is a pretty big deal. The kids who win prizes always get into really good colleges and win scholarships and things like that. A week later, on Monday night Ellen and I had a display table near the door to the gym—there were students from three regional high schools competing—so the judges looked at our project first, but that didn't end up helping. They took some notes and moved on to the next exhibit pretty quickly. "Not a good sign," Ellen said with a sigh.

While we waited for the judging, we took turns wandering around the gym, looking at other people's projects and getting sodas at the concession table. I stopped to talk to Jon about his homemade telescope. "You're going to win," I predicted. He'd set up a really ingenious experiment to track comets.

"I'm not so sure," Jon replied. "Did you see the girls from Kent with the solar-powered robot?"

I walked over to look at the robot. A lot of kids from South Regional were at the fair to see how their friends did and just to check out the cool exhibits. I couldn't believe it when I saw Jack walking my way.

He must have come here to see me! I thought, my heart pounding. He changed his mind—he wants to stay friends after all. "Jack," I called.

He must have heard me—we weren't *that* far apart—but instead of continuing toward me, he pivoted and headed in a different direction. "Hey," I heard him say to someone. "How's it going?"

My cheeks crimson, I hurried back to my booth, hoping no one had witnessed me getting totally iced by my ex. A few minutes ago I'd been feeling pretty good. My life seemed to be getting back to normal. But Jack blowing me off like that was like a knife twisting in my heart. Without his friendship, there was an empty place in my life that I didn't think would ever be filled.

Jon won a prize, but Ellen and I didn't, not even honorable mention. Ellen was disappointed, but I wasn't really surprised. You don't win if you don't give something one hundred percent. That was what Daisy always said, and that was how she'd lived her life.

I was starting to believe I'd never win at anything.

Thirteen

Rose came home one weekend in early May for her long-awaited bridal shower. I'd arranged with Griffin to use the WRC on a Sunday, when it's usually closed.

Lily and I went over early to decorate the picnic tables by the creek with tablecloths and balloon bouquets. "The weather's great," she observed. "That's lucky."

"Yeah," I agreed, glancing upward. The sky was blue, so it looked like I didn't have to worry about rain, but I was nervous about everything else. "What if she doesn't like it, though?"

"She's going to get tons of presents," Lily replied. "What's not to like?"

I still wasn't sure about my choice, but it was too late to back out now. I'd gone with my gut and decided to make the bridal shower nontraditional, like me. There wouldn't be any china or silver. We were going to have bagels and cream cheese and fruit salad on paper plates, with deer and raccoons and a fox and a moose watching us from the other side of the lawn.

I was excited in spite of myself. I wanted Rose to like the shower so badly!

"Let's head back to the apartment," I said to Lily. "I've made the dough, but I still need to bake the cookies."

Back at the apartment, I was a nervous wreck. I kept trying—and failing—to do a hundred things at once. I thought I'd have enough time to fix my hair while the cookies were baking, but the smell of something burning as I was tying up my braid proved me wrong. I ran down the stairs to find Lily pulling the cookies out of the oven—and blowing the smoke off them.

"They aren't badly burned," she told me.

"Well," I said, eyeing my singed desserts, "they'll have to do. I don't have time to make more."

At ten-thirty I was back at the Wildlife Rescue Center—the bridal shower guests started arriving at eleven. I'd invited Mom and Lily, of course, and Rose's high school friends Cath and Rox and their mothers. Mita was there, although *her* mother lived in Boston now and couldn't make it because she had to work at her Indian restaurant. Rose's BU roommates, Beverly and Julia, came, and Stephen's mom and sisters.

Everyone exclaimed about the WRC. "Isn't this a lovely setting?" "How unusual!" "Are those animals tame?"

I hadn't told Rose beforehand where the party was going to be, and I was chewing my nails as I waited for her reaction. To my vast relief, she gave me a big hug and said, "This is fantastic, Toad."

"It's going well, don't you think?" I whispered to Lily a little while later. The guests were eating bagels and chatting—things seemed to be going smoothly.

"You pulled it off," Lily whispered back.

That's when the guests discovered the cookies.

"Ooh—chocolate chocolate chip!" Val Mathias said. "My favorite!"

I was about to warn her that they weren't double chocolate chip—they were just regular chocolate chip set on "extra crispy"—but she had already taken a big bite. So had Mita and Mrs. Mathias. I have to say that their expressions would have been hilarious if I hadn't been so embarrassed.

"Let's do the presents," I suggested as everyone grabbed napkins and tried to dispose of their cookies as discreetly as possible.

Rose smiled. "I'm ready."

There were two tall stacks of packages, all wrapped in glittery paper with lots of ribbons and bows. I handed Rose the first present . . . just as the first raindrop fell.

Hurriedly we all moved inside—but we weren't fast enough. Rose opened her gifts in the charmless lobby of the WRC while the rest of the guests tried to dry themselves off. I don't even remember what Rose got—I was only concentrating on trying not to burst into tears.

When the party was over and only Mom, Lily, Rose, and I were left, I put my hands to my face. "I can't believe I wrecked your one and only chance at a bridal shower," I groaned.

Rose looked surprised. "What are you talking about?" she asked.

"See?" I turned to my mother. "You were right not to let me help at your parties, Mom. I can't do anything right. I'm going to drop my bouquet and trip going down the aisle, Rose, I just know it. I'm such a spaz."

"Toad, I *loved* my shower," Rose said.

I rolled my eyes. "Please. You don't have to lie about it."

"Seriously," she insisted. "Maybe it wasn't perfect, but it was special! I'll never forget it."

"It was very original," Mom put in. "I'm impressed that you did it all yourself—the locale, the food, the invitations. You didn't even ask me for help!"

"I didn't want to bother you," I explained. "You're too busy as it is."

"Well, I thought it was offbeat and perfect," Rose declared, giving me a hug. "You put a lot of yourself into it, and that's what means the most to me. I only hope I have half as much fun at my wedding!"

I sighed. There was no use crying over spilled milk or soggy bagels. "Let's go home," I said.

I wouldn't let Rose clean up, so she and Lily went to look at Lefty while Mom helped me out. She and I ran out into the rain to get all the trash off the picnic tables. We carried the leftover food and supplies and Rose's gifts to the car. We didn't speak until everything was done. Then, before I could call Rose and Lily, Mom put a hand on my arm. "Laurel, sit down for a minute," she said.

We both sat down on chairs in the lobby. I looked at her apologetically. "I know the party was a mess," I began. "I should have asked you and Sarah to cater it. I really hoped that if for once I did it myself, it—"

Mom lifted a hand. "The party was fine, Laurel. Is that really what you think people think of you, though? That you can't do anything right?"

I hung my head, biting my lip.

"Laurel, I didn't want you to help with the catering because I didn't want to stress you out." She let out a sigh. "Do you remember, after Dad died, how hard we had to scramble? I leaned hard on your big sisters, especially Daisy. It was too much for her—she ended up cracking under the strain."

"You mean junior year, when she went through that rebellious stage? That wasn't your fault, Mom."

"It wasn't?" Mom shook her head. "I felt very much to blame at the time."

"Daisy just needed to let off steam," I said. "She'd always been so perfect."

"That's just it," Mom exclaimed. "I made her feel she *had* to be."

"And she was. Whereas I don't even come close, no matter how hard I try."

I hung my head again and struggled not to cry, embarrassed that Mom was witnessing me feeling so sorry for myself. When Mom put an arm around my shoulders, though, I couldn't help it. A tear trickled down my cheek.

"I think you're a very able person, Laurel May Walker," she declared.

I sniffled. "That's not how I feel."

"Laurel, you have your own special qualities and abilities." Mom gave me a squeeze. "It's true that you'll never be like Daisy, but I wouldn't want you to be. You're you, and a lot of people love you exactly as you are. Including me."

We were both thoughtful for a minute. Then Mom said, "I *am* too busy, aren't I?" I couldn't deny it. "The problem is, I've found it's the only thing that helps. If I work constantly, I don't have as much time to grieve. Do you know what I mean?"

I thought about how I'd sought refuge in my relationship with Jack. "I think so."

"It's crazy." Mom's arm tightened around me. "I've been missing one daughter so much that it's made me neglect the ones I still have. I'll make some changes, Laurel," she promised. "I'll get my work schedule under control. And if you really want to help with the business, I'd be more than glad to have you. There are a lot of things I think you could do very well."

I cracked a smile. "Like, if you need any wild animal acts."

Mom laughed. "Seriously. I don't want you not to try things just because you're afraid you might trip and fall. We all trip and fall sometimes. That doesn't mean you won't succeed sometimes, too."

"Thanks, Mom," I whispered.

She still had her arm around me. I put my head on her shoulder. "You can lean on me, too, Mom."

She tipped her head so it rested lightly on top of mine. "Okay," she said, "I will."

T HE RAIN CLEARED by dinnertime. After we ate, Rose went over to Rox's house, Lily sat down at the computer to write a story—she'd sworn off chat rooms for the time being— and Mom and Hal settled down to watch the news on public television. I took Snickers out for a walk.

It was seven-thirty and still light. Halfway between the spring equinox and the summer solstice, the days were getting longer and longer. I let Snickers run around in the park for a while—she was getting so big, she almost didn't look like a puppy anymore—and then walked with her through town. I was feeling better than I had in a while, thanks to my talk with Mom. Now that I looked back on it, the bridal shower hadn't been all *that* bad. Maybe I'd never be the most polished, self-confident person on the planet, but that *didn't* mean I couldn't handle things. When I forget to be afraid, I do okay, I thought, remembering the flood at the WRC.

At the end of the commercial part of Main Street, I found myself turning left on Lighthouse Road. "The sun won't set for half an hour," I told the dog. "Let's go to the beach."

With Snickers loping beside me, I followed the road around a big curve. My family's old house stood tall behind a hedge of lilacs. The apple trees in the backyard were in bloom. Do the bluebirds still come back to the birdhouse Daisy helped me nail to the trunk of the beech tree? I wondered.

I kept walking, savoring the way the world was suddenly full of color and sound again. Frogs croaked and chuckled in the pond. Mayflies buzzed. Weeds and wildflowers were sprouting on the roadside: dandelions, chickweed, thistles, coltsfoot. The sight of them was as welcome as an old friend.

At the bottom of a long gravel driveway, I stopped. The sign hanging from the mailbox said Windy Ridge. I peered up the drive at the house on the hill, wondering. Is he home? I thought. I shouldn't show up without calling first. Not that there's any point calling—he'd refuse to talk to me.

I considered turning around. Then I chided myself for being a coward. What are you afraid of? I asked myself. You have nothing to lose.

I headed up the driveway.

"Mr. and Mrs. Harrison will flip," I warned Snickers. I hadn't seen them since Jack and I broke up, and I was sure they hated me. Snickers just tugged on the leash, wanting to chase a rabbit munching clover on the hillside.

When I got to the front door, I hesitated again. It wasn't too late to run back down the driveway. Instead I took a deep breath and rang the bell.

Jack answered the door himself. His expression wasn't exactly welcoming. "What do you want?"

Snickers bounced against the screen door that separated us, barking happily at the sight of Jack. "Can we talk?" I asked.

Jack shrugged. He opened the screen door, and Snickers proceeded to jump all over him. When he bent to rub her ears, she licked his face.

"I was heating up some leftover pizza," Jack said. I followed him into the kitchen. "Want a soda or something?"

"No, thanks. Are your parents around?"

Snapping open a can of root beer, he shook his head. "They drove down to Boston for the symphony."

"Oh," I said.

"What do you want, anyway?" he asked again curtly.

I looked at Jack and tried to pretend this was a normal conversation and not one of the most uncomfortable moments of my life. "I just wanted to, you know, see how you're doing. And Rose's wedding is in three weeks, and I thought maybe, well, since you're such an old friend of the family, you should really be there. I know Rose and Stephen would like that. So you should . . ." I gulped. "Come to the wedding. With me. You know, as friends."

We were standing on opposite sides of the trestle table in the Harrisons' big kitchen. "I don't think so," Jack said finally.

I gripped the back of the chair in front of me. "Can't we get past this?" I pleaded. "I miss you. Can't we be—"

His jaw muscles tightened. "You really don't get it, do you?"

"But it's not just anybody—it's Rose and Stephen. You've known them forever and—"

"Okay, I'll spell it out for you," he interrupted me, flushing angrily. "You broke my heart, Laurel. I don't want to be around you, especially not at a wedding."

His face was red; mine turned pale. "What will it take for you to forgive me?" I whispered.

"I don't know if I ever will."

There was nothing else to say. Jack didn't walk me to the door. I let myself out, then jogged home with Snickers, trying not to cry as I hurried along Main Street. Bursting into the apartment, I almost tripped over Lily. "What's the matter?" she asked when she saw my miserable expression. "Laurel, what happened?"

Not answering her, I dropped the dog's leash and ran upstairs. Slamming the door to my room, I flung myself onto my bed. Instead of crying, though, I just lay there with my face in the pillow. I'll get over this, I told myself. I'll get over this, I'll get over this. . . .

H E'S *GONE?*"
I was at the Wildlife Rescue Center the following Saturday, staring into Lefty's empty pen. Carlos stood beside me. "We knew it had to happen sooner or later," he reminded me. "He'd outgrown us—he needed a real tank to swim in so he could get ready for the ocean. Griff had the aquarium come and get him yesterday."

I turned away from the pen. "I didn't even get to say good-bye."

"I'm sorry, Laurel. Griff and I should've called you." Carlos rested a hand briefly on my shoulder. On any other occasion I would have been thrilled by this contact, but not today. I drew in a deep, shaky breath. "It's . . . just . . . so . . . *hard.*" I was crying a little—I couldn't help it. "Lefty was like one of my pets. I wanted to keep him with me forever."

"I know. But sometimes you have to let go of someone you love because that's what's best for them."

I thought about my futile visit with Jack the Sunday before. "Maybe," I said, unconvinced.

We got to work. I tried to focus, but it was useless. I was supposed to be helping him splint the wing of an osprey with a minor injury, but every time he asked me to hand him some supplies or instruments, I gave him the wrong thing. "You're really distracted, Laurel," Carlos said. "Thinking about Lefty?"

"Actually, I'm thinking about Jack." Flipping my hair aside, I looked at Carlos. "Remember him? The guy I was going out with."

"Yeah, I remember," said Carlos.

The bird's wing was finished. I followed Carlos as he carried the osprey back to its cage. "Well, it's been almost a month since we broke up, and he's as mad at me as ever. I'm *not* sorry we broke up," I added so Carlos wouldn't get the wrong impression. I wanted him to know I was unattached, just in case. "But I'm afraid we'll never be friends again. Why can't we go back to the way we were before we started dating? It doesn't make sense!"

Carlos laughed as he turned away from the cage. "Who said relationships made sense? Take me and Emily."

Emily? I thought. His sister? His cat? His hairstylist? "Emily?" I asked.

"My girlfriend."

"Oh." I felt myself blush, and I prayed Carlos would

never, ever guess that for a minute there I'd actually imagined he could be a little bit interested in me. Of course he has a girlfriend, I thought. You idiot, Laurel.

Carlos handed me a tub of bird feed. We moved along the row of cages, filling seed trays. "We keep playing these dumb games. Like, she was mad because I didn't go to Florida for spring break with her. I just didn't have the cash. And now I'm trying to figure out a way for us to be together over summer vacation and she acts like she couldn't care less about that."

"She probably wants to be with you," I commented, imagining how I'd feel in Emily's place. "Maybe she's worried that you'll take her for granted or something."

"That's my point," Carlos said. "Who knows, right? She has her own private heart. And I have mine and you have yours and Jack has his."

"You and Emily are working things out, though, right?"

"We broke up for a while last fall and then got back together," Carlos answered. "I guess my advice about Jack is just to let things take their course. What's meant to be will be."

At the end of the day Carlos sat down at the desk in the office to type up some notes while I went outside to play with a pair of orphaned coyote pups. The trees were getting really leafy, and it was fun to watch the pups pounce on the shifting patterns of sun and shade on the ground.

I sat on the grass, leaning back on my hands, and looked up into the sky. Suddenly I started to laugh. Carlos and me as a couple, I thought. Yeah, right! Straightening up, I wrapped my arms around my knees and glanced toward the parking lot.

Carlos was climbing into his car—he waved in my direction. Who knows, though? I mused. What had he said? What will be, will be? Maybe someday . . .

I put the coyotes back in their pen and brushed the grass and dirt off the legs of my overalls. I'd walked to work that morning, and I headed home by way of the beach.

In the late afternoon light the ocean was brilliantly blue. A couple of sailboats zigzagged along the horizon. The beach, deserted and seaweed strewn in winter, was dotted with people. Summer was just around the corner.

I stopped to watch a little girl playing catch with her father. They were both wearing Boston Red Sox caps, and all at once I felt a stab of grief so intense, I had to sit down on a rock.

I remembered Dad teaching Daisy how to throw. I could picture us all, as vividly as if it had been yesterday. We were all outside in the grassy yard of the big house one summer evening. Dad tossed grounders for Daisy; she scooped them up in her glove with ease. Rose had been helping Mom in the garden. Lily was playing with her dolls while I collected fireflies in a mason jar.

I turned my head to look out at the ocean. The water was calm. Hard to believe on a day like this that the sea could turn into a monster that devoured fishermen and their boats.

Closing my eyes, I took a deep breath of sea air. It filled my lungs with salty, cool freshness. "I miss you, Dad," I whispered. "I miss you, Daze."

With a sigh, I stood up. The little girl and her father had gone home.

Walking along the shore, I stopped every few yards to study a tide pool or pick up a clamshell. Gulls screeched and sandpipers skittered along the edge of the surf, stabbing their pointy beaks into the wet sand in search of food. I stopped to take off my sneakers and socks and roll up my pants. Then, with my shoes in my hands, I walked a few steps into the waves.

The Atlantic felt like ice. I sucked in my breath as my toes went instantly numb. I stayed in the water, though, waiting for it to happen. And it did. As the wild peace of the sea filled me, I felt something deep in my bones. I knew I'd always miss my father and my sister, but I would make it without them. I'd make it without Jack, too, if I had to, and I wasn't even really that disappointed that Carlos had a girlfriend. Maybe I didn't march to the same drummer as most people, but I could do things on my own and do them well. That was what I'd learned, little by little, in the year I turned sixteen. I was complete by myself.

Which wasn't to say I didn't need people. When my feet were dry, I put my shoes back on and hurried toward town. Mom had taken the weekend off to spend time with me and Lily—she was probably already cooking dinner. Lily would be writing a story, and Snickers would be waiting for her walk.

I couldn't wait to get home.

Fourteen

THE REST OF May passed in a whirl. The weekend before
the wedding Mom, Lily, Hal, and I went down to Boston
for Rose's and Stephen's commencements. We were so proud
of Rose in her black gown and mortarboard, and when her
a cappella group sang at a big postgraduation party, I was
pretty sure I had the prettiest, coolest, most talented sister in
the world.

The first Friday in June, back in Maine, Stephen's parents hosted a rehearsal dinner at the Harborside. Later on at
home, even though it was after ten, we were all still running
around. "I'll never be able to sleep," Rose said as she checked
over her to-do list. "I'm getting married tomorrow!"

Mom was steaming shrimp. "Here's a project for you,
then," she told Rose. "Check in with Sue Smith about the
flowers."

Mrs. Smith, an old Lighthouse Road neighbor and Mom's good friend, was doing the bouquets and centerpieces. While Rose got on the phone to call her, Lily and I went upstairs. "Let's wrap our present," she suggested.

We'd pooled our savings to buy a gift for Rose and Stephen: an engraved picture frame for them to put their wedding photo in. Lily took the box out of her closet, along with a roll of pink-and-white wrapping paper. "I think they're really going to like it," she predicted.

I looked at the frame one more time while Lily cut the paper. "I think so, too."

Lily put the lid back on the box and started to wrap it. Then she stopped and gazed at me with sad eyes. For a moment we were pensive and still. Would anything ever feel right without Daisy?

"I still miss her all the time," Lily said.

I nodded. "Me too."

Lily sighed and then got back to work. She taped the package briskly while I took a roll of ribbon and made curls with the scissors blade. "How many people do you suppose will come to the wedding tomorrow?" she asked.

"Rose said about seventy."

"Hmmm." Lily gave me a sly look. "I wonder if there will be any *surprise* guests?"

I raised my eyebrows. "You mean, gate-crashers?"

Lily giggled. "No. Well, I guess we'll see, won't we?"

"I guess so," I said, even though I had no idea what she was talking about.

We tied the ribbon onto the package and then took turns writing in the card. When Lily handed me the pen, I read what she'd written: *To the most wonderful big sister in the world and the sweetest brother-in-law I could ever hope for. Wishing you a lifetime of happiness together. Love, Lily.*

I hesitated. Lily had said it all; what could I add? Then I thought of something. For once I found the words to fit what I was feeling. "Thanks for always being there, you two," I scribbled. "I love you both so much. And Rose, let's be best friends as well as sisters forever."

THE FIRST SATURDAY in June dawned sunny and clear. "Hallelujah," Rose exclaimed at breakfast. "It was so muggy last night, I was sure it would be pouring today. But look at that glorious blue sky!"

None of us could eat much. We were all too excited. After breakfast Rose went for a jog to calm her nerves. Then she was in the shower for about an hour. Then it was time to get ready.

I let Rose have my room and I changed in Lily's. Lily and I were putting on our shoes when Rose called out to us, "Hey, guys. I need your help."

Lily and I crossed the hall. Rose was standing in the middle of my room, half in the wedding dress. "Will someone zip me?" she asked.

I zipped Rose up. She fidgeted with the sleeves of the wedding dress, pushing them off her shoulders a little bit. "Time for the hair," she announced.

Rose had decided to wear her hair in a loose French twist. Lily helped her pin it up, and then she positioned the hair comb from which the long veil fluttered. "'Something old, something new, something borrowed, something blue,'" Lily recited.

"Thanks for reminding me," Rose said. She handed me a strand of pearls. "These are Mom's. Something borrowed."

"What about something blue?" I asked as I hooked the pearls around Rose's neck.

She grinned. "My underwear."

"The dress is old," Lily said.

"And the veil is new," Rose said. She patted the necklace. "There. I'm ready."

Lily and I stood on either side of Rose in front of the mirror. We looked at our reflection. Rose smiled. "What do you think?"

I stared. I couldn't believe this was my sister, the girl I'd grown up with, the girl with long hair and bare feet who was always singing. Because she wasn't a girl anymore; the long white dress had transformed her into a woman.

I thought about how we all still missed Daisy more than we could bear sometimes. There should have been four sisters gazing together into the mirror and into the future. But the more we worked at it, the better we were getting at being just three. I felt closer to Rose and Lily all the time.

"You look beautiful, Rose," I said, my eyes damp.

Lily was misty, too. "Oh, Rose."

Lily and I leaned close to Rose, and we had a group hug.

"Don't make me cry," Rose grumbled. "My mascara will run!" But she held us tightly for a minute, as if knowing that when she let go, she would step away from us into another identity, another life.

"Look at you."

The three of us turned to see Mom standing in the doorway. She was beautiful, too, in a cornflower blue chiffon dress. "Oh, Rose," she said, echoing Lily. "I can't believe it. My oldest girl is a bride."

Smiling through their tears, Rose and Mom embraced for a long moment. "The limo's here to take you to the church," Mom told Rose. "Are you ready?"

Rose looked at me and Lily. We stepped to her side, and she took our hands, giving them a squeeze. "I'm ready," she said.

P EEKING THROUGH THE door to the chapel with Lily while Val and Elizabeth helped Rose adjust her veil, I could see that the little church was full. The organist, Mrs. Enright, was playing an introit. Flanked by his groomsmen, Stephen stood at the altar with Reverend Beecher, his hands clasped in front of him and a nervous, expectant smile on his face. "One more minute," I whispered to Rose. "Everyone's here!"

We lined up in the hall: Lily first because she was the shortest, then Valerie and Elizabeth, and finally me, the maid of honor. Rose was last. Mom and Hal had offered to walk with her, but she'd decided to walk down the aisle by herself. "Daddy will be with me in spirit," she'd said. "I won't be alone."

Now Mrs. Enright started playing the Handel piece Rose and Stephen had chosen for the processional. "This is it!" Val whispered.

Clutching her bouquet, Lily looked over her shoulder at me. I nodded. "Go ahead."

One by one, the bridesmaids proceeded down the aisle. I knew Lily was nervous, but it didn't show—she looked elegant and calm. When my turn came, I waited an extra beat. Standing behind me, Rose touched my arm. She knew why I'd waited. It was Daisy's turn. Daisy was here in spirit, too.

I began walking down the aisle, wishing I had Lily's grace and poise. I almost didn't make it to the altar because I spotted Mr. and Mrs. Harrison sitting in the third row on the left side . . . and Jack was with them. When his eyes met mine, I was so startled, I tripped a little. Just what I'd been most afraid would happen! Luckily I managed to recover enough to avoid falling flat on my face, and I made it to the altar in one piece, although I was beet red from the neck up.

At the front of the church, the bridesmaids lined up opposite the groomsmen and everyone turned to face the door. When Rose appeared, a vision in her long white gown with the bouquet of pink rosebuds held before her, a collective sigh filled the church. I saw Gram start crying and Hal hand Mom a handkerchief. The most wonderful thing of all, though, was Stephen's face. He'd known Rose since she was sixteen, but at that moment it was as if he were seeing her for the first time and he couldn't believe his good fortune. Joy, amazement, and gratitude radiated from his eyes. And love. Most of all, love.

Rose reached the altar. Stephen held out his hand to her and she stepped to his side, her gaze never leaving his. "Dearly beloved," the minister began.

WE ALL CRIED during the ceremony because weddings are emotional and because it was impossible not to remember the last time all our friends and relatives had gathered together in this church—for Daisy's funeral. By the time we arrived at the Mathiases' house for the reception, though, the mood had lightened.

"We're married!" Rose squealed, throwing her arms around Stephen even though they were supposed to be posing for a formal portrait. "Yippee!"

Stephen's parents' sprawling backyard was bordered by formal gardens—the perfect setting for a wedding. There were buffet tables set up under a white-canopied tent, and Mom's catering assistant, Sarah, was circulating among the guests, passing out glasses of champagne. I saw Jack standing with Lily. I knew I should go talk to him. I still couldn't believe he'd come.

Feeling shy, I made my way over. "Hi, Jack," I said. Before I could stop her, Lily melted away into the crowd, leaving us alone.

"Hi," Jack said.

We stood there, holding our glasses of sparkling punch. "Wasn't it a nice ceremony?" I asked after a long pause.

"Rose is a beautiful bride," Jack replied.

"So. I didn't expect you to be here. I'm glad," I added softly.

Jack nodded in the direction Lily had gone. "You can thank your little sister."

"Lily?" I wrinkled my eyebrows. "What do you mean?"

"She came over a couple of days ago," Jack explained, "and practically begged me to come to the wedding. She said I had to, or you'd be too upset to properly carry out your maid of honor duties."

So that was why she was so mysterious, hinting about surprise wedding guests! I thought. The corners of Jack's lips twitched a little. Was he actually going to smile? "What a meddler." I shook my head.

"She meant well."

Just then I spotted Lily watching us from a distance. When she caught my eye, she blew me a kiss. "It's true. She did," I agreed. Silence fell over us again. "Well," I said.

"Well."

"Thanks. I *am* glad you came."

He turned his head away. "Um." He cleared his throat. "I think I'll go get some food."

"And I should talk to my grandparents. See you later?"

"Yep."

Jack strode off toward the tent. That wasn't so bad, I thought, wistful for the days when Jack and I could talk for hours. A little stiff, but it could've been worse.

Lily appeared at my elbow. "Well?"

"You're a busybody, you know that?"

"Are you going to be friends again or not?"

I looked after Jack. Weddings make you feel good about

the future, and a tiny flower of hope blossomed in my heart. "I think we might," I answered.

M OM AND SARAH and our other friends who'd helped cook did a great job—the food was delicious. When everyone had eaten, it was time for Rose and Stephen to cut the cake, which was devil's food with white butter cream icing and a garnish of pink sugar rosebuds.

More champagne was poured, and it was time for toasts. Mr. Mathias went first. "On behalf of Anne and myself, thank you, Maggie and Hal, for putting together this splendid party," he said, lifting his glass. "We already thought of Rose as our daughter, and we're delighted to welcome her officially into our family."

Hal said a few words, and so did Stephen's best man, his college roommate, George. Then Stephen himself stepped forward. "In case anyone here doesn't already know it," he began, slipping his arm around Rose's waist, "I am the luckiest man alive."

"Here, here!" everyone cried.

"My best friend, Rose Annabelle Walker, is now my wife. I can't imagine greater happiness."

Stephen and Rose kissed. Everybody clapped.

"I had an ulterior motive in marrying Rose, though," Stephen went on, a twinkle in his eye. "This way I get to be part of her family forever, and as you've all experienced today, her mom, Maggie, is the world's best cook. I plan to enjoy many, many meals at her table in the years to come."

Stephen winked at Mom. There was more laughter. "And as if the two I had weren't enough, I also get two new sisters," Stephen said. "I think Lily and Laurel both know how special they are to me. And today I know we're all remembering Rose's sister Daisy and how much she meant to us. Her memory will always be Rose's and my most precious possession."

For a moment we were all silent. I felt a hand on my shoulder. Turning, I saw that Jack had stepped up behind me. Lifting my hand, I placed it over his.

"Finally, I'd like to thank you all for being here to witness our vows," Stephen concluded. He smiled down at his bride. "There's no backing out now. You're stuck with me, Rose!"

Stephen and Rose kissed again. There was more clapping and laughing, and then the band started playing Rose's favorite Beatles song, "If I Fell." Stephen led Rose to the dance floor that was set up at one end of the tent and took her gently in his arms.

Alone, Stephen and Rose circled the floor. Jack had taken his hand from my shoulder and moved a few steps away. Lily was standing next to me now. "Their first dance as husband and wife," she said with a sentimental sniffle.

Watching Rose and Stephen, I got sniffly, too. "They're so perfect together," I said.

Lily nodded. "Someday you'll get married to the perfect person, too."

That day seemed a long, long way off . . . which was fine with me. When the first song ended, other couples crowded onto the dance floor. Jack came back over. "Would you like to dance, Laurel?" he asked formally.

We danced one song, holding each other at arm's length. Still, the fact that he asked me at all was a gesture I appreciated. Then Jack asked Lily to dance, and I moved onto the grass to watch.

I want to save this moment, I thought, trying to memorize every detail of the scene. Rose in Mom's wedding gown with her bridal veil whirling out behind her as she and Stephen spun on the dance floor; Lily and Jack dancing awkwardly and laughing, Mom and Hal lifting their champagne glasses in a private toast; the lush, romantic scent of roses in the air; overhead, the sun bright in the flawless June sky; and in the distance the deep, timeless blue of the sea.

My expression grew pensive as I thought about the great adventure my older sister and her husband were embarking upon. My future will be an adventure, too, I reflected. School was almost over, and another long summer stretched out ahead of me. I'd be working full-time at the Wildlife Rescue Center, and since I'd already taken all the science classes offered at South Regional, I also planned to register for a course at the community college—I'd get a jump on my college credits.

Then it will be fall again, I thought. My senior year in high school. I'll turn seventeen. An ache entered my heart. Along with my birthday would come another anniversary . . . one year since Daisy's death.

"What are you thinking about, Toad?"

I blinked. I hadn't even noticed that the music had stopped

and my sister, the bride, had come over to me. "I was thinking about Daisy," I admitted.

Rose put her arms around me. "I miss her today, don't you?"

I nodded. "But I hate being sad on your wedding day."

We stepped apart again. "It's okay," she said. "I'm a little sad, too, underneath the happiness. Daisy wouldn't want us to mope, though. She'd say, 'Get out there, girls, and *party!*'"

I knew Rose was right. Our family had experienced more than our share of tragedy, but we also seemed to have more than our share of love.

I smiled at Rose. "Then let's party."

Rose hooked her arm through mine, and together we walked back to the celebration.

Lily

For my grandmother,
Eunice Butler Schwemm

One

*T*HE DAY I *turned sixteen was the most wonderful of my life! My devoted older sisters Rose and Laurel showered me with jewelry, gift certificates to the mall, and the complete works of Shakespeare in leather-bound volumes. As if that were not enough, my mom, the beautiful, recently remarried widow Maggie Walker, doubled my allowance and announced that from then on I wouldn't have chores or a curfew because I'd be going to boarding school in Paris."*

"The end," I said out loud, scrawling the words at the bottom of the page. Then I slapped my notebook shut and tossed it on my desk. I had to laugh. "Yeah, right. I wish."

There couldn't be a worse time of year for my birthday: in between Christmas and New Year's, where it gets completely lost in the holiday shuffle. I get totally ripped off in the present department, or at least that's the way it *seems*, because people are always giving me "joint" Christmas and birthday gifts. But sixteen, I figured, is special. It had to be a big deal this year.

Throwing my bathrobe on over my nightgown—it was late morning, the day after Christmas, and I'd slept in—I ran downstairs to see what everyone else was up to. Mom and Hal were in the kitchen, drinking coffee and looking at some papers spread out on the table. "Catering business stuff?" I asked.

Mom nodded at me, then turned back to my stepfather. "Hal, I've been thinking about overhead. Maybe we can cut it back if we . . ."

She leaned over to point something out to him. As her blond hair swung close to his face, he took the opportunity to kiss her cheek. Mom laughed, blushing. "Oh, Hal," she said, but she sounded pleased.

Rolling my eyes, I headed for the family room. Mom and Hal had just gotten back from their honeymoon a few weeks before Christmas, and you'd think they were twenty the way they were always gazing adoringly at each other and kissing in public. Mom looks great for her age, but she *is* in her forties, and Hal's at least fifty, and they've both been married before and have grown-up kids.

"The lovebirds?" Rose guessed when she saw my expression.

Rose and her husband, Stephen, and my other big sister, Laurel, were sitting on the couch with their coffee, watching the morning news. The room was still littered with scraps of wrapping paper and satin ribbon.

"Aren't they a little old for that?" I asked. "I mean, it's not like they just met. Mom's known Hal forever. They never *used to* act this way."

"Getting married is romantic," Stephen said, slipping an arm around Rose's waist and pulling her close.

"Not you guys, too," I groaned as they smooched. "You've been married for a whole year and a half. Can't you show a little self-control?"

"I think Mom and Hal are cute," Laurel remarked as she pushed her unruly brown hair behind her ears. She clicked the remote control, switching to the public television channel and some boring nature show. Typical.

"Yeah, well, you don't have to live with them," I pointed out a little wistfully. I was the only sister still at home. Laurel's a freshman at the University of Maine—she's prevet. Rose is a singer and actress; she and Stephen settled in Boston after graduating from college. I'd had a third sister, Daisy—she was in between Rose and Laurel—but she was killed in a car crash when she was nineteen. "It's no fun at the dinner table lately, believe me. When they're not drooling over each other, they're talking about Mom's new store. I might as well be invisible."

Actually, this wasn't really true. Hal is a great guy and pays me a lot of attention. It was nice—having a father again, I mean.

"The store's a big deal, though," Rose said. She was now leaning against Stephen's propped-up knees so he could comb her long blond hair with his fingers. "Mom and Hal are investing a lot in it, and there's a ton of work to do beforehand."

My mom is a caterer. She started doing that to make a living after my father died eight years ago—his fishing boat was lost at sea in a sudden storm. At first it was tough for her to make ends meet, but now she's really successful—so successful, in fact, that she's going to open a gourmet food shop in town this summer. Hal's an accountant, and he's going to help manage the finances.

"I know it's a big deal," I said, nudging Laurel aside so I could sit, too. The show was about coral reefs, and there was a pretty hunky guy scuba diving with the tropical fish. "It's just a constant topic, you know? There are other important things happening these days."

"Like what?" Rose asked.

"*You* know," I said.

Rose wrinkled her forehead and turned to Stephen. "What do you think Lily's talking about?"

He shrugged. "Got me."

"I'm stumped," Laurel put in.

"I know. The after-Christmas sales at the mall," Rose guessed.

"You idiots!" I exclaimed. "Tomorrow's my birthday!"

"Your *birthday!*" Rose slapped the heel of her hand against her forehead. I caught her winking at Laurel. "I totally forgot. How old will you be? Fifteen?"

I knew she was pulling my leg, but I still got worked up. "*Sixteen,*" I corrected indignantly.

"And it's tomorrow?" Laurel shook her head. "That doesn't leave much time to shop. Is it okay if I make the Christmas present I gave you, like, a joint present?"

"Absolutely not!" I declared. "Haven't you guys planned a party?"

"Ask Mom," Rose answered. "Stephen and I are planning to stick around for your birthday, but we need to leave late tomorrow afternoon. Remember I told you my agent, Carol, got me the audition with the touring company of a Broadway musical? I need to rehearse. Speaking of which . . ." She got to her feet and stretched her arms over her head. "Shower time."

Laurel stood up as well. "I have to leave tomorrow, too," she told me. "Do you think you could have your party in the morning?"

I scowled. "I'm not giving myself a party—you guys are supposed to do it!" Honestly. Didn't anyone care?

Rose finally took pity on me. "Don't worry, Lil. Mom's putting together a brunch, and we'll all be there with bells on."

"Brunch is perfect," Laurel said, heading for the door. "I'll call Carlos and tell him I'll be back in the afternoon."

"Your boyfriend's more important than my birthday?" I shouted after her, but she didn't answer. Which is just as well because obviously she would've said, "Yes." Duh, I thought. Carlos is a senior at U. Maine, and he's gorgeous. He and Laurel met years ago working at the local wild animal shelter, but they just started dating, and I couldn't exactly blame Laurel for wanting to hurry back to campus!

I trailed into the kitchen. Hal had disappeared, but Mom was still there. "Does brunch sound okay?" she asked, glancing up from her paperwork. "With just the family?"

"I *was* kind of hoping for a real party," I admitted. "Twenty or thirty people, semiformal attire, champagne punch . . ."

I wasn't kidding, but Mom laughed, anyway. "Oh, Lily," she said. "Your sisters' sixteenth-birthday celebrations were pretty low-key. That's our tradition."

"Well, I *guess* it's okay if it's just us," I said with a disappointed sniff. "Will there be a cake at least . . . with butter cream frosting?"

"Butter cream frosting," Mom assured me.

"Three layers?"

"Three layers."

I was satisfied. "All right. No joint presents, though," I told her.

Mom laughed again. "Heaven forbid!"

I ate breakfast and then went up to my room, which Laurel shares with me if Rose and Stephen are visiting. I changed into a high-waisted rayon dress and pinned my long, wavy blond hair up with the antique silver-and-garnet comb Rose and Stephen gave me for Christmas. I've always liked dressing up in funky, unusual clothes—lately I've been feeling kind of turn-of-the-century.

I went over to the window and looked out in time to see Laurel walking her dog, Snickers. People were going in and out of our building—we live on Main Street above Wissinger's Bakery, one of the busiest stores in our little southern Maine town, even in the winter, when it's just us locals. When I was really young, my family had a big beautiful old house on Lighthouse Road. It had been in the family for generations, but after Dad died, we had to sell it and move into town.

Our apartment is nice, though, with three bedrooms on two floors. It feels like home to me now. Hal used to rent the apartment next door, but he moved in with us when he and Mom got married.

I stayed at the window, my eyes taking in the view. The Hawk Harbor marina was empty of all but fishing boats—the summer people's yachts were in dry dock—and beyond the marina the ocean was steel gray and choppy. I could see to the end of Rocky Point, where the country club is, and down the pine-covered coast a ways. In summer Hawk Harbor gets really crowded and busy. A lot of tourists vacation here, and fancy restaurants and boutiques have popped up all over the place—Mom's future store is a good example. Off-season, though, more than half the stores close and Hawk Harbor reverts back to being a small town. I like it that way. I love living in an old-fashioned place that's full of history and tradition.

I went over to my bookshelves, thinking I'd start reading one of the novels I'd gotten for Christmas. On the way I looked at two framed photographs on my desk.

I don't know anybody my age who's lost so many close relatives. One picture was of my father, Jim Walker, who died when I was eight, and another was of my older sister Daisy, who died when I was thirteen. If she were still alive, Daisy'd be a junior at Dartmouth. She died right after Laurel's sixteenth birthday, and that autumn and winter were possibly the worst time of my life. Of all our lives.

Daisy was so special, I remembered, lifting the picture to study it more closely. In the photo she was holding a softball bat—her arms tanned and strong. Her blond hair was summer bleached, and her eyes sparkled with good humor. And Dad, I thought. I bit my lip. I hated to admit it, even to myself, but if it weren't for that picture on my desk, I might have forgotten what Dad looked like. It made me sad, but I couldn't help it. He'd been gone for half my life.

I was still holding the picture of Daisy, and now I studied it again. I have a whole album of photos of her, which I look through all the time, but for some reason this one means the most to me. It's just so *Daisy*. I don't like thinking about how her story ended—the rainy night, the car sliding off the slick road—so instead I cherish this single moment, Daisy and her softball bat, her beauty and strength preserved forever. She was so together—smart, athletic, popular, caring, independent, *genuine*. She'd been the backbone of our family after Dad was gone. She took care of me. She could fix anything. Anything at all.

In a weird way I felt closer to Daisy than ever now that Rose and Laurel didn't live at home anymore and I was the only sister left. "I still miss you all the time," I whispered.

I kissed Daisy's picture, then carefully placed it back on the desk. I tried really hard not to think about the fact that my favorite sister hadn't lived to see me turn sixteen.

MOM'S THE BEST caterer in the state of Maine. Brunch the next morning was delicious and elegant: eggs Benedict, a basket of fresh-baked muffins, fruit salad, a cake on a pedestal, candles, good china.

At the end of the meal Rose said, "I bet Lily's ready for her presents. That's always *my* favorite part, anyway."

I blinked innocently. "There are presents for *moi?*"

"Yes, let's do presents before we cut the cake," Mom said.

Hal carried a pile of gift-wrapped boxes over to the table. There was a book from Laurel, a scarf from Rose and Stephen, and a DVD from Hal. "Um, not to seem greedy," I said to Mom, "but I was expecting something . . . else."

"Of course," she answered, smiling as she handed me a small velvet box. "I knew you were waiting for this."

I opened the box eagerly. On their sixteenth birthdays all my sisters had gotten gold charms from our great-grandmother's bracelet. What would mine be? I wondered.

"Oh, it's beautiful," I exclaimed when I saw the little gold book on a slender chain.

"You can open it up," Mom explained. "It's a locket."

I opened the locket. "I'll have to find a tiny, tiny picture to put in here. Thanks, Mom."

"Cake time!" Laurel said, hopping out of her chair. "I'll light the candles."

Everybody sang "Happy Birthday" and I blew out the candles. My wish, of course, was that someday I'd get to go to Paris. I felt as if I had everything else I could want.

As soon as brunch was over, Laurel, Rose, and Stephen had to rush around, packing stuff and tossing it into their cars. Mom handed them care packages of food, and then there was a flurry of hugs and kisses and they were gone.

Back to their real lives, I thought as I stood at the living

room window, watching Rose and Stephen buzz off in the old
Saab Stephen's been driving since high school.

I grew up in a big, lively family. Sometimes Rose, Laurel,
and I get on each other's nerves, and sometimes I complain
about being the youngest, but I like having my sisters around.
Now my sixteenth birthday was over almost before it had
begun.

I was an only child again.

O N NEW YEAR'S Eve day Noelle Armitage came over to
listen to music and read beauty magazines with me.
Noelle and I were neighbors when my family lived on Lighthouse Road, and we've been friends off and on forever. I'll
admit that in sixth grade, I thought she wasn't cool and I
started hanging out with some other girls. But in junior high
we got close again. We both read a lot and love fashion. Noelle
has excellent taste in clothes.

"What's with this?" Noelle asked, tossing a magazine my
way. We were sitting on the floor of my room, our backs against
the bed, a bag of pretzel sticks open between us. "Lavender lip
gloss?"

"Easter egg colors are in. Look. *These* models have *yellow* lips."

"Maybe I should rethink my makeup for tonight. I was just
going to wear *red* lipstick."

"Red's always acceptable," I assured her. "It's classic. And
on New Year's Eve you want to look classic."

Stretching her arms over her head, Noelle let out a happy
sigh. "Seth Modine."

I nodded. That was all there was to say. "Seth Modine," I agreed, somewhat grumpily.

Noelle had been invited to Seth Modine's New Year's Eve party and I hadn't. She didn't rub it in, and it wasn't like I was *devastated,* but it did bug me a little. Seth's part of the It crowd at South Regional High, and the fact that I wasn't on his guest list meant I wasn't. Not that I care about that sort of thing. Well, maybe I do—a little.

"Why did he invite you, anyway?" I asked Noelle. "I didn't even know you guys were friends."

"I think his bud, that Timothy guy, likes me. We're all in the same history class."

"Timothy Pratt? He's cute."

"He's okay." Noelle's pretty cute herself, with wide blue eyes and dead-straight, chin-length, pale blond hair.

Jumping up, she went over to my closet. "So, what can I borrow?"

I helped Noelle pick out a short, sexy black dress that I got as a hand-me-down from Rose. "What are *you* going to do tonight?" she asked.

"I don't know." I watched Noelle try on my shoes. I wasn't dating anyone special. "Mickey's going to a party at Daniel Levin's and she said I could go with her, but I can't get too excited about it."

Mickey is McKenna Clinton, another close girlfriend of mine. She's fun, but some of her other friends, like Daniel, are kind of quiet. "A party at Daniel's." Noelle laughed. "Isn't that an oxymoron or something?"

"Can you imagine Daniel busting a move on the dance floor?" I agreed.

Noelle shook her head and stuck out her right foot, modeling a black-beaded high heel. "Can I borrow these, too?"

"Sure," I said. "Someone might as well look hot tonight since I'll probably be sitting home, watching TV."

And that's what I ended up doing. Mom and Hal invited me to go with them to the annual New Year's Eve party at the Harrisons', but I couldn't picture myself there dateless. It was okay when I was a kid, but not now that I'm sixteen. I dressed up, anyway—I put on my Emily Dickinson gown and some fake pearl earrings, made microwave popcorn, and watched old Katharine Hepburn–Spencer Tracy movies on the family room TV.

Usually I'm as happy on my own as I am when I'm surrounded by people, but tonight, as the hands of the clock moved toward midnight and I had no one to kiss and wish Happy New Year, I felt kind of sad. The apartment, which had seemed so cramped when my family first moved in years ago, felt big and empty. The only people home, I thought, are me, myself, and I.

I didn't want to be lonely, not on New Year's Eve, so I turned on the secondhand laptop computer Hal gave me for my birthday last year and opened up a file called Journal.

"Me again," I typed. *"It's 11:55 on December 31st and I'm not at Seth Modine's party wearing high heels and lavender lip gloss. 'Why, Lily Rebecca Walker,' you declare in astonishment. 'How could he have overlooked you when he made up his guest list?' Good question. I guess he just hasn't noticed me yet."*

I stopped typing. My gaze wandered from the computer screen to the dark window. If Seth hasn't noticed me, I thought, then that makes him the only one. I'd always made it a point to be hard to miss. Whenever I change my style or my attitude or my friends, Mom says I'm going through a "phase." Once Rose called me a chameleon, but Laurel pointed out that I was the opposite—I don't change color to blend in with my environment, but to stand out from it. What a perfect Laurel comment—she always has to turn everything into an opportunity for nature education.

Now I tilted my head thoughtfully to one side. Maybe there are different ways of getting noticed, I mused. So, what do I have to do to get noticed the right way?

I went back to my journal. *"My big sisters make it seem easy,"* I wrote. *"Rose knows exactly who she is and what she wants to do in life, and so does Laurel, and so did Daisy. I wonder if now that I'm sixteen, I'll figure out who I am, too."*

Just then the clock on the mantel struck twelve. "Happy New Year," I whispered to myself.

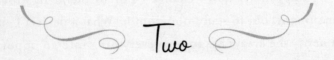

Two

S ECOND SEMESTER OF junior year brought new classes and new teachers. Noelle and I were in first-period oceanography together, and before the bell rang, we slumped down in our back-row seats and whispered about Timothy Pratt. "He called the day after Seth's party and asked me out," Noelle confided.

"No kidding!"

"We're going to a movie this weekend."

"Wow!"

"I don't know, though." Noelle doodled with her mechanical pencil on the first page of a new narrow-ruled spiral notebook. We both love mechanical pencils and narrow-ruled paper. "I thought I had a crush on him, but now I'm not so sure. He gave me this quick kiss at midnight at the party and his lips felt kind of slimy."

I laughed. "He was drooling. Maybe you should be flattered."

Just then Mr. Hashimoto came in. Sitting down at his desk at the front of the room, he started taking attendance. He raced through the list pretty fast, but when he got to my name, which is always one of the last ones, he looked up to study me over the rims of his gigantic rectangular-framed glasses. How come teachers always sport the most unfashionable eyewear? I wondered.

"Walker? Laurel's sister?" he asked.

"Yes," I replied.

"I had her in class last year. She was an outstanding student," he commented.

I just nodded. What was I supposed to say?

Noelle rolled her eyes. "Doesn't that drive you crazy?" she whispered.

"I'm used to it," I whispered back.

It was true. When you're the youngest of four kids who've all gone to the same schools, you hear that kind of thing all the time. For some reason, though, today it was worse than usual. First there was Mr. Hashimoto. Then in fourth-period English, Ms. Gates, who's been the drama adviser at South Regional for about a hundred years, went on and on about Rose. On my way into gym class I had to look at the pictures of Daisy with her sports teams and see the plaque dedicated to her. After class my gym teacher, Larry Wheeler, pulled me aside to reminisce about how great it had been coaching Daisy in softball and soccer, how she was the best athlete he'd ever seen at South Regional, and how he still missed her.

We spent a few minutes being sad together. "Everybody still misses her," I told him, a little choked up.

"She was extraordinary," Coach Wheeler replied, giving me a comforting pat on the back.

As I walked down the hall to my locker to grab a book for my last class, I had a weird sensation. I felt like a ghost.

I'm not Rose or Daisy or Laurel, I wanted to shout, so stop comparing me to them! But that was the problem. I'd tried on a lot of identities over the years but still hadn't found one that fit. I knew who I *wasn't*—my sisters—but I didn't know who I *was.*

I studied the other kids walking by me in the hall. Jock, I thought, mentally labeling each of them. Nerd. Bohemian. Cheerleader. Marching band. Everyone seemed to have a niche . . . everyone but me.

Mickey was waiting for me at my locker. "It's time to make my mark," I announced.

"What are you talking about?" she asked, flipping her long, frizzy brown braid over one shoulder.

We walked to class together, matching strides, while I tried to explain about feeling invisible, about not fitting in, about just being viewed as Rose and Laurel and Daisy's kid sister. "I'm always on the fringe of things. I feel like a lot of kids at school avoid me because they don't know what crowd I belong to. I'm too eclectic or something."

"That's what makes you unique," Mickey pointed out. "You have so many interests."

"I need *one* interest," I decided. "I have to start thinking about college, you know? My sisters all got scholarships. What makes *me* stand out? What am *I* good at?"

Opening the door to the stairwell, Mickey said, "You're losing it, Lily. I really don't think you need to worry about this stuff." Mickey frowned a little. "Besides, it's not like you don't have friends. You have me and Noelle. Why do you need to be part of a crowd?"

I found myself picturing Daisy. She was my definition of success, and *she'd* had a crowd. "Maybe because it would help me figure out who I am," I explained. "And it's time. You know what my life's been like the last eight years, Mickey. We're in good shape now. Secure. *Normal.* My family makes sense again." I paused before adding, quietly, "Now I just need to make sense of myself."

THE NEXT WEEK Mickey and Noelle came up to me in the hall after school one day. "Have I got something to show you," Mickey said as she grabbed my arm and hauled me down the corridor. Noelle strode after us. "Take a look at this," Mickey said.

She stood me in front of a poster on the wall outside the computer lab. I read it out loud. "'New creative-writing workshop . . . two days a week, one-half English credit for juniors and seniors . . . register with Mrs. Cobb by January fifteenth.'"

I looked at Mickey. "Why are you showing me this?"

"Are you kidding? It's perfect for you!" Mickey jabbed Noelle with her elbow. "Isn't it perfect for her?"

Noelle nodded, her white blond bangs bouncing. "Totally."

"I don't think so because—," I began.

"*This* is your identity. You have that stash of stories in your closet," Mickey interrupted. "You're *always* writing something."

"Yeah, but—"

"Let's go to Mrs. Cobb's office right now and sign you up," Noelle decided.

They tried to drag me off again, but I dug in my heels. "I don't think I want to sign up," I said.

"Doesn't it sound like fun?" Mickey asked. "I'm going to sign up."

"Yeah, but the thing with my writing is, I never show it to anyone," I reminded her. "Not even you guys. No way am I going to let a class full of total strangers read my stuff."

"It might not be total strangers," Noelle remarked. "Now that I think about it, I remember Timothy saying something about it. Something about *Seth* wanting to do it. I think we should all sign up. It would be cool to take a class like that together."

I went on shaking my head stubbornly. Seth or no Seth, I couldn't see it happening. Let other people read my stories? No way. "Come on, let's go. I feel like a burger at Cap'n Jack's."

We headed out to the parking lot and the baby blue VW Bug Noelle borrows from her brother sometimes. She likes to be seen in it because it matches her eyes *and* her retro Twiggy look. As we drove off to Cap'n Jack's, Mickey and Noelle started chatting about the movie we'd all seen last weekend in Kent. I didn't join in because I was still thinking about the creative-writing workshop. It does sound interesting, I thought as I looked out the car window at a brown, stubbly field bordered by skeleton-branched trees. But I wasn't exaggerating when I said that I never show my stories to anyone.

Writing was a private thing for me. What would it be like to share it with the whole world?

W HEN NOELLE DROPPED me off at home later, I found Mom in the kitchen, pureeing something pink in the food processor. "What are you making?" I asked, pouring myself a glass of seltzer.

"Roasted bell pepper and lobster bisque," she answered, "for the wedding lunch I'm catering this weekend. Would you toss me the pepper grinder, honey?"

I gave her the pepper grinder. "So, Mom," I said, pulling a stool up to the counter so I could nibble leftover cooked lobster. "I'm in this dilemma."

"What about?"

"Well, I'm a little bit good at a lot of things but not great at any one thing like Rose and Laurel are and like Daisy was," I concluded. "Daisy especially. How am I ever going to get a scholarship for college?"

"I know Hal and I have been talking a lot about finances lately," Mom said as she ladled hot broth into a big kettle, "about how we're putting all our eggs in one basket with the store. But I don't want you to think we can't afford to pitch

The Year I Turned Sixteen

in for your college tuition. You'll get financial aid, and we'll help you all we can."

"It's not just that," I said. "I need to *focus.*"

"You have plenty of time to decide what you want to be when you grow up."

"But Daisy knew she wanted to be a doctor and—"

"Oops!" Mom jumped back as some broth splashed onto the range top. "Lily, would you throw me a dishcloth?"

I helped her clean up the spill. "I want to find my identity," I went on, even though Mom was too distracted to pay much attention. "There's this new creative-writing class at school, but . . . I just don't know."

"Well, you love clothes." She gave the broth a stir and stepped over to open the refrigerator. "How about fashion design?"

"I can't draw," I reminded her.

"I wouldn't worry about it if I were you," Mom concluded. "Something will strike you sooner or later. You're only sixteen."

Only sixteen, I thought as I clumped upstairs to my bedroom. Mom makes it sound like I'm still in kindergarten!

Later I took my laptop to bed and wrote in my journal for a few minutes before turning out the light. *"No one understands me these days. Mom thinks I should be perfectly content being the baby of the family forever. But I'm ready to grow up."*

I stopped typing. Lifting my eyes from the keyboard, I met those of the blond girl in the photo on my desk. "What do *you* think, Daze?" I asked her. "I want to be famous but . . . at what?"

I remembered what Coach Wheeler had said the other day about Daisy. He'd called her "extraordinary." I shook my head, discouraged. Among the three of them my older sisters had done it all—there was nothing left for me.

I'm the baby of the family, I thought glumly, and I'll always just be ordinary.

Three

BY LUNCHTIME ON Monday I had made my decision. I let Mickey and Noelle drag me to Mrs. Cobb's office to see if there were still openings in the new writing class. It hadn't started yet because it was just for partial credit, meeting twice a week, on Tuesdays and Thursdays during lunch period. "She wants to sign up for the creative-writing class," Noelle announced.

Mrs. Cobb looked at me, one salt-and-pepper eyebrow lifted. "Can she speak for herself?" she asked.

Noelle nodded. "Sure."

When I didn't speak, however, Mickey jabbed me with her elbow. "Um . . . ," I began.

"We're *all* taking the class," Noelle went on. "If there's still room for us."

"I can just squeeze you in," Mrs. Cobb replied. "Let me get your names."

Noelle and Mickey wrote their names on Mrs. Cobb's list. Then the pen was in my hand—the moment of truth.

I froze, my fingers clutching the pen. I stared at the sheet in a panic. I couldn't take this class. I couldn't let people read my stories. It would be like letting them see me naked!

Then I focused on a name at the top of the list. He had intense, dramatic handwriting. Seth Modine, I thought. It sounds like poetry.

Taking a deep breath, I scrawled my full name at the bottom of the sheet: Lily Rebecca Walker. I had practiced my signature a lot, and it looked pretty distinguished. Almost as stylish as Seth's.

"Just in time," Mrs. Cobb said, giving me a smile. "The first class is tomorrow. See you there."

I SIGNED UP for a new writing class they're offering at South Regional," I said. I'd gone to the cemetery after school. I do that every now and then: visit my dad's and sister's graves. And okay, call me crazy, but I talk to them.

Now I buttoned my coat up to the neck. It was a gray, bitterly cold afternoon. "I'm nervous about it, Daze. All the stories I've written up until now are so juvenile. What if people laugh at me?"

I was silent for a minute, listening as the wind rustled the last dry, papery-brown leaves on the branches of the beech tree next to the fence. A crow circled overhead, cawing mournfully. "You never had doubts like this, did you?" I asked finally. "I remember the way you used to look on the soccer field. Pure determination. I need to be more like that." I sighed. "Well, thanks for listening." I gave the two headstones a good-bye wave. "Love you, Daze. Love you, Daddy."

As I walked toward the gate snowflakes started to fall. "I'll let you know how it goes," I promised over my shoulder.

I WAS NERVOUS about the writing workshop, but that didn't prevent me from dressing for the occasion: a narrow, knee-length skirt and a belted jacket, with my hair pinned up. Very 1930s and literary, I thought—Dorothy Parker. "I still can't believe you guys talked me into this," I hissed to Noelle and Mickey as we took seats in the next-to-last row of the classroom on Tuesday.

"You're going to love it," Mickey whispered back.

At that moment Seth and Timothy came in with a girl named Loryn Baker. I guess this is the right place to describe Seth Modine—not that mere words can do him justice. He's tall and lean, with one of those long, graceful bodies that clothes hang on really well. His hair is golden brown and longish, and he wears it swept back from his forehead in a very striking way. Behind his oval-rimmed glasses his eyes are dark gray, and he has a little cleft in his chin. He always wears trousers—never jeans. Today he was wearing a black mock turtleneck. He's way too cool for small-town Maine.

Timothy, Seth, and Loryn sat down right in front of us. "Hey," Timothy said to Noelle. She smiled at him. Seth met my eye briefly before dropping into his chair. My heart did a back flip.

"Yeah, maybe, I will" I was about to whisper back to Mickey, but I kept the thought to myself. She'd leaned away from me to say something to Daniel Levin, who's also a tall, lean type but with reddish hair and blue eyes.

"Writers," Mrs. Cobb began, addressing us. "All of you are writers or want to become writers. The secret of writing is that anyone can do it. Talent is a mystery, but craft isn't. You learn by doing."

Mrs. Cobb talked for a while about what our assignments would be: recording conversations, brainstorming off different one-word topics, writing first-person essays and fiction. Sometimes we'd work in pairs so we could critique each other's stories.

"Today we're going to start with a loosening-up exercise," she went on. "We'll do these every class, and you'll do them on your own, too. The goal is to get you churning out a dozen pages a day. You won't love all of it—in fact, most of it will end up in the trash. But the more bad stuff you write, the more good stuff you'll write—the deeper you'll be digging into the well of material that everyone has inside. So, pick up your pens and turn to a blank piece of paper. Write a page about your bedroom. Describe things. Be concrete. I want to know what's in there, what it says about you."

I turned to Noelle. She wiggled her eyebrows. "What about *who's* in there?" she whispered.

I stifled a giggle.

"Let's not waste time chatting," Mrs. Cobb suggested, eyeing our part of the room.

Seth bent his head and started writing. I gripped my mechanical pencil, my own fingers itching. What had Mickey said? "You're going to love it. . . ."

I am, I realized. The assignments sounded fun, and it wouldn't kill me to spend fifty minutes twice a week staring at the back of Seth's head. And I could write a *book* about my bedroom.

I started scribbling. *"My room smells like faded roses and old books. It's jammed with stuff because I never throw anything away—broken dolls and tired stuffed animals perch on my windowsill, comfortable in the knowledge that I could never part with them."*

I filled a page and flipped to the next. I couldn't believe I'd had doubts about taking this class. I can do this, I thought, exhilarated. I'm a writer. *That's* who I am!

AFTER DINNER I spent half an hour upstairs in my room on the phone with Noelle and Mickey, talking about the writing assignment. Then I sat at my desk with a new mechanical pencil and a narrow-ruled legal pad, waiting for inspiration. Mrs. Cobb wanted us to write about the ocean: either fiction or nonfiction, five pages. She figured that wouldn't be hard because we live right on the Atlantic—it's our world. Mickey had said she was going to write about clamming in Kettle Cove, and Noelle was going to write about this lifeguard she had a crush on one summer, but I didn't want to write about things that had actually happened to me. How boring.

Which isn't to say there aren't some dramatic episodes in

my family history, I reflected. Dad's boat lost at sea, Daisy's car crash . . .

I shivered. I couldn't write about *that* stuff. It cut way too close to the bone. Maybe someone else's heartbreak, though . . .

I clicked my pencil twice so just the right amount of lead stuck out and started to write.

M Y SHORT STORY, "Doomed," was ten pages long instead of five.

"Jeez," Noelle said, sneaking a peek before I handed it in to Mrs. Cobb. "What'd you do, write the Great American Novel?"

"It's pretty good," I had to admit.

"What's it about?" Mickey asked.

"It's a gothic romance set in nineteenth-century England," I told them. "This guy and this girl fall in love when he saves her from a shipwreck off the coast of Cornwall in which the rest of her family is drowned. But they keep getting separated by fate, and in the end, just as they're about to be reunited, she's run over by a train."

"Wow," Noelle said again. "You have an amazing imagination, Lily."

"Well, I borrowed the train part from *Anna Karenina*. I just hope Mrs. Cobb likes it," I said. "I think it's the most gripping story I've ever written."

The class spent the hour talking about "voice," and I spent the hour wondering what Seth Modine would look like with his black collarless shirt unbuttoned to the waist. I was also rehearsing what I'd say to Mrs. Cobb when she returned my assignment and said it was the best story in the class and she thought I should submit it to *The New Yorker*.

When Mrs. Cobb handed my story back next class, though, she didn't say anything about *The New Yorker*. She hadn't graded the assignment, and as I read her comments, I realized that was a lucky break. *"Unconvincing emotions . . . stilted dialogue . . . contrived situations,"* I read silently. *"Next time write in your own voice, Lily, and see what happens."*

I frowned. Write in my own voice . . . what does *that* mean? Isn't pretending to be someone else what fiction is all about?

I planned to ask Mrs. Cobb about this at the end of class. At that moment she was looking for volunteers to read their assignments out loud. When no hands went up, she said, "Everyone will read eventually. Come on. Who's feeling brave today? I'd rather not have to call on you."

Mickey, Noelle, and I slumped down in our seats. Luckily Daniel saved us from a fate worse than death. "I'll read," he said.

"Excellent." Mrs. Cobb beamed at him. "Come on up and stand at the podium."

Daniel had written a nonfiction piece about going fishing with his grandfather. It was funny—the part about his grandfather bailing water out of the leaky old rowboat—and sad, too, because at the end it turned out his grandfather had just died and now Daniel had to go fishing by himself. "That was good," I whispered to Mickey. "Wasn't that good?"

Mickey nodded. "He had a lot of guts to go first."

I glanced at Daniel. He has that really fair complexion that auburn-haired people always have and he'd turned kind of magenta while he was reading, but now that he was back in his chair, he looked relieved. Our eyes met—his are dark blue—and I smiled. He smiled back.

I'll tell him I liked his story, I decided, but at that instant Daniel and his grandfather and the rowboat went right out of my brain. Mrs. Cobb had asked for another volunteer, and Seth had raised his hand.

Seth's story was about a spiritually tortured jazz musician living on the Left Bank in Paris. "I thought we were supposed to write about the ocean," Mickey hissed into my ear.

"Well, the Left Bank's on the Seine," I hissed back. "That's a body of water, anyway."

Seth's protagonist spent most of his time at cafes in soul-searching conversation with his equally tortured musician friends. I had no idea what Seth was getting at, but I loved the way he made intense eye contact with his audience, including me once or twice. Also, he had sprinkled real French throughout the dialogue. Basically I couldn't concentrate on much besides trying not to drool.

Seth finished reading. Mrs. Cobb said something polite, and he walked back to his seat.

At the end of class Mrs. Cobb randomly paired us up with writing partners. The idea was to get together with our partners between classes to share ideas, do writing exercises, and critique each other's stories. I held my breath as Mrs. Cobb read through her list. When she called out, "Lily Walker and Daniel

Levin," I couldn't help letting out a sigh of disappointment.
The very next pair was McKenna Clinton and Seth Modine.
Mickey, who wouldn't even appreciate Seth at all!

"No way!" I hissed to Noelle.

"Life's so unfair!" she hissed back. Noelle hadn't even
gotten a guy partner—she was paired with Beth Jacobs, a very
serious, jockish girl.

The bell rang and I went up to Mrs. Cobb's desk. "I have a
question," I said, waving "Doomed" at her. "You said to write
in my own voice, but I'm not sure what you mean by that."

"Remember what we were talking about in class a few days
ago?" she asked.

I didn't remember. I'd been too busy imagining what I
would say to Seth if I ever got to speak to him. "Umm . . ."

"When you write in your own voice, you use language that
comes naturally to you. You write about things you've experienced firsthand or situations you can fully imagine yourself in."

"You mean like Seth writing about jazz?" I asked.

At that moment Seth and Timothy walked by on their way
to the door. Seth heard me talking about him and gave me a
knowing half smile. I blushed furiously.

"Not exactly," Mrs. Cobb told me. "I don't mean that you
should restrict yourself to everyday subjects. Fantasy is okay.
Listen to yourself talk sometime, Lily. The rhythm, the dic-
tion. I liked the description of your bedroom. Try for some of
that idiosyncratic flavor in your next story."

I thanked her for these pearls of wisdom even though I had

no idea what she meant. Noelle and Mickey were waiting for me at the door. So was Daniel.

"Howdy, pardner," he cracked.

"Howdy, yourself," I said.

"Want to make a date?" He blushed when he realized what he'd said. "I mean, to get together and write?"

"Sure," I agreed. "I need all the help I can get!"

Daniel and I picked a time and place and he took off.

"Didn't Mrs. Cobb like the story you wrote?" Noelle asked me.

"She trashed it," I replied.

The three of us headed to our next class. "Wasn't Daniel's story good?" Mickey asked.

"How about Seth's?" Noelle countered.

"I thought Daniel's was better," Mickey said. "What did you think, Lily?"

I couldn't compare the stories because I didn't remember now if Seth's had been any good. "I liked Seth's use of *visual* imagery," I said meaningfully.

My friends laughed.

At my locker I glanced again at Mrs. Cobb's comments on my shipwrecked-lovers story. Then I tossed the pages in with all the other junk on the locker floor.

Maybe being a great writer wasn't going to be as easy as I'd thought.

Four

THAT WEEKEND LAUREL came home from college for a visit. On Saturday she and Mom and I bundled up and went for a walk with Snickers along Lighthouse Road.

"I'm feeling down," Laurel announced when we got to the place where the road curves and there's a great view of the ocean.

Mom stopped to take off her gloves and hat. The sun was out, and it was turning into a mild winter afternoon. "What's wrong, honey?" she asked Laurel.

Laurel bent to pick up a stick. "I can't get over how bad my grades were last fall." She tossed the stick and Snickers bounded after it, barking. "My classes this semester are even harder. I'll probably flunk out."

"Your grades were *not* bad," Mom said firmly. "You're just not used to getting B's."

"And C's," Laurel said.

"It was *one* C-plus," Mom reminded her, "and in economics, which isn't even your major."

"But veterinary schools will look at *all* my grades," Laurel said glumly. "I'll never get in anywhere."

Mom hugged Laurel around the shoulders, laughing. "You're only a freshman—you have three more years to get that grade point up. College is harder than high school, that's all. You'll get the hang of it."

We kept walking. Maine is beautiful in the winter—in some ways I almost like it better than in the summer. With the trees bare you can see things more clearly, like the tumbling-down stone walls that zigzag through the woods, marking the boundaries of long-ago farms. Without green to compete with it, the sky and the water seem to have more color.

"Maybe you two can help me with something," Mom said. "The store needs a name. Any ideas?"

I thought about it. "Spice of Life," I suggested.

"Not bad," Mom said.

"The Sizzling Skillet," Laurel offered.

"The Plentiful Pantry," I said.

Mom laughed. "Don't get *too* carried away. I like the idea of a one-word name. Something simple but catchy."

Laurel lifted her shoulders. "I can't think of anything."

"It should be inviting, right?" I asked. "Something that makes people feel like they're sitting down to dinner with friends. How about . . . Potluck?"

"Potluck." Mom smiled. "I like that, Lily." She said it again. "Potluck. Yes, that could be it."

I got an unexpected thrill out of solving Mom's problem. "Anything else you need help with?" I asked.

"Actually, there is." She looked at Laurel rather than me, though. "I wanted to ask you about working for me this summer, Laurel. I know the Wildlife Rescue Center will have a job for you, but I'd like to make you assistant manager at the shop. I have a feeling that I'll really need the help."

"Really?" Laurel beamed. "I'd love to work at Potluck."

"What about me?" I broke in. "I'm sixteen. I could work for you, too, Mom. How about co-assistant manager?"

She was putting her hat back on; we were getting a sea breeze now and it was colder. "I'm sure there will be something for you to do, sweetheart," she said vaguely. I tried not to let my disappointment show.

At the driveway to the lighthouse we turned around. "How's school for *you* this term, Lil?" Laurel asked.

I told her about the writing class and Mrs. Cobb's not-so-hot response to my first story. "Your own voice, huh?" Laurel laughed. "That *would* be hard since you've always been the Girl of Many Disguises. I mean, how are you supposed to settle on just one?"

I sighed. "I have no idea. I have a writing partner now, though. This guy from the class—Daniel. I'm counting on him to help me. He's really good."

"Sorry for interrupting, Lil, but look." Mom pointed at something. "I didn't notice when we walked by in the other direction. The old place is for sale."

We peered through a brambly hedge at the three-story Victorian house where I'd lived as a child. It was a bed-and-breakfast now, the Lilac Inn, and a For Sale sign was planted on the lawn. "I can't believe it!" Laurel said.

"Why do you think they're going out of business?" I asked. "There are always tons of people staying there, at least in the summer."

Mom shook her head. "You never know. It might have nothing to do with how much money they're making. Things happen in people's lives that they have no control over." I knew she was thinking about Dad, remembering how tough it had been for us to make ends meet at first without him, and I reached for her hand.

"Who do you suppose will buy it next?" Laurel wondered, clipping Snickers's leash back on her collar. "Another inn-keeper?"

"Maybe *we* could buy it!" I exclaimed.

"Wouldn't that be something?" Mom smiled wistfully. "Even if it's priced reasonably, though, we couldn't afford it right now. Hal and I are putting every penny into the new store."

We walked on toward town. I took a last look at the house over my shoulder, still holding Mom's hand. The wind was rocking the old porch swing—one of the few things the inn-keepers had left unchanged when they fixed up the house. I remember sitting in that swing one summer day with Rose, I thought. We'd been stringing beads to make bracelets. Daisy was bouncing a ball against the barn wall, Mom was gardening,

Dad was mending his fishing nets, and Laurel was climbing an apple tree.

Our house, memories and all, was for sale again.

SHOULD WE GET something to eat, or are you worried about smearing french fry grease on your special narrow-ruled paper?"

"French fries sound great," I said. Daniel and I were settled in a booth at Patsy's, the local diner, our writing stuff spread out in front of us. "But you'd better not make fun of my special paper, or I'll make fun of your pencil case covered with smiley face stickers that must date back to, like, second grade."

Daniel widened his eyes, playing dumb. "Pencil case? What pencil case?"

I smiled and shook my head. Actually, now I had to admit how lucky I was to have Daniel as a writing partner—even though he wasn't Seth, Daniel was nice. Plus I wasn't as distracted with him as I would have been with Seth. We ordered a basket of fries and some sodas. "Okay, so I'm totally clueless about this assignment," I told him. It was Sunday night—we had five pages to write for Tuesday. "Mrs. Cobb is so obtuse. Write about disappointment. What does *that* mean?"

Daniel laughed. He has a nice laugh. "You've never been disappointed?" he asked, raising one sandy-red eyebrow in this very comical look.

I laughed, too. "Yeah, sure. But I mean, do we write about one disappointment or about disappointment in general?"

"I guess you write about whatever it means to you," Daniel replied. "I think that's why Mrs. Cobb gives these open-ended assignments. She leaves room to experiment."

I sighed. "I'd feel better if she spelled it out. I bombed out last time—I don't want to turn in another crummy piece."

"Well, I'm not sure what to write about, either. Maybe we should start with one of those brainstorming exercises." He shoved a couple of fries in his mouth, then reached for his notebook and a pen. "Let's brainstorm on the word *disappointment* for five minutes and see what we come up with."

I grabbed my pencil. "Ready, set, go."

We both paused for a second, thinking, and then started writing as fast as we could. The brainstorming thing really does work. When you brainstorm, you don't really pay attention to the words you're putting on the page—they just pour out. Then you read it afterward and it's kind of a surprise.

"Five minutes are up," Daniel announced after what felt like five seconds. "Do you want to read yours out loud first or shall I?"

"Read it out *loud?*" I repeated.

"Sure. That's what we're supposed to be doing. That's how we can help each other."

I shook my head. "I think I'll just look this over at home later and see if it gives me any ideas."

"Uh-uh," Daniel said firmly. "We're writing partners, Lily. Believe me, I feel dumb about reading mine out loud, too. In class the other day I almost passed out, I was so nervous. But it's really helpful." His voice softened. "You can trust me. I won't say anything harsh."

I looked into Daniel's eyes. He looked totally sincere and kind. "Well . . . okay," I said. "Let me eat some french fries first, though. I want to die on a full stomach."

We finished off the fries. Then Daniel read his page of brainstorming. Then I read mine. And you know what? It wasn't the worst thing in the world. I blushed a little and I couldn't stop fidgeting with a strand of my hair, but I read the whole thing.

"That's the first time in my *life* that anyone's heard something I've written," I told Daniel, "except for the time my big sister Rose found my story notebook when I was about eight and read the whole thing."

"Well, how'd the exercise feel?" Daniel asked.

"A little embarrassing," I confessed. "But not as embarrassing as I expected. I mean, I didn't even realize I'd written that stuff about being the last one in my junior high clique to get my ears pierced."

Daniel and I high-fived each other. "Now we just need to figure out what would be a good story idea. You're going to write about that junior high stuff, right?" he kidded.

I groaned. "A work of genius in the rough," I joked. But honestly, being with Daniel, I somehow felt it might be.

DANIEL AND I spent about fifteen more minutes at the diner. Back at home later I turned on my computer to write in my journal. *"What's shaking?"* I typed. *"Mrs. Cobb hated my first story. Was it really that bad? I thought the train crash scene was particularly vivid and gory, and the period costume details were excellent. Actually, Mrs. Cobb did like the costume stuff—she's into specifics, like the way things smell and feel and taste. But it all comes back to the voice thing. I forgot to ask Daniel's opinion about that. What kind of voice am I supposed to use? Should I scream? Whisper? Whine? Yodel?"*

I spent a few minutes describing my walk with Mom and Laurel and my writing date with Daniel. *"Daniel's a really good writer,"* I typed, *"and he's also a good listener. He doesn't make snap judgments. Which isn't to say that he only said nice things about stuff I wrote tonight, but he was constructive. I think I lucked out getting him as a writing partner. I still haven't decided what to write about for class, though."*

I switched off the computer and sat at my desk with pencil and paper. I'm not sure why, but that's how I do it: I type my journal and handwrite everything else. Now I closed my eyes, trying to visualize a story and a voice telling that story. It needs to be completely different, I thought. Not gothic and romantic like "Doomed." Something totally nontraditional.

I experimented with a sentence or two. "The girl stood at the bus stop in the rain. Her shoulders were hunched, and wet strands of dirty blond hair fell over eyes that were blank with despair. She waited."

I frowned down at the page. "It needs more drama," I said to myself. "What if I . . ."

Tearing off a new sheet of paper, I rewrote it without using capitals or punctuation, "the girl stood at the bus stop in the rain her shoulders were hunched and wet strands of dirty blond hair fell over eyes that were blank with despair she waited."

I smiled. I like that, I decided. Talk about different!

* * *

M Y NEW WRITING style seemed to require a new look, so on Tuesday, I wore a short, shapeless black dress and tights with holes in them and pale makeup with very dark lipstick. I pulled my hair back in a tight ponytail and wore earrings that were so long, they almost hit my shoulders. The finishing touch was a pair of glasses with black rectangular frames and clear lenses that I'd picked up at Second Time Around.

"Wow. Look at you," Noelle said as we met at my locker before writing class. "Why so ghoulish?"

I hesitated for an instant, then thrust my pages at Noelle and Mickey. No point in being shy. I'd already read it over the phone to Daniel, and Mrs. Cobb would see it soon—it was time for my story to fend for itself. "Here. Read this."

Mickey and Noelle stood side by side to read together. "Do you like it?" I asked hopefully when they got to the last page.

Mickey nodded. "It's grim and bleak and depressing. You can really feel the emotions, you know? And the way she doesn't have a name. She's just 'the girl.'"

"It's cool," Noelle agreed. "Like something you'd read in a magazine. Sophisticated."

I beamed. I thought so, too. "I'm glad you guys like it. Daniel wasn't so positive."

"What does he know?" Noelle asked.

"Anyway, it's the exact opposite of my other story stylistically," I explained, "so Mrs. Cobb is bound to like it."

"You should read it aloud in class," Mickey said.

I shook my head.

"Come on," Noelle urged.

"I'm not ready," I said as we headed into the room.

"*I'd* volunteer if my story were that good," Mickey said.

We sat at the opposite end of the third row from Seth and Timothy because Timothy had asked Noelle out again and she'd said no. Apparently even though he was *almost* as good-looking as Seth, Timothy's lips were simply too gooey. Noelle had also decided he was atrociously stuck on himself.

As Mrs. Cobb chatted about today's focus, the character arc, I thought about my friends urging me to read. I kept turning my head to gaze at Seth's gorgeous profile. At one point he looked my way and our eyes met, and he actually gave me a little smile.

I slumped in my chair, clutching my story with sweaty hands. I'd love to impress Seth—especially with my writing. But what if I fell flat on my face? He was so intellectual. My story had *no* references to philosophy or French or foreign films or anything like that, like Seth's had the other day. If he thinks it stinks, I'll die, I thought.

Mrs. Cobb finished writing on the blackboard and turned to face the class. "Who'd like to read first today?"

I was sitting in between Noelle and Mickey—I got an elbow from each side. "Ouch!" I whispered.

"Go for it," Noelle whispered into one ear.

"Everyone has to sometime," Mickey hissed into the other ear.

I cast an anguished glance at Seth, who was drumming his fingers on his desk in a bored fashion. Mickey was right. I had to read sometime. Why not get it over with?

"I—I'll read, Mrs. C-Cobb," I stammered, raising my hand.

"Lily. Wonderful."

I walked up to the podium, painfully conscious that all eyes in the room were on me. My legs buckled slightly. So that's what it means to have your knees knock, I thought, doing my best not to trip.

I stepped behind the podium and then turned around to face the class. "Uh-hmm," I said, clearing my throat. "My story, on the theme of disappointment, is titled 'Runaway to Nowhere.'" I pushed my fake glasses up on the bridge of my nose. "Before I start, I want to say that there's something you won't get by just listening to this, but it's all in lowercase with no punctuation." I caught Daniel's eye, and even though I knew he thought my story was crummy (well, he'd put it much nicer, but that had been the general idea), he gave me an encouraging smile. "So maybe just think about how that might affect the story's mood, you know? Okay." I cleared my throat yet again. "Here goes."

I started reading, keeping my voice flat and somber to match the all-lowercase/no-punctuation thing. I read really slowly to give all the words the proper emphasis. "The girl stood at the bus stop in the rain her shoulders were hunched and wet strands of dirty blond hair fell over eyes that were blank with despair she waited."

I paused, daring to look up at the class. Seth's expression was unreadable; Loryn was studying a chip in her dark blue fingernail polish. At least Daniel, Noelle, and Mickey appeared interested. "when the bus pulled up the girl got on without even looking at the destination she didn't care where it was headed as long as it took her away from her life her painful lonely desperate life."

I kept reading, my manner exaggeratedly serious to go with the material. Then I heard a sound—the worst possible sound you can hear when you're reading one of your stories out loud in class for the first time in your life.

Someone snickered.

Mrs. Cobb murmured, "Sshh."

Swallowing, I went on reading.

Someone else snickered.

"Please listen quietly," Mrs. Cobb requested.

My face turned red with mortification, but I was stuck up there, less than halfway through my story. "she thought it would be different in a new place with new people but she'd brought her problems her fears her disappointment with her," I read. "the loneliness was larger than an ocean and sucked her down like a vortex she struggled against the current but she was helpless helplessly struggling helpless."

Someone laughed out loud. It was Loryn. She slapped a hand over her mouth, but she couldn't stop giggling. I kept reading, but the more serious and sad the stuff in my story was, the more people laughed.

Mrs. Cobb, Mickey, Noelle, and Daniel seemed to be the only ones in the whole room with straight faces. Mickey darted angry glances at the laughers; Noelle bit her lip. I could tell she was feeling awful for me. My eyes prickled and my throat grew tight. It's not supposed to be funny! I wanted to cry out.

I wanted to burst into tears and run out of the room, but I knew that would make me look even more like an idiot. I stood there, frozen, for what felt like a year but was probably only two or three seconds. What am I doing wrong? I wondered. I kept reading mechanically as my mind spun. Why is this different from when Daniel and Seth and other people stood up to read? Why don't I ever hit the right note?

Then suddenly I thought about a story Loryn had read last class. It had been kind of mean—she'd been making fun of a fat girl who went to the same diner every day and ordered the same enormous meal and ate all the food in the same order and folded her napkin in the same exact way every time. People had laughed, but not *at* her, the way they were now, with my story. Maybe I'm taking myself too seriously, I thought. Being sincere is uncool.

All at once I had a brilliant idea. I kept reading my story and the class kept laughing, so I started playing it that way, as if I'd *meant* to be hilarious. "she stood on the banks of the river and thought about throwing herself in how the cold water would close over her head and she could finally forget the other deeper coldness of the people who didn't care." I made my tone ironic and raised one eyebrow slightly. "but she lacked the courage to take that ultimate step she lacked the courage even to get back on the bus and return to the place where all her unhappiness had begun."

I threw in some body language and changed my voice to

sound a bit more like Cruella De Vil. I heard the laughter change, they were laughing *with* me, as they had with Loryn. Seth leaned forward to listen, his elbows on his desk, his lips curved in an appreciative smile. My story had turned into a comedy routine. I was a hit.

When I read the last sentence—"she'd learned nothing gone nowhere become no one"—the class actually clapped. I gave a bow and went back to my seat. "Awesome, Lil!" Noelle whispered, squeezing my arm. "We were worried about you for a minute there, but you really pulled it off."

I darted a glance down the row at Seth. He smiled at me, an interested light in his gray eyes. That was a Look, I thought, my heart cartwheeling around in my chest. Seth Modine just gave me a Look!

After class a bunch of kids surrounded me at the door. "That was *so* funny," Loryn declared. "My sides are still aching."

"You should try out for the talent show," suggested Rico Chivetti, this cute theater guy who's part of the It crowd. "I'm one of the judges. You'd be a shoo-in."

"I'll think about it," I said casually.

Usually I walk to my next class with Mickey, but today I was part of a big, lively, laughing group. Seth and Timothy kind of brought up the rear, but you would definitely have had to say that we were walking together. I'm part of a group with Seth, I thought dizzily.

"See you, Lily," Loryn said when we got to her locker.

Seth's locker was a couple down from Loryn's. "Later, Lily," he said.

"Bye," I replied, breathless with happiness and disbelief.

"Don't forget the talent show," Rico called.

I gave him a wave. The talent show, I thought. He wants me to try out for the talent show! And Seth spoke to me! He said my name!

I'd been teetering on the edge of disaster, but miraculously I'd turned things around. Noelle and Mickey had been right when they'd talked me into taking the writing class.

I'd finally found a way to stand out. And I planned to keep it that way.

Five

IT WASN'T HARD to immerse myself in my new identity. I went to Second Time Around with an armful of Victorian-style dresses and came home with all black clothes. I wore the rectangular glasses all the time and dark eyeliner and lipstick that Noelle and Mickey told me was "scary, but in a good way." And I wrote all my stories for Mrs. Cobb's class in lowercase letters with no punctuation, and they were all about alienated kids, and they all sounded depressing on paper but were hilarious when read aloud in a certain sarcastic tone that I was rapidly perfecting, and I volunteered to read aloud all the time now even though I didn't have to. Because the class *loved* my stories.

One Wednesday, when I didn't have writing class during lunch, I walked alone to the cafeteria. Right outside the door I bumped into Daniel. "Hey," he said.

"Hey," I said back.

"Getting something to eat?"

"The thought had occurred to me," I replied.

He held the door open for me. "That's a lot of black you've got on."

I shrugged. "They're clothes. They cover my essential nakedness."

Daniel laughed. We stepped into the food line, and he gave my shoulder a playful little bump. "You don't have to put on an act with *me*, Lily."

I bumped his shoulder back. "What act?"

"For one thing, the glasses." He pointed to them. "I thought they were just a prop, for your story. But you're still wearing them."

I lifted a hand to touch the glasses self-consciously. "Eyewear is an accessory just like, you know, a belt or earrings."

"Oh. I see," Daniel said.

He was still smiling. I tried to give him a withering glance, but I couldn't. Instead I felt like giggling. The glasses *were* a little over the top. "Who are you eating with?" I asked. "Do you want to have lunch?"

"Actually, I'm grabbing a sandwich to take with me to the computer lab—I have a project to finish," Daniel said. "Rain check, okay?"

"Rain check," I agreed warmly.

Daniel paid for his lunch and took off. There was a very brief interlude where I was standing alone with my tray, feeling dopey about the fact that I had to look for someone to join, and then Loryn swept me off to her table. *Seth's* table.

Not only was I sitting at the see-and-be-seen crowd's usual highly visible table by the window, but I was sitting next to Seth. I wasn't exactly sure how that happened, if it was an accident or on purpose. Anyway, there I was, trying to look casual while inside I felt like a six-year-old who'd managed to get her paws in an impossible-to-reach cookie jar.

"You're going to *die* over this," Loryn said to the group in her typically bored tone. "I've been asked to join the *prom* committee."

"The prom committee," Rico said. "What an honor."

Loryn rolled her dark-lined eyes expressively. "Isn't it? Staci Shipman asked me herself." She launched into an imitation of Staci, the unbelievably perky president of the pep club. "'You'd be *really* good at picking the chaperons, Loryn, because you're *really* smart and all the teachers *really* like you! Just remember it's *really* important to have *really* cool chaperons so we can all *really* have fun at the dance that will, like, *really* be our very best memory of high school!'"

"Does Staci always sound like she just sucked the helium out of a balloon or what?" Timothy wanted to know. "I hope you have a great time working with her on the prom committee."

"I can't wait to join—it's going to be hilarious. I've always wanted an inside look at the pep club. I mean, how do these people *think?*"

"Do they think, period?" Rico wondered.

"Anyway, I have some great ideas for chaperons." Her eyes twinkled darkly. "Mr. Adams."

Everybody hooted. Mr. Adams is the very large, very hairy metal shop teacher. He rides a Harley.

"And Mrs. Balicki," Loryn went on. More laughter—Mrs. Balicki is about eighty.

"Mr. Simonides," I suggested. This went over well, too. Mr. Simonides is the social studies teacher who must smoke three packs of unfiltered Camel cigarettes a day.

"Ms. Carpenter," Timothy put in. "I bet she can really dance."

There were more chuckles, but my own smile faltered. This didn't strike me as funny at all. Ms. Carpenter uses a wheelchair.

Before I could speak up, Seth told Loryn, "Make sure you ask Mrs. Cobb."

"Right, and I'll tell her that in between the band's sets, we all want to pair up for brainstorming exercises. Speaking of Mrs. Cobb, who here has a lame writing partner?" Loryn asked, raising her own hand.

Seth raised his. "You don't like working with Mickey?" I asked, surprised. Mickey's about the nicest, most thoughtful person on the planet.

"I'm sorry, I know she's your bud, but she can't write," Seth said. He leaned back in his chair, his linked hands clasped behind his neck. "And if you can't write, you can't give a legitimate critique. Not that that stops her. But *you're* stuck with Levin." Seth made a *tsk, tsk* sound with his tongue.

I thought about how I could defend my friends in a tactful way that didn't make me sound like a puritan. But I was too busy feeling relieved. Thank goodness Seth didn't see me in the lunch line with Daniel before, I thought.

We spent the rest of lunch period ripping apart Hawk Harbor. I've always liked my hometown, but Seth and his buddies had a much hipper attitude. Hawk Harbor was provincial, boring, tacky, and anti-intellectual. That's why they hung out at a coffee bar in Kent instead of at one of the usual teen spots like Pizza Bowl or the Rusty Nail. "Our goal is to live in Maine without actually *living* in Maine," Seth explained to me. "No lobster fishing for us."

"You're expatriates," I said.

He laughed. "Exactly."

We looked at each other. I was kind of spellbound by how brilliant his eyes looked behind those glasses.

Apparently he was looking at my glasses, too. "Nice specs," he said.

"Oh, these." I prayed he couldn't tell that the lenses were fake. "Thanks."

"So, come with us sometime," Loryn invited me. "To the coffee shop."

I breathed deeply to keep myself from clapping with glee. "Sure," I said.

I CAN'T BELIEVE you sat with those guys at lunch," Mickey said later as we rode the school bus.

I shrugged. "It's no big deal."

"Just don't forget about your old friends, okay?"

"Of course not." I punched her lightly on the arm. "Don't

be silly." I felt momentarily disloyal, remembering how I'd let Seth and Loryn's cracks about Mickey and Daniel slide. "Next time I'm with them, you could sit with us," I offered, even though I kind of hoped she wouldn't. "You don't *have* to hang out with Daniel and the geeks."

Mickey gave me a stern look. "Daniel's not a geek," she said. "He's my friend. Okay?"

"I'm just kidding," I assured her. "I like him. But you should really spend some time with me and Loryn and Rico and Seth." I blushed a little, just saying his name. "They're really fun to be around."

"I'm sure they are," Mickey said. I couldn't read her expression.

The bus stopped on Main Street a block away from my apartment. Mickey was coming over to work on a math problem set with me.

We settled down in the family room with our math textbooks and notebooks spread open. Every time we started to make some progress on the homework assignment, though, the phone would ring. First it was Loryn, "just calling to talk before tackling the intellectual challenge of homework." Then Rico called to remind me about the talent show tryouts the next day. Finally Fiona Sullivan called.

"Hi," I said, surprised. I couldn't imagine why Fiona would be calling *me*. She's possibly the coolest junior girl at South Regional. We're in the same homeroom, but we hardly ever talk to each other. The only connection between us is that about a million years ago, her older brother

Brian dated my big sister Rose. "What's up?" I asked.

"I wanted to tell you I'm having a party Friday night," Fiona said. "You're not busy, are you?"

"No. I mean, I don't think so," I added, so I wouldn't sound *too* available.

"Good. Seth will be there. Bring some friends along if you like. It'll be fun."

"Great. Thanks."

"See you in homeroom."

"Right. Bye, Fiona."

Mickey's dark eyebrows arched up so high, they almost disappeared into her hair. "Fiona?"

I nodded.

"Fiona *Sullivan?*"

"Yep."

Mickey shook her head. "Wow. You *have* arrived."

"She's having a party on Friday, and she said I should bring some friends. Do you want to come with me?"

Mickey shrugged. "I wouldn't know what to do with myself at a party at Fiona's. I mean, I'm not that good at talking to Beautiful People."

"That's ridiculous," I said. "They're not Beautiful, and you talk to them just like you talk to anybody." Even as I said this, though, I knew it wasn't true. Fiona and Seth and their circle *were* Beautiful—capital *B*. And I never *used* to know how to talk to them, I thought. Not until lately. Not until reading my story in creative-writing class changed everything.

Mickey and I got back to work. When we were done with

math, we sat on the couch with our writing notebooks and read each other our stories in progress. "Your stuff is getting wilder and wilder," Mickey commented when I finished reading my latest masterpiece, which was about this girl who goes from guy to guy seeking love and self-affirmation, but it doesn't work, and along the way she gets anorexic. In the end she starts eating again and gives up boys, and there's just the faintest hint that she might figure herself out. "At least that one has sort of a happy ending."

"Don't you think it's funny?" I asked. "You're supposed to be laughing your head off."

"I smiled a little," Mickey said. "What did you think of *my* story?"

I gave Mickey my most constructive criticism in case she read her story to Seth at some point. She's pretty imaginative, but for some reason that doesn't always come out in her writing. After she left and before dinner, with my stomach growling in appropriate fashion, I put a few finishing touches on "Hunger" and then called up Daniel to invite him over later for microwave popcorn and a critique session. He suggested going out someplace in town, like the diner again, but I didn't really want anyone to see us together even though we *were* just writing partners.

When he showed up at seven-thirty, I introduced him to my mother and Hal and then we shut ourselves up in the family room. As we got comfortable on the couch, kicking off our shoes and slumping side by side into the pillows with our feet on the coffee table, Daniel joked, "Aren't they going to wonder what we're up to in here?"

"Please." I rolled my eyes, Loryn style. "Are you ready to hear my latest?"

He nodded. "Hit me."

I read the story in my most dryly sarcastic tone, the one that always made people laugh. Daniel didn't even crack a grin. "You're grumpier than Mickey," I complained. "How about a chuckle or two?"

He let out a long sigh. "I guess I don't get it," he confessed. "I know everybody else thinks the stuff you're writing these days is a riot, but it leaves me . . . I don't know." He shrugged. "It feels hollow or something. Like you're not writing about people you care about. It's just to get a laugh."

I blew out a frustrated puff of air. "But I'm trying so *hard.*" I wasn't sure why, but I wanted Daniel to like my story. "Are you sure you don't think it's a *little* funny?"

"Why does it have to be funny?" he countered.

"I don't know." I thought about it. "Because I like making people laugh?"

I phrased it as a question, but Daniel didn't answer me. "What does Mrs. Cobb think?" he said instead.

I blew out another puff of air. "She's still coming down hard on me. You know what she's like. She always makes a point of saying a couple of nice things. But most of her comments are negative. You know what, though?" I slapped my notebook down on the couch. "I don't care. Everyone else will like it, right?"

"What about you, though? Do *you* like it?"

"I wrote it," I reminded him.

"Yeah, but that doesn't mean it *moves* you."

I lifted my notebook again, covering my face with it. "Can we not be so New Age touchy-feely?" I begged.

When I peeked around the edge of the notebook, Daniel was grinning at me, one strand of auburn hair flopping into his eyes. "I just want you to be in harmony with your inner music."

I groaned. "Okay, if you're so harmonized, read me what *you* wrote."

Our assignment was to write about food, which is how I'd come up with my anorexia theme. Daniel had written about a Thanksgiving dinner at his cousins' when he was ten. It was a sweet, touching story, and when he was done, I actually sniffled.

"You're good at doing that twist thing at the end," I said. Daniel offered me a tissue from the box on the end table. "You know, how we think it's going to be sad because the dog just died and then your uncle who nobody's seen in years shows up and surprises everybody."

"Yeah, well, thanks." Daniel's cheeks turned pink; he sounded pleased.

"Not that it's perfect." I didn't want him to get lazy. "You need to use more action verbs, and you've *got* to get rid of that passive voice stuff, like, 'the ball was thrown by so and so' and 'the feeling was experienced by such and such.'"

"Right." Daniel scribbled something in his notebook. "Thanks."

Twenty minutes later I walked Daniel to the door. "Night," I said.

"Night," he echoed. "Uh, Lily?"

"Yeah?"

"Would you ever want to . . . uh . . . instead of just getting together to write . . . maybe try to . . . um . . ."

I waited patiently, but he didn't go on. "Was that a question?" I prodded.

"Sort of." He blushed furiously. "But I think I'll ask it some other time. See you tomorrow."

"So long," I told him, thinking how weird guys could be.

As soon as the door closed behind him I got it. Daniel was about to ask me out! I decided it was just as well he hadn't gone through with it because of course I couldn't say yes. I hope things don't end up getting awkward between us, I thought.

I didn't dwell on it for long. I was concentrating on rereading my story. Daniel and Mickey didn't like it, and Mrs. Cobb probably won't either, I mused, but I bet the rest of the class will think it's great. "And Seth's the one who speaks French and wants to go to film school," I said to myself as I stapled the pages together. Mrs. Cobb and Daniel were entitled to their opinions, but I wasn't going to cry over them. What did *they* know?

I THOUGHT I'D find you here," a voice behind me said.

I whirled around. Lately instead of pulling my hair back in a severe ponytail, I'd been wearing it down, kind of hanging over my face. Now it whirled with me like a windblown curtain, and my rectangular spectacles slipped halfway down the bridge of my nose. "Seth," I squeaked. "Hi!"

I was standing in the back of the high school auditorium, watching kids audition for the talent show. I'd already had my tryout, and I thought it had gone pretty well. Rico and the rest of the judges had laughed really hard at my poem, "Up and Down and Down Some More."

Seth dropped into a seat near me, slumping down comfortably. He was wearing charcoal gray trousers with a muted dark teal and black plaid oxford buttoned all the way up. He had his glasses off and was twirling them kind of the way a lifeguard twirls a whistle. As those intense eyes drank me up, I felt like I was onstage again. Onstage without any clothes on.

"How'd it go?" he asked.

"Okay," I said, thinking, Thank goodness he didn't show up *before* my audition. I'd have been dumbstruck. "We'll see, right?"

"Right." Seth glanced at the stage. A girl was twirling the baton. "She should do the world a favor and toss that thing in the harbor," he said.

I had to laugh. "Cut her some slack. It takes guts just to get up there."

He nodded, his eyes on me again. "True, I suppose. Were *you* nervous?"

Not as nervous as I am now, I thought. "No," I said nonchalantly. "If I get a spot, great. If not, I'll live. Why are you here, anyway? Are you auditioning?"

Seth laughed. "And what would I do?"

As far as I was concerned, Seth could just get up onstage and let people look at him. But when I thought about it, I couldn't actually picture him performing. "I'm stumped," I admitted.

"My point exactly," Seth said.

"But if you really wanted to, I'm sure you could juggle or whistle or sing, couldn't you?" I teased.

"I love all the junk people consider talent. It's so unbelievably clichéd. Except for you. You're a cut above the rest."

"Yeah?" I couldn't believe Seth was saying such nice things about me—and I was dying to hear more.

He didn't disappoint me. "You project so much wit and acuity."

I made a mental note to look up *acuity* in a dictionary later. "Well . . . ," I murmured, my eyelashes lowered modestly.

"So, Lily, the real reason I'm here . . ." Seth dropped his voice. It was as warm and deep as velvet. I wanted to *wear* it. "Would you like to go to Fiona's party with me tomorrow night?"

"W-what?" I stammered, convinced my hearing had failed me. Or maybe I was just losing my mind.

"Fiona's party tomorrow night. She told me she invited you. Do you want to go together?"

The lights in the auditorium were dim, but I could tell my face was glowing like a neon sign. "Uh . . . yes," I finally managed to say. "Sure. It sounds like fun." I bit my lip before I could say any more dorky-sounding things.

"I'll pick you up at eight. Where do you live?"

"In town, right over Wissinger's Bakery. The name's on the bell."

Getting to his feet, Seth touched my arm lightly. "See you in school tomorrow."

"Yeah," I managed to choke out.

I watched him walk out of the auditorium. I still hadn't decided what was more amazing about him: his body or his wardrobe. The combination was devastating, that was for sure.

Oh, wow, I thought, sinking weakly into a seat. If I'd been a heroine in a nineteenth-century novel, I would have fainted dead away. I have a date tomorrow night with Seth Modine!

I HAVE A date with Seth Modine tomorrow night!" I screamed over the phone to Noelle half an hour later.

"I can't believe it!" she screamed back.

We screamed for another minute. My body was so full of adrenaline, I could have sprinted to Portland and back without breaking a sweat. I still couldn't get over what had just happened.

"So, wait," Noelle commanded. "Tell me again, word for word. I want to know every single thing he said, what he looked like, what you said and what you looked like, et cetera."

I repeated the story, going into as much delicious detail as possible. "I can't believe it!" Noelle screamed again at the end.

"Me either!" I screamed.

I was still hyped about it the next day. When Seth sat next to me in creative writing, I nearly fell off my chair. Every time I glanced through my clear lenses at Mickey and Noelle, who were sitting on the other side of me, they wiggled their eyebrows and I'd almost burst out laughing. Having Seth so close made my temperature rise about ten degrees. I literally felt feverish.

Then at the end of the day, the principal announced the names of the kids who'd gotten spots in the talent show. I stood by my locker with Noelle and Mickey, listening. The three of us held hands, and when we heard my name, we lifted our joined hands in the air and screamed. There'd been a lot of screaming going on lately.

"You did it, Lil!" Mickey shrieked.

Noelle flung her arms around me. "Congratulations!"

We spun in a circle, all hugging. "I can't believe it," I said.

"Things are totally clicking for you these days," Noelle observed.

I nodded. It was almost too much to take in. The talent show and Seth. "I can't believe just a few weeks ago I was feeling like a nobody."

"And look at you now," Mickey said. "Queen of South Regional!"

"Mickey was only half joking," I wrote in my journal later on at home. *"I don't want my old friends to think my ego's getting out of control, though, so I assured her it was just 'Queen for a Day.' But you know what, Diary? I'll take my fifteen minutes of fame. It's so great to be in the center of things instead of on the outside. To know for the first time in my life that other people are looking at me with envy. Maybe that's totally shallow. So, shoot me. It's the way I feel."*

I exited my journal and shut down my computer. "Now I know what it was like to be you," I said softly, my eyes on Daisy's picture. "To be a winner."

I SPENT ABOUT two hours getting ready for my date with Seth. It wasn't like I'd never had a date before—I'd gone out with plenty of guys, a couple of whom had even qualified as boyfriends. But I'd never gone out with anyone as sophisticated as Seth. He was in a completely different league, and I didn't want to blow it. I wanted him to ask me out again. And again and again and again . . .

I wish I had a big sister around, I thought in the shower. Even Laurel would have been better than nothing, even though her fashion sense is nonexistent. But it was really Daisy I longed to share this with. I wanted her to see how well I was turning out.

I washed my hair and shaved my legs and scrubbed myself all over with this foamy peach-scented body wash I borrowed from Mom. Afterward I blew-dry my hair so it would be really straight and put on body lotion and deodorant. Finally, wearing a bra and underwear, I went into my closet.

This was the hard part. I had so many great clothes. What should I wear?

I fingered a green velour swing dress. That was cute. Or what about hip-hugger jeans with a really cool top? My suede-fringed skirt looks good on me, I thought, and so does that white sailor-collar blouse. But I also liked the electric blue jumper and the green wrap miniskirt and the . . .

Then I remembered. Seth had started paying attention to me when I started dressing in black and wearing spectacles and acting cynical. Nobody in the It crowd sported cowboy boots. If I wear pink, I realized, Seth won't recognize me.

So I put on a short black skirt, a skinny black T-shirt, black tights, and black shoes. Even my earrings were black. The only thing that wasn't black was my hair, which I wore parted in the middle and combed straight down so that it hid half my face. I didn't put on perfume—it seemed too adolescent.

"I thought you had a date," Mom said as I sat down next to her on the living room couch to wait for Seth.

"I do."

Mom frowned a little. "That's what you're wearing?"

"What's wrong with it?"

"You have so many *pretty* clothes."

"Mom, I'm nervous," I said. "Please don't give me a hard time."

"Sorry, hon." She gave me a hug, carefully, so that she wouldn't mess up my hair. "I just didn't recognize you. You're usually so colorful."

"Black is always in style," I reminded her.

When the doorbell rang, I shot to my feet as if I'd been launched by a space shuttle rocket. "It's *him*," I announced, my voice cracking inelegantly.

Mom followed me into the hallway. "Do *I* get to meet him?" she asked.

"Of course," I said, but my hand was shaking too much to turn the knob. "Help me, Mom," I whispered.

Mom opened the door. "You must be Seth," she said, giving him a warm smile.

They shook hands. "It's a pleasure to meet you, Mrs. Walker," Seth said. "This is a great apartment. It must be intense living over the bakery—all those evocative smells. Like Proust and his madeleines, right?"

"Proust?" Mom asked.

He's so smart, I thought, hoping Mom was soaking it in. I tried not to look too smug. I really couldn't get over this. A cultured, gorgeous, ultracool guy was here to take *me* on a date. Unbelievable!

Seth explained his Proust reference, tossing out lots of long words along the way. Mom nodded. "I see what you mean," she said with another smile.

I stepped forward, clutching my coat and purse. "Ready to go?" I asked.

I got over my nervousness pretty quickly during the car ride to Fiona's. Seth and I started talking, and it was just like reading my stories in Mrs. Cobb's class. I put on a careless, cynical tone and joked about everything. I made Seth laugh.

I kept it up at Fiona's party. It was a little harder because Seth put his arm around me and that momentarily short-circuited my brain, but pretty soon I was back in the groove. It was like there was a CD inside me and someone had pushed the play button. No matter what people were talking about—music, movies, school—I had something sarcastic and unexpected to say on the subject. Together Seth and I were definitely the It couple of the evening.

Not that this was necessarily quite the thrill I'd expected it to be. I'd never partied with these people before, and I'd thought they'd be a little more . . . lively. A little more fun. No one danced, though, and when I suggested ducking outside for a moonlit walk—Fiona lives a block from the ocean—Seth just yawned. "I'm happy here," he said, indicating his place on the couch. "Moonlight's overrated, if you ask me."

So we sat on the couch with a bunch of his friends and talked. And talked. When I was sure we'd covered every topic in the universe we found some new ones and talked some more. It was exhilarating to talk to people who had so much to say, but it was exhausting, too. Because I knew I had to stay on my toes. Say the right thing, everybody loves you, I figured out. Say the wrong thing, and next time *you'll* be the one they rake over the coals.

Seth drove me home at quarter to twelve because I had a midnight curfew. "We still have a few minutes," he said, parking by the curb in front of the bakery and turning off the engine.

I unbuckled my belt and turned a little in my seat to face him. "Thanks for the fun evening," I said softly.

"Thank *you.*" Seth put out a hand and gently brushed my hair back from my face. "You know, you're as beautiful as you are sharp. That's a rare combination."

"Oh, well," I said nonchalantly.

Seth's hand moved to my shoulders. He pulled me gently toward him. "May I kiss you?"

I nodded yes. We tried a brief, experimental kiss . . . and

liked it. So we tried another one. Seth wasn't the first boy I'd kissed, but he was far and away the sexiest. Kissing him wasn't like anything I'd ever experienced. Our mouths fit together perfectly, and so did our bodies, and when he wrapped me up in his arms with his lips on mine, I felt pretty sure I'd died and gone to heaven.

"Look," Seth said. He'd left the key half turned in the ignition so we could read the clock on the dashboard. It read 12:00.

"Time flies," I said with a sigh.

He mussed my hair. "There. Now you look like you've really been up to something you shouldn't."

I laughed. "Thanks."

We kissed again, just a light brush of the lips that still felt remarkably electric. "See you," I said casually.

"Maybe later this weekend," he agreed. "I'll call you tomorrow."

I could have done cartwheels. Seth was going to call me! We might go out again . . . twice in one weekend!

With admirable self-restraint I said good night, got out of the car, and strolled into the building. Inside, though, when I knew he couldn't see me, I hugged myself and spun around in an ecstatic circle.

My lips were still burning from Seth's kisses as I started typing in my diary a few minutes later. *"I'm describing this for posterity: my first date with Seth Modine!"* I typed in the names of the other people who'd been at Fiona's. *"To be honest, the party was a little on the dull side. But I am not complaining. Being with Seth was totally amazing. I*

sort of feel like I'm putting on an act when I crack those cynical jokes and with the
black clothes and all, but . . ." I touched my lips with my fingertips.
"Those kisses were for real."

I turned off my computer. I figured I'd try to go to
sleep. Not that I needed to dream. My dreams had come true
already.

Six

WINTER THAWED INTO early spring, and there was a picture of Seth Modine in my birthday locket. We were going out, and I was popular in a way I'd never been before. I got invited to parties every weekend—I was the It girl of the moment. I was too busy to feel lonely about being the only sister left at home anymore. I was too busy for a lot of things, like homework.

"And like your old friends," Noelle said one night over the phone.

It was the week before the talent show, and I'd been rehearsing my poem in my bedroom. "What are you talking about?"

She sighed. "I don't want to whine, Lil. Mickey and I are just sad, that's all. We thought we were your best friends, but we never see you anymore."

"Don't be ridiculous," I said. "You *are* my best friends.

That hasn't changed. Don't I always get you invited to the parties I'm going to?"

"You get us invited, but that doesn't mean we're welcome," Noelle said.

I knew she had a point. Either you were It or you weren't, and their friendship with me wasn't quite enough to make Noelle and Mickey It. They just weren't intellectual enough. But I still liked them, of course.

"We'll do something together soon, just the three of us, okay?" I promised.

"How about this weekend? Maybe Saturday?"

"Talent show," I reminded her. "There's a party at Rico's afterward. I'll make sure you're on the list."

"Okay, Lil. Thanks. Well . . . later."

"Later!"

My telephone rings at least five times a night these days—Hal finally sprang for a second line out of desperation. As soon as I hung up with Noelle, Loryn called. Then Seth. The call after that was from Daniel.

"Hi!" I said with genuine pleasure. For a while he and I had been talking on the phone or getting together once or twice a week. Lately I hadn't heard from him. "What's up, pardner?"

"Uh, is this okay?" he asked.

"Is what okay?"

"You know, calling you. Should I still do this now that you have a, you know, boyfriend?"

I really didn't see any connection between having a boyfriend and talking to Daniel about writing. There'd been that time he almost asked me out—if that had even been his intention—but that was ancient history now. "Sure," I said. "Of course you should call. Seth wouldn't mind, if that's what you mean. Why would he?"

"No reason," Daniel said. "So, what are you writing about for the next assignment?"

I was kind of in a rut in writing class. All my stories sounded the same, and every time I got a paper back, Mrs. Cobb's comments sounded the same, too. But I wasn't worried about it. Seth and I were in sync. Why would I obsess about the fact that I'd never clicked with Mrs. Cobb?

"I'm writing a sequel to my piece for the talent show," I told Daniel. "A longer piece, not a poem this time. Listen."

I told him my idea. As usual he wasn't wild about it, and as usual I didn't care. When we hung up, I tried to do some writing. The sequel just wasn't happening, so I turned to a clean page of narrow-ruled paper.

I looked over at the picture of my father. Suddenly I had a strong impulse. I never write about Dad, I thought. There were so many stories I could tell about him! But who'd want to hear them?

Instead I made an entry in my journal. "*I gotta admit it's getting to be a strain, churning out these stories for class,*" I typed. "*It's a relief to write in my diary and use capitals and punctuation. 'Then try something else for a change,' Daniel would say. Hey, you don't mess with success.*"

I turned off my computer and went over to the window. It was almost April, and a gentle spring rain tapped against the panes. April showers bring May flowers, I thought. And what did Daisy used to say? She had her own rhyme—something about opening day in the major leagues.

Cupping my chin in my hands, I propped my elbows on the windowsill and tried to remember Daisy's rhyme. I couldn't. A weird longing came over me. "Why couldn't she speak to me one more time?" I whispered.

Turning from the window, I went to my bookshelf and pulled out my Daisy photo album. I hadn't looked through it in a while. I hadn't visited the cemetery recently, either. It seemed childish, somehow—having conversations with my sister's gravestone. I would've died of embarrassment if anyone had ever seen me.

Now I looked at my photos of Daisy. There she was, shooting a goal during a soccer game, posing with Kristin and Jamila in their South Regional High graduation gowns, on a toboggan with me and Laurel, popping a wheelie on her bike, blowing out the candles on her birthday cake at her sweet-sixteen clambake.

"You wouldn't believe how great my life has been since *I* turned sixteen," I told her. "You should see me, Daze. I used to be an oddball, remember? Not anymore."

My sister smiled out of the graduation photograph. I squinted, trying to see into those eyes. Usually I felt some kind of bond, but it wasn't there tonight.

In fact, I didn't feel anything at all.

ROSE AND STEPHEN came home the first weekend in April so they could go to my talent show on Saturday night and then to a coed bridal shower for Rose's old friend Cath Appleby and her fiancé on Sunday morning. When they got in around five on Friday, I greeted Rose at the door with a Euro-style cheek-to-cheek air kiss. "No hug?" she asked.

I raised an ironic eyebrow. "Do we need to be so sentimental?"

Rose grabbed me, anyway. No sooner had she pulled me close, though, than she pushed me away again. "What's with the specs?" she asked.

"I need glasses," I said. It wasn't *really* a lie—I did need them. For my image.

"Since when?"

"Since recently."

"Oh," she said, still looking puzzled.

She and Stephen had arrived in time for dinner. Hal brought home Chinese food—he likes to give Mom a break from cooking now and then. "I'm so psyched Cath's getting married," Rose said, dipping her mini-spring roll into sweet-and-sour sauce and then popping it into her mouth. She chewed and swallowed. "Now I won't be the only one in our old crowd who's settled down." She nudged Stephen with her elbow. "You know, tied to the old ball and chain."

"Gee, thanks," he said.

"Is anyone going to eat that last spring roll?" Rose asked, reaching for the carton. "Because if not . . ."

"Help yourself," Hal said, even though she already had.

"Hey, whatever happened with the Broadway show?" I asked.

Rose put up a hand in a just-a-minute sign so she could finish chewing. "I didn't get a part," she said a minute later.

"That's too bad," I commiserated.

"I'm sorry, Rose," Mom said. "You must be disappointed."

"Yeah, but it's for the best." Rose certainly didn't *look* disappointed—she had a huge grin on her face. "I'm not too bummed about it because . . . I'm going to have a baby. I'm pregnant!"

For a moment nobody spoke. Then Mom jumped out of her chair with a delighted shriek. She and Rose hugged, talking a mile a minute. "Just barely pregnant," Rose told Mom. "I'm not due until November."

"Are you having morning sickness?" Mom asked.

Rose shook her head. "No. I'm hungry all the time, though."

Mom laughed. "I noticed. Oh, Hal, can you believe it? We're going to be grandparents!"

Rose turned to me. "And you're going to be an aunt, Lil. Aren't you excited?"

I *was* excited, but I wasn't about to start jumping up and down like an idiot. Wearing black all the time makes a person a lot less demonstrative—it just goes with the territory. "Sure," I said casually.

My underwhelmed response didn't really matter because everyone else was so enthusiastic. Rose called Laurel to tell her the news, and we could hear Laurel exclaiming on the other end of the phone. Laurel was still at U. Maine— she hadn't been able to get away for the talent show because she had a big chemistry test coming up the next week.

When she hung up after speaking with Laurel, Rose was smiling. A second later her eyes brimmed with tears. "I really wish I could share this with Daisy, too," she said.

Mom and Rose embraced again. I felt an ache under my ribs. But I didn't cry or join the hug fest. I don't know; I just couldn't get into the Hallmark moment. I wondered what Seth would have thought of the whole scene.

The next day Stephen took his law school books over to the town library for a couple of hours. Mom and Rose discussed layettes and nursery decor. I hung out with them, figuring that listening to baby talk beat stressing over the talent show, which started in just a few hours.

"What do you think about a stenciled border of yellow ducks and blue sailboats on the wall," Rose asked Mom, "and a yellow-and-white-striped crib bumper?"

"Cute," Mom said. "You'll have to take the old rocking chair, Rose. It's the one I rocked in with you girls when you were infants."

"How about names?" I asked.

"We're thinking about David for a boy and Jane for a girl," Rose told me.

"Jane?" I wrinkled my nose. "That's so boring."

Rose laughed. "What names do you like?"

"How about Bianca?" I suggested. "Or Victoria?"

Rose lifted her eyes skyward. "Why did I ask?"

"All right, are you girls ready for a project?" Mom got to her feet, "Come up to the attic with me."

The three of us went upstairs. Mom pulled down the folding ladder in the hall ceiling and we took turns climbing up it. "What are we looking for?" Rose asked once we were standing in the attic.

"There's a trunk here somewhere with old baby things, Rose," Mom said. "You girls all wore a beautiful hand-embroidered christening dress that my grandmother made when my mother was a baby. Let's see if we can find it."

The attic was musty and cluttered. I shifted some boxes to get at a beat-up old trunk, coughing at the dust I'd kicked up. Meanwhile Mom lifted the latch on another old trunk. "What's in here?" Rose asked.

Mom pulled out a cardboard shoe box. "Old family papers and photographs. I keep meaning to come up here some rainy day and sort through it all, but I never get around to it."

Rose and I went over to take a look. "What gorgeous curls," Rose said, pointing to a sepia-tinted photograph of a child in an old-fashioned pinafore.

"Who's that little girl?" I asked.

Mom turned the photo over and laughed. "It's a little boy," she said. "Your dad's grandpa Simon."

"Why'd they put him in a dress?" I wondered.

"That was the style back then," Rose said.

"Look at this one," Mom said. "Do you recognize *that* little boy?"

In the faded color snapshot a man in a waterproof slicker and boots stood on the deck of a fishing boat with his hand resting proudly on the head of a freckle-faced boy. The boy was holding a bucket full of cod and grinning. He was missing a front tooth. "It's Dad," I said, "with Great-uncle Ted."

"Can I have that?" Rose asked. "I'd like to put it in a frame."

"Of course," Mom said. Rose took the picture, handling it carefully. "Let's see if we can find some others as good for Laurel and Lily to take."

Mom opened another shoe box. Inside it were small, leather-bound books. She lifted one up. "It's a diary," she said.

I stepped closer, curious. "Whose?"

She turned to the first page. "'This diary is the exclusive and very private property of Flora Elizabeth White,'" Mom read, "'and is not to be perused by strange eyes on penalty of death.'" Mom smiled. "Sound familiar, Lily?"

I used to label my own journal notebooks with dire warnings like that. "Maybe we shouldn't read this, then," I said.

Mom laughed. "Oh, I think it's okay. Flora Elizabeth White grew up to be your great-grandmother Flora Walker. She's been dead for twenty years."

"Great-grandma Flora—the one with the charm bracelet?" I asked.

Mom nodded. "That's right."

"She was pretty prolific," Rose observed. "Look at all these volumes."

"I didn't realize she was a writer." Mom looked at me. "I bet you'd enjoy reading them, Lily. Maybe they'd give you some ideas for stories."

I shrugged. I was kind of curious about the diaries but didn't want to show it. As I've said, enthusiasm wasn't a virtue in the crowd I was currently hanging with. "I'm sure it's mostly pretty boring," I said in a disinterested manner.

Mom put the box aside. "Let's bring them downstairs, anyway."

We continued hunting for the baby stuff. Rose opened up a trunk. "Dress-up clothes," she said as she sifted through the things. "Remember this ratty old velvet cape, Lil? And these cardboard swords decorated with plastic jewels?"

"For playing The Three Musketeers," I said.

Mom laughed. "Remember when Lily wore her D'Artagnan costume for a week straight and the only thing we could get her to say was, 'All for one and one for all'?"

"Here's another Lily special," Rose said, digging out a moth-eaten mouse costume.

"That was another one you kept on for a week," Mom recalled, "and ate nothing but cheese the whole time."

"I'd change the ears sometimes," I said, "and the tail. I could be a rabbit or a horse or an elephant."

"You were wild," Rose concluded. "We never knew *what* to expect from you."

Rose sounded nostalgic for the old days, and suddenly I felt nostalgic, too. It was fun having a personality that changed all the time, I thought somewhat wistfully. I looked down at the clothes I was wearing now—black jeans and a black T-shirt— and for a second I felt trapped. My current look and attitude didn't leave me much room to grow.

"Here are the baby outfits," Mom announced.

She and Rose began to ooh and ah over tiny sweaters and crocheted booties. I closed the lid of the costume trunk. No more make-believe, I decided.

I'd found the real me at last.

Seven

OR HAD I?

Mom, Rose, Stephen, and Hal came to the talent show that night. Afterward in the crowded, noisy hall outside the high school auditorium, they showered me with hugs. "You were great!" Rose exclaimed.

"A riot," Stephen agreed.

"It went okay, didn't it?" I asked, trying not to grin from ear to ear.

"The audience laughed like crazy," Hal said.

"Yep, you're ready for off Broadway," Rose concluded.

Mom was the only one who hadn't spoken up. "What did *you* think, Mom?" I asked.

"The poem was definitely . . . interesting. Surprising." She smiled wryly. "I must just be an out-of-touch old lady."

"You didn't get it?" I said.

She shook her head. "Well, I sort of got it. It was about a girl who couldn't find a date for the prom, who didn't fit in at school. She was practically suicidal. Yet it was supposed to be . . ."

"Funny," I supplied. "You know, ironic. It's black humor, Mom."

"Well, anyway, I'm proud of you." Mom gave me another hug. "And we're taking you out for dessert to celebrate."

We went to the Harborside. Seth came along. It was the first time Rose had met my new boyfriend, and for me this was almost as important as performing in the talent show. I wanted her to approve of him. But for some reason, they didn't hit it off. It was sort of like Mom and my poem. Rose just didn't seem to get Seth.

I knew it for sure halfway through my cheesecake. Seth kept making fun of kids who'd performed in the talent show, and in a playful way Rose challenged pretty much every remark he made. He didn't let up, though, and finally Rose just said, "Hmmm," while Stephen stuffed a huge bite of lemon meringue pie into his mouth to hide his smile. They think Seth's full of it, I realized.

Suddenly I was dying to get out of there. I pushed my plate away and refolded my cloth napkin, then stood up. "Seth and I are going to a party at Rico's," I told Mom. "Can I stay out a little later than usual? You know, to celebrate?"

Mom glanced at Hal. He shrugged. "Sure," she decided. "You can stay out until one."

"Thanks." I bent over to kiss Mom's cheek. "See you all tomorrow."

Seth and I made our getaway, leaving the others to finish their coffee. "I like Rose," Seth said as we drove to Rico's. "She's cool."

"Yeah." I found myself telling a bald-faced lie. I didn't want to hurt his feelings. "She liked you, too."

Seth slipped an arm around my shoulders and smiled an of-course-she-did smile. I couldn't quite smile back, so I turned my head away to look out the window. Seth *is* full of it, I thought. I don't blame Rose. He really came off as a pompous jerk.

I was about to tell him he could be a little more charitable toward kids who'd had the nerve to get up onstage in front of hundreds of people when he abruptly pulled the car over to the side of the road. I glanced at him, startled, and he put his arms around me and kissed me on the mouth. "You were phenomenal tonight, Lily," he murmured. His lips explored my jaw and then my throat. "I can't believe you're mine."

After that I mellowed out. Why pick a fight? I decided. Seth thought I was phenomenal, and that summed up my feelings for him, too.

Our impromptu make-out session made us fashionably late for Rico's party. It was big—fifty or more people. Half an hour into the party, though, it occurred to me that there were quite a few faces missing. "I thought Rico invited everyone who was in the talent show," I said to Seth and Loryn as we cracked open our sodas. "Where are Ginny Lauer and Andrew Hunt?"

Loryn laughed. "Are you *kidding?*"

"No," I said. Out of the corner of my eye I spotted Mickey and Noelle. They looked like they were getting up their nerve to approach a group of people, including Fiona and Rico. "And those AV guys who did the lights—Izzy and Clay?"

"They didn't make the final cut," Seth said.

I looked at him, my head tilted to one side. "What final cut?"

"Rico wanted to keep the party exclusive," he explained.

"You mean Rico didn't even invite them?" I asked. I could see Noelle and Mickey being squeezed out of Rico and Fiona's circle.

Loryn rolled her eyes. "Of course not!"

"But this is supposed to be the official talent show cast party," I said. "It's not really fair to leave people out."

"You were going to spend the evening getting to know Izzy and Clay?" Seth teased. "Yeah, they seem like true Renaissance men."

"We knew they wouldn't come," Loryn said to me.

"So we just made an executive decision," Seth finished.

"I still think you should've invited them," I said crossly.

Seth put an arm around my waist. "This is really touching, Lily," he joked. "I didn't know you harbored such tender feelings for your fellow man."

Have a sense of humor, I told myself, but tonight I didn't feel like laughing at someone else's expense. Everyone in the talent show had worked equally hard. So what if Clay, Izzy, Ginny, and Andrew weren't the coolest kids in Hawk Harbor?

I wiggled free of Seth's embrace. "Be right back," I muttered. "I need to find someone."

I hadn't had a minute to talk to Noelle and Mickey yet, and by the time I caught up with them, they were putting on their jackets and heading for the door. "Where are you going?" I asked.

"Walk us out to my car," Noelle invited.

When we were outside, I said, "What's up, guys?"

"We're heading over to my house to watch cable," Noelle said.

I didn't really have to ask, but I did, anyway. "Aren't you having fun?"

Noelle laughed. "Lil, it was great to see you in the talent show. We're really proud of you. But these parties . . . no one talks to us."

"Well, come back in and hang with me and Seth. I'm sure people will talk to you if you give them a chance," I urged.

Mickey shot Noelle a sideways glance. "No, thanks," she said.

I felt hurt, and I guess I looked hurt, too. "No offense, Lil," Noelle assured me. "We still love you."

"But when you're with that crowd, you're not yourself," Mickey said. "We don't really feel welcome."

"Hey, don't try to spare my feelings," I said sarcastically. "Tell it like it is."

Mickey bit her lip. "I'm sorry, Lil, but that's how it feels on this end."

"Well, you *are* welcome to join us, but it's your choice, obviously." I crossed my arms across my chest.

"See you around," Noelle said, and she and Mickey climbed into the car.

I turned on my heel and stormed back to the party. They're so high maintenance, I fumed. Why do I even bother? But I knew that was the point. I hadn't been bothering for a while. Seth's friends *weren't* Mickey and Noelle's friends, and since I'd started going out with Seth, I'd shut my old friends out of my life. Now I was paying the price. *They* were blowing *me* off.

Once I was back inside, everything felt normal again. People bugged me until I recited my poem from the talent show one more time. When Rico got out his camera, we all posed for pictures, Seth and I with our arms wrapped around each other, and even though I'd been kind of mad at him before, now I pressed my cheek against his and thought, This one will be in the yearbook. Coolest junior class couple.

At 1 A.M. Seth drove me home, where we shared a final, passionate good-bye kiss. In the apartment I tiptoed upstairs. Everything was dark and quiet. After washing up and getting into my nightgown, I turned on my laptop and started typing.

It was a relief to be curled up in bed, alone with my diary. *"Rose wasn't too impressed by Seth,"* I wrote in my journal. *"The whole time at the Harborside she was either yawning or being confrontational. Maybe she was just tired,"* I added hopefully. *"Pregnant women are always tired, right?"*

I decided this was the best explanation for Rose's behavior. But it didn't necessarily explain Seth. *"We had a fight at Rico's,"* I typed. *"Well, not really a fight. We didn't see eye to eye about something. It wasn't a big deal, though. I'm over it."*

I paused, staring at the sentence I'd just written. Was I, though? Over it?

I turned off my computer. I didn't want to write in my journal anymore. I didn't want to ask questions that didn't have easy answers.

So I didn't write this question down, but as I turned out the light and tried to fall asleep, it buzzed in my brain, anyway. If this is the real me at last, why is it suddenly such hard work to be Lily Walker?

I T WAS MAY, and the school year was almost over. "I can't believe the prom is this weekend!" Noelle exclaimed one Wednesday in the cafeteria.

I'd barely spoken to Mickey and Noelle since that scene at Rico's party, but today was Mickey's birthday, so we were celebrating. Well, *they* were celebrating, I was moping. "I know," I said, licking frosting off one of the cupcakes Noelle had brought. "And Seth's home sick with a stomach flu."

"He'll be back on his feet by Saturday," Mickey predicted.

"He'd better be," I said.

But he wasn't. In fact, his stomach flu turned out not to be stomach flu at all—Seth ended up in the community hospital having his appendix removed. I went stag to my first prom, sharing a limo with Loryn and Fiona and their dates, Dylan and Brett.

"Poor Seth," Fiona said, slouching elegantly in her seat. She was wearing a slinky midnight blue strapless dress with chunky high heels.

The Year I Turned Sixteen

"It's a major bummer," Brett agreed, adjusting his bow tie.

I was wearing a black slip dress and my birthday necklace with the charm from my great-grandmother's bracelet. Now I took the necklace off and opened the book-shaped locket so I could see the little picture of my boyfriend inside.

"Look," I said with a sigh, showing it to Loryn.

"Even when he's not with us, we somehow feel his presence," she joked in a preacherly tone.

I took the locket back. Seth gazed up at me. He had a half smile on his face, and his eyes were narrowed. He was sticking his chin out a little. He always does that in pictures, I thought now for the first time. That kind of rugged, cool chin thing. I frowned. He looks like a model. A little too posed.

I closed the locket quickly. I shouldn't be having such mean thoughts about my poor sick boyfriend. "I took him his boutonniere in the hospital," I told Loryn and the others. I didn't tell them that Seth had acted like he couldn't have cared less about the whole thing.

Plenty of kids were at the dance without dates, so even though I missed Seth, I wasn't a wallflower. I got asked to dance a lot, and by some really cool guys. Seth's buddy Bob Sokolov came over to me just as the band kicked into a particularly excellent song. We started dancing, and he wasn't bad. He also had a very cool tux, complete with collarless shirt. But he spent the entire time looking everywhere but at my face, as if he were checking the crowd to see who might be watching us. It was a bore.

When the song ended, I politely asked him if he wanted to

dance another one, praying he'd say no. Lucky for me he was ready to hit the refreshment table. I took another route to the same destination, bumping into Daniel on the way. "Hey," I said, a wide smile spreading across my face.

"Hey, yourself," he replied, grinning back at me.

He handed me a cup of punch and then took one for himself. "Who are you here with?" I asked.

"I'm flying solo," he answered.

I realized I didn't know much about Daniel's social life, even though we'd become buddies in writing class. "You procrastinated too long and Princess Charming said yes to someone else?" I kidded.

"Something like that." He looked down into his punch cup. "How about you? Where's Mr. Modine?"

I told Daniel about Seth's appendectomy. "Ouch," Daniel said, wincing. "Bad timing, huh?"

"Actually, he didn't seem that torn up about missing the prom," I told Daniel. "He thinks the whole concept is totally bourgeois."

We finished our punch and tossed our cups in the trash. "Want to dance?" I asked.

Daniel lifted his hands palms outward in a "no, no, not me, never" gesture. "Two left feet," he explained. *"Three* left feet."

I laughed. "It's the *prom,* Daniel. You have to dance with somebody."

"Well . . ." He smoothed his hair back self-consciously.

I grabbed his arm. "Come on!"

We danced a couple of fast songs. Daniel actually had some nice moves. He was relaxed and limber, not totally stiff like a lot of guys. "You're a great dancer," I told him, shaking my head. "I can't believe you tried to feed me that stuff about left feet."

Daniel shrugged. I lifted my shoulders, too. We started moving our shoulders back and forth in rhythm, which made me laugh. "You make it work," he said. "I have two left feet and you have two right ones."

Whatever it was, we melded pretty well. Daniel was a decent slow dancer, too. When the music changed, he hesitated for a split second before taking me in his arms, but then he didn't wimp out. He didn't hold me at a distance, like we were waltzing in sixth-grade ballroom dance class—he pulled me close and moved with me in a self-assured way.

"I can't believe you don't have a date," I told him, surprising myself.

Daniel raised his eyebrows. Two red spots popped up on his cheeks. "Truth *is* stranger than fiction."

"No, seriously. You're so sweet!" I patted his lapel. "*And* you look okay in formal wear. There are so many girls at school who didn't get asked to the prom and who would've been totally psyched to go with you. You should've done someone a big favor."

"But then I wouldn't be available to substitute for hospitalized boyfriends, would I?" he pointed out.

"True."

I *was* selfishly glad that Daniel didn't have to run off and pay attention to another girl. It was tons more fun dancing with him than with a guy like Bob. Daniel was actually interested in me, not in how he looked dancing with me.

"Isn't it great that Mrs. Cobb decided not to give a final?" Daniel asked.

We were still slow dancing. "Yeah," I agreed as we swayed back and forth. "Although I wouldn't have minded a chance to pull my grade up a little. Looks like I'll be getting a B."

"That's not so bad."

There didn't seem much point in telling him about how high my hopes for the class had been back in January. "Mrs. Cobb just never warmed to my writing."

Daniel tried some Fred Astaire stuff—he lifted my right hand in the air, then placed his other hand on the small of my back and spun me neatly under his arm. "What about next year?"

Mrs. Cobb had just announced that she'd be teaching a continuation of the creative-writing class next semester. This time people would have to try out for a limited number of spaces by submitting a manuscript over the summer. "It sounds pretty intense," I said.

"I think I'll take a shot at it, anyway. You should, too, Lily."

I shrugged. "Who knows? Fall's a long way off."

We were quiet for a minute. I tuned in to the music, which was lush and hypnotic. With a contented sigh I rested my head on Daniel's shoulder.

An instant later I jumped back. "Oops!" I said. Now I was

the one with pink cheeks. "Forgot where I was for a minute there."

"It's okay," Daniel said softly.

I looked into his eyes. Next thing I knew, the song was over, and Loryn and Fiona and their dates swooped down on me, and the whole pack of us were dancing, and Daniel had disappeared. I guess it was a good thing that the song had ended when it did. I *had* almost forgotten something. It was so easy to be with Daniel and so much fun, I'd almost forgotten that he wasn't my prom date.

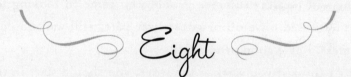

Eight

SUMMER VACATION STARTED one week before Memorial Day. "I need to look for a job, don't I?" I asked Mom and Hal one night as we ate a picnic supper in the park down the block.

When they turned sixteen, my older sisters had all gotten jobs to start saving money for college. Daisy's first real summer job had been at the hospital (where Seth had his appendectomy)—she had worked as a receptionist. That's what sparked her interest in studying medicine. Even though she'd taken a year off in between high school and college to work full-time and help out the family, she'd never lost sight of her goal. She'd been totally dedicated and focused.

"Might not be a bad idea," Mom said, scooping some pasta salad onto a plastic plate and handing it to me.

"You know what I'd really like to do," I told her. "Work for you at Potluck."

The gourmet shop's grand opening was scheduled for Memorial Day weekend, when tourism season starts in earnest in Hawk Harbor. Mom opened a Tupperware container and nibbled a strawberry. "I remember you mentioning that. It's a possibility."

I pictured myself behind the counter at Potluck, hobnobbing with wealthy summer people who came in looking for basil-infused olive oil or goose liver pâté. "I'll wait on customers. I have good people skills."

"I think if you work at the store, you should start in the kitchen, helping Sarah," Mom commented.

"You mean Laurel gets to be assistant manager and I get to chop carrots?" I asked in an offended tone.

"Laurel's an adult now," Mom said, unruffled. "She's ready for the responsibility—she has some experience under her belt."

"Taking care of mangy wild animals," I mumbled. "Are you sure you want her handling food?"

I couldn't change Mom's mind, though. I could be a prep cook at Potluck, working behind the scenes—she reminded me that Laurel had done that sort of work for her off and on for the last couple of years—or I could look for another job. I decided to accept her offer, even if it did mean having to play second fiddle to my older sister.

Laurel was home from college for the summer, but Carlos had a summer job a couple of hours away in a lab at Tufts University, near Boston. Laurel was brooding like crazy.

Despite that, it was nice having a sister at home again.

She'd taken over her old bedroom, and already it had that familiar zoolike odor, thanks to Snickers the dog, two birds, and a mini—lop-eared rabbit named Ebenezer. Animals are not my thing, but I could put up with them if it meant having Laurel around. It was nice having someone to talk to.

One Friday after dinner Laurel, Mom, and Hal sat down at the kitchen table to go over lists of things they needed to do before Potluck's grand opening. I lurked nearby, hoping someone would ask for my opinion.

"You seem distracted," Mom said to Laurel. "You know, I don't want to ruin your summer. If you think being assistant manager will put too much pressure on you, we can change your job description a little."

"It won't be any pressure at all compared to school," Laurel said, sticking her hands into the pockets of her overalls and slouching in her chair. "I guess I should just put it behind me, you know? Start fresh next fall. But I keep thinking about how I blew my math final."

"You didn't blow it," Hal said.

"I got a C," Laurel insisted, "and it pulled my semester grade down to a B."

"I think you should be proud of yourself," Mom declared. "Your second-semester grades were better than your first-semester ones. Next year you'll do even better."

"Next year. Huh," Laurel huffed. "I'll tell you one thing about next year. I'm dropping out of the prevet program. Everyone in those classes is super-competitive. I hate it."

Mom put the Potluck papers aside, and she, Laurel, and

Hal continued talking about Laurel's academic career. I wandered off, drinking my iced tea thoughtfully. Nature Girl was having an identity crisis. Interesting!

Later I barged into her room without knocking, the way I always do. "Are you really going to drop prevet?" I asked, flopping onto her bed.

Laurel was sitting at her desk, writing a letter—to Carlos, I guessed.

She turned in her chair to look at me. "Yeah, I am," she said. "I mean, I hope I don't sound like a baby, whining because I didn't get straight A's, but I busted my butt all year and I feel like I don't have anything to show for it. I might still major in bio, but at least I won't have to take so many other hard-core science classes."

I wondered what Daisy would have said at a moment like this. She'd been the family cheerleader. "What about your furry and feathered friends?" I gestured at Laurel's menagerie. "You owe it to them to become a vet. You *love* animals. I used to think you *were* an animal."

"I can still have pets," Laurel pointed out.

"Okay, so what about Carlos?"

"What *about* Carlos?"

"I thought you guys were going to have related careers, like when you used to work at the Wildlife Rescue Center."

Laurel tapped her pen on the desk, frowning. "I don't know anymore. He graduated magna cum laude—he's going to Tufts for grad school. How can I compete with that? Maybe I'm not smart enough—maybe we don't belong together."

"That's the most ridiculous thing I ever heard," I declared. "You *are* smart, and you and Carlos are perfect for each other. It shouldn't make a difference if you don't both end up going to graduate school. Anyway, you still might. It's a couple of years away."

"You're right." Laurel turned back to her letter. "Who knows what will happen?"

This conversation struck me as so odd that I couldn't get it out of my mind. The next morning Rose came up to Hawk Harbor for the day—Stephen had just finished his second year of law school, and he had an orientation for his summer job at a firm in Boston—and I felt I had to talk with her about Laurel.

"You should give her some advice," I told Rose. "She'd listen to you because you actually have real-life experience."

Rose heaved a sigh. We were sitting on the family room couch, watching the Saturday morning cooking shows on public TV, and she was resting her folded arms on top of her stomach, which was starting to stick out. "How can *I* give her advice? It's not like I have it all figured out or anything."

"Are you kidding?" I said. "You're the most together person I know."

To my surprise, instead of being flattered, Rose burst into tears. "Are you okay?" I asked worriedly. "Are you nauseated or something?"

"I'm not nauseated," Rose blubbered, "but I'm not okay, either."

"Well, what's wrong?"

"I just don't know if I'm ready to have a baby, Lil. What if I don't know how to take care of it? What if my career is sidetracked forever? What if I'm a t-terrible m-mom?"

I patted my sister's shoulder while she sobbed noisily for a minute. "You'll be a great mom, Rose, and your career *won't* get sidetracked," I said with certainty. "There are lots of singers and actresses out there with babies and stuff, and it doesn't slow them down one bit."

Rose sniffled. "Like who?"

"Like Madonna," I said, "and Uma Thurman and Jodie Foster. And there are athletes and supermodels who have babies and then go back to work, too. Everybody does it these days."

Rose wiped her eyes on the sleeve of her maternity T-shirt. "Don't think I'm crazy, okay? It's just the hormones. I'm extremely volatile lately."

"What can I do to make you feel better?" I asked.

She gave me a wry smile. "How about a glass of milk and some Pop-Tarts?"

"My sisters are wacko these days," I typed in my journal an hour later. *"We're talking certifiable. Like, they have really great lives: Laurel's a freshman at a good university with a totally gorgeous, devoted boyfriend, and Rose has a cool career and a great husband plus she's expecting a baby. But for some reason they're both freaking out about stuff and having all this self-doubt. I don't get it."*

I stopped writing and looked pensively out the window. The trees lining Main Street were lush and green, and in the distance the peaceful blue harbor was spotted with sailboats.

How can Laurel just suddenly decide that she doesn't want to be a vet? I wondered. When she's wanted to be one all her life? It was totally confusing. And Rose, talking about quitting her singing career to stay home with the baby. What was *that* all about?

My sisters aren't done growing up, I realized. It was a revelation. I'd just assumed that by the time people graduated from high school or at least college, they were done with that kind of stuff. Apparently not.

I'd always taken Daisy for my model. She knew exactly who she was and what she wanted to do with every hour in every day, for the rest of her life. *"But maybe it's not always that easy. Maybe for some people identity is a learning process,"* I typed in my journal. *"Rose and Laurel are still figuring out who they are."*

I hit the return key and started a new paragraph. *"And if they're still figuring out who they are . . . then what about me?"*

Nine

S UDDENLY IT WAS the official beginning of summer and Mom was in a total panic.

"Relax," Stephen said, pouring Mom a glass of wine. He and Rose were home for Memorial Day weekend. Carlos was visiting, too—everyone wanted to be on hand for Potluck's grand opening the next day. Rose had made dinner, and we'd forced Mom to sit down at the table with us. "You and Hal are the most organized people on the planet," Stephen went on. "You've thought of everything—it'll go great."

"I don't know." Mom chewed her lip anxiously. Hal pushed her wineglass closer to her, but Mom didn't touch it. "What if no one comes to the store? Or what if they just browse and don't buy anything?"

"You did tons of market research," Rose reminded Mom

as she set a platter of broiled halibut on the table. "There's no other store like it for miles."

"I just don't know," Mom repeated. She toyed with her silverware, straightening the knife and spoon until they were precisely parallel. "I was up half the night, looking at the numbers again." She shot a glance at Hal. "We've really stretched ourselves to finance this. What if Potluck flops?"

Hal gave Mom a hug. "If it flops, we'll start over—you've done it before. But it *won't* flop," he said. "I guarantee you're going to be so busy tomorrow, your head will be spinning."

We started eating. "Great fish, Rose," Carlos said. Laurel's boyfriend has short black hair and dark eyes and a killer smile, but he's a man of few words. If he said the fish was great, you better believe it was.

"Thanks." Rose was already serving herself seconds. She was eating like a horse. Make that a team of horses. The big kind. "Anyone else want more?"

We passed the fish and side dishes around the table. I scooped a little more rice pilaf onto my plate.

"I was biking down Lighthouse Road earlier," Laurel said, taking a platter from me. "The Lilac Inn is still for sale."

"Supposedly they had an offer a month or so ago, but the deal fell through," Hal said.

Rose looked at Mom. "You and Hal are thinking about buying a house, aren't you?"

Laurel's eyes lit up. "Wouldn't it be fun to live there again?"

"They're not asking a bad price, either," Stephen put in.

Rose glanced at Stephen. "How do *you* know?"

"I called the realtor," he confessed, shrugging. "Just curious."

"Let's do it, then!" I exclaimed. "Let's buy our old house back!"

Mom shook her head, laughing. "You kids are too much," she said. "It wouldn't be the right house for me and Hal even if we had the money right now. Three floors and six bedrooms! Not exactly practical, with only one of you girls at home."

I heaved a dramatic sigh. "Dreams don't come true if you're always being *practical,*" I said.

Mom smiled again. "Be that as it may."

"So, we have a present for you, Mom." Rose hopped to her feet and went over to the sideboard, retrieving a large, flat, gift-wrapped box. "Here."

"What is it?" Mom asked.

"Open it," Rose said, smiling.

Mom ripped off the paper and opened the box. She lifted out something and started to unfold it. "What . . . ?"

She held it up. It was a green twill apron with the word *Potluck* embroidered on it in bright yellow. "Look at this," Mom said. "It's adorable!"

"There's one for each of us," Laurel explained.

"We picked the colors to match the sign and the menus," I contributed.

"It's the perfect touch," Mom said. "You girls are so thoughtful. These aprons make having my own store seem real."

"It's real, all right," Rose agreed.

After dinner Rose and Stephen went out with some old high school friends. Laurel and I cleaned up the kitchen while Mom and Hal took turns making phone calls to people Mom had catered for, reminding them to come to the grand opening. "Are *you* nervous?" I asked Laurel as I rinsed a plate and stuck it in the dishwasher.

Laurel's always been kind of shy. "You know me," Laurel replied, putting a platter in the sink and squirting dishwashing liquid onto it. "I'd rather be behind the scenes. But I'm flattered that Mom thinks I can contribute something." Laurel cracked a smile. "Her mistake, right?"

"It's not a mistake," I surprised myself by saying. I'd been about to launch into a complaint about how unfair it was that Laurel had a job that I'd be a hundred times better at. Instead I decided to try to make my big sister feel good about herself. She *should* feel good. "You're really smart and reliable. And you'll look good in the apron," I added, "because it's green . . . Nature Girl."

We both laughed.

SATURDAY MORNING BEFORE Memorial Day the excitement was at a fever pitch in the new store. Laurel and I ran around, scrambling to help customers and keep the shelves stocked. Rose stayed for the day, too, helping the cooks and popping out of the kitchen frequently to talk to people she knew. The store was packed with customers all day long. I tried to keep track of how much stuff we were selling—half a dozen bottles of raspberry vinegar, pounds and pounds of Mom's fresh salads, cooking utensils, gourmet salsas and chutneys in pretty jars, fresh-baked scones and brownies, dish towels, cookbooks—but after a couple of hours I lost track. All I knew was that we didn't have a quiet moment, and when six o'clock came, there were still people in the store, so we stayed open an extra twenty minutes.

When the front door was finally shut and locked, Sarah started cleaning up the kitchen, and the rest of us collapsed out front. Rose literally lay down flat on her back on the rug.

"What a day!" Laurel said. Hitting a few buttons on the computerized cash register, Hal came up with the grand total of the day's receipts. When he said the number out loud, we all screeched.

"Are we going to be rich, rich, rich beyond our wildest dreams?" I asked my mother.

Mom laughed. "This was just the first day," she reminded me, "and it's a holiday weekend. We'll have to see how the rest of the summer goes. But we made twice what I expected we would!"

With a grunt Rose got up from the floor. "If Daisy were here, she'd say you'd hit a home run, Mom. I think this calls for a celebration. Let's eat."

"Let's go out," Mom said with a grin. "I think we've had enough of our own cooking for the day."

Ten

FOR THE NEXT couple of weeks the scene at Potluck wasn't as crazy as it had been over Memorial Day weekend, but business was still lively. The shop was a success by any measure.

I found that I really liked working with Laurel. One day, after taking care of a customer who wanted a pound of tabbouleh and half a dozen lemon squares, Laurel came out from behind the counter and helped me unpack a crate of our old neighbor Sue Smith's homemade jams and jellies. "I like this shop, don't you?" I asked Laurel.

She nodded. "Everything's so appealing. No wonder people can't come in here and buy just one thing. Mrs. Smith's jams are selling really well."

"I think it's great that Mom's selling a lot of local stuff."

"Me too," Laurel agreed.

"So, who gets the first lunch break today?" I asked. She and I had been taking turns.

"I don't mind waiting," she answered.

I got to my feet. "I'll head out, then."

"Where are you going?"

"Probably the bookstore. How about you?"

"I think I'll run up and get Snickers and then take a quick walk in the park," Laurel said. "That's the only thing I don't like about working here—being cooped up inside all day."

"See you later," I said as I headed out the door.

I'd been spending most of my lunch breaks at Harbor Light Books since it was right across the street. Daniel worked there, and he always had some new book to recommend to me, and I'd write down the title so I could look for it at the library. If I found something I just had to own, he'd pretend he was buying it for himself so he could give me his employee discount. Some days I went to visit Seth; he worked down by the beach, at a surf shop. They sold cool sunglasses and stuff, and Seth said that being near the ocean was like "standing beside the muse." But I didn't feel like going to see him today.

I jogged up to the Down East News and Drugstore to buy a candy bar. Back at Harbor Light Books, I paused outside to look at the window display and then sailed in, ready to greet Daniel with a smile. Instead Mr. Ballard, the elderly guy, was behind the cash register. "Hi, Mr. Ballard," I said. "Is Daniel around?"

"He just headed out on his lunch break," Mr. Ballard answered, adjusting his bifocals.

"Oh." My smile faded. "Do you know when he'll be back?"

"He's usually gone for an hour."

We only took half-hour breaks at Potluck. I won't see him today, I realized, strangely disappointed. Not that it should matter. I could look at books just as well without him. "Thanks, Mr. Ballard," I said. "I'll just browse around." It was odd to realize that I'd been counting on seeing Daniel.

I wandered up and down the aisles for a few minutes, then headed back outside to the sidewalk without buying anything. The bookstore wasn't nearly as much fun without Daniel there to joke around with.

I still had twenty minutes left in my break, but it wasn't really enough time to run to the surf shop. Or maybe it was. But hanging out with Seth isn't all that relaxing, I admitted to myself. He'd want to read me some of the indecipherable poetry he wrote when he wasn't selling Teva sandals and Bollé glasses. Or we'd have to rehash our analysis of the plot of the obscure foreign movie we'd rented the night before. Plus I wasn't wearing black today—I'd thrown on a flowered shirt and pink shorts. *And* I'd forgotten my glasses.

Instead I went back to Potluck to eat my yogurt and then check the display case to see if there were any lemon squares too crumbly to sell to customers.

DANIEL CALLED A couple of nights later. "Sorry I missed you at the store the other day," he said.

"It wasn't a big deal," I assured him, in case he could somehow sense that at the time I'd been bummed.

"Are you writing these days?" he asked.

"I'm totally blocked," I said with a gloomy sigh.

"Really?"

"Really. I sit down with paper and pencil, but nothing happens. I've tried some different things—writing first thing in the morning, writing during my lunch hour, writing before bedtime, listening to music, eating a snack while I write, taking my notebook to the park—but nothing works."

"Why don't we get together and do writing exercises like we used to for Mrs. Cobb's class?"

"You and me?"

"Yeah." He hesitated. "Unless you don't want to. Maybe you'd rather do something like that with Seth."

"Seth informed me yesterday that he's not trying out for Mrs. Cobb's class. He's 'grown beyond it.'"

Daniel laughed. "Not me, man."

"Okay, sure, let's do it," I said. "How about this weekend?"

We picked a time to meet at his house. To be honest, I couldn't wait. Just because I wanted to get back to writing, of course.

In my bedroom I sat down at the desk with a narrow-ruled legal pad and a new mechanical pencil. I put the lead to the paper, but my hand didn't move. Write a story about anything, I told myself. It doesn't have to be brilliant. You don't have to make people laugh.

Five minutes later I gave up with a sigh. No story had materialized—not even the first sentence of one. I turned on my laptop, figuring I could at least write in my journal. I never get blocked writing in my journal.

Five minutes later the screen was still blank. I turned off my computer and got up from the desk. The sun had set. Standing at the window, I stared down at Main Street. As I watched, the streetlights came on one by one. My room was still dark, though, and so was my mood.

If I'm a writer, then how come I can't write? I wondered. I didn't like to admit it, but I was counting on Daniel's help.

Eleven

ON SATURDAY, I drove my stepfather's Subaru to Daniel's house—his family lives a couple of miles inland. I parked it in the driveway and ran to the porch so I wouldn't get soaked.

Just as Daniel was opening the door, a bolt of lightning zig-zagged across the charcoal sky. A few seconds later we heard the crack and boom of thunder. "Come inside," Daniel advised, "before you get electrocuted."

I'd never been to his house. "This is nice," I said as he walked me down the hall to the den. "Is it old?"

"Nineteen-ten or something like that."

"We used to live in an old house." I stopped to look at a family portrait on the wall. "Is that *you?*"

I pointed to a little kid with buck teeth and a carrot-colored crew cut. Daniel groaned. "Don't remind me, okay?

I'm always after my parents to take that down, but they think it's cute."

"Are your folks home?" I asked. "Can I meet them?"

"They went to the hardware store," Daniel answered. "They should be back before you leave."

"How about your brother and sister?" From the picture it looked like Daniel was the middle child.

"My big sister's in summer session at Dartmouth," Daniel said, "and my little brother's at sailing camp."

"My sister went to Dartmouth," I said. "Daisy. The one who died."

Daniel nodded. "I think I knew that."

We didn't speak as we walked into the den and sat down on the couch. Suddenly I shivered.

"Are you cold?" Daniel asked. "I could get you a sweatshirt or something."

I shook my head. "That's okay. It was just . . . weather like this always gets me down. Storms and rainy nights can be pretty bad luck."

Daniel's forehead creased. "I'm sorry I reminded you about your sister. That must make you really sad."

"Sometimes," I admitted. Bending over to hide the tears that were gathering in my eyes, I pulled a notebook from my backpack. "Should we start writing?" I asked, taking a deep breath to regain my composure.

Daniel must have sensed that I didn't really want to talk. "Yes, let's write," he said.

We sat at opposite ends of the sofa, sitting sideways facing each other with our feet up on the cushions and our notebooks propped against our knees. "Let's try some warm-up exercises," Daniel suggested. "How about I give you a topic to write a paragraph about and you give me one? Then we can read our paragraphs out loud."

"Okay." Lightning flashed and thunder rumbled, closer together this time. "Why don't you write about learning how to ride a bicycle?"

"And you write about a visit to the orthodontist."

We wrote our paragraphs, then read them to each other. They were pretty good—full of concrete detail, the way Mrs. Cobb liked them. "Let's do another one," I suggested.

"All right." Daniel gave me a mischievous smile. "This time write about your most embarrassing moment."

I laughed. "Are you kidding?"

"Absolutely not."

"You really want to hear about the time I—"

"No, no," he interrupted, "just write it."

"Okay, then *you* write about your first kiss."

Daniel turned a little red, and I thought he was going to confess that he'd never kissed anyone. Instead he said, "You asked for it!"

I giggled as I wrote my paragraph. Daniel was grinning, too. "You read first," he said.

"Okay." I cleared my throat. "'Picture the scene,'" I began. "'The junior high gymnasium. Songs from the *Grease* soundtrack blast through the crowded room. It's the seventh-grade sock hop. I'm wearing a pink poodle skirt and a fuzzy white cardigan buttoned up backward and my very first bra.'"

Daniel laughed pretty hard when I got to the part about Noelle spilling punch all over my sweater while I was jitter-bugging with Jamie Buckingham and Jamie trying to dry me off by pawing my chest with a paper towel. "Let's hear yours," I said when I was through.

Daniel smiled wryly. "Actually, now that I think about it, my first kiss could also qualify as my most embarrassing moment."

"Doesn't everyone's?" I said reassuringly.

He cleared his throat. "Okay. Here goes."

Daniel's first kiss was at the beginning of ninth grade with Martha Cabot. "Martha Cabot?" I exclaimed. Martha's kind of pretty, but she's about six feet tall. "How did you reach her lips?"

"This is hard enough as it is," Daniel said. "Don't inter-rupt me."

Covering my mouth with my hand so I wouldn't laugh, I let him finish. He and Martha had been working on the school yearbook together, and one day in the darkroom she'd put the moves on him. Daniel had been so surprised, he'd knocked over a basin of developer.

"That's terrible," I sympathized. I couldn't bump his shoulder because of the way we were sitting, so I nudged his bare foot with mine. "You know what, though? I don't think it should count. Your first kiss should be one you were psyched about. Write another paragraph."

644   The Year I Turned Sixteen

"You write about yours, then," Daniel said.

Instead of writing, I clasped my notebook to my chest, "I was in eighth grade," I recalled. "I kissed Sam Lovejoy at Alyssa Chamberlain's Halloween party."

Daniel hugged his notebook, too. "Okay, so I guess my first *real* kiss was with Debbie DeBernardo. I took her to the Christmas dance when we were freshmen."

Debbie had moved away sophomore year—Ohio or someplace like that. "Did you guys date? Did you like her?"

"She was nice," Daniel said. "We weren't a couple, though."

"Have you ever been a couple with anyone?" I asked.

Daniel blushed a little. "I guess not."

I nudged his foot again. "That's okay. Being a couple isn't always all it's cracked up to be."

"I figure it'll happen when it happens." Daniel looked at me. I'd never really noticed how blue his eyes were. "When the right person comes along."

"That's absolutely the right attitude," I said, trying to sound like I didn't have any doubts.

But Daniel never misses a trick. "Is that how it is with you and Seth?" He was still looking at me intently. "He's the right person?"

"I don't know. I guess so." For some reason I didn't want to talk about Seth. "Back to Debbie D. Was she your dream girl?"

"Not really. She wasn't imaginative enough. What about Jamie Buckingham? Are you still heartbroken that things didn't work out with him?"

I giggled. "Yeah, right. He had the worst taste in clothes! His socks always clashed with his pants."

"What a crime," Daniel kidded.

"Well, it matters to me," I said. "I can't help it."

"Do *I* pass the fashion test?" he asked.

I checked out his faded navy polo shirt and rumpled khakis. "You're conservative, but yes. You match."

"Good."

"Okay, I have another one for you," I said. My knees were getting stiff from being bent, so I stretched my right leg out along the edge of the sofa. My foot was next to Daniel's hip but not touching him. "I've heard about your first kiss. What was your *best* kiss?"

Daniel lifted his eyes to the ceiling. "What's happening here? We're not even writing. It's like truth or dare or something."

"It's fun," I said. "Isn't it?"

"Kind of." He thought for a while, then smiled crookedly. He'd put his notebook down, and now he folded his arms across his chest. He has a decent body, I found myself noticing. Not as skinny as I thought. "I don't think I've had my best kiss yet," he said. "I'm still waiting for it. What about you?"

"Has to be my first kiss with Seth," I said, but suddenly I wasn't so sure. *Was* that my best kiss? Or was I still waiting, too?

While we'd been talking, lightning and thunder had continued to flicker and rumble while rain lashed the windowpanes. Daniel's house seemed to be right in the middle of the storm. Now, all at once, there was a brilliant flash at the window, accompanied by a resounding boom. Instantly the lights went out.

I let out a startled squeak.

"There goes the power," Daniel observed.

"I hope it doesn't start a fire or anything."

"Don't worry. Our power's always going out. There are too many trees around here with branches leaning on the lines. Should I light a candle?"

"If you want."

He didn't move, though. We stared at each other in the dim light. We were still sitting on the couch, and now he put a hand on my bare ankle, the one that was closest to him. I nudged his toes with my other foot. The room seemed full of electricity; a serious shiver ran up my spine. "Lily," Daniel said softly.

"Don't say anything," I whispered.

I'm not sure what possessed me. Maybe it was all that talk about the perfect kiss and the sudden convenient darkness. Maybe it was just something I'd subconsciously wanted to do for a long time. Anyway, I shifted on the couch, getting on my knees so I could reach over and rest my hands on Daniel's shoulders. Then I kissed him.

If he was surprised, he didn't act it. He grasped my waist in his hands and kissed me right back. With the storm rumbling around us, we kept on kissing. And it was a *great* kiss. Possibly the best kiss ever.

* * *

L AUREL, I NEED to make a confession," I told my sister that
night.

"What do I look like, a priest?" she joked.

The two of us had gone out for pizza because Mom and
Hal were at a dinner party. Now I looked over my shoulder to
double check that there was nobody I knew in Pizza Bowl to
overhear this. "I kissed a guy," I said, lowering my voice. "A
guy who wasn't Seth."

Laurel raised her eyebrows. "Interesting."

"Interesting? It's awful. It's cheating! I cheated on my
boyfriend." I clapped a hand over my mouth. "Oh no! What if
someone heard me say that?"

"No one heard," Laurel assured me. "Just tell me what
happened."

I gave her a brief sketch of my afternoon at Daniel's,
including the abrupt ending: His parents had gotten home
from the hardware store and, despite the storm, I'd taken off
like I'd been shot from a cannon. "I don't know what came
over me," I concluded. "There must have been some weird
charge in the air from the storm."

"Maybe you like him," Laurel said, reaching for another
slice of pizza.

"Sure, I like him, but I don't *like* him."

"Why not?" She'd met him a couple of times. "He seems
like a neat guy to me."

"Well, first of all, he's not as good-looking as Seth," I told
Laurel. "I mean, Daniel's just average."

"So?" she said. "Looks don't mean everything."

"You can afford to say that because Carlos is a total stud."

Laurel shrugged. "He's cute, but that's incidental. I fell for him because we bonded over stuff. We care about the same things. We look at the world in the same way."

I thought about it. What kinds of things did Seth and I bond over? What did he care about? His clothes, his reputation . . . "Wait a minute," I said, confused. "Let's get back to the cheating thing. I'm going out with Seth. I shouldn't be kissing another guy no matter *who* he is."

"That's true," Laurel agreed, "but you can't go back in time and undo it, so you might as well try to understand why it happened. Why *did* it?"

I thought back. "Well, we were just having this really fun time writing and talking, and after a while it got personal. And our feet were touching." I told Laurel about how we were sitting on the couch. "Then I started to get this tingly feeling, like I was more aware of him physically. And it's not that Daniel and I see things in the exact same way, like you and Carlos. We disagree a lot. But we have fun arguing."

"Well, let's talk about Seth," Laurel suggested. "Do you and he have fun talking?"

"Yeah, sure," I said.

"What do you talk about?"

"You name it. We're *always* talking about intellectual things. And we talk about other people. We're sarcastic together."

"Is that enough?" Laurel asked.

I stared at her. "What do you mean?"

"I mean, does it make you happy? Maybe you kissed Daniel because there's something missing in your relationship with Seth."

I wrinkled my forehead. "How could there be? Seth's gorgeous and cool, and Daniel's not."

Laurel shrugged again. "You're the one who kissed Daniel, not me."

We finished our pizza in silence.

Walking to the car in the parking lot, I asked Laurel, "So what do I do now?"

"You mean about the guys?"

"Yeah."

"I guess you either stay with Seth because you like him best and write the other thing off as a fluke, or you break up with Seth and possibly explore something new with Daniel."

"Well, which?"

Laurel laughed. "*You* have to decide, Lil. I can't figure out your feelings for you. Believe me, it's hard enough most of the time figuring out my own."

We drove home, listening to the radio. Laurel was behind the wheel, so I stared out the window at the dark night woods and tried to decode my feelings. It was trickier than you might think. On the surface, it seemed like a no-brainer. I was dating Seth Modine, and in the world of Hawk Harbor, that was about as good as it gets. But if that was true, then why had I kissed Daniel . . . and why did I think that if I had the chance, I'd do it again?

*   *   *

I'M COMPLETELY CONFUSED *about my love life,"* I typed in my journal early Tuesday evening. *"I'm avoiding Seth and Daniel—I just can't deal with either of them right now. Seth wanted to come over tonight, but I lied and told him I have a fever. Daniel must've been as flipped out as I was about our kiss on Saturday during the thunderstorm. He hasn't called to talk about writing or anything else. And I'm not sure how I feel about that. Maybe I'll try writing a story so that if he calls, we'll have something to talk about besides us."*

I put away my computer and got out a pad of paper and a mechanical pencil. Moving my desk chair over by my bed, I sat with my feet propped on the mattress and my face turned to the view through the window of the harbor in the last light of a clear summer day. "What should I write about?" I asked a sailboat with a deep green hull. My heart was so full—I wanted just to pour it out onto the page. I clicked my pencil and began scribbling, but when I saw the first two words I'd written, I stopped. *"Dear Daisy . . ."*

I tossed my notebook and pencil on the bed and hugged my knees to my chin, rocking myself and crying. "I miss you so much right now, Daze," I whispered. "I've never felt this alone before."

I looked out the window again, my eyes blurry with tears. The green sailboat was at its mooring now, and its sails were being reefed for the night. I didn't feel Daisy's presence—I felt alone, more alone than I'd ever felt in my entire life.

Twelve

I WAS DRYING my hands on a dish towel when the phone rang. Laurel and I had just cleaned up from dinner. I picked up the receiver. "Hello?"

"Lily? It's Daniel."

"Hi, Daniel," I said. I shot a glance at Laurel. "What's up?"

"I thought maybe we could get together. Just to talk."

"You mean tonight? Right now?"

"Yeah, if you're free. I'll buy you an ice-cream cone," he offered.

"Okay," I agreed. "Meet you at the Corner Ice Cream Shoppe in half an hour."

I hung up the phone. "You made a date with Daniel?" Laurel guessed.

"Ice cream doesn't count as a date," I said. "But we *are* going to 'talk.'"

"What are you going to say to him?" my sister asked.

I heaved a troubled sigh. "I have no idea."

I was on the way out the door to meet Daniel when the phone rang again. This time when I picked it up, I heard another very familiar male voice. "Lily, I haven't seen you in days," Seth said.

"It's been kind of busy here."

"Let's go out and you can tell me about it."

I hesitated. Since I didn't know what I was going to say to Daniel, I didn't know how long our nondate would take. But I probably needed to "talk" to Seth, too. "Why don't we meet in an hour?" I suggested. "By the surf shop—we can take a walk on the beach."

"See you there."

As I walked down the street to the ice-cream place, I struggled to understand my emotions. They were all over the map. What do you want, Lily Rebecca Walker? I asked myself. Did I want to stay with Seth? I liked being his girlfriend well enough, but was well enough *enough?* Now that a few months had passed, the initial thrill had worn off a little. I still found him incredibly attractive, but I had to be honest with myself. His friends were starting to get on my nerves. They were cool, but they never had any fun. Seth was smart, but even so, our relationship didn't have a whole lot of depth.

Still, everybody at South Regional will think I'm crazy if I break up with Seth to go out with Daniel, I thought. It will blow my whole image. My image. That phrase stopped me. I'd been cultivating this image the whole year since I'd turned sixteen. The black clothes, the too-cool-to-care cynicism, the anything-for-a-laugh poems and stories. Now I touched the rectangular glasses perching on my nose. I was tired of them and everything they symbolized.

Maybe it's time to ditch the image, I thought. Maybe other people's opinions have nothing to do with this. Maybe I need to do what's right for me.

Outside the Corner Ice Cream Shoppe, I paused. I saw Daniel inside, sitting at one of the little wrought iron tables. He didn't see me, though—he was looking up at the list of flavors posted on the wall—so I had an extra minute to think. For a few seconds I was overcome with longing. I wanted to muss Daniel's rumpled auburn hair with my fingers and have him say sweetly comforting, encouraging words. Daniel, who'd liked me, I realized now, since the winter day we became writing partners.

But even while half of me wanted to fling myself in Daniel's arms, the other half panicked. I got a nervous, sick feeling in my stomach. I can't do it, I thought. I couldn't break up with Seth and start fresh with Daniel or anybody. Things had been going so well for me—was I really ready to throw it all away?

I pushed open the door and a bell jingled. Daniel turned around. "Hi, Lily," he said, his cheeks getting kind of pink.

"Daniel, I'm not really hungry for ice cream," I said. "Can we just take a walk instead?"

"Sure."

We headed outside and turned down a quiet side street. I started talking before Daniel could say anything that would end up making us both feel worse than we were bound to feel, anyway. "Daniel, after this . . . I can't see you again."

There was a pause. "Oh," he said finally.

I looked at him. He was staring straight ahead, his jaw clenched. "I'm sorry," I went on quickly. "I know the other day it must have seemed like I . . . had feelings for you. But I don't. Kissing you was a mistake. I'm still Seth's girl-friend."

"I see."

"You do?"

"Yeah, it's pretty clear," Daniel said simply. "I made a mistake, too. I thought you could see beyond the superficial stuff. But I was wrong. Sorry I'm not cool enough for you, Lily."

His voice was full of pain, and my heart ached. I hated hurting him, especially because I knew that *he* would never hurt *me* like this.

He'd turned sharply around to walk back to town. "Daniel, wait," I called after him. I couldn't take back my words, but I wanted to make things better somehow. "It's not like that. I swear."

He didn't wait, though. And I wasn't so sure that it wasn't "like that."

I stood on the sidewalk, watching him go. My eyes were dry; it's possible, I'd learned lately, to be too sad to cry.

I checked my watch. I still had some time to kill before my beach date with Seth. My talk with Daniel—our last, I guessed—had taken a lot less than an hour.

* * *

T HE NEXT DAY during my lunch break I rode my bike to Mrs. Cobb's house. I was hoping she wouldn't be home, so I could just stick the envelope in her mailbox, but when I rang the bell, she came to the door. "Lily, hi," she said with a warm smile. "Are you submitting a manuscript for the writing class?"

I nodded. "I didn't write much all summer, but last night for some reason I got motivated." After finishing my journal entry, I'd stayed up until midnight writing a tragicomic story about a teenage girl who gets amnesia after a bizarre electrolysis accident.

"Well, you're just in time," Mrs. Cobb told me. "I'm almost done reading the submissions. I'll be able to let you know in a couple of days whether you'll have a spot in the class."

"Not much chance, huh?" I asked glumly.

"There's a perfectly good chance."

"But you don't even really like my writing."

"That's not true," Mrs. Cobb said. "I think you have a vibrant, colorful imagination and a rich vocabulary." She gave my envelope a shake. "I'll look forward to reading what's in here."

"Well . . . thanks." I kicked at a loose brick on the walkway. "Did, um, Daniel Levin try out for the class?"

"Yes, along with about thirty others, including you."

"Thirty?" I gulped. "For a class of fifteen?"

She nodded.

I said good-bye to Mrs. Cobb and rode my bike back to town. With that much competition I didn't have a prayer of getting into the writing class. It was hard not to care, even though I tried.

TOWARD THE END of summer Laurel and Mom started having whispery conversations that they'd cut short the moment I entered the room. I had no idea what was brewing until the weekend Carlos came up from Tufts for a visit.

Carlos was cheerful with the rest of us, but I couldn't help picking up on some extremely tense vibes between him and Laurel. After lunch one Sunday, Mom went up to her room for a rest, and Laurel and Carlos ducked into the family room. They didn't close the door all the way, so naturally I took this as an open invitation to eavesdrop.

"I can't believe you're dropping out," Carlos said to Laurel.

My eyes widened. Dropping out?

"I'm not dropping out," Laurel countered. "I'm taking time off. That's a completely different thing."

"How is it different?" Carlos asked. "It sounds the same to me."

"I'll go back for spring semester," she told him, "or next fall at the latest. I won't lose that much time. I just need to get my head together. And my mom needs me—the store is only starting to get off the ground."

"Of course you want to help your mom," Carlos said, his tone softening. "But I'm worried that you're using the store as an excuse because you were bummed about your grades last year. I'm worried that taking time off will make it easier not to go back at all."

Laurel was quiet for a minute. I held my breath, waiting for her response. "I don't think I'm looking for an excuse," she said at last. "I don't feel like I'm wimping out. I just feel like I don't know what I want right now. Can you accept that?"

Carlos must have given her the kind of answer that doesn't require words because the room fell silent. I tiptoed away. That's the big secret, then, I thought. Laurel's taking time off from college to help Mom. It was hard for me to see that as a problem. As far as I was concerned, it would be great to have my sister around a while longer. What about me, though? Why did Mom need Laurel's help so badly? Wasn't *I* good for anything?

Thirteen

THE NEXT NIGHT Laurel and I talked about my new work schedule. She was practically running Potluck now, with Hal's help—he'd cut back his accounting practice so he could be more involved with Mom's businesses. Mom was focused on the catering end.

Since school was about to start, Laurel had me down for just the Saturday shift. "I could do more, you know," I told her.

"Let's see how it goes," she replied. "With college interviews and applications and the creative-writing workshop on top of everything else, you'll be pretty busy."

I'd gotten into Mrs. Cobb's writing class—that had been a pretty nice surprise. Mickey had gotten in, too, and I was glad I'd have an excuse to see her more. Other than that, for the first time in my life I wasn't that psyched about a new school year.

Seth picked me up on Monday morning. As we drove along, Seth cranked the volume on the jazz station. I stared out the window.

The lobby of South Regional was packed with excited bodies. Everybody was talking a mile a minute, laughing, shouting. Seth waded into the mob with all the confidence of a senior.

I trailed after him as he greeted his friends and bumped right into him when he stopped abruptly. "Who's that?" he asked, staring.

I followed his gaze. A girl I'd never seen before was standing at the foot of the big staircase. She was pencil thin with very short, black hair, pale skin, and huge doe eyes. Her mouth was a dramatic slash of dark lipstick. "I don't know," I said.

Rico loomed up behind us. "Simona van der Wilde," he reported into Seth's ear. "Sophomore. Just moved here."

"Simona van der Wilde?" I couldn't help giggling.

"Hmmm," Seth murmured.

I didn't pay much attention to Simona van der Wilde. Maybe I should have. Four days later, after school on Friday, Seth took me for a drive.

And dumped me.

"I'm really sorry, Lily," he said. We were parked near the lighthouse. "I don't know how it happened. There's just this intense spiritual and intellectual connection between me and Simona. And you and me . . . it's not there anymore. I want to get to know her better, and I'm not about to go behind your back."

"Oh," I said, stunned. Seth was watching me, and I felt like I should show some emotion—start screaming or crying or hitting him or something. But I didn't feel anything except an absurd desire to laugh. Spiritual and intellectual connection? I'm sure! "Wow."

"If you ever need a friend, I'll still be there for you, okay?" Seth traced my cheekbone with a gentle finger.

"Okay."

Seth hugged me. "I knew you'd be objective about this. Thanks."

We headed back to town. Seth stopped in front of my building. Before I got out of the car, he leaned over and kissed me on the cheek. "Take care of yourself, Lily."

"I will."

I stepped out onto the curb. Then after Seth drove off, I experienced a major delayed reaction. It's over, I thought, tears springing to my eyes. We broke up. And because of someone named Simona van der Wilde!

As I walked up to the apartment, though, I knew it wasn't totally Simona's fault. Seth was right—he and I hadn't been clicking for a while. At least he'd been honest about wanting to date someone new.

I dumped my book bag on the floor in the front hall and shuffled into the kitchen. There was a plate of Potluck brownies on the counter—I helped myself to one, along with a glass of milk. I was sitting at the table with my snack, trying to take Seth's picture out of my locket, when Mom came in, wearing a bathrobe. "What's up?" she asked.

I dug at the little photo with my fingernail, and it finally popped out. "Gotcha," I declared.

Mom sat down next to me and watched me tear the tiny picture to shreds. "Did you and Seth have a fight?"

I told her about Simona. "It's not like it was a match made in heaven," I said, sniffling. "But we were a *couple.* I could depend on that. Now I'm on my own again."

Mom patted my shoulder. "I know what it's like. Even when you've outgrown a relationship, it always hurts to say good-bye to someone you've cared about."

"I hadn't necessarily *outgrown* the relationship," I said. "No?"

We sat in silence for a minute. I kept sniffling and Mom kept rubbing my shoulder. "Well, maybe I had, a little," I conceded. "It wasn't working, anyway."

"You know what I think?" Mom said. "Remember when you were younger, you were always going through phases? Well, I think Lily Walker is about to enter a new phase."

I looked at her with my arms folded. "A new phase. Great," I groaned.

Mom laughed. "What's wrong with that? Why should you have to stick to just one?"

"Because I felt like I'd finally settled down," I said. "People knew who I was. It's like how it was for Daisy."

"Daisy?" Mom said, puzzled.

"Daisy had her act together," I explained. "She was in control of her destiny. She knew what she was good at, and she knew what she wanted to accomplish, and people liked and admired her for it. Nothing bothered her," I added. "She was so strong."

Mom shook her head. "No one loved Daisy more than I did, but she was *not* perfect."

"I didn't say she was *perfect,*" I said. "Well . . . maybe."

"Daisy went through phases, too," Mom reminded me. "Remember when *she* was sixteen? She tore those ligaments in her knee and had to sit out soccer *and* basketball seasons. She had a hard time finding the right way to mourn your father. And I—all of us—were putting too much pressure on her always to be strong, cheerful Daisy."

"She kind of went wild," I recalled. It was true. But she'd gotten over it and come out stronger.

"She went through a phase," Mom said. "And do you know what?"

"What?"

"If she were alive today, chances are she'd be going through some other phase."

"I don't think so." I pictured the photograph on my desk. "Not Daisy."

"Yes," Mom insisted. "It could have been anything. She might have decided she was tired of sports. Maybe she would have spent her junior year abroad or taken time off from college altogether for some reason, like Laurel. She might have changed her mind about being premed and decided to be a teacher or a banker or an . . . an astrologer instead."

I laughed.

"My point is, Lil, we *all* evolve. It never stops. Daisy might seem unchanging and somehow larger than life because you remember her as she was at nineteen, and that's all we'll ever know for sure. She didn't *get* to live out her life. But if she had, I guarantee there would have been some surprises in it."

I looked at my mother. There were lines etched around her large blue eyes—lines she had earned caring for me and my sisters, and starting a business, and learning to be independent—but they were warm and beautiful eyes.

Suddenly I knew whose picture I wanted to put in my locket. I wanted a picture of Mom, as she was right at this moment. She held out her arms to hug me, and I rested my head on her shoulder. "Thanks, Mom," I whispered.

IT WAS UNBELIEVABLE how fast the It crowd dropped me after I stopped dating Seth. "Easy come, easy go," I said to Mickey and Noelle one day at lunch in the school cafeteria.

"Who needs them?" Noelle declared loyally. I couldn't believe how nice they were being. After all, I hadn't treated them that well last spring. But as Noelle had said the night I called to tell her that Seth and I broke up, "Good friends know how to forgive and forget."

I cast a glance at a table halfway across the cafeteria. I was trying not to get bummed out about the spectacle of my ex sharing a chair and a cappuccino with Simona van der Wilde.

Unwrapping my tuna salad sandwich, I said in my noblest tone, "I don't really hold a grudge. I hope they'll be very happy together."

Mickey and Noelle stared at me for a second, then burst out laughing. I had to laugh, too. "Yeah, right!" they said.

We finished our sandwiches, treating ourselves to candy

bars from the vending machine on our way out of the cafeteria. "You know, there is at least one good thing about you and Seth breaking up," Mickey commented as we walked down the hall toward our lockers.

"What?" I asked.

"You're wearing fun clothes again instead of all that basic black."

I looked down at my outfit: rainbow-striped tights and a red jumper. At breakfast that morning Laurel had told me I looked a little like Ronald McDonald. Best of all, I'd tossed out those glasses.

The previous winter and spring I'd created a new persona for myself: I was the girl who entertained people with her sarcasm and who dressed like a chic but colorless waif. By summertime I hadn't really wanted to be that Lily Walker anymore, but I was stuck with her because she was the one who was dating Seth Modine. Now I was free again to be whoever I wanted to be.

Which brought me back to the same old dilemma. Who am I? What kind of stories do I want to write?

That night at home I tried to work on my creative-writing assignment. The topic was to write a story based on an epigram, like "forgive and forget" or "make hay while the sun shines," but as usual lately I was totally blocked. *"Make hay, make hay,"* I scribbled over and over in my notebook. *"Forgive and forget, forgive and forget, forgive and forget."*

I wanted to call up Daniel like in the old days, but we weren't really speaking much even though he had to know

I wasn't seeing Seth any longer. He was taking Mrs. Cobb's class, too, and he was polite to me, but that was about it.

I thought about writing the kind of story I'd churned out for class all last spring, but I couldn't bring myself to do it. That had never been my real voice, whatever my real voice was. And Mrs. Cobb had told me she let me into the class because I had potential and she wanted me to discover it. I owed it to her to try.

I sat on my bed for a minute, gazing pensively into space. My window was open, and a mild September breeze stirred the curtain. Suddenly I found myself remembering the day Mom, Rose, and I had climbed up to the attic to look for old baby clothes. Mom had found my great-grandmother's diaries. What had she said? "Maybe they'll give you some ideas for stories. . . ."

Hopping off the bed, I walked over to my closet. I'd stuck the cardboard box under a pile of old sweaters. Now I moved the sweaters aside and reached into the box, pulling out a small, leather-bound volume.

I opened it up. Flora Elizabeth White had written her name, the place, and the date on the inside cover in a cursive as flowery as her name. People really shouldn't read other people's diaries, even if they *have* been dead twenty years, I thought, but I turned to the first entry, anyway.

"My dear Diary and Friend," Flora wrote. *"Today is my sixteenth birthday. Sixteen! Doesn't that sound old? We're celebrating with ice cream— my little brother Billy will have to turn the handle all by himself—and a picnic by the sea. I'll wear my new bathing dress, which shows quite a bit of leg . . . sure to*

scandalize this buttoned-up town! Do you suppose that now that I'm a grown woman, Mama and Papa will allow me to receive suitors as they did Eleanor when she turned sixteen? I know Simon Walker is dying to pay me a call!"

Four pages later Flora's tone grew more serious. *"It is as we feared, Diary. As you know, my sister Eleanor's health hasn't been good for some time. Last week the doctor made the dreaded diagnosis: galloping consumption— tuberculosis. Since then Eleanor seems to fade more each day. I worry that she's giving up hope. We must believe she'll be cured! How could I go on if she were taken from me?"*

I almost couldn't believe what I was reading. It seemed so immediate, so present. It's exactly like what I went through losing Daisy, I thought. I turned the page quickly. I had to find out. What would happen to Eleanor? Would she be all right?

There was an entry dated a month later. *"Mother and Eleanor left yesterday on the train, heading west to Arizona, where they'll stay two months. It's hard to be separated from my only sister, but maybe it's for the best. I need to learn to be less reliant on her and more reliant on myself. But it's difficult, Diary. She's not just my sister; she's my dearest friend."*

I found myself nodding as I read. Yes, I thought. I know exactly what you mean.

Flora continued, describing the reason for the trip. *"The doctor says a dry climate is the best thing for Eleanor's condition and that the damp summer air in Hawk Harbor is terribly unhealthy. I took a walk by the sea this afternoon, waiting for Papa to return on his fishing boat, and it's very hard for me to believe that the salty breeze is anything but wholesome. But Dr. Lovejoy must know best, mustn't he?"*

On the next page Flora's mood lightened up. *"Simon Walker*

paid a call this evening. Didn't I tell you he would? He didn't enjoy himself as much as he might have, however, because Harding Quayle got here first. You should have seen me, Diary! Calmly mending Papa's fishing nets on the porch swing while Harding and Simon argued about politics. Two suitors in one evening! Harding is a better conversationalist, but I suspect that sometimes he speaks just to hear the sound of his own voice."

"Sounds familiar," I said aloud.

"Whereas Simon seems more thoughtful," Flora wrote. *"And I know I'm not supposed to judge a book by its cover, but Simon also happens to be the handsomest boy in Hawk Harbor."*

I couldn't stop reading. When I finished one volume, I dove immediately into the next. Flora's diary was better than a novel. There were so many ups and downs. Eleanor returned from Arizona, her health improved, only to die of scarlet fever a year later. The pages where Flora wrote about that were tear-stained and, reading about it, I cried, too. *"It's as if my heart has been torn from my body,"* Flora mourned. I knew exactly how she'd felt.

I kept reading. Flora's family survived hard times and easy ones. Simon kept on courting Flora even though there were always other guys hanging around, and he even got up his nerve to propose to her, but she turned him down.

"Why did you do that?" I exclaimed. "You *have* to marry him, Flora. He's my great-grandfather!"

Sure enough, after Simon went off and proposed to another girl (Dorothea Lovejoy, the doctor's daughter), Flora came to her senses and told him she *did* love him in a scene that poor Dorothea happened to witness, so needless to say, she broke up with Simon, who then reproposed to Flora, who finally said yes.

Flora's diaries covered it all: baptisms and funerals, blizzards and croquet games, tea parties and presidential elections. She liked clothes as much as I did and described what she wore on every occasion. I felt like I'd made a new friend.

It got a little less interesting after she had babies, though. Closing the diary, I put it on my shelf with the other volumes. "I'll finish reading this a few years down the road," I promised my great-grandmother, "when I can relate to it a little more. In the meantime maybe Rose would get into it!"

I sat at my window, looking out at Hawk Harbor in the moonlight. Flora's diaries had put a lot of things in new perspective, like my breakup with Seth. It was weird, thinking that the young woman who'd kept that journal had grown up and grown old and finally died. Weird, but natural. She coped, I thought. Life brought her bad as well as good, but more good than bad. She flourished even without her big sister around to take care of her. She had a long, interesting life.

A feeling of peace entered me. I decided I didn't want to write anything of my own just then—I wanted to absorb what I'd read.

What I'd learned.

Fourteen

"THOSE DIARIES SOUND cool. I *would* like to read them," Rose said.

It was early October, and Rose had come up for the weekend because some of her old Hawk Harbor friends had thrown her a baby shower on Saturday. After the party she, Laurel, and I were sitting on a park bench, enjoying the afternoon sunshine.

Rose placed a hand on her round belly. "Did Flora write anything about what it feels like to have a baby? You know, labor and delivery?"

I shook my head. "No details. She didn't even write that she was *pregnant*. All of a sudden the first baby just *appeared*."

"I guess people didn't talk about that stuff as much as we do nowadays," Rose mused.

"How does it feel?" Laurel asked, kind of shyly. "I mean, this part. *Before* the labor and delivery."

"Well, it feels like—," Rose began. Then she grabbed Laurel's hand and placed it on top of her sweatshirt where it was stretched over her stomach. "See for yourself."

They sat like that for a few seconds. Then Laurel's eyes widened. "Is that the *baby?*"

Rose laughed. "Yep."

"What's it doing?" I asked.

"Back flips!" Laurel said.

I took a turn. I felt something shaped like an elbow sticking up from Rose's abdomen. It swam from one side to the other. "It's like a horror movie," I said. *"Alien."*

"Gee, thanks," Rose said dryly.

"Isn't it incredible?" Laurel still looked amazed. "There's a *person* in there. A new person."

"I know." Rose nodded, suddenly solemn. "He or she is going to be the start of the next generation of our family."

We all thought about that for a while. "Wow," I said.

"Don't think I'm crazy," Rose went on, "but sometimes I get this eerie feeling. Like I'm a link between the past and the future. Some part of everybody is in me: Mom and Dad, my grandparents, my *great*-grandparents. And it's all going into this baby. He—she—*is* the future, but the past is in her, too."

"That's not only crazy, it's depressing," Laurel said.

Rose shifted position on the bench, then brushed a strand of blond hair off her forehead. "Why?"

"Don't you sometimes want to forget the past?" Laurel asked. "Or parts of it, anyway? It's not like we have the happiest family history."

"That's true," Rose admitted. "But you know what I think? We wouldn't be who we are without our past, even the painful parts. Even the mistakes we've made and the losses we've experienced. It's all part of who we are."

"I wish Daisy were here," I said softly.

Rose took my hand and pressed it. "Me too." Then she laughed. "How did this conversation get so cosmic?"

"If Daisy were here, she wouldn't let us just veg out like this," Laurel speculated. "She'd have you on your feet doing prenatal aerobics."

We all laughed. "Can you imagine?" Rose said, slumping more comfortably on the bench.

"Back to the past stuff," I said. "If Daisy were here—"

"But she *is* here," Rose interrupted. "She's always with us, in a way."

"What way?" I asked.

"Oh, I don't know." Rose thought. "Like when I'm sad about something or scared. I think about Daisy, and not because she had all the answers or anything like that. Not because she was brave, even though she was. I think about her because she loved me and I loved her. It's that simple. I think about *all* the people I love, especially you guys. That's what gets me through."

I looked at my sister, my eyes bright with tears. I wanted to tell Rose how much her words meant to me, but I couldn't speak. "It's all right, Lily," she said softly as she took my hand again. "You can remember Daisy any way you want. Just keep her with you."

I nodded.

Laurel was sniffling. "Can we be a little less heart wrenching?" she asked. "Before we all start bawling in the middle of the park?"

Rose smiled. "Okay, here's some news that will cheer you up. Guess what I've been working on?"

"What?" I asked.

"I cut a demo," she said. "An album!"

Laurel and I both shrieked. "An *album?*"

Rose nodded. "I wasn't going to tell you unless something came of it, but you might as well know so you can be rooting for me. This friend of mine who works at a recording studio got me some time there, and I recorded a bunch of songs. Stuff I wrote and covers. Just me with this guitarist—very bare bones. But people who've heard the tape really like it, so my agent's taking it around to a bunch of music industry people to see if anyone will give me a contract."

Laurel and I shrieked again.

Rose laughed. "Nothing's happened yet. Believe me, you'll be the first to know."

I patted Rose's stomach. "You should be very proud of your mommy, little Jane or David," I declared.

"It's not little Jane or David anymore," Rose said. "Stephen and I realized we weren't wild about those names."

"Who's it going to be, then?" Laurel asked.

"We still haven't decided." Rose's eyes grew dreamy. "All we know is that we want our perfect baby to have a perfect name."

"You've still got some time," I said. "You're not due for seven or eight weeks."

"Right," Rose agreed. "Plenty of time."

The next day after church Rose drove home to Boston. While Hal worked on the computer, Laurel did some reading, and Mom took a nap, I rode my bike to the cemetery with three small pots of gold and russet mums in the handlebar basket.

It had been a long time since I'd visited Dad's and Daisy's graves. I just got so busy when I was dating Seth and so into the whole It scene, and sitting in a cemetery talking to your dead sister would *not* have seemed cool to those people. Why did I ever care what they thought? I wondered now.

The graveyard was peaceful. Fallen leaves and cloud shadows danced among the headstones. I placed a flowerpot on Daisy's grave and another one on Dad's. "We miss you guys a lot," I said after a moment, "You watch over us, though, don't you?"

The only answer was the sound of a gray squirrel chattering on a fence rail. "I need to believe that you're still with me, Daze," I said, "the way Rose and Laurel and I were talking yesterday." A tear rolled down my face and dropped silently onto my sister's grave.

I sat right down on the short, golden grass and buried my face in my hands and cried. I cried about breaking up with Seth and losing Daniel's friendship, about Daisy, and about Dad. "I'll never grow up, will I?" I asked. "I'll always be the baby of the family."

That's when I felt it. It's not like I had a visitation or anything like that. I don't believe in ghosts. But all of a sudden I felt this presence. This love.

My sister's love.

Suddenly everything finally made sense because, paradoxically, I finally accepted that it never *would* make sense. That's life. It's not all wrapped up with a tidy bow—it's crazy and disorganized and unpredictable, and so are the people who live it. Growing up doesn't happen overnight—it takes years, decades, a whole lifetime.

I sat for a few more minutes, savoring this feeling. Then I got to my feet, touching Daisy's headstone lightly with my fingertips as I did so. "Thanks," I whispered.

Back at my bike, I remembered the third pot of mums. I picked it up and wandered back into the graveyard, looking for something in particular. Looking for some*one*.

I found her in the far northwest corner of the cemetery, her simple granite headstone in the shade of a red maple. Flora White Walker, it read. And there was Simon's stone, too, right next to hers.

I placed the flowers halfway between the two graves. "I feel like I know you," I told them softly, "even though we never met. You're part of me, like Rose was saying yesterday. I'm glad."

I pedaled back toward town. Instead of going straight home, though, I found myself cruising down Lighthouse Road.

When I got to my old driveway, I stopped. The Lilac Inn was still for sale. The grass in the front yard was overgrown, and the driveway was carpeted with leaves. I used to live here, I thought as I pushed my bike up the driveway and then propped it against the barn, so it's not *really* trespassing.

I never go anywhere without paper and pencil—there was a notepad in the bike's basket with a mechanical pencil stuck through the spiral wire. Sliding it into my back jeans pocket, I walked across the lawn to a grove of gnarled, ancient apple trees.

I plucked an apple from a low branch and dropped to the grass, sitting with my back against the tree's scratchy trunk. I rubbed the apple clean on my shirt and took a bite.

As I crunched the apple I gazed around the yard that used to be my playground when I was a child. It had been so long since we'd moved—almost eight years—but something about this autumn day, with its misty, earthy smells and ripe colors, made my memories feel vivid and fresh. Something about the conversations I'd had recently with my sisters and my mother, and reading Flora's journals, made the past feel very much alive.

Half closing my eyes, I pictured my younger self, dressed in various silly costumes—cowgirl, pirate, princess—and playing tricks on my big sisters. I remembered one fall day Daisy had spent hours raking up the leaves. I'd ticked off Rose by hanging her underwear and bras on the front porch railing when I knew one of her boyfriends was coming over, so she'd chased me around the yard, and we scattered the leaves all over the place. Laurel kept a bunch of wild animals in hutches by the barn, and I used to feed them Froot Loops because I knew that would make her mad. "We'd go to McCloskey's Farm to pick a pumpkin for Halloween," I reminisced out loud. "Dad helped me carve the best jack-o'-lanterns—one year we made a salty old fisherman with Dad's cap and a Popeye wink and a pipe in the corner of its mouth."

Right about then I got a really peculiar feeling. It was kind of like the one I'd felt at the cemetery—the presence—but even more intense. Voices and images and scents and textures rose up from deep inside me. I grabbed my notepad and flipped it open to the first blank sheet.

I couldn't write fast enough. I remembered conversations with Mom, games I'd played with my sisters, boat rides with Dad. I wrote down funny things and sad things, dialogue and description. That could be a story, I found myself thinking as I scribbled notes about the time I stole a pie Mom had just baked for a party and Noelle and I ate the whole thing and then got in huge trouble, or that, or that . . .

Later, back at home, I read over the things I'd written. Then I put my mechanical pencil to a clean sheet of narrow-ruled paper. I wrote five pages without stopping: a story in the form of an imagined conversation between me and my great-grandmother Flora Elizabeth White.

I knew it was good even before I turned it in on Tuesday. I guess that's how it is when you find your writer's voice—it's like coming home after a long trip and unpacking your suitcase and finally getting to sleep in your own bed again. Everything feels comfortable and effortless.

When Mrs. Cobb returned the story to me during class on

Thursday, she gave me a warm smile. "I've been waiting for this, Lily," she said. "Thanks."

I glanced at her comments on the last page. *"Original . . . moving . . . insightful. Would you read this aloud for the group?"*

I looked up. Mrs. Cobb was sitting on the edge of her desk. "We need some volunteers to read this morning." She met my eye. "Lily?"

I hadn't read aloud yet this semester, and as I walked up to the podium I remembered the first time I'd read *last* semester, how nervous I'd been and how I'd salvaged a near-disastrous moment by turning what I'd intended as a serious, if lame, story into a joke. That had been the beginning of my long-running, one-woman show. Today I knew I could count on Mickey's approval. As for the rest of the class . . . This time they can laugh if they want, I thought. I don't care if they like it. I don't care if they like *me*. I like the story, and that's what matters.

But as I cleared my throat and got ready to read, I realized that I *did* care about one person's opinion. My eyes darted to the second desk from the left in the third row. What would Daniel think?

"Um, before I start," I said to my classmates, "I just want to say that the character of Flora in the story is a real person—my great-grandmother, in fact, and she died before I was born, but I feel as if I know her because I have some of her old diaries. So I didn't make her up, but I made up the situation, obviously. Okay." I took a deep breath. "Here goes. This is called 'An Apple Tree for Eleanor.'"

I read my story, about a chance meeting in the orchard between the narrator—me—and sixteen-year-old Flora White, who was distraught over her sister's illness. Together Flora and I talked about our experiences and plotted ways to make Eleanor well again. The story was open-ended; in the last sentence I described myself watching Flora and Eleanor walk off through the misty grove of trees, their arms linked, their long skirts swishing against the dewy grass, and disappear back into the past. The story was upbeat, though. You didn't know if Eleanor would be cured or not, but the possibility was there. The important thing was the connection: between the sisters, between the present and the past. The important thing was hope.

When I finished reading, I lowered my stapled notebook pages and looked shyly up at the class.

Mickey started spontaneously clapping, and a bunch of other people joined in. Daniel smiled—just for a second, and then he made his expression neutral again, but a second was long enough. I clutched my story to my chest and, my heart soaring, went back to my desk. "I really, really liked that," Mickey whispered, giving my bicep a congratulatory squeeze.

I smiled at her, and I smiled at Mrs. Cobb writing about metaphor and simile on the blackboard, and I smiled at the back of Daniel's head. It felt amazingly good, having shared a story that expressed my true feelings and dreams. And it turned out that after all my struggling, it was easy to be myself. I didn't have to put on an act to impress people or wear a costume to get attention. Although I'll always love dressing up, I thought, glancing down at my bandanna print skirt and cowboy boots.

Maybe I'd be dressed in black again tomorrow. Who knew? That was the fun of it.

A couple of other kids in the class read stories, and then we did some writing exercises, and then the bell rang. Mickey hooked her arm through mine, like Flora and Eleanor, and we walked to the cafeteria together.

T HAT FRIDAY, CARLOS drove up from Tufts. Laurel and I went to the Village Market to buy stuff for a special dinner.

"Lily," she said as I inspected a melon, "I have to tell you something. Mom and I have talked about it, and I think I'm going to register for the spring term at school."

"That's really great," I told her. Then when I realized what she was saying, I asked, "You're leaving me?"

"Oh, Lily," Laurel replied. "You know I'll always be there if you need me. But I really need to get back to school. Being away from it made me realize I miss it—and how committed I am to the prevet program."

I nodded, even though I still felt kind of sad. "I'm glad, Laurel. You *have* to be a veterinarian. It's what you were born to do."

Laurel smiled, her cheeks pink with pleasure. "You think so?"

"Definitely."

We tossed a shrink-wrapped package of chicken in the cart,

and a bag of rice, and some vegetables. We hit the ice-cream aisle, too.

We paid for the food and headed back out to the car. "I bet Carlos is glad you're going back to school, huh?" I asked.

"Yep," Laurel answered as she turned the key in the ignition. "He's really focused on the future, you know? So he was bummed out about me taking time off. He thought my whole college career was going to be derailed. Now, though, I think he really understands why it's important for me to do what I'm doing. And look what's happening, you know? This looks like a turning point for me."

I sighed. "You and Carlos are so intense."

Laurel laughed. "Is that good or bad?"

"It's good," I assured her as we drove south on the Old Boston Post Road. "You're so involved with each other. So committed."

"Well, yeah," Laurel said. "That's what it means to be in a relationship."

I thought about Seth. Obviously he hadn't ended up feeling too committed to me, or me to him.

Turning onto Main Street, Laurel glanced at me out of the corner of her eye. "Whatever happened with Daniel?"

"Nothing," I said with another sigh. "I stayed with Seth, remember?"

"But you and Seth aren't together anymore. Are you still interested in Daniel?"

"I think about him a lot," I admitted. "He's in the writing class. But I really hurt his feelings. I don't know." I shrugged.

"Maybe it's better not to have a boyfriend right now. I'm finally figuring out some stuff about myself. I'm building a closer relationship with Mom. That's enough."

"Yeah, but if you really like Daniel . . ."

"I didn't say I really like Daniel," I argued, but I couldn't help picturing that thundery day on the couch at his house, the way I'd leaned over him to give him a kiss. A pretty hot kiss at that. "Okay, I do really like him. But he won't even talk to me."

"Does he still work at Harbor Light Books?" Laurel asked.

"I think so. On weekends."

"There's this book I really want for my birthday," she said, flashing me a smile. "I'll write down the title. You should probably buy it tomorrow because it's a bestseller and that way you'll make sure to get a copy."

So that's how I came to be in the bookstore on Saturday during my lunch hour. Mr. Ballard was behind the counter; Daniel was arranging a new display in the front window. "Hi," I said to him.

Daniel looked up. When he saw it was me, he blushed a little, which I took as an encouraging sign. He wouldn't blush if he didn't care, I thought hopefully. "Hi," he replied.

"So, um, I'm looking for a birthday gift for my sister." I read the title off the scrap of paper Laurel had given me. "Do you have it?"

"Sure. Over here."

I followed him back to a shelf labeled New Hardcover

Nonfiction. He pointed to a volume in a glossy cover. "There you go."

I lifted the book down, weighing it in my hand. "Thanks."

"Sure."

I expected him to sprint up to the front of the store again. He didn't, though, so I took that as another encouraging sign and forged ahead. "Um, Daniel. Do you think we could, uh, if you haven't taken a lunch break yet, maybe, er . . ."

Daniel made a big show of checking his watch. "Yeah, I'm about due for a break," he said casually. "I wouldn't mind grabbing a bite to eat."

"Great," I said.

Daniel put my book behind the counter so I could pay for it later, and we walked outside. It was a blustery fall day; the wind whisked leaves along the sidewalk and whipped my long hair into a tangle. "Patsy's?" Daniel asked, pointing up the block.

Did he remember that was where we had our first writing partners date? I hoped so. "Perfect," I replied.

Patsy's wasn't crowded—no place in Hawk Harbor is after Labor Day. We could have sat pretty much anywhere, but without consulting about it we gravitated to a corner booth. Another good sign, I thought. He wants privacy as much as I do.

When we'd ordered our food—a turkey club for me, fish-and-chips for him—I said conversationally, "How do you like Mrs. Cobb's class this year?"

This got the ball rolling. We talked about the project Mrs. Cobb had assigned—to research and write a piece of historical fiction—and argued about whether anyone in the class had done a decent job with the poetry assignment, and debated the virtues of doing anonymous written critiques of our class-mates' work instead of having one-on-one writing partners as we'd done in the spring.

Our food came, but we were too busy talking to eat. "Back to the historical fiction thing," I said. "I'm going to use my great-grandmother's diaries and then do some additional research about town history and stuff. Do you think that's kind of cheating, you know, because the diaries aren't really history?"

"They are history," Daniel replied. "Totally. A first-person account. You should definitely work with them and write more stories as good as that other one."

I blushed happily. "You thought that was good?"

"It was great."

We were quiet for a minute. Daniel fiddled with his fork, not quite meeting my eyes. Talking about Mrs. Cobb's class is one thing, I realized. We still have a long way to go on some other topics.

And it was up to me to make the first move. "Daniel, I'm sorry," I said. "I blew it over the summer. I was feeling really scared and confused and dependent on Seth. I wish I hadn't hurt your feelings. I wish I'd known myself better then."

Now he did look up at me, in that incredibly direct way he has. "Why? What would you have done differently?"

"Well . . . that night we met at the Corner Ice Cream Shoppe," I said. "Our walk was pretty . . . short. I would have taken a much longer one." I kicked his foot a little. "You know what I mean?"

He nudged mine back. "I think so."

We started playing footsie, just like that day on the couch. Then Daniel slid around the bend in the horseshoe-shaped booth and I inched over, too, until we were sitting next to each other behind the little rack that held the ketchup and the salt-and-pepper shakers. We bumped shoulders in our old way, and then I got the nerve to turn my head to look at him. For a long moment we just stared into each other's eyes, and his eyes were so warm and sweet that I found myself wondering, How could I have ever thought this guy wasn't cute?

Then Daniel kissed me. Fast, and next to my mouth rather than on it. Still, it was a kiss, right there in Patsy's Diner. We'd never gotten around to eating, so we had our lunches wrapped to go and walked back to the bookstore. I was late returning to Potluck, but I figured Laurel would understand.

"You know, I wasn't *really* expecting to kiss and make up when I dropped in for that book," I told Daniel.

He laughed. "Yeah, right."

"Well, why did you forgive me?"

He tipped back his head, looking up at the cloud-swept sky. "Because—and I know this is going to come as a huge surprise, Lily—I *like* you."

"Even after everything?"

Daniel shrugged. "Yeah, even after everything. I figured that sooner or later you'd come to your senses and realize that Seth wasn't right for you and I was."

"Really?"

"No, not really." Daniel glanced at me. "Would you have broken up with him if he hadn't broken up with you first?"

I thought about it. "Eventually."

We both thought this over. Then in front of Harbor Light Books, I stopped and turned to face him. "I didn't know what I wanted back then," I said softly. "I do now."

"Yeah?"

"Yeah."

I stood on tiptoes and kissed Daniel lightly on the lips, right in the middle of Main Street. He turned red. "How am I supposed to go back to work now?"

I giggled. Glancing over my shoulder, I saw Laurel watching us from the window of Potluck—she gave me a thumbs-up sign. "I'll kiss you again after work. Think about *that.*"

Fifteen

IT WAS LATE October—Laurel's nineteenth birthday weekend. Mom tried to talk Rose and Stephen out of driving up from Boston for the party because Rose was eight months pregnant and Mom thought she should stay closer to home. "This *is* home," Rose reminded Mom, laughing, as she and Stephen dumped their bags in the front hall on Friday night. "And this is nothing, Mom. My friend Sophie from childbirth class is flying to Chicago this weekend for a wedding!"

Mom rolled her eyes. "She'll be sorry if she has that baby at thirty-five thousand feet, with a flight attendant acting as midwife."

On Saturday morning Sarah worked my shift at Potluck so I could stay home and help Mom bake a carrot cake with cream cheese frosting for Laurel.

"Tonight's going to be the best birthday party ever," Rose

predicted. "I don't even care that I'm not the one getting the gifts."

"Speaking of which, who'll do the decorations?" Mom asked. She looked at Rose and Stephen. "How about you two?"

Rose glanced at Stephen. "Actually, we have an . . . appointment. Here in town, right after lunch. I'm not sure how long it'll take."

"An appointment?" I said, but Rose didn't volunteer details.

I ambushed her at the door when she was putting on her coat—one of Stephen's, actually, because his coats were all that fit her now. She buttoned it over her front—it looked like she had a basketball under there. "An appointment with whom?" I asked.

Rose looked over her shoulder. When she was certain no one else was around, she whispered, "A realtor."

"A realtor?" I whispered back.

Just then Stephen, Laurel, and Carlos stepped into the hall. "We're late," Stephen said to Rose.

"Tell you about it later," my sister promised, giving me a conspiratorial wink as she sailed out the door.

I'D ASKED LAUREL if I could invite Daniel to her birthday party and she'd said yes. He showed up promptly at six, wearing a tie and carrying a big bouquet of autumn wildflowers. "Think Laurel will like these?" he asked, tugging on the knot in his tie.

"She'll love them," I assured him.

Laurel did love the flowers—she put them in a vase in the center of the table. She also loves Mexican food, so Mom and I had cooked up a feast of her favorites: pico de gallo, tortilla soup, stuffed chilies, and fajitas. When we were all around the table, about to dig in, I looked across at Rose. "So?" I asked.

She raised her eyebrows at me. "So what?"

"Your appointment! Are you going to tell us about it?"

Rose smiled. Actually, she'd been smiling since she and Stephen got back from town half an hour ago—her smile just broadened. "Okay, we do have some news," she began. She caught Stephen's eye, and he nodded. He was grinning, too. "We met with a realtor. You know Mrs. Geisler, with the office on the corner—Maribeth Geisler? Anyway, we—"

Abruptly Rose stopped talking. She frowned, a pained grimace on her face, one hand touching her abdomen. "What's the matter?" Laurel asked.

Rose didn't answer right away. She sat tensely, her breath a little bit ragged. Then she let out a big sigh. "Oof," she said. "I don't know; it's weird. I've been having these fake contraction things, Braxton Hicks, all afternoon, but now they're starting to get worse. It's only been like five minutes since the last one."

She shot a puzzled look at Stephen. His mouth dropped open. "Rose, maybe they're not fake contractions," he said, sounding panicky. "Five minutes apart . . . in childbirth class the teacher said . . . what if this is the real thing?"

"It can't be," she said, "because I'm not due until—"

She stopped speaking, her face contorted. "Rose, can you talk during this contraction?" Mom asked.

Biting her lip hard, Rose shook her head no.

Mom smiled at Stephen. "Then this *is* the real thing," she said. "Why don't you get a few things together while I call the emergency room at the hospital and tell them we're on our way over?"

It was a pretty exciting night. Laurel never got around to opening her presents; the cake sat untouched on the kitchen counter under a glass dome. We all went to the hospital, even Daniel, and after an intense two-hour labor Rose gave birth to a baby girl.

We took turns crowding into the labor-and-delivery room to view this newest member of the family. "Look at her," Mom said happily, holding the swaddled infant so Hal could admire her. "Isn't she precious?"

Stephen was grinning from ear to ear. "I'm a dad," he said. "I'm a dad!"

Carlos hugged Stephen, pounding him heartily on the back. Daniel stepped over to shake Stephen's hand. "I feel like I should be handing out cigars," Hal said.

"How about ordering a pizza instead?" Rose suggested. "I'm starving!"

"Someone else may be ready for a meal, too," Mom observed, handing the baby back to Rose.

The nurse who'd helped deliver the baby stuck her head into the room. "That's right, Rose. Why don't you try nursing her?"

"Oh, right. Okay." Rose waved one hand. "Everybody out!"

We crowded back into the hallway so Rose could have some privacy while she breast-fed her new baby. Later we kissed Rose, Stephen, and the baby good night and went home.

"How soon can we go back in the morning, do you think?" I asked Mom after Daniel took off. "Seven? Eight?"

Mom smiled. "Why don't you see when you wake up? You may sleep later than you think."

I was sure it would be like Christmas, and I'd wake up at the crack of dawn. Instead when I finally lifted my groggy head from the pillow, the clock on my night table said ten-fifteen. "Mom!" I yelled, leaping from the bed and racing out into the hall. "Laurel! Are you guys still here? Did you leave without me?"

I looked down the stairs. Laurel and Carlos were standing at the foot, wearing their jackets. "Throw something on and go with us," Laurel invited.

For the first time in my life I got dressed without even looking at the clothes I was putting on. On my way out the door Carlos gave me a strange look. I glanced down. I was wearing a plaid skirt with a striped top. My tights were purple; my shoes were green. "Oh no," I said. "I'd better change. I want to make a good impression on my niece!"

Laurel laughed. "Come on." She grabbed my arm and dragged me out the door. "Supposedly babies can only see, like, six inches in front of their faces. It doesn't matter what you wear."

This was a relief. I didn't want the baby to think I was crazy or anything. "The baby," I said out loud as we drove to the hospital in Carlos's car—Mom and Hal had already gone over. "Do you think they've decided on a name?"

"We'll find out," Laurel replied.

When we got to Rose's room, she and Stephen were alone with the baby, who was sleeping in a little bassinet on wheels. "Mom and Hal went to the cafeteria for a cup of coffee," Rose explained. "Sit down, you guys."

I pulled my chair close to the sleeping baby. "Does she have a name yet?" I asked.

Rose glanced at Stephen and then back at me and Laurel, smiling. "Yes, she does. Her name is Daisy."

"Daisy," Laurel whispered. She was standing by the bassinet, and now she put out a hand to touch the baby's forehead. A tear trickled down Laurel's cheek. "Daisy," she said again.

"Daisy Margaret Mathias," Rose said. "Margaret after Mom, of course."

"It's beautiful," I said. My own eyes full of tears, I thought about the conversation the three of us had had a few weeks ago in the park. "It *is* the perfect name."

Stephen glanced at Carlos. "What do you say we get a cup of coffee, too, and let the sisters have a minute by themselves?"

Carlos nodded. "Good idea."

The guys left and it was just us three. Make that four. "I wish so much that Daisy were here to see my baby," Rose said. "But I feel as if giving the baby her name will keep her memory close forever. And I want baby Daisy to take after my sisters." Rose smiled. "All of you."

Just then the baby began to rub her face with her tiny red

fists and make funny little squeaks that sounded like a cat meowing. "May I?" Laurel asked.

Rose nodded, and Laurel lifted Daisy up. "She's so small!" Laurel exclaimed.

"Six pounds, fourteen ounces," Rose said. "Not bad for a month early."

Laurel carried Daisy over to Rose's bed. Rose laid the baby on her back across her own lap. I sat on one side of Rose with Laurel on the other, and we all gazed at Daisy. "I still can't believe it," Rose said in an awed tone. "I have a daughter."

"It had to be a girl," I pointed out. "What would we do with a boy in this family?"

We all laughed. Rose lifted Daisy up and held her facing outward. "Take a good look," she instructed the baby. "These are your aunts. Very important people."

"We'll help take care of you," I promised my niece.

"I'll take you bird watching," Laurel said, "and teach you the names of wildflowers."

"I'll tell you stories and take you clothes shopping," I said.

Rose smiled. "She won't lack for attention, that's for sure. She'll be spoiled rotten."

Just then Mom, Hal, Stephen, and Carlos came back into the room. "What do you think of Daisy Margaret?" Mom asked, as if she couldn't tell the answer by the smiles on Laurel's and my faces.

"I think it's the prettiest name in the world for the prettiest baby in the world," I declared.

"Ditto," Laurel said.

"Are you ready for some more good news?" Rose asked. "As if Daisy isn't enough?"

"What could it possibly be?" Mom wondered.

"I started telling you about it last night at the dinner table, right before I went into labor," Rose reminded us. "About meeting with Maribeth Geisler, the realtor."

"Right," Hal said. "What was that all about?"

"Well." Rose paused dramatically. She always does that when she has something important to say—it's her trademark. "Stephen's grandparents left him some money in their will, and we decided we wanted to use it for the down payment on a house in the country, up here near our families." She paused again. "We knew exactly which house we wanted, too. So yesterday we took a look at it with Maribeth, and we made an offer on the spot." Another pause. "The owners came back today with a counteroffer, and Stephen just called Maribeth to tell her we'd accept it."

"Where's the house?" I asked.

Rose was smiling at Mom. Mom smiled back at her, a look of disbelief in her eyes. "Is it the house I think it is?"

Rose nodded.

"The Lilac Inn!" I shouted.

"Our old house!" Laurel exclaimed.

We all started talking at once. "We'll use it on weekends and holidays," Stephen said to Hal, "when we need a break from the city."

"Wait'll you see the apple trees I used to climb," Laurel

said to Carlos, "and the old porch swing is still there, isn't it, Rose?"

"We'll have Daisy's christening party out on the lawn in the spring," Rose decided, "and you guys know that whenever you visit, you can have your old bedrooms."

"I can't believe it," Mom said. "I just can't believe it!"

Rose turned to Mom. "It's okay, isn't it? At first I worried that maybe it would feel strange. I wondered if I'd ever be able to stop thinking of it as *your* house."

"I know what you mean. But so much time has passed since it was my home." Mom glanced at Hal, and he took her hand. "We'll probably end up buying a place here in town. And we don't need anything nearly so big. That's a house for a young, growing family."

"Will you come for Christmas dinner, though?" Rose asked. "And help me make the roast beef and bake apple pies?"

Mom smiled. "Of course."

For a minute we were all quiet. I looked at my older sister with her husband at her side, holding her baby in her arms. And not only were they parents, but they'd bought a house! I can't believe Rose is so grown up, I thought. And Laurel's going back to college, and I'm almost seventeen. This time next year I'll be in college, too.

Suddenly I thought of something. "I'm not the baby of the family anymore!" I said. "Isn't that awesome?"

Everybody laughed.

I kissed my niece on her pink button nose. "Thanks, Daisy."

Epilogue

FIVE WEEKS LATER, on the day before Thanksgiving, Rose, Stephen, and baby Daisy drove up to Maine to take possession of their new home. We were all so excited about having the house back in the family, we decided to celebrate Thanksgiving there. We cooked at the apartment and then carted the food over to Lighthouse Road, along with folding chairs and card tables because the old place was still unfurnished.

"I brought some tablecloths and candles," Mom said as we set up the card tables in the dining room. Hands on her hips, she gazed around the room. "Would you look at that wallpaper? Yuck!"

"Let's take a tour before we have dinner," Rose suggested.

"We need a tour?" I asked. "Rose, we used to live here."

She laughed. "Yeah, but if you think *this* wallpaper's gruesome, you should see the rest of the house!"

While Hal, Stephen, and Carlos tossed a football on the front lawn, the Walker women strolled through the old house, exclaiming over the changes. "They fixed the broken banister on the staircase," Mom observed, shifting baby Daisy to her other shoulder.

"They kept the house in pretty good shape," Rose agreed. "It has a new furnace and a new roof. But their taste in interior decoration was dismal."

The owners of the Lilac Inn had been heavily into purple and cherubs. "Look at Laurel's room!" I squealed when we were on the second floor.

Laurel groaned. "Fuchsia with a heart border. Gross."

"Oh, come on," Rose teased. "Isn't it romantic?" She went to the window and pushed up the sash. "Hey, Carlos, get up here!" she shouted. "Wait'll you see Laurel's old bedroom. It's a total make-out palace!"

We went to my old room next. "Wow," Laurel said. "It looks like a bordello."

I put out a hand to touch the wallpaper. It was dark blue and velvety. "I like it," I said. "It's kind of gothic. Would you keep it like this, Rose?"

"Are you kidding?" she hooted. "As soon as Daisy's old enough for one of those baby swings, I'm sticking her in it so I can start stripping wallpaper. This room'll be the first to go."

At the end of the hall we came to the master bedroom. "This is the only room they didn't change," Rose commented as we stepped inside. "I think the innkeepers must've slept here."

Mom and Dad's old room had tall windows facing out over the apple orchard. The wallpaper was pale blue with tiny white flowers.

We all fell silent. I could picture the room as it had been: Mom and Dad's four-poster bed against the far wall, the big dresser between the two windows, Mom's dressing table and mirror next to the closet, an easy chair with ottoman and floor lamp in the corner. I remembered coming in here on mornings when Dad didn't get up early to go out on the boat. He'd want to sleep late, but I'd bounce on top of him and tickle him. And when I had bad dreams, Mom and Dad would let me sleep in between them. Their big bed had seemed like the safest spot in the whole world.

I looked at Rose. "This will be Stephen's and my room," she said quietly. "I don't plan to change anything about it,"

Mom patted the baby on the back. She nodded wordlessly, then turned to step back into the hall.

The innkeepers had updated the bathroom fixtures, which we all agreed was great. While Rose asked Mom's advice about refinishing wood floors, Laurel and I wandered back downstairs. "Do you think it's weird or wonderful?" I asked her.

"Both," she said.

Fifteen minutes later we'd set the card tables and put out the food. Before taking our chairs, we stood at our places, clasping each other's hands with our heads bowed as Stephen said grace. "I know we're all ravenous," he said, "but I want to drag this out a little longer. We all have so much to be thankful for today. Why don't we each say something?"

He looked at Rose. She nodded. "Today and every day, I am thankful for my wonderful family," she said.

Mom smiled at Rose, her eyes sparkling with tears. "I'm so glad to have such a beautiful grandchild." She gave Rose, Laurel, and me a playful look. "I sincerely hope someday to have many more."

"I'm thankful for Rose's recording contract," Laurel put in. "I think my sister is the best singer in the world, and I know she's going to be a big star."

Rose beamed. The contract had come through just the week before. "And I thought I'd never have a career after the baby," she said.

"As for you, Laurel," Stephen put in, "we're psyched that you're going back to school in January."

Laurel smiled. "I've signed up for a tough course load, but every time I start worrying about it, I think about Mom. If she can run a business, I can beat biochemistry!"

Carlos was looking at Laurel. "Are we going to tell them?" he asked her.

She looked back at him, blushing. "You mean now?"

"Sure," he said. "What time could be better?"

Laurel nodded. "You're right." She turned from Carlos to look at Mom. "Mom, I know you're going to think I'm too young, but—"

"You're engaged," Mom said quietly.

Her eyes bright and her cheeks pink, Laurel nodded.

"Oh, sweetheart." Mom crossed to Laurel and clasped both of her hands. "I'm so happy."

Personally, I was so thrilled, I was about to burst.

"Don't worry, Mom," Laurel said as she and Mom embraced. "We're going to wait till after I graduate to get married."

"I think that's a good idea," Mom said.

"Has everyone had a chance to be thankful?" Hal asked.

"Nope, nope," I said. "I'm thankful for a lot, too. For all the same things you guys have mentioned, but a few others as well. I'm thankful that I have the world's greatest boyfriend. . . ." Daniel and I had been a couple for more than a month now, and I was pretty sure we'd be going out forever. "And the world's greatest writing teacher, who came up with the world's greatest idea for a book."

"What book?" Rose asked.

"Tell them about it, Lil," Mom said.

"I'm going to edit Great-grandma Flora's diaries and turn them into a book, with my own reminiscences in there, too," I explained. "It will be a family history of the Walkers over the generations."

"That is the best idea ever," Rose said.

"I'm glad you think so," I said, "because I have to interview all of you for stories to put in the book."

"Okay," Hal said, his eyes twinkling. *"Now* can we eat?"

For a few minutes there was a lot of noise: chairs scraping, platters and bowls being passed, people saying "please" and "thank you." Then the room grew still except for the sound of silverware clinking on china.

When Stephen took his first bite of Mom's stuffing and

gravy, he lifted his eyes with a sigh of appreciation. "Now *that's* something to be thankful for," he declared. "This may be an unconventional Thanksgiving in some ways, but Maggie's cooking is as awesome as ever."

Hal had been pouring wine into the glasses—just a drop in mine so I'd have something to toast with. "Here's to many more holiday meals together," he said, lifting his glass.

"Here's to family," Rose said, looking at the baby, who was sleeping in a basket on the floor next to the table.

"Here's to sisters," Laurel said, smiling at me and Rose with her heart in her eyes. We held each other's gaze for a long moment. I have the best sisters in the whole world, I thought.

"And to brothers-in-law," Stephen added with a wink at Carlos.

"Here's to much happiness for Rose and Stephen and Daisy in their new-old house," Mom said.

"It's everybody's house," Rose said. "I really want us all to spend time here together. That's why we bought it."

Mom turned to me, and we clinked our glasses. "Lily and I will be over here all the time, won't we?"

I pictured myself sitting under an apple tree, writing stories. I'd baby-sit Daisy and take her for stroller walks on summer days. When she got bigger, I'd show her all my great old hiding places. I'd even help strip wallpaper!

I nodded, a big smile on my face. "Definitely," I said. "Welcome home, everyone."

For more girl bonding and boys,

check out **BEACH BLONDES**

by Katherine Applegate.

"I hate my life. I hate my life. And I hate Sean Valletti."

The school bus had dropped Summer Smith six blocks from her home, and now she had frozen slush in the tops of her boots. Her toes were numb. Her ears were painful. Her lips were chapped. Her face was stiff from the cold and stung by the wind whipping her blond hair. Her gloved fingers, wrapped around her eleventh-grade biology text and a three-ring binder, were weak claws. Her blue eyes streamed tears as she faced into the bitter wind that tore at her, teased her, sneaked through every opening in her clothes to slither along her goose-pimpled flesh.

As for Sean Valletti, she hated him because he was incredibly gorgeous, very mature, and did not know that she existed. Despite the fact that Summer had often stared longingly at the back of his head in the school lunchroom, despite the fact that she'd sat next to him in biology five days in a row and had even had an actual dream about him, Sean did not know she existed.

And today, as Summer was leaving school after the last bell, he had stopped in the doorway, looked out at the cold, miserable world outside, and said, "Hey, you live near me. Why don't I drive you home in my car? That way you won't have to walk from the bus stop and get cold."

Yes, he had said those very words. He had said them to Liz Block. He had not said them to Summer Smith. If he had, Summer would now be loving her life instead of hating it.

Just another two blocks to her home, Summer told herself. Two blocks she would not have had to walk if Sean Valletti had asked her to drive with him. Another five minutes of spitting out snowflakes under clouds so low you had to duck to get under them.

There was no sun. There never had been a sun. It was made up by science teachers. And there was no true love, not in the real world. True love existed only on TV. In the real world it didn't matter how young or even how perfect you were: no true love. Maybe she should have told Sean about the dream she'd had. Then he'd know she existed. He'd think she was bizarre and possibly dangerous, but he'd know she existed.

Summer had told most of it to Jennifer Crosby, her best friend, who was not known for her subtlety. Jennifer had told her she should march right up to Sean and say something like, "You're the man of my dreams. Literally." Right. Jennifer had also suggested that Summer get Sean's attention by "accidentally" bumping into him. Summer had actually tried that. The bruise had healed after a few days.

Summer smiled ruefully at the memory. Okay, so maybe it wasn't a genuine tragedy that Sean Valletti didn't know she existed. A genuine tragedy would be if he *did* know and was deliberately avoiding her.

She was carefully duckwalking up the icy driveway of her house when the wind caught her. She wobbled. She fought for balance. She lost. And Summer's already bad day suddenly got worse.

Ten minutes later she finally opened her front door. And now she really hated her life.

"Is that you, sweetheart?" Her mother's voice.

Summer closed the door behind her, shuddering with relief. She dropped the wet wad of notebook paper on the carpet. Her biology notes, all in loopy blue handwriting, were blotching and running together.

Her mother stepped out of the living room, carrying her reading glasses in one hand and a book in the other. "It *is* you," she said. "How was your day?"

"Oh . . . fine," Summer said. "Except for the part where I fell on my face, scraped my knee, banged my head against the bumper of the car, and had to chase my biology notes across the yard." Summer dug a handful of slush out of her collar.

"Your aunt Mallory called," her mother said.

"Uh-huh."

"She wants to know if you'd like to spend the summer down in Florida on Crab Claw Key. You know, she has that big house there now, practically a mansion, so there's plenty of room. And it's right on the water."

Summer stood very still. The wad of slush was melting in her hand. "You mean . . . You mean, she's asking if I want to spend the summer on the beach, in the sun, swimming and . . . and being warm and lying out in the sun and getting tan . . . and going to beach parties and getting windsurfing lessons from sensitive guys with excellent bodies? She wants to know if I'd like that?"

"Well, would you?" her mother asked.

* * *

There it was! Summer literally bounced in her seat as she looked out the window of the plane. The clouds had broken up, and the plane had emerged into clear sunlight so bright that Summer scrunched up her eyes as she looked down below at a scene so perfect, so intensely beautiful it made her want to cry.

She noticed the guy in the seat across the aisle looking at her and grinning—the guy who looked exactly like Jake Gyllenhaal. She'd heard him tell someone his name was Seth.

Summer blushed and quickly turned sideways in her seat to press her nose against the plastic window, avoiding making eye contact with Jake/Seth.

No more bouncing, she ordered herself. Cool, sophisticated people do not bounce. And from the very first moment in Florida she was going to be the new, improved, much cooler Summer Smith. The sweet, nice, average, boring Summer Smith whose big whoop in life was hanging out at the mall with the same guys who'd known her all her life was going to be left behind.

Below her was a line of islands, green irregular shapes like mismatched jewels strung together by the wavy line of a single highway. Tiny green islands fringed by white surf. Larger islands with houses in neat rows and the white cigar shapes of boats clustered around the shore.

And in every direction the ocean, the Gulf of Mexico, blue where it was deep; green, even turquoise where it was less deep. Here and there the sun reflected off the surface, making a mirror of the ocean.

The plane sank lower. The water was so clear, Summer could see the shadows of boats on the sea bottom. So clear that in places it was as if boats were floating in air, suspended over ripply sand. Scattered on the water were bright splashes of color—crimson, purple, and buttery gold in the sails of windsurfers. And there were long white trails drawn by Jet Skis and motorboats across the blue.

They were over Crab Claw Key, and Summer laughed.

"See something funny?" the woman in the seat beside her asked.

"It's shaped just like a crab's claw," Summer said.

"What is?"

"Um, you know, Crab Claw Key. It's shaped like a . . . like a crab's claw." She formed her hand into a crab shape and opened and closed the pincers a few times.

"I think maybe that's how it got the name," the woman said.

Very good, Summer told herself. Already you're on your way to impressing the local people with your brilliance. She slid her crab hand down to her side. She was regretting the decision to wear jeans and a purple University of Minnesota sweatshirt. First of all, she was going to be too hot, judging from the blazing sun. Second, it was like wearing a sign that said "Hi, I'm a tourist from the Midwest. Feel free to mock me."

"You here for the summer, huh?" the woman asked. "Maybe you have a job here, or family?"

"An aunt," Summer said. "And a cousin. But I don't have a job, at least not yet, although I definitely have to get one. Mostly I'm just here to lie on the beach and swim and stuff."

The woman nodded seriously. She was an old woman with a face that had the stretched face-lift look, as though each eye was a little too far around the side of her head. "Here to meet boys, too, right? Find romance?"

Summer glanced at Jake/Seth, hoping he had not overheard that particular part of the conversation. "Maybe," Summer admitted in a low voice. "I mean, it would be okay if I did, but that's not why I'm here."

The woman reached inside a voluminous shoulder bag and pulled out an oblong box. "Would you like me to read your cards? No charge, so don't worry."

"Excuse me?"

"Tarot, honey. Tarot cards. That's what I do; I have a little studio just off the main wharf. Normally I'd have to charge you twenty-five dollars." She began laying brightly illustrated cards on the tray. "We'll have to make this quick; we're getting ready to land."

"I guess you know that because you're a fortune-teller, right? About landing soon, I mean."

The woman did not acknowledge the joke. She was laying out the cards.

"Ahh," the woman said.

"Ahh?"

"Hmmm."

"What?" Summer didn't believe in things like tarot cards, but this was hard to ignore.

"You will definitely meet some young men this summer," the woman said.

"Well, I always *meet* guys; I mean, there are guys at school. Half the people there are guys, so—"

"You will meet three young men, each very different, each very important in your life."

Summer glanced at Jake/Seth. Please, let him not be able to hear this. "Well, thanks, ma'am," Summer said brightly.

"Three young men," the woman repeated. "Maybe some more, too, but at least these three."

The pilot announced that they were beginning their approach. The woman sighed and began gathering up her cards.

Summer fidgeted for several seconds. She really didn't believe in superstitious things like tarot cards. But what would it hurt to find out what the woman knew? Or thought she knew. Or, at least, pretended to know.

"Three guys, huh?"

"Three." A knowing, almost smug nod. "Each very different. One will *seem* to be a mystery. One will *seem* to represent danger. One will *seem* to be the right one."

Crab Claw Key rushed up toward them suddenly, each house visible, cars and boats, and then, people lying out on the beach, tiny brown stick figures seeming to stare up at the plane. The shadow of the plane raced across them.

"Seem?" Summer said.

"The future is always shifting," the woman said. "Is your seat belt fastened?"

The wheels touched down. The plane taxied toward the little terminal, and Summer began to feel nervous. "Just act cool," Summer told herself. "Just don't act like some dork from Bloomington."

"What?" the lady asked.

"Nothing," Summer said, not convincingly.

"You watch out for the bad one."

"The bad—"

"One will represent mystery. One will be the right one. But that third boy—you'd better watch out for him."

As soon as the plane had come to a stop, Summer pried her carry-on bag from the overhead compartment and shuffled toward the door with the rest of the passengers. The flight attendants were smiling and chattering, "g'bye, havaniceday, bubbye, g'bye" like happy robots, but Summer barely heard them. She was still turning the woman's words over in her head.

She reached the door to the plane, and blazing heat jumped on her like a wild animal. It glued her University of Minnesota sweatshirt to her skin.

Hot. Very, very hot. Hot like crawling inside an oven.

A breeze like a blowtorch caught Summer's long blond hair and lifted it from the back of her neck. She pried open one eye and saw a world of blazing light. Somehow the plane had flown from the earth straight into the sun.

Jake/Seth squeezed past her on the stairs, jostling her with his bag. "Sorry," he said.

"No, it's my fault. I was just looking around," Summer said. "I should have kept moving."

"First time here?" he asked. His eyes were behind very dark shades. His smile was very nice. His smile was very, *very* nice.

"Uh-huh. Yes."

They had reached the bottom of the stairs. Jake/Seth moved away, walking quickly across the tarmac. Then he turned, walking backward. "Hey, Minnesota, my name is Seth. I'm from Wisconsin. How long you staying and what's your name?"

"Summer!" she yelled.

"Great," he said. "I'm here for the summer too." He waved and turned away.

LOOKING FOR THE PERFECT BEACH READ?

SiMONTEEN

Simon & Schuster's **Simon Teen**
e-newsletter delivers current updates on
the hottest titles, exciting sweepstakes, and
exclusive content from your favorite authors.

Visit **TEEN.SimonandSchuster.com** to
sign up, post your thoughts, and find out what
every avid reader is talking about!

Margaret K. McElderry Books

SIMON & SCHUSTER BFYR

SIMON PULSE